Praise for Jen Doyle

"Sexy and sweet and packing some serious heat. *Calling It* is a debut home run."
—Marina Adair, bestselling author of *Summer in Napa*

"Ms. Doyle's fresh writing just lit a fuse that I didn't want to end. I'm in awe that *Calling It* is her first novel. She absolutely killed it!"
—*The Romance Reviews*

"I really enjoyed this book and the author's voice. I look forward to more from her."
—*Smexy Books* on *Calling It*

"If you dig well written, sweet, [and] funny...romance with a firm HEA, do yourself a favor and pick this series up!"
—*The Romance Reviews* on *Called Up*

"If you're looking for books with that small-town feel, a story filled with tough, sexy [and] sweet guys...strong and independent women, and a story that you'll find yourself completely invested in, then look no further. Jen Doyle's fun, lighthearted books full of sweet and sexy moments are definitely what you need to pick up next!"
—*Fiction Fare* on *Called Up*

"Jen Doyle hit this one over the wall, out of the park, and probably broke a windshield in the parking lot because *Called Out* is a home run of epic proportions."
—*Guilty Pleasures Book Reviews*

**Also available from Jen Doyle
and Carina Press**

Calling It
Called Up
Called Out
Holiday House Call

JEN DOYLE

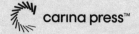

carina press™

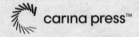 carina press™

ISBN-13: 978-1-335-66127-2

Recycling programs
for this product may
not exist in your area.

Calling It

Copyright © 2016 by Jennifer Doyle

www.CarinaPress.com

Printed in U.S.A.

To Diana,
who put the map in front of me and said, "Go."

Chapter One

They were crucifying him on sports radio. Again. Tonight's theme was NateGate: Is Baseball's Hawkins Out For Good? and, considering that he was the Nate Hawkins they were talking about, he was an idiot for listening in the first place.

"So the team's doctors have just come out and said he'll be fine to play in the spring, but I have to be honest, Jim. We're supposed to believe that he'll be good to go when pitchers and catchers report in less than a month? He's not a twenty-two-year-old kid anymore. Bones that old don't heal the way they used to."

That old? He was thirty-three, for fuck's sake.

"Marco, I'm not too worried about his knee..."

Exactly. His knee was freaking fine.

"What's bothering me are the rumors I'm starting to hear about the Breathalyzer test results being faked."

"Are you *shitting* me?"

And now he was arguing with the radio.

Perfect. Good thing it was practically the middle of the night and his was the only car on the highway. It would be just his luck to have someone snap a picture of him as he was yelling at his dashboard.

"I mean, the guy's SUV rolled, what, seven times?

That doesn't just happen. And we're getting nothing from team management despite the fact that they've invested a bucketload of money in him, plus nothing from the man himself... Things are not adding up. Let's go to the phones."

Listening to guys who were paid to stir up shit was bad enough. But the callers? Hell, no. He had to shut it off.

And yet he let it go on for another fifteen minutes. It was like driving by a wreck on the highway: nearly impossible to turn your head away.

So much for his adoring public. Christ. He was actually grateful to see the red-and-blue lights of a police car flashing behind him. He'd clearly sunk to a new low.

With relief, he shut off the radio and pulled over.

He was reaching for his license when a familiar voice came over the speaker. "You bringing your shitstorm to *my* town? Get out of the car, Hawkins."

Nate grinned at the familiar voice, despite the fact that the whole point of fleeing to his mom's house was to go off the grid for a while. "Tuck," he said, hand outstretched as they came face-to-face. "Last time I saw you..."

The other man grabbed Nate's hand and pulled him into a one-armed hug. "Thirteen years ago?" Tuck said. "Damn, you and Wash were on fire during that game. Don't get me wrong, watching you behind home plate isn't a chore. But seeing you on the court..."

Nate worked hard at not letting his smile fade as he allowed the words to die their own quiet death. He had enough on his plate without inviting the past to edge its way in, too.

After a moment, Tuck shrugged. "Guess basketball wasn't the same without your boys behind you."

His 'boys.' Right. Wash, Jason, Deke and Cal, teammates who had been as close as brothers, but with whom Nate had barely spoken in over two years. New subject. "I thought you moved to Denver. I didn't know you were back."

"No reason you would." Tuck's eyes dropped, a standard reaction these days. "You've been a bit preoccupied."

That got a genuine—if harsh—laugh out of Nate. He leaned back against his car and crossed his arms in front of him. "Can't imagine where you heard that."

Which was a joke, of course, the radio show being case in point. The car accident itself had been bad enough, but when you were the all-star catcher for one of Chicago's baseball teams and had just recently signed with the city's new expansion team in a record-breaking deal, that bought you headlines nationwide.

Tuck leaned against the car, as well. "Shit, Hawk. You okay?"

Talk about a loaded question. The car accident in itself had sucked. His career being potentially over sucked shit. But to have his name still being dragged through the mud after it was all said and should have been done? He'd been in self-imposed exile for six fucking weeks and was still afraid he might just lose his shit and hurt someone.

But he'd been in the public eye long enough to know that even one grumble made you come off like a spoiled, out-of-touch asshole. "I've had better months." He forced a shrug and tried not to sound bitter. "So is this about the drinking and driving thing? You want me to walk the line? Recite the alphabet?"

He'd even taken a Breathalyzer test, although that was the biggest laugh of all. One of the few things he remembered about the accident was that he'd been stone-cold sober. The results that proved it had been released weeks ago—and yet as they'd said on the radio, there was a vocal camp stirring up rumors that he'd faked it. Because the story about his (now) ex-fiancée sleeping with his (now) ex-best friend wasn't juicy enough.

Tuck smiled. "No tests." He nodded at the car. The limited edition Porsche Nate's ex had given him. "This guy I used to coach apparently got himself one of these. Had to see it up close."

That one earned a genuine smile—it felt like ages since someone had just been nice. "It was an engagement present." One he had no love for. Which was fine because, as it turned out, Nate apparently had to give it back. Pete, his attorney, had texted that little bit of info an hour ago.

For a minute, Tuck just looked at him. Then, having obviously gathered Nate wasn't in a mood to chat, he gave a slow nod before saying, "Heading out to your mom's?"

"It was a last-minute thing," Nate said. "I thought I'd surprise her."

This time Tuck was the one crossing his arms in front of his chest. "Well, then, you might want to make other plans."

"Why? What's wrong with my mom's place?"

Tuck shrugged. "This didn't come from me, but I heard she had company tonight. I figure that's not something you want to find out the hard way."

"Company?" Nate repeated, belatedly realizing what Tuck meant. "My *mom*? *Who?*" That was…disturbing.

"Not my business." Tuck straightened up and smiled, signaling an end to the discussion. "The boys' basketball team is having a run that would make The Dream proud. You should stop by. They'd be over the moon."

Normally Nate wouldn't hesitate—though he'd made his living playing baseball for the past twelve years, basketball was where it had all begun. But a packed-to-the-gills gymnasium wasn't at the top of his Places I Want To Be list. He gave as noncommittal an answer as possible, said goodbye and then got back into his car, waving as Tuck drove off.

As he started up the engine, he considered where to go next. One of his sisters would be his best bet. They weren't happy with him for being so out of touch over the past couple of years, but they wouldn't turn him away, either. Ella was most likely asleep since she was up at dawn with her horses, so she was out of the question. And Jules, though potentially still awake, tended to have the strongest opinions about the way he lived his life. So that was a no.

Which left Fitz. She might razz him a bit, but she wouldn't push. She might even let him hide out for a few days. Plus, he owned the apartment she lived in and had his own key. He gunned the gas and headed into town.

Chapter Two

Dorie stepped into her bathroom and smiled. The lighting was low, the steam was rising as water filled the tub and the candles were lit. In her old life, meaning three weeks ago when she'd still been living in Boston with her brothers Christopher, Seamus, and Jack, those would not have been good things. If the lighting was low there, it was because Seamus had blown a fuse. Steam rising from the tub meant that Jack's dog had gotten sprayed by a skunk again. And as for candles being lit? Necessity, not choice.

In her new apartment in Iowa, it was an entirely different story. Lights were low because she'd dimmed them, steam was rising because she was about to have an actual bath and the candles were purely for relaxation purposes. All she needed now was to choose from not one but three bottles of bubble bath. There she'd been, standing in the health and beauty aisle of the Hy-Vee, when the girlie subconscious she'd ignored for thirty years had risen up and seized control.

Having gone straight from her parents' house to the apartment she'd shared with three of her six older brothers, she'd never had a bathroom to herself. Never had the luxury of bubble baths, never even had bath products to speak of.

Well, one time she'd been given bath beads, but Seamus had decided to use them for some kind of sex thing with one of his girlfriends. That in itself was enough to convince Dorie to stick to showers. Since Christopher and Jack had followed that up with a series of pranks on Seamus—which was, yes, hilarious, but that also required the rest of her supply—she never even had a choice.

With a sigh, Dorie picked up one of the bottles—strawberries and cream—and added a capful to the tub. Her brothers had driven her crazy—had driven her halfway across the country, in fact. But she missed them. *So* much. Forcing back the wave of homesickness, she closed her eyes and reminded herself she was following her new life plan.

Here in Inspiration they didn't see her as the baby of the Donelli clan. She wasn't the one cleaning up after her brothers—physically or metaphorically—or tagging along behind them, or standing by as they lived their lives and she only existed in hers. Here, she was just Dorie, the fully grown woman they took seriously enough to hire to run their library.

Damn straight. And she was going to be *awesome*.

So, yes, maybe it freaked her out a little that she was completely on her own. That wasn't something anyone here needed to know.

At least, she hoped no one knew. She'd tried to be cool and professional at dinner tonight with her new boss—aka Mayor Gin—but she may have told a few too many stories about her family or talked about Boston too much. The mayor had laughed at all the appropriate times but, to be honest, Dorie wasn't entirely confident she'd managed to pull off the I-am-confident-and-competent-woman-hear-me-roar thing. Or, considering she was the new town librarian, hear-me-assert-myself-quietly-but-with-total-authority.

Dorie laid her robe to the side of the ridiculously large Jacuzzi tub and took a deep breath as she got into the water.

Of course, she thought as she sank down into the water, she might also be a little bit unsettled due to the fact that Mayor Gin's full name was Virginia Hawkins. As in, mom to *the* Nate Hawkins of Iowa-Dream-high-school-basketball-and-now-Major-League-Baseball fame. Nate Hawkins, incidentally, who filled out his pin-striped baseball pants so well that if she wasn't soaking wet already, she would be now.

As the bubbles floated across Dorie's skin, it wasn't too much of a stretch to imagine him letting his towel drop to the floor and sinking down into the bathtub with her. Okay, so it was no stretch at all. She'd been fantasizing about him since she was thirteen, when the sixteen-year-old version of Nate had been the cutest boy her middle-school self had ever laid eyes on.

She'd been a little too obvious about her crush, though, and her brothers had teased her about it to no end. They still did. At least now they were a thousand-plus miles away and therefore unlikely to show up on her doorstep, despite their ongoing threats. Her brothers were overprotective enough that even her fantasy men needed to be able to stand up to them. She smiled. Nate Hawkins was a catcher in the Major Leagues. Six large, angry men coming at him was just another day on the job.

Letting her thoughts run wild, Dorie stretched her arms out along the tub's sides and turned up the jets until the water rippled and pulsed around her. Just as she was reaching down between her legs to help all that pulsing move along, she froze. Yes, she was in a Nate Hawkins haze at the moment, but she could have sworn she'd heard someone say, "Honey, I'm home."

She sat up when that was followed by, "Chili cheese casserole? Hot *damn*."

Blindly reaching for her robe—literally, since she'd taken her contacts out and couldn't see a freakin' thing—Dorie stood up. The water cascaded down her body, taking her happy thoughts with it.

Seriously?

Had her brothers really done it? Planned a surprise visit just to check in? They were so ridiculous she honestly wouldn't put it past them.

"To-*mmyyyy*!" she roared. Because of all of them, he was the most blatantly obnoxious. With a huff, she knotted the belt around her waist, then yanked open the bathroom door and stormed down the hall. "*My* casserole, Tommy. I left enough meatballs for you to eat for a month. Get your hands out of my—"

She stopped suddenly when the man in her kitchen muttered, "Shit."

That wasn't Tommy's voice, and it sure as hell wasn't his stocky build. Tommy was only a few inches taller than her. The man standing in her kitchen was over six feet tall and all lean muscle. That much she could tell even without her glasses.

She squinted, trying to see which of her brothers' friends this could be—there was something about him that seemed familiar even in all of his blurriness. Plus,

all of her brothers' friends always went straight to the
fridge. There was Sean's college roommate, who was
from Des Moines, and she was pretty sure that one of
Jack's old bandmates lived in Omaha, two and a half
hours away. It was highly possible one of them had been
recruited. "Okay, give. Who are you, and which of my
brothers sent you?"

An eternity of silence passed before the man answered. "You don't know who I am?"

Um, hello? Who came into someone else's house—
Ate. Her. *Food.*—and then had the nerve to sound offended that she didn't know who he was. She took
another step forward, trying to get close enough to see
him better. "All I know right now is that you're the guy
who's eating my dinner. Except I didn't get to have it
for dinner because N—"

She cut herself off. No. She was not allowed to think
that ever again. The mayor was her boss, not "Nate
Hawkins's mom." "Because my *boss* asked me to have
dinner, so I didn't get to eat it, but I was planning on
having it for lunch tomorrow and…" Trying to make out
his face, she squinted again. "And I know all of three
people in this town, so, no, I have no idea who you are
other than the guy who's eating *my dinner*!"

So maybe she was overreacting. But she'd been having a really good—and on its way to being even better—
bath. "I swear. Whichever one of my brothers sent you
to check up on me can just go fu—"

He coughed.

No, that hadn't been a cough. It was much more like
a…

"You're *laughing*?" she asked. "You eat my—"

"Dinner?" he said. Definitely laughing.

Her eyes narrowed.

"Sorry," he said, wisely getting himself under control. "Although I'm pretty sure I'd happily eat anything you offered."

Dorie's mouth dropped open. Was he…? Did he mean…?

For heaven's sake. So what if his voice had dropped down nice and low? It was just her overly active imagination moving her Fantasy Train from Nate Hawkins Land straight to hot-guy-in-my-kitchen territory. Which wasn't the worst thing. Although she tried to avoid hookups with her brothers' friends, Jack's bandmate wouldn't be the worst way to spend an evening. A touch of home and all that.

He stood up straighter and she forced herself to refocus on what he was saying.

"Look, I have no idea who your brothers are, and I'm really sorry about your dinner…"

Um… "I'm sorry?" He had no idea who they were?

So if her brothers hadn't sent him—if, in fact, he had no connection to her family—then she was standing dripping wet in her living room, naked except for her robe. With a total stranger, no less.

Thanks to a lifetime of defending herself in wrestling matches with brothers who couldn't care less that she was a) a girl and b) smaller than them, she could take him down regardless of how big he was. Or how, um, solid. It would ruin her relaxing evening to the point of no recovery, however. She took a step back.

"Don't," she snapped. "Don't come any closer."

She reached down behind her, groping for the phone but finding something else instead. A baseball bat, of all things. It belonged to her landlord, as did all the furniture and a surprising number of baseball-related knickknacks.

Could be worse. There was one of those big foam hands around somewhere.

Hauling the bat up into a swinging stance, she warned, "Come any closer and I swear to God I'll take your head off faster than you can say *casserole*."

His hands went up in the air and he took a step back. "Uh, okay. Looks like we've had a bit of a misunderstanding." Then he sat on one of the stools. "Damn, woman. You sure have a thing about food."

Hell, yes, she had a thing about food. She'd grown up with six brothers, every one of whom could eat an entire lasagna faster than she could wrap her hand around the serving spoon. "It's an awesome casserole."

"That it is," he murmured appreciatively, sending a bolt of heat directly down to where she did *not* need it. Her nipples puckered, but she blamed it on the fact that she'd just been living in major imaginary sin. She took another step back. His eyesight was probably better than hers. But, oh boy, did the man smell good.

Then again, maybe it was just the casserole.

"You should go," she said. It came out much more hoarsely than she'd intended.

"I, uh…" His voice had the same raspiness. "I could use a minute."

There was no doubt in her mind why he needed a minute, especially when she realized her robe had slipped when she'd lifted the bat, and he had a grade-A view of, well, everything. She lowered the bat and snatched her robe closed. "Maybe you could use that minute to tell me who you are."

"Right. Or maybe we could just cut to the chase," he

said, no longer giving off that somewhat amused vibe. It had pissed her off, but she preferred it to the turn things had just taken.

"You break into my place and you're giving me attitude?" Asshole. No more nice librarian. Using the I-mean-business trick the nuns at St. Mary's had used, she rapped the bat on the floor for emphasis. "So let's go back to 'who are you' and then move on to how you got in."

"You really don't know." This time, it was more a statement than a question.

"I really have no idea." And her patience was wearing thin. "Should I?"

"Fitz didn't tell you?"

"Fitz, as in my landlord?"

"Your landlord?" he snapped. "She moved out?"

He'd asked that in kind of the way a...

Oh, great—was she standing here half-naked with her landlord's boyfriend? Or maybe ex-boyfriend, given that he seemed to have no clue Fitz had moved out a month ago.

Even though she hadn't gotten any crazy or dangerous vibes—something she was pretty attuned to after all the years of dealing with her brothers' exes—she clutched the handle of the bat and adjusted her stance a little. Just to be safe.

Reading her body language far too clearly, he dialed down the agitation. She actually felt it happen, like the air rushing out of the hole in a balloon.

"D.B.," he said.

"Huh?"

"My name." He gestured. "On the bat. D.B. My bat. My place."

She looked down. Brought the bat up closer to her face. Yes, there were the initials *D.B.* carved right in. "Oh. But…" She raised her eyes to his—or, rather, in the general direction of his. "So then who is Fitz?"

"My sister," he said, sounding kind of…sad? He recovered quickly, though. "I needed a place to crash tonight. Didn't realize she'd moved."

Oh, that wasn't playing fair. Except if he didn't know her brothers, much less that she had any, then he also probably had no clue that playing the sister card would get her every time.

"I just moved in a few weeks ago," she explained, feeling the need to reassure him.

The air changed again. Although she still couldn't make out his features, she had absolutely zero doubt that he was staring at her.

And suddenly all the tension was back, albeit in an entirely different way. It crackled in the air around her.

She nearly jumped when he cleared his throat and stood up, saying, "Look. This has been—" his laugh sounded as resigned as it did bitter "—fun. But I'll go. Like you said. I'll—"

"*Wait.*"

The word was said so adamantly Dorie almost didn't realize it had come from her own mouth.

Because it was asinine. Foolish. A mistake in a whole host of ways.

He was her landlord's brother, but that didn't mean he was harmless. Yet she heard herself saying, "It's late. It's, uh, your apartment. And probably your bed. You should sleep in it."

When he started to protest, she said, "Really. Stay. Just let me grab some clothes and then the bedroom's all yours." She turned and walked down the hallway before she offered up anything else.

Like dessert, for example. After she dropped her robe.

For heaven's sake. Maybe her brothers were right to worry and she truly shouldn't be trusted to be on her own.

The first thing she did was detour into the bedroom and grab her glasses—if the man was going to spend the night with her, she was damn well going to see what he looked like. And she'd call her landlord. Confirmation that the man was actually Fitz's brother was still required.

She pulled on a T-shirt and a pair of flannel PJ bottoms and then grabbed her phone before crossing to the bathroom. While she let the water drain from the tub, regretfully swirling her hand in the bubbles that were left, she made the call. There were voices on the other end when Fitz picked up. Sounded like a poker game.

"Hi. I'm trying to reach Fitz?"

"You've got her" was the answer. "Who's this?"

"Fitz, hi. This is Dor… Um, Lucinda. Lucinda Donelli." Feeling a frightening urge to babble, Dorie shut herself up. The woman didn't care that Dorie went by a nickname.

After a few beats of silence, Fitz finally answered, "Oh. Is everything okay?"

"Yes. I just…" Dorie leaned back a little so that she could make sure the guy was still out by the kitchen. He was. She shifted forward again, softly asking, "Do you know someone named D.B.?"

"What?" Fitz snapped so sharply that Dorie straightened up.

Dorie nudged the bathroom door closed. "This guy

just kind of showed up. Your brother? He said he actually owns the apartment and—"

"He said his name is D.B.?" Fitz asked. "Can I talk to him?"

"Of course." As the last of the water disappeared, she opened the door again and went down the hallway. The man still had his back to her. He was on one of the stools at the island, kind of slumped down, his head in his hands. Just for the record, with her glasses now on, it was clear his body was exactly as built as she'd envisioned it.

"Fitz is on the phone," Dorie said, holding it out to him.

And as he turned, she realized with a start that she did know who he was. He was so far beyond vaguely familiar that, if the circumstances were different, it would have been laughable. Even, possibly, thrilling. Because the man in her kitchen was…

Holy good lord.

The man in her kitchen was Nate Hawkins.

Chapter Three

Over the course of his career, Nate had met thousands of women. It wouldn't be a stretch to say he'd been up close and personal with hundreds of them. But he was pretty damn sure that he'd never even been half as turned on as he'd been when the woman living in Fitz's apartment brought the bat up over her shoulder and her robe began to slip.

Hearing that Fitz had moved out was enough of a surprise that he'd managed to keep his tongue in his mouth until she'd disappeared down the hall. The back view was as good as the front, though, and it was with a groan that he rested his elbows on the counter and buried his head in his hands. The past six weeks since the accident were the longest he'd gone without sex since he was sixteen years old. He was due for something nice and physical. No strings attached.

When he caught the sweet scent of her coming up behind him—when he turned and was nearly struck speechless—he almost threw caution to the wind. But then his eyes went to the phone she held in her hand and he realized she was saying it was Fitz.

Damn.

Yes, he'd chosen Fitz's place to escape to, but with

the exception of her phone call after his accident, all of their recent conversations had been short but tense conversations about his Thanksgiving and Christmas plans.

Bat Woman handed the phone over and then walked quickly away. At least there wouldn't be any witnesses. He did take one last look, however—holy Christ, yes—before letting his head drop back down. "Fitz. Hi."

After a moment of heavy silence, she said, "So you're invoking the D.B. clause."

Right.

It wasn't that he'd lied. D.B. was a nickname of sorts, one bestowed on him by Fitz when he'd started to believe his own press. "*Just calling a spade a spade, Nate. If you want to be a douche bag, I'm going to call you one.*"

"Yep. I guess so." Not that Nate had truly thought through the consequences of saying that was his name. He'd been ridiculously happy to have someone not have any clue, and then the woman's feistiness had thrown him entirely. He'd latched on to the first name he could think of. The bat with the initials carved on it had been a gift horse whose mouth he hadn't looked too far into.

Fitz finally said, "You're here?"

Though it wasn't the most enthusiastic greeting, it also wasn't hostile. He'd take that as a good sign.

"Yeah," he said. "So when did you move out? *Why* did you move out?"

She sidestepped both questions. "I can still cover the rent."

Like he cared about that. She shouldn't even have been paying him rent in the first place, but she'd insisted. It just got donated to the town anyway. "Where are you?" he asked, hating himself for not having a clue.

"Deke's place."

"You're living with Deke?" Nate snapped. Max Deacon, more of a player than Nate had ever been, and Nate's baby sister? Hell, no.

Okay, so he hadn't been the best at staying on top of things. And he was pretty sure Fitz would say he had no right in the first place. But if Deke had gone against the sister rule and was now shacking up with Fitz, there were going to be words.

But she laughed and said, "No, I am not living with Deke."

Thank the Lord.

"Poker night," she reminded him.

The poker night he'd started with Wash, Jason and Deke. Hell, Cal might even be there and out of the army by now for all Nate knew. They were his friends—his *brothers*. And he hadn't so much as texted them in two years. It wasn't a surprise she hadn't invited him to join them. He'd chosen Courtney over them and burned that bridge.

"What are you up to tomorrow?" he asked.

She hesitated for a moment, then replied, "How about you come out to Wash's place for lunch if you're free?"

Wash's place. The farm that had been Nate's grandparents' but that Wash now ran. "Is Wash okay with that?"

There was a muffled conversation, followed by Fitz laughing. "Sure. He just says that D.B. better be bringing some work boots."

"Done," Nate said. "Fitz…" Fuck, this shouldn't be so hard. But as his coaches tended to say, if it didn't hurt, it wasn't working. So… "I've missed you."

She didn't answer right away, and he had the sense

he'd taken her by surprise. There was a hitch in her voice when she told him, "I've missed you, too. Love you, Nate. I'll text you a time for tomorrow."

"Sounds good." The fact that he was suddenly looking forward to mucking out stalls was frightening. "Love you, too."

It wasn't until Nate looked down to turn off the phone that he remembered where he was—that the woman who lived here was down the hall. Hell, she'd probably barricaded herself in the bathroom in order to keep a locked door between her and the stranger who'd barged in on her in the middle of the night.

And ate her *dinner*, he thought with a quiet laugh.

He'd give her back her phone and let her know he was leaving. Nowhere to stay, but he had a very expensive tiny car he could sleep in.

He found her in the bedroom, changing the sheets, which he would have told her she didn't have to do if his heart hadn't just lodged itself directly into his throat, cutting off any possibility of speech. Her pajama pants and T-shirt weren't nearly as revealing as the robe had been, but her bending over the bed and straightening out the corner stirred up something deep inside of him. And now the only thing running through his mind was how soft her hair would be when he wrapped it around his hand; how warm and wet she'd be when he buried himself inside her.

"Christ, woman," he groaned. He grabbed the doorjamb above his head and he clutched it so hard he practically splintered the wood.

She gasped as she straightened up and spun around, her hand flying to her chest. "I was…I was just…"

She bit her lip and sank down until she was sitting

on the edge of the bed. Her eyes met his, and he had to tell himself he couldn't take her right here. He needed to focus on climbing out of this hole—he didn't have the time to fall further in, no matter how enjoyable that might be.

But he couldn't look away.

Her eyes were a deep dark brown, the same color as the hair piled on top of her head. He wanted to trace the golden skin along her collarbone to the hollow of her throat, wanted his tongue on every part of her. And the glasses she now wore almost undid him.

If she'd been wearing those with the robe? When she'd hiked that bat up over her shoulder?

Holy. *Shit.* Turned out he liked a woman who would take him on without even blinking an eye. Who knew?

He especially liked it when her interested gaze traveled down his chest, past his waist… He liked it too much, actually. Only the quickly summoned thought of David Ortiz slamming into him at home plate stopped him from embarrassing himself in a way he hadn't since he was practically a kid.

Even that almost wasn't enough when she said, "I, um, changed the sheets. So you can take the bed."

All control vanished as the words just came pouring out of his mouth. "The only way I take the bed is if I take you in it with me."

His heart nearly raced its way out of his chest in the seconds before she replied, "I bet you say that to all the girls." Laughter danced in her eyes and a wicked grin came over her face when her eyes again dropped to his cock and then quickly came back up. She bit her bottom lip before whispering, "Hungry?"

Miguel Cabrera. Adrian Beltre. Derek *fucking* Jeter.

He gripped the doorjamb tighter.

"I could eat," he answered as evenly as he could manage.

For a moment they just stayed where they were, staring.

When she stood and walked toward him, he almost blinked. This was a dream. It had to be. Or some elaborate setup that Pete had come up with in order to get Nate's mind off everything else. Put this fantasy of a woman in front of him—feisty and looking so innocent and cute while she offered up anything he wanted to take—until he was so goddamn spent he could finally get over himself and start living his life again.

Except then she brushed past him as she walked out of the room, pausing only to whisper into his ear, "I think you need another minute."

Chapter Four

Making conversation with the object of her seventeen-year-long obsession wasn't easy. It was even harder, Dorie was realizing, after nearly getting herself off while fantasizing about him in the bathtub only moments before meeting him in the cold, hard flesh.

Or, rather, in the not-at-all cold, but mouthwateringly hard flesh.

That she'd managed not to lay herself down on that bed and invite him to join her was a miracle. Either that or the dumbest thing she'd ever done in her entire life.

Really. A night with Nate Hawkins? Who turned down a chance like that?

Dorie Donelli, apparently.

The problem, she realized as she headed to the kitchen, was that she'd seen the haunted look in his eyes when she'd handed him the phone. She knew more than enough of his backstory thanks to the media being all over him for the past six weeks, plus there was the whole obsession thing. Put all that together and it equaled Bad Idea. In flashing red letters.

"So how about some meatballs?" he asked from so close behind her that he almost made her jump. Again.

She turned to look at him. Holy crap, the man was truly that beautiful. "I'm sorry?"

"Meatballs," he said again. "Unless you're saving them for Tommy, of course."

Losing every ounce of cool she'd managed to maintain up to that point, she blurted out, "Tommy's my brother. In Boston. And please don't use the word *balls* again." Then she whirled around and opened the fridge.

She got out the meatballs, threw them in some gravy on the stove and made Nate Hawkins a sandwich. After he ate that one, she made him two more. At various points, she also managed to speak. But it was the most surreal experience of her life. And, possibly, the most difficult. Because he was *funny*. Nice. Not at all the cold-ish, aloof Master of his Domain-type he'd seemed like in recent years.

"So, um, time for bed." If she didn't remove herself from his presence soon, she'd lose her resolve and jump him right here.

Maybe she would have if he'd admitted who he was, bad idea be damned. He was Nate Hawkins, after all. But he didn't, which meant she couldn't, and so she resolutely ignored his grin, glared and then directed him to the couch before locking herself in her room.

When she woke up the next morning to find him gone, she was grateful. She wasn't sure she'd have been able to keep up the charade, especially when she came upon the thoughtfully folded stack of sheets and blankets. The bat was sitting on top of them, holding a note in place: *Thanks for keeping me off the street. And thanks for the meatball (hoping you'll make an exception for my use of the word here) sandwiches.* Rather than a signature, there was an arrow pointing to the initials on the bat. She was not at all pleased that it made her laugh out loud.

She spent her first two hours at work in a daze, finally calling it quits when she realized she'd shelved fourteen infant board books alongside some erotica. Thank goodness she still had a few weeks before there were patrons around.

Taking her cup of coffee into her office, she sat in her chair and booted up her laptop. Plugging *Nate Hawkins* into Google pulled up the headlines from the past six weeks: the picture of the upside down SUV at the top, right next to one of Courtney, clearly shaken, being escorted out of the hospital by a bodyguard the following day, then one of them together in happier times.

Moving past the accompanying headline, Courtney Smacks Hawk Down, she skimmed through all the Nate-Gate ridiculousness, the heartbreaking part about Courtney losing her baby and the speculation over whether his career was over due to the injury of his knee in the crash—and whether that meant the end-before-they'd-even-begun of the Chicago Watchmen, who had signed him as an anchor of their new expansion team. Instead, she skipped down to the part about the Iowa Dream.

The story of five high school boys from tiny Inspiration, Iowa, had taken the country by storm seventeen years before. Literally. They'd come out of nowhere to win the Iowa state high school basketball championship despite the fact that most of their town had been destroyed in a horrific tornado right before the season had begun. Wash Fairfield, Max Deacon, Jason Pike, Cal Turner and, of course, Nate Hawkins.

The story probably would have faded if not for the fact that they'd all chosen to stay together, turning down offers from bigger, well-known schools in order to attend the tiny Finley College, only forty miles from their home. There was a movie about them. Several books. And now, every time Nate Hawkins made the news the story came out all over again.

Dorie swirled her chair so that she was looking out her window at the town's central green, now picture-perfect with the falling snow. Though she'd already had a good job in Boston, the job ad for Inspiration's library director had jumped out at her, taking her back to those years of watching the little-basketball-team-that-could. She'd come home that night to find a living room full of obnoxious men—several of whom she was related to— watching mud wrestling. The kitchen was full of dirty dishes and no fewer than five people demanded "Beer!" when she went in. Ignoring them, she had gone into her room to find some random guy passed out on her bed.

She'd sent her résumé in the next day.

She'd never expected an interview, much less the actual job. And although she'd done enough homework to know that the Iowa Dream Foundation underwrote half the library's budget—as well as that of a good deal of town services—it was also clear they were very hands-off. She figured she'd eventually meet one or two of them. But having Nate Hawkins himself sleep on her couch?

Not even in her wildest dreams.

Turning away from the window, she shut down the browser, closed her eyes and took a deep breath. In the light of day, it was hard to believe it had actually happened. She didn't usually bother to flirt. She was blunt, a little clumsy at times and sometimes snorted when she laughed. She did *not* say things like, "I think you need another minute." Not to men like him.

Except she *had* said it. And even though she'd fantasized about him for years, it frightened her how normal he'd seemed. How easy it would be to forget that his real world was nothing like hers and that it was currently all-consuming. How easy it would be to fall into bed with him—to actually fall for him—and think he was falling back. And that was without even touching on the fact that he was her boss's son.

Oh, wow. Things had been so much less complicated when he was in dream form.

Ugh. She knocked her head against the desk.

"Um… Hello? Are you Dorie?"

Dorie whirled around so fast that her chair almost shot out from under her. "Yes. Hi." Chimes. She needed to get some door chimes. Plastering a smile on her face, she launched into the spiel for the occasional droppers-by. "I'm so sorry, but we're not actually open quite yet. There will be a grand reopening in February. If you'd like to give me your name and address, I'll make sure to send you an invitation."

Undeterred by Dorie's attempt at a send-off, the woman came forward and stuck her hand out. "Sorry. I should have called first. I just dropped by on a whim." They shook hands. "We spoke last night. I'm Fitz."

Oh. Dorie jumped up. "*You're* Fitz?" She knew she shouldn't have sounded so surprised. She just hadn't expected someone quite so young. "Was there a problem with my rent check?"

Fitz shook her head and smiled. "Nope." She took an envelope out of her messenger bag. "I actually have a check for you. I think Mama Gin mentioned that the

Foundation had approved five thousand dollars in seed money?" Handing over the envelope, she added, "We can't wait to see what you do with it."

Taking the check, Dorie looked down at it. "You and me both."

As they'd told her before she accepted the job, the library had suffered nearly a decade's worth of neglect and there was an overwhelming amount of work to be done. That, more than anything, was what had sold her on it. She wanted to put her mark on something, and this library was perfect. "Thanks."

Fitz nodded. "If you have any questions, feel free to come to me." She came farther into the room, wandering in an aimless sort of way as she looked around.

Or, rather, not quite aimless—more like she was procrastinating. Before she could say anything else, a phone rang. With a frown, Fitz answered it. "I know," she mumbled into the phone. "Yes, I can do it." She turned away and practically growled, "I've *got* it." She hung up the phone and faced Dorie again. "Sorry. That was, um…"

Rather than finish the sentence, she dug into her bag and took out another envelope and handed it to Dorie, although this one was much bigger than the one with the check. Dorie took it from Fitz and opened it. "A confidentiality agreement?" she asked. "For the seed money?"

With an embarrassed laugh, Fitz shook her head. "Not quite." She gestured for Dorie to read the document.

As Dorie began to leaf through the papers, a phrase caught her attention. She supposed she shouldn't have been surprised. Nate Hawkins wasn't just a man, he was a multimillion-dollar industry. Of course they'd want to protect him. But still, it took a lot of nerve to ask someone to agree to pay one million dollars if they didn't provide their own protection during sex.

"Are you *serious*?" Dorie put it back in the envelope and pushed it across her desk, right back at Fitz.

The corner of Fitz's mouth twitched, and from the glint in her eye, Dorie could have sworn she was in complete agreement. Without looking away, she took out her phone and dialed a number; a few seconds later, she said, "Sorry, no go." After a short pause, she handed Dorie the phone. "Your turn."

Um, okay. "Hello."

"Ms. Donelli, my name is Peter Morales. I represent Nate Hawkins. Do you know who he is?"

As much as she hated to admit it in front of Fitz, she answered, "Yes, I know who he is."

Fitz stiffened, then looked away.

"Then I'm sure you understand," Pete was saying, "that this is a standard agreement. It isn't anything personal."

A laugh escaped. "Who he sleeps with and what he does with them isn't *personal*?" She looked at Fitz.

Fitz's mouth twitched again, but this time the smile didn't quite reach her eyes. She reached for the phone. "I'll call you back, Pete."

Dorie could hear Pete's squawking as Fitz ended the call. The man wasn't happy.

Neither was Fitz, who said, "So you lied last night."

"I didn't lie." Dorie kept her tone as even as possible. "But if I'd known I'd have company while I was taking a bath, I would have kept my contacts in so I could see more than two feet in front of me." And if she'd had any idea that Fitz was his sister—of which he had three: Daniella, Juliette and Angelica, i.e., not someone named Fitz—she probably would have handled everything differently.

Although Fitz's nod pretty clearly said touché, what she actually verbalized was, "Did you sleep with him?"

"*Really?*" The word was out of Dorie's mouth before she could stop it.

Dorie took a deep breath and walked over to the window. "He said his name was D.B. You agreed. By the time I could actually see well enough to realize who he was, it was late and I wasn't exactly in a position to call you both out."

That sounded like the lamest excuse ever, especially as she heard herself say it out loud. But she had no memory of handing him the phone or walking down the hallway. She'd just found herself in the bedroom changing the sheets. And then she'd turned to see him framed in her bedroom doorway, clenching every muscle in his body tight as he'd watched her, holding himself in place.

Even if she'd wanted to tell him she knew who he was at that point, it would have been impossible. *Breathing* had been impossible.

So, yes, she'd taken the easy way out, although it wasn't like either Nate or Fitz had seen fit to contradict her in the first place. Hell, they were the ones with the D.B. thing. But she may have sounded a bit defensive when she added, "I don't know why he said what he did or why you went along with it. All I did was make him a meatball sandwich—" *or three* "—and then I went to bed. *Alone.*" With a sigh, she turned back to Fitz. "I came here for a job, not to make trouble for a man who has more than enough already. Nothing happened. And I can't imagine we'll ever cross paths again."

Honestly? She was even more sure now that she didn't

want them to. Having him as an imaginary boyfriend was clearly much less complicated than the real thing.

As if that was even an option.

There wasn't even a hint of apology in Fitz's voice. "I don't want to see him hurt."

"Then maybe next time you should ask him to join you at poker night rather than leave him fending for himself," Dorie snapped.

Fitz's face flushed. But rather than snap back and tell Dorie to mind her own beeswax, she turned away and quietly said, "It's complicated."

Right. And no matter how much about him she'd read, Dorie really didn't know anything about the man behind the stories. What she did know very well, however, was what it was like to have brothers. And between what she knew of The Dream and their history, the little she'd heard over the phone last night and her own useless attempts at keeping the peace between six volatile and hot-tempered Irish-Italian men, she empathized with the woman standing in front of her.

Leaning back against the windowsill, she said, "Families are hard. I know. But you guys obviously care about each other. I'm sure it will work out."

With a quiet exhale, Fitz said, "I sincerely hope so." Then she stood up and walked out the door, ending the conversation about Dorie's nonillustrious night with her superstar no-longer-completely-imaginary boyfriend.

And that, Dorie was sure, was that.

Chapter Five

So much for a few low-key days at home. Nate's first night had definitely not gone as planned. Knowing he couldn't spend another moment near Dorie, whose name he'd finally pried out of her—and having hours to kill before he was due at Wash's—he'd headed to his oldest sister's spread around 5:45 a.m. Ella raised horses on the outskirts of town, where the sunrises were unreal and the people were few and far between. But as he was driving past his aunt and uncle's farm and saw the huge tree that looked like it had come down in the previous week's blizzard, he took a detour.

He'd been there an hour when his uncle came out of the farmhouse with a pair of work gloves in his back pocket and a Thermos in his hand. "Thought you were Wash for a while there," he said, making his way down to where Nate was chopping wood. "Your aunt Laura said I should convince you to come inside for breakfast, but I told her there must be some reason you chose to be out here in the cold."

"Uncle A." Although warmth spread through Nate as the man neared, he was too out of sorts to say much more. That his own uncle's first thought was of *Wash*, not Nate, did nothing to help matters. He swung the ax one last time so that it was resting in the stump. "Looking good for an old man."

"Seventy-eight years young—and don't you forget it." He uncapped the Thermos and poured a cup of steaming coffee, then handed it to Nate.

Nate drank from it gratefully, closing his eyes as he tasted home. Plus, the caffeine was welcome. He'd tossed and turned on the couch all night, not so much because it was uncomfortable, but because it had taken every ounce of willpower he had not to follow Dorie back down that hallway and climb right into that bed with her.

To be honest, the whole thing had freaked the hell out of him. She intrigued him in a way that went beyond the usual physical response. He wasn't sure if it was because she wasn't the type he usually went for or in spite of it. She seemed a little more innocent than he was used to; nicer, for sure. There wasn't any fake flash to her, no jaded glint in her eye. Not that he had a problem with women like that—he'd actually come to find comfort in them. They had their agenda, he had his and everyone got what they wanted.

Dorie, however, was a question mark. There'd been interest on her part—of that he had no doubt. Yet she'd stayed on the flirting side rather than taking it further. It wasn't something he was used to, he had to admit.

He'd actually kind of liked it. He liked *her.* And he liked the way the air had hummed around her, the sense of energy and anticipation he usually felt right before stepping out on the field. He probably should have felt bad that he'd kept saying yes to more food just to keep her talking, even though the casserole had been more than enough to make up for the dinner he hadn't had in Chicago, but he wasn't ashamed. Not one bit.

"We didn't expect you home anytime soon," Uncle A said, pulling Nate back into the moment. "Those city folks getting on your nerves?"

Uninterested in going into details, Nate handed the cup back and took the gloves being offered. "Something like that." He pulled the ax out of the stump and set up a new log to split.

"And your knee?" Uncle A asked, raising the question of the moment. What the whole world had wanted to know since the accident six weeks before.

It was a fair question; it truly was. Especially from the man who was more of a father to Nate than his own had ever been. So he didn't attempt to shrug it off. But he was also kind of sick of hearing about it since the only answer he had was what every single doctor had told him after every conceivable test had been run. "They think it's fine—" and they'd finally gone on record saying so, "—but you know the way they are. There are no guarantees." The cold, hard truth was that only time would tell for sure. And beyond his current PT regimen, there was nothing anyone could do until spring training started up and he was actually playing again. "It feels good. Stiffer than I'd like, but no pain."

Uncle A, having already talked more than he usually did, just nodded as he started stacking the wood in the shed. They worked in silence until the pile of logs was done.

His coach might not be too happy with Nate doing anything that counted even remotely as a strain on his still-healing body, but it had been exactly what he needed. His head was feeling clearer than it had in a very long time. "I don't suppose Aunt Laura has any of those cinnamon rolls lying around?"

"Oh, lord, I hope so," Uncle A answered, pulling a tarp over the wood. "I only get to eat those things when you kids are here."

Laughing at the idea of still being considered a kid, Nate secured the tarp and followed his uncle inside, happily sitting down to a breakfast of pancakes and bacon and eggs—which he was told in no uncertain terms that he had to eat before getting to the cinnamon rolls; God help him, he was going to put on ten pounds today alone—when Aunt Laura said, "So, then, tomorrow at ten."

"Sure," Nate said. "Sounds good." Except then he realized he had no idea what he'd just agreed to. "Wait. What?"

"The *library*," Aunt Laura said with exasperation. "Lucinda is such a tiny thing. I don't know what possessed you to let her take on a job like that."

Nate paused, a piece of bacon halfway to his mouth. "Who's Lucinda? And how is it my fault?"

"Because you boys basically hired her. That foundation of yours." Aunt Laura began stacking dirty dishes. "That building's practically falling down around us. And that was before the storm last week. The poor girl has to take care of all of it."

Sitting back in his chair, Nate tried to remember what Ella, his proxy for pretty much everything Inspiration-related, had told him. "The library reopening thing," he murmured. "In a few weeks?"

His aunt went on about bookshelves being thrown out and new ones being put in. Carpets to be pulled up and replaced; painting to be done.

"You have no idea how many boxes of books she's moved already," she said, planting herself in front of

Nate, a plate of freshly iced cinnamon rolls so close he could practically taste them. "I mean, unless you're not supposed to be doing anything because of your kn—"

"My knee is fine," Nate snapped. Christ. If "tiny" Lucinda was able to manage, he could damn well do the same.

Seeing the hurt flash through his aunt's eyes, he made sure his voice was gentler as he added, "How about tomorrow at ten? Anything else you guys need done around here?" More labor might not be doctor-approved, but damn if he was going to just sit around like an invalid and let his almost eighty-year-old uncle do it all instead.

He drew it out as long as he could, working himself up to being ready to face whatever crowd Fitz and Wash had rounded up. He was ashamed to admit how much he dreaded facing his family and friends. Not because he was afraid they'd come down on him for, well, whatever, but because he knew they wouldn't. Just like his aunt and uncle, they'd be nicer to him than he deserved. And since they'd started treating him with kid gloves even before the Courtney years, they probably wouldn't even lay on the guilt.

"Take the truck, too," Uncle A said as Nate was leaving. He handed over a set of keys, grumbling, "That fool car isn't going to help matters any with Wash. Plus now I've got this perfectly good truck and ain't got no reason to use it."

Nate hid his smile. The "perfectly good truck" was a fifteen-year-old Chevy that had a habit of breaking down on roads in the middle of nowhere. Knowing his uncle would never accept a flat-out replacement, Nate had instead given everyone in his family a new car after he'd gotten his signing bonus. It was easier that way.

But when Nate stowed the Spyder in the barn and climbed up into the truck, he found himself just sitting there.

He already missed what Dorie had given him the night before: attitude. Friction, with a little bit of a smile on the side. And although he didn't like the feeling that he'd lied to her, it had been heaven to just sit and laugh and talk without the specter of who he was and the whole NateGate thing hanging over the room.

Leaning his head back against the seat, he smiled at the vision of her in that robe, swinging the bat over her shoulder. Decided he was going to get some more of that. And with the smile still on his face, he gave a quick wave to his aunt and uncle, then headed out to the road.

Chapter Six

"You're living in Nate Hawkins's apartment? *Seriously?*"

Even though Christopher was the brother Dorie was closest to, she was regretting saying anything. She just hadn't been able to get him to shut up about her niece and nephews, and she already felt homesick without the additional guilt trip of hearing stories about them.

"You can't tell anyone," she said. "You have to promise."

"Oh, shit," he answered, laughing to himself in the exact same way Nate had the night before. "I don't think I can do that. I mean…" The laughter grew louder. "Shit, Luce. This is just too good."

Luce. They completely refused to call her Dorie, no matter how much she tried. Why that bothered her even more than all the other teasing, she had no idea. She jerked the fridge door open. "Okay," she sighed. "Name your price." She wasn't above buying his silence.

"An autographed ball." There wasn't even a second of hesitation.

"Really?" Her brothers were die-hard Red Sox fans. They'd followed The Dream just like every other kid in their neighborhood, but they had no particular love for Nate Hawkins. No hate, either, though. He wasn't a Yankee, after all.

"Are you kidding?" Chris said. "He's Hall of Fame. No doubt. As long as his knee is okay."

She checked to see if the tuna she'd made a few days before was any good. Nope. Her eyes watered and the smell almost knocked her over. She threw it away, container and all. "He seemed to be fine when he was chowing down my casserole," she muttered. Maybe she'd just have Doritos for dinner. Doritos didn't go bad.

She grabbed a handful of baby carrots—her mother would kill her if she didn't have a vegetable with every meal—putting them on a plate as she kicked the refrigerator door shut. Then she poured out some chips.

"You *met* him?" Chris exclaimed. "Great way to bury the lead." Then he sighed. "Please tell me you didn't sleep with him already."

Christopher was the only of her brothers who even acknowledged she'd had sex, much less that, up until her recent move, she'd been having it regularly. Still… She had standards—she was holding on to them by a thin thread, but they were there. "He barely even knows my name." And she may not have been a card-carrying member of the you-have-to-love-a-guy-to-sleep-with-him club, but she was big on complete honesty between both parties. She may have understood why he hadn't told her his real name—and he might even have understood why she hadn't come clean either. But it didn't sit right.

"Hold on," she said, frowning when she heard a knock on her door. She glanced at the clock. Too late for UPS, but it was Iowa, so who knew? And she wanted her Amazon package of new books. Badly.

With a laugh, she said, "Chris, you didn't figure out a way to airlift me some of Shay's pizza, did you?" She went to the door and flung it open. "What I wouldn't do for some of that hot, melty good—"

Her mouth snapped shut. Because there, in all his God-given glory, stood Nate Hawkins.

He was wearing the kind of clothes her brothers wore all the time—faded jeans and running shoes, and a dark blue long-sleeved T-shirt with racing stripes down the arms. But oh, lordy, was there a reason why the man had graced more than his share of magazine covers. With his sandy brown hair tousled and slightly damp, it was next to impossible not to think about what he would look like after an afternoon in bed. She might have actually gulped.

"Speaking of hot, melty goodness," Adonis—er, Nate Hawkins—said as he held up two grocery bags. "I owe you a dinner. Can I come in?"

Although a strangled squeak came out of Dorie's throat, she did manage to nod and then get out of the way as he stepped inside. Damn it. If this was going to be a regular occurrence she was going to need to get better pajamas. Then again, if this was going to be a regular occurrence she'd probably end up institutionalized. Or maybe she was already hallucinating.

"Christo," she said hurriedly into the phone, "I gotta go."

"What? Why? Is everything okay?" When she didn't answer he hesitated only for a few seconds before saying, "Wait. Holy *shit*. Is he there? Did Nate Hawkins just knock on your door?"

"Not. A. *Word*," she whispered. "I'll kill you."

She hung up the phone before he could reply. When

she closed the front door and turned around, she half expected to find an empty kitchen. There was no way in hell Nate Hawkins had truly just shown up to make her dinner.

But, no. There he was, standing on the other side of the counter separating the kitchen from the living room and emptying out the grocery bags.

"Was that one of the brothers?" he asked with a devilish grin. And, yes, his body was exactly as perfect and beautiful as she remembered. She'd been hoping that had only been a figment of imagination from her fantasies last night. That she still wanted to lick him irritated her to no end. "What makes you think it wasn't my boyfriend?"

His head jerked up and the smile disappeared. "Do you have a boyfriend?"

"Um… No." Okay. So she wasn't that good of a liar and all of her energies were directed toward not becoming a babbling idiot in his presence. And walking over to the kitchen counter. "But I totally *could*."

The grin came back and her knees actually went weak. She sank down onto the stool.

"It's the brothers," he said, going back to the bags. "Six, right?"

She'd told him that last night? She honestly had no clue.

He took the last few items out and folded up the paper bags, then stowed them with the others in the cabinet under the kitchen sink. He reached down for a cutting board and then took one of the chef's knives out of the block on the counter. Completely unaware of the fact that she was barely able to breathe as she watched him begin haphazardly chopping an onion, he just kept talking.

"Any guy that even looks at one of my sisters has to pass through me first." The knife paused as he frowned. "Well, I mean they used to." He shrugged. "Take that times six... I'm guessing it can be a little intimidating."

Intimidating? *That* was intimidating?

He looked up at her. "Right?"

"Uh..."

She had to get ahold of herself. He was obviously planning on sticking around for a little while, crazy as that seemed. If she wanted to make it through the evening, coherent communication was a requirement.

Forcing herself to pretend he was someone other than Nate Hawkins, she shook her head and stood up. "That's not how you cut an onion." She went around the counter to join him. If there was one thing she knew how to do, it was cook. "Let me."

Not even the slightest bit defensive, he handed the knife over, then reached into the fridge and took out two beers. He waited for her to finish with the onion and rinse off her hands before he handed over a bottle.

The problem was, take away the Nate Hawkins part and he was still the most beautiful man she'd ever seen. He made her throat go dry; made her burn from the inside out.

He'd clearly made a mistake. There was probably some gorgeous, leggy blonde in the next apartment over and he'd just somehow ended up here instead. Except she lived over a storefront and the next apartment over was in another building.

And he was looking at her. Smiling at *her*. If he'd made a mistake, it was sure taking him a long time to figure it out.

"To big brothers," she said, managing to find her voice.

"And the sisters worth fighting for," he answered gruffly.

His fingers brushed hers as their bottles touched. It took everything she had to keep herself from jumping back as a frisson of heat darted through her.

Um… Why wasn't she considering the one-night stand thing again?

Oh, right. Because she was lying to him. And whether he had a good reason or not, he was lying right back.

He stared at her for a second and then took a step back. She had no idea if there had been an actual moment between them or if she'd just imagined it. "What else can I do?" she asked.

"Nothing." He opened the package of ground beef. "I'm making *you* dinner, remember?" He got out a frying pan and started browning the meat. "It's only fair I make you another one of Aunt Laura's casseroles."

So caught up in the surrealness of it all, it took Dorie a few seconds to realize what that meant. When she did, she almost spit out her beer. "Mrs. Grimes is your aunt Laura?" As in Mrs. Grimes, one of the two staff members she'd inherited when she took over the library, Mr. Grimes being staffer number two. "Oh, my God. Could they be any cuter?" She *loved* them. They'd been so welcoming and warm that she almost felt like they were related to her.

"Yeah," he answered. "They'll be married sixty years next month."

Dorie had been trying so hard not to get lost in the way the muscles rippled across the man's back that she almost missed his smile turning wistful. Almost. Her mouth popped open as she stared. If you put raw sex and power together and then wrapped it up with a guy's guy, Alpha Male bow, you'd get Nate Hawkins. Nothing she'd ever seen or read had even hinted at his having a romantic side. Even his relationship with his now ex-fiancée had always come off kind of, well, cold.

"What?" he said warily, turning to look at her.

"Uh, nothing," she gulped. "I was just afraid you were about to start talking about true love or something like that."

Oh, God, she had not just said that. He'd just been through one of the most public breakups known to man and she was mocking him. She was an *idiot*. And unfortunately, from the way his entire body tensed, he hadn't missed that fact at all.

But rather than act in any one of the ways her brothers would—offended, angry, twisting her arm until she recanted—he just looked at her with a gaze so intense that her breath caught and her heart started pounding and she suddenly understood what it must be like to be caught in the gravitational pull of the sun. Knowing that any second you would burst into flame yet not caring one damn bit because oh, how glorious that moment of combustion would be.

Then his lips twitched into a smile as he turned back to the stove and the spell was broken. "You don't believe in true love?" he asked.

On a cosmic level, yes. In her own personal experience, however, the closest she'd ever come to being in love was when she'd hung his poster on her bedroom wall. "Jury's still out," she mumbled.

"Huh." He looked at her over his shoulder with a

twinkle in his eye. Then he turned back to the stove and his broadening smile nearly took her breath away. Again.

She jumped to her feet. Agitated, she got out the flour and sugar and salt. She could at least make dessert.

"What are you doing?" he asked. She couldn't tell if that smile meant he was laughing at her or with her. Of course, she wasn't laughing.

"Baking. I cook when I'm nervous," she said to her annoyance. Telling him so wasn't going to help. In fact, all it would do was force the question...

"I make you nervous?" He turned down the gas and faced her, his arms going across his chest as though he was pulling himself in. "Why?"

Seriously? "Because you're—"

Thankfully she stopped herself from blurting out his name. As she'd told Fitz, she hadn't deliberately been hiding the fact that she knew who he was, but it was also far too late to throw it out there now. "Because you're gorgeous," she answered. Which was only marginally better.

The man actually blushed.

"Oh, please." She glared at him as she gathered the rest of what she'd need for chocolate cupcakes. "You're obviously aware of that fact."

"Do you always say exactly what you're thinking?" he asked. She didn't need to be looking at him to know he was laughing again; she could hear it in his voice.

"Only when I'm nervous," she muttered. The fact that she'd brought it up for a second time being case in point.

The silence lasted so long that she was sure he'd turned away. But when she spun around to reach for the eggs, he was right there. Then his hand—oh, God, his *hand*—went to her hair, slid down her jaw and tilted her head up gently so that she had no choice but to look up at him.

"I don't want to scare you," he said softly. "Just say the word and I'm gone."

Forgetting the counter was right behind her, Dorie took a step back and came right up against it.

This was crazy.

Ludicrous.

Her heart was pounding so loudly in her ears that she couldn't hear herself think.

Sex was one thing; being so unsettled by a man's presence was another entirely. She obviously needed to put a stop to this. She'd tell him to leave.

But what came out of her mouth instead was a whispered, "If I wanted you gone, I'd knee you in the balls and then chase you out with that bat over there."

And there went the moment. Leave it to her to mention kneeing a guy's balls when the lips of one of the most eligible bachelors in the world—angel with fallen wings or not—were about three inches away from hers. But that's who she was. Better to scare him off now, she supposed.

Except rather than freak out or even look at her strangely, he laughed as his hand left her hair and he took a step back. "I like you, Dorie Donelli. I think I might like your brothers, too."

Now that there was no longer skin-on-skin contact, she was able to breathe again. Dizzy enough to have to clutch the edge of the counter, but at least she could breathe.

Chapter Seven

What. The. *Fuck* had just happened?

Nate's heart was racing so fast he was practically sweating. It made no sense. She wasn't his type. Blondes and redheads were definitely more up his alley. And she was short. At six foot three, he tended to date women who were on the taller side. He was a professional catcher, for Christ's sake. He spent hours out of every day crouching; the last thing he wanted to do when he came home to a woman was bend down.

Dorie was around five foot five, five foot six and she didn't seem the type to wear Jimmy Choo shoes, yet he found himself thinking that he couldn't care less. All he really wanted to do was lift her up, wrap her legs around him and then bury his head right there at the curve of her neck until she begged him to—

"Can I be doing something right now?"

Her voice startled him enough that he almost dropped the skillet he'd just lifted to drain.

"Uh, no," he answered quickly, just to be safe.

He wanted to kiss her. To thrust his hands in her hair and pull her up against him and take it directly from there. But rattling around in the dark recesses of his brain was the notion that going down that road right now would be a mistake of the highest order. And, for reasons he couldn't even begin to name, that scared him. The only thing he *did* know at the moment, in fact, was that in the past twenty-four hours he'd barely thought at all about the accident or anything that came after it. The contracts teetering on the edge of disaster, the questions about his knee, the whole damn Breathalyzer thing…

None of it.

Instead, his mind kept drifting back to her. To *here*. To this apartment and the fact that it seemed to be the one place in the entire world where the past six weeks were history. Where, in fact, he couldn't stop smiling.

Hell.

"Almost done." He threw in some seasoning and then turned the gas down to low. "It just needs to simmer for a few minutes, then we should be good to go."

Although she frowned, her eyes sparkled with amusement. "Except for the part where it has to be in the oven for an hour."

He made his shrug as casual as was humanly possible. "There is that."

Leaning back against the counter, she folded her arms across her chest. The look in her eyes was, it seemed, utter and innocent bewilderment. "So what exactly were you planning to do to pass the time?"

Fuck her into oblivion would have been his honest-to-God answer up until about three minutes ago. He almost laughed when the words, *Get to know you*, nearly came out of his mouth instead.

With some nerves of his own—which was ridiculous; he didn't get nervous—he reached for his beer, actively fighting the urge to down the entire thing. "Tell me how you came to have some of Aunt Laura's casserole in the first place."

A sad smile came to Dorie's face as she looked away. "She thinks I'm lonely. And like any self-respecting grandmotherly type, she wants to feed me to make me feel better."

"Are you lonely?" he asked without thinking. Whispering almost.

She looked up quickly, clearly not expecting that to be his response. Or maybe just not expecting the intensity of it. Hell, neither had he.

She gave a self-conscious laugh, but her shrug was answer enough.

He wanted to touch her again. To take her in his arms and kiss her—tell her she'd never be lonely again.

Then she shook it off and gave a huge smile. "Between the brothers and the wives-slash-girlfriends and my parents, etcetera, etcetera…" She rolled her eyes. "If it means I get to live my life and not get any grief for a little while? I'm good. Besides, I like hanging out with Mr. and Mrs. Grimes. They're totally my speed."

"Mine, too." He tipped his bottle toward her in a mock toast. "I'll be spending all day tomorrow hanging out with them in the library. Come find me there to see for yourself."

She froze, beer halfway to her mouth. "Wha…?"

So, okay. A little bit more of a reaction than he'd expected, but whatever. He shrugged. "There's a new librarian in town, I guess. And a lot of heavy lifting. She, uh… Dorie?"

Her gaze was focused somewhere over his shoulder and it was pretty clear she hadn't heard a word he'd just said. Then she met his gaze. "You're coming to my library tomorrow?" she said, partly curious, and partly, well...partly horrified. Except then she gave another one of those little laughs from the back of her throat and said, "Of course you are."

No way. "*You're* the librarian?" That was unexpected. Not unwelcome by any means—just...intriguing.

He turned back to the stove and went about getting the chili finished so it could go into the casserole dish, cheese and all. It was easier to talk when he wasn't looking at her. "Then who's Lucinda?" He was pretty sure that was the librarian's name.

"Right," Dorie muttered, almost to herself. "Your aunt seems to have an issue with names. I keep telling her I go by Dorie, but it doesn't seem to stick."

"Tell me about it," Nate answered, laughing. "She's only ever called me Nathan. Even my mom rarely calls me that." So caught up in what he was doing, it wasn't until Dorie replied that Nate realized what he'd just done.

"Nathan, huh?" The smile in her voice sent ice up through his veins. "Not D.B.?"

Shit. *Shit.*

He truly hadn't meant to deceive her. He'd just been so grateful she hadn't recognized him—and, okay, yes, completely turned on—that he'd wanted that moment for himself. To not be someone whose face had been plastered on the news for the past two months. Not be the rich and spoiled athlete some people still insisted on believing had been driving drunk—and definitely not be the guy Courtney had cheated on.

Was D.B. the best choice? Hell, no. It had just come out. But he was pretty sure that if he'd been honest about who he was, the night would have turned out a whole lot differently.

"D.B. is a nickname," he mumbled, concentrating really hard on putting the finishing touches on the casserole so he could put it in the oven.

"Maybe I could call you Nathan instead?" she asked, still smiling from behind him.

"Or Nate," he said, dreading the look of recognition that was sure to come into her eyes and yet partly wanting that very thing. "Most people call me Nate."

He finally turned around, straightened his shoulders and looked at her. She was standing there within arm's reach. He could feel the heat coming off her skin.

"Okay," she said, looking up at him from underneath those long, dark lashes. The smile finally reached her eyes. "Nate."

It was like a bomb went off in Nate's head. Chest. *Heart.* Whatever. Nothing had ever struck him the way it did when Dorie looked at him and truly smiled.

He snatched up his beer. Wanting to get to know a woman was a new thing for him. He needed something for his hands to do that wasn't trailing up and down her skin.

"So, Dorie-not-Lucinda," he finally said. "Any other names I should know about?"

She smiled again, and this time he managed to keep his reaction a little more subdued.

"My brothers all call me Luce," she said, "which can be incredibly annoying…"

"Hey, what's wrong with Luce? I like that."

"Because I *asked* them to call me Dorie," she said, all little-sister attitude.

Hell, he liked that, too. He grinned as she continued, "It's short for Dorinda, my—well, one of—my middle names."

"One of? You have more than one middle name?"

She nodded. "Five."

"Five? You have five middle names?"

"Well…"

"You know I have to ask…" he added when she didn't elaborate.

Rolling her eyes, she said, "Lucinda Dorinda Yaz Yaz Tommy Sue Donelli."

Beer halfway to his mouth, he paused. "Yaz-Yaz? That counts as two?"

"Well, it's Yaz once, then Yaz again."

He laughed. "Is that a family name?"

She hiked herself up to the counter. "Yaz, as in Carl Yastrzemski."

Ouch.

"You're a Red Sox fan?" For the first time in his life he cared more about whether or not she actually watched baseball—hoping for the *not* right now—than he did about who she rooted for.

"Well, duh," she answered. "From Boston. Hello." She gave a cute little frown. "Shay, my brother, was five when I was born, and he loved Yaz, so that's the name he picked. And since Colin didn't have a thought of his own until he was, like, fourteen, he just picked Yaz, too."

"Wait," Nate said, holding his hand up. "They picked your names?"

"I know, right?" she said. "When my mom went into labor my dad couldn't get anyone to take care of my brothers so he had to bring them all to the hospital until my grandparents could come pick them up. He bribed them into behaving by promising them they could name me. It didn't occur to him that they'd all want to pick a name of their own."

For as exasperated as she seemed with her brothers—with the story itself—the love and affection that came through her voice as she spoke was almost overwhelming. It pulled a smile out of him even though that earned him another frown. "So, Yaz Yaz," he said, holding back his laugh. "And the rest?"

Her glare diminishing only slightly, she answered, "Sean—he was nine and thought Lucinda sounded like a princess, so he decided on that. Jack decided that since Dorinda rhymed with Lucinda, that must be a princess, too. You know the Yaz Yaz part. Tommy was three when I was born, so the only name that came to mind when they asked was his own."

"That's five," he said, catching the surprise as she looked up at him. "Sean, Jack, Shay, Colin, and Tommy." Her eyes widened even further. Hell, yes, he was paying attention. "Who's number six?"

"Christopher. He wasn't really talking yet. He babbled something and they decided it was 'Sue.'"

Nate did some quick math. "So seven kids in nine years?" He refused to acknowledge that he kind of liked the sound of that.

"Go ahead, you can say it," Dorie said, rolling her eyes in a way that made it clear she'd had this conversation a million times. "That's way too many kids. Overpopulation and all that," she mumbled, peeling the label off her beer bottle. "Or you could say something about the Catholic thing. The Irish-Italian one. Or maybe even that they could have just gone for two more and gotten a baseball team out of it."

Her voice trailed off, which made him realize that he was staring at her again. That he was thinking about how different she was from Courtney—from any woman he'd ever known.

And it scared the ever-living shit out of him.

"I, uh…" He ran his hand through his hair. "I need to…"

Go, he was going to say. Except he couldn't force that final word out when she hopped to the floor, almost looking relieved, as she no doubt knew exactly what he'd been about to say. That was his moment. Where he should have grabbed his coat and gone. But his feet were rooted to the floor.

And he was so fucking glad that she didn't push him toward the door. Instead she wrapped her arms around herself and looked down at the floor. "So." She kind of shrugged. "I don't suppose you'd be up for some GTA?"

It was so unexpected a segue that it threw him for a minute. "Grand Theft Auto?"

She got that prickly look, which amused him to no end, even—or maybe especially—when she said, "And by GTA, I mean GTA. All clothes are staying on."

From the way she then immediately clamped her mouth shut, it was clear she was feeling the same push and pull he was. To his complete surprise, it made him laugh. "You're on."

She kicked his ass and made no bones about enjoying every minute of it.

Granted he was distracted. Not because of the way she looked, although he couldn't deny his attraction. It was more the determination painted all over her face as she went all in. The glint in her eye when she made a move, the enthusiasm and joy as she leaped to her feet, lording it over him when she won.

By the time dinner was over and dishes were cleaned

up and put away, he realized it wasn't just that he'd made a terrible mistake—he'd made a fatal one. It wasn't the part about him wanting so badly to get a woman out of her clothes—it was how much he wanted to be there when she got back into them.

Chapter Eight

For the second night in a row, Dorie didn't sleep; and for the second morning in a row, she found herself sitting in her office, staring out at the street. Unlike the night before, she'd gotten past the part about whether it had all been real. Obviously it was. The problem now was that she had no idea what to do about it. She'd spent a whole lifetime building the fantasy of him up into the ideal man—what on earth was she supposed to do with the true-to-life one?

And now even her potential-one-night stand idea had become complicated. She was almost afraid to admit how much she liked him—definitely more than most of the guys she'd slept with, and that was even without the Nate Hawkins factor. In fact, she'd almost blurted out that she did know exactly who he was so that they could just get on with it.

Yes, she was resolved to do that very thing, especially since they could then acknowledge his pre-Courtney reputation for one-and-done hookups, actually do the hooking up, and then both move on. He was clearly here to lick his wounds before heading back to Chicago where he'd either go back to his old ways or be on the search for his next Courtney, so it should work out fine.

Right.

But even if he never spoke to her again, she'd deal. That she'd had the chance to hang out with him at all was a dream come true. And if against all odds he did speak to her after she'd come clean, well, she didn't plan on doing much speaking. In fact, she would happily provide any necessary licking services whenever and wherever required.

Shaking off the completely useless tingly feeling that thought brought about, she glanced at the clock. Mrs. Grimes had said that her nephew—no name mentioned—would be here by ten, which was an hour away. And Dorie had a whole lot of things to get done: on top of the normal erasing-ten-years'-worth-of-neglect to-dos, last week's blizzard had taken out two windows in the main reading room. The resulting four-foot snowdrift had taken out most of *Fiction, Do—H* and had broken Dorie's heart. Right up until she realized what an incredible opportunity it was. She got to buy books—hundreds of them. And new furniture. New carpeting. They just had to determine what could be salvaged first.

It was half an hour later when she heard the door chimes she'd installed the previous afternoon. She'd managed to wedge herself into the area of the room with the most damage and was balanced on the bottom shelf of a bookcase that had fallen against the wall.

"Back here!" she called out loudly enough for Mrs. Grimes to hear her from the circulation area out in front. "Could you make up a few more boxes for me?"

"My pleasure," answered someone who was very obviously *not* Mrs. Grimes. "How many do you need?"

Dorie spun around at the sound of Nate's voice. Given how precarious everything was in the first place, that meant she very ungracefully kept going, losing her balance in the process and falling face-first into the pile of books on the floor. As if that wasn't bad enough in itself, she was pretty sure the view he had was a direct one of her ass pointing up in the air.

Sure enough, he chuckled and said, "Can't say I mind seeing you like that." As he got closer, though, his voice turned to concern. "Dorie, *Jesus*—are you trying to get hurt?"

It wasn't until he was pushing himself between her and the now-dangerously wobbly bookcase so that she could get herself out from underneath it that she realized she'd gotten herself in a little bit over her head. She made her way around the piles of books on the floor and then watched as he carefully repositioned the bookcase against the wall. "It wasn't *that* bad." At least it hadn't seemed to be when she'd gotten herself started.

He wasn't listening, though. Instead he was looking around the room. "Did it maybe occur to you that you shouldn't be dealing with this alone?"

"I'm sorry," Dorie snapped. "I could have sworn I left my brothers back home." The room looked much worse than it actually was. With the exception of this back area, actually, everything was organized and packed away. But the toppled shelves were pretty bad. And the stacks of still-soggy books were definitely taking on an unpleasant smell. Still… "I can manage the cleanup from a snowstorm."

"Did a tree come through?" he asked, walking past her to the so-spanking-new window it still had stickers on it.

It gave her the chance to look at him, here in the light. It was hard not to. She knew his stats—hopefully she'd never have to admit that she hadn't needed to look them up. But although the numbers told how long and lean he was, they didn't do that body justice. Actually, she wasn't sure anything other than a private showing could do that body justice. The only thing that came to mind was the *Vanity Fair* photo from a few years before— he was sitting in a dugout, no shirt, but the bottom half of his uniform was still on. The pinstripes emphasized the muscles in his legs, stretched out in front of him and practically begging a woman to come and straddle him.

Like he'd need to ask.

One arm rested along the back of the bench beside him, a big and obviously strong hand curled around a baseball; the other arm was relaxed at his side, his wrist resting on his thigh, catcher's mitt positioned directly over what she suspected to be a very fine endowment. He wore his catcher's helmet, mask flipped up, his eyes sparkling with laughter. Though not actually smiling, his lips curved just enough to extend an invitation.

"Dorie?" he asked, and she had to deliberately remind herself that it wasn't her place to run her hands down that gorgeous chest of his, maybe rest her cheek against his abs as she took a quick nip at his skin. Still, a sound escaped from the back of her throat. And she was pretty sure she'd just licked her lips.

"*Dorie...*"

Her gaze flew up at the sound of her name being torn from his throat all needy and raw. She took a shaky step back as she saw the intent and desire in his eyes; it took everything she had not to retreat farther as he came closer. She tilted her head up just as he bent his down and...

"Nathan! *There* you are."

Rather than pull back as his aunt came into the room—as Dorie instinctively did—Nate just watched as her whole world tilted. Then, as if nothing had happened, he walked past her and greeted his aunt and uncle.

It took Dorie a few seconds to catch her breath again, seconds during which she had to fully concentrate on keeping herself from crumpling into a boneless heap.

Holy. Hell.

She made herself turn around, plastering a smile on her face in expectation of facing Mr. and Mrs. Grimes. But instead, the gaze she met was Fitz's. It wasn't a happy one. And that was nothing compared to the icy daggers being sent Dorie's way from the woman standing next to Fitz.

The woman was, like Nate, cover-model gorgeous. Her long, caramel-colored hair was pulled back into a ponytail, and she was tall and thin, yet curvy in the right places. And, God, how Dorie was hoping this was one of Nate's sisters.

"Jules," Nate said, his voice full of both challenge and trepidation as his hands fell to his sides. "What are you doing here?"

"Nate," she answered, the ice transferring from her eyes to her voice as she turned to look at him. There was a flash of emotion—an aching sadness gone so quickly Dorie may have imagined it—before Jules folded her arms across her chest. "I was afraid that if I waited for you to come find me I'd be waiting another two years."

With a brief glance at Dorie, Nate stepped forward. "Missed you, sis," he murmured. "You come here to yell at me, or to tell me you missed me, too?"

From inside his embrace, Jules pulled her arm back, bringing it forward in a quick and very unladylike punch. Then she threw her arms around him and gave a huge hug. "Of course I missed you. Although there sure have been a lot of things to yell about lately."

Visibly tensing, he pulled away and said, "Maybe we don't need to go into them here."

She glared at him but didn't push, saying instead, "So do I get to see you at some point today, or do you have other plans?"

Trying to ignore her disappointment, Dorie almost missed the look he gave her—as though he was asking *her* permission. It surprised her enough that she turned to see if there was someone else standing behind her.

There wasn't.

"I, uh… No," he said. "Not after I'm done helping here."

"And that would be when?" Jules asked, her question directed to Mrs. Grimes.

Who, despite being her aunt Laura as well, presumably, just smiled. In an absentminded kind of way, the older woman gestured at the mess. "No earlier than dinnertime, I'm sure. But Lucinda is in charge, so it's really up to her."

For once Dorie didn't bother to make the correction. "An hour, maybe? I can manage it from there."

Nate gave an irritatingly patronizing smile. "No, you can't."

Seriously? "Yes, I can."

Before Nate had a chance to reply, Fitz spoke, albeit reluctantly. "I have to say, I agree with Nate. I had no idea it was this bad back here. You really do need some help—more than just Nate, I think." She reached into her bag and took out her phone, then put her hand on Jules's arm and began to lead her out. "What do you say, Jules? Can we count on you to handle lunch?"

With the kind of aggrieved sigh Dorie had used on her own brothers more than once, Jules just nodded. Taking out her phone, she gave Nate a heated yet also forgiving glare. "It's going on your tab," she said as she left the room.

That clearly didn't bother him at all. In fact, it only made him smile.

After Jules left—followed shortly by Fitz and Mr. and Mrs. Grimes—Dorie found herself facing Nate again. And as any decent person should do, she said, "You should go be with your sister, Nate. Not here."

As his gaze went to the doorway everyone else had disappeared through, he murmured, "Yeah. Probably."

And the walls came crashing down around her.

She recognized that look in his eyes because she'd felt it deeply for years. It was longing, plain and simple. But the urge she'd just felt to comfort him was truly terrifying. It had taken everything she had to drag herself away from the safety and comfort of home in order to get herself here. She could *not* get sucked into his drama, no matter who he was. She just couldn't.

And yet when he looked up and grinned, all traces of turmoil gone as he said, "But I'd rather be with you. I like it a lot better when *you* yell at me."

Oh, *damn*. She stared up into his eyes. "What would she want to yell at you about?" she asked, descending into a rabbit hole of trouble.

There was a long pause, which didn't surprise her; and then an answer, which did. Quietly, he said, "She doesn't like the way I live my life."

"Do you?" she asked as the air rushed out of her

lungs. She didn't want to like him this much. Didn't want to see the man behind the superstar, the funny, not-afraid-of-a-kitchen-loves-his-family-even-though-they-obviously-drive-him-crazy man. "Like the way you live your life?" she added even as his eyes narrowed.

He straightened up further, and she was suddenly reminded that he was a six-foot-tall hunk of muscle who regularly had other six-foot-tall hunks of muscle running with all of their might straight at him. It was quite a sight—in an awesome, breathtaking way that had nothing to do with how beautiful he was. And she knew that the smart thing would be to retreat. Quickly.

But she stood her ground.

"Do you?" she asked again, almost a whisper.

He stared at her for a minute and she was afraid she would break when he took a strand of her hair. His eyes dropped as he watched it pass through his fingers.

"You just call it like it is," he murmured. "Don't you?"

She wasn't generally taken in by a pretty face. They were a dime a dozen, as far as she was concerned. Good for a fun night or two, but not really worth much beyond that. But put that pretty face on a guy who didn't shy away from her directness—who actually seemed to appreciate it? Bam, all her lady parts were ready to go.

She had to swallow over the lump in her throat when he let his hand fall away and said, "No. Not so much these days."

"Is there anything I can do?" she finally managed. Because, yes. She could offer sex. She was in. Her goddamn conscience could go right on out the newly repaired window.

After what seemed like forever, all the tension in his body evaporated—just like that—and he gave his easy smile. "Just keep cooking for me and I'll be happy." He reached down for an empty box, went over to the shelf he'd rescued her from and started packing books away.

Well, okay, then.

It took a few minutes for Dorie to catch her breath. Then she forced herself to turn back to her own books. "I only cooked for you once. And that doesn't count, because it wasn't really for you. It was just what I had in the freezer."

"You made me cupcakes last night," he corrected.

"I made *us* cupcakes." She grinned. "You were the one who cooked."

"Huh," he said. "You're right. So I guess now it's your turn. Too bad I already have plans for tonight. So what are you doing tomorrow?"

Wait, like an actual date? With all these crazy emotions and strange *feelings* swirling around them? It was one thing to hang out. To banter and tease. To strip naked and do his bidding. "Uh… Um…"

She wanted sex with her imaginary boyfriend come to life, with the gorgeous fantasyland superstar baseball player. She did not—*could* not—allow herself to think beyond that. Not when the true-to-life man was so much more than she'd ever dreamed—so much more that she could see herself losing focus. Getting caught up and taking her eyes off her own goals. And if Courtney Knight, billionaire trust fund baby, beautiful muse for, at last count, three musicians and one painter, and brilliant morning news anchorwoman, was now primarily known as Nate Hawkins's Ex-Fiancée, well, Dorie Donelli did not stand a chance. It was so against her New Life directive that it wasn't even funny. "I, um…"

Saving her from making what was sure to be a pathetic excuse, Fitz's voice rang out from behind her. "Tomorrow's trivia night. Nate—the guys are already planning on you being there."

Oh, thank God.

"Really," Nate said. It was a statement more than a question.

"Yep," Fitz answered, clearly choosing not to acknowledge the suspicion in his voice. Ignoring it entirely, in fact, and turning to Dorie. "I've called in the cavalry. We'll have this place cleaned out in no time. Nate—can you help Aunt Laura and Uncle A with the boxes? We're gonna need a bunch more made up."

Nate looked from Fitz to Dorie, then to Fitz again, not at all happy about being so obviously dismissed. He didn't question her, though. With one final glance at Dorie, he left the room.

Waiting until he was safely out of hearing distance, Fitz whirled around and looked at Dorie.

"What?" Dorie asked as Fitz remained silent.

Fitz hesitated for another minute before saying, "That was interesting," and coming farther into the room. "He seems, I don't know, *happy*." She was clearly surprised as she stared thoughtfully at Dorie. Then she briskly said, "You should come to trivia night. Join us on the ladies' team."

Dorie's eyes bugged out. *Really?*

"So now you want to pimp me out to make him *happy*?" Not exactly contradictory to Dorie's own ideas, but still…

That didn't seem to offend Fitz at all. She just ignored Dorie's words as she give a little bit of a shrug.

Dorie shook her head. "No." No, no, no, *no*. She was *not* doing this.

Fitz changed the subject by saying, "So Wash is coming by with a couple of the guys from the farm."

Oh. Oh, lord. This was not helping. Wash Fairfield? This was getting even crazier. *C-R-A-Z-Y.*

"Oh, *God.*"

Plus…windows aside, Dorie did have a conscience, especially if there was more hanging out to be done. But how could she tell Nate the truth when Wash Fairfield was standing there next to him? She resisted the sudden urge to put her head between her knees.

"Boxes," she said to herself, nearly forgetting the other woman until Fitz looked up and said, "Huh?"

"Boxes," Dorie repeated, this time with assurance since avoidance was absolutely the way to get through this day. "And paint." Shit. "You do have Home Depot here in Iowa, right?"

Ignoring the fact that Fitz was clearly amused by all this, Dorie headed toward her office with a quickly jabbed finger point at Fitz. "You're not leaving me alone here. You do realize that, right?"

Fitz laughed and shook her head again. "Wouldn't miss this for the world."

Which was a damn good thing. Because Dorie had no intention of making a fool of herself in front of Nate Hawkins, Wash Fairfield and whoever else they could drag up. But someone was going to need to remind her to keep breathing.

Chapter Nine

Nate watched the sun come up through his mother's kitchen window. He'd let himself get more and more caught up in "the life," as Wash used to call it, and then he'd allowed Courtney to become an excuse for not coming home. Being here in his mom's house, spending time with Fitz and Wash—even Jules—was reminding him that he actually loved it here. That it nourished him. Breathed life into what had been turning into a brittle shell. The only problem right now was that the lack of sleep was beginning to take its toll.

Sleepless nights one and two had been due to Dorie, so he didn't totally mind. Number three was a little more complicated, thanks to his dinner at Jules's. That she and her husband weren't doing well had been plain as day. He hated seeing his sister unhappy, but since he'd grown up with his brother-in-law and never been a big fan, he actually thought she'd be better off without the guy.

But it had brought Nate right back to those last few months with Courtney. The barely concealed tension, the lack of any warmth… The general sense that something was about to blow—and not really caring enough to fix it. It had also exposed nearly every raw nerve he'd been dealing with for years, starting with his own parents' broken marriage thanks to his father's drinking and infidelities.

Maybe this irrational attraction to Dorie was more about what he'd never really had as opposed to what he wanted from *her*.

Or, hell, maybe it was just a simple rebound thing. That was the most likely explanation. Whatever it was, he'd made every attempt to resist it last night by deliberately not giving in to the temptation to go by her place again last night and instead heading directly back to his mom's.

After tossing and turning all night, when it was finally light enough to stop pretending he was asleep, he'd opened his eyes and been more than a little unsettled at how much he'd missed seeing her. Especially since she'd spent most of yesterday afternoon running errands with Fitz—an excuse, he was pretty sure, to avoid him after whatever it was that had happened between them in the morning.

Putting that out of his head, he took out his phone. There were nearly a dozen emails, the most urgent of which, of course, was from Pete about management. They wanted to "discuss NateGate." They weren't happy that it hadn't gone away—as if he was over the moon about it. But there was good news, too. Pete's contact at the police department said they'd be releasing a statement today that would officially clear Nate of all charges. To be honest, that was more of a relief than he'd like to admit. He hadn't been drunk—he knew that without question—and he'd wanted to believe he hadn't been at fault. But he had almost no memory of the accident itself, so knowing for sure that he hadn't caused it was a huge weight off his chest.

Except now Alexis, his publicist, wanted to put out a statement *ASAP* and Mark, his agent, was already lining up new endorsements for a star reborn, none of which he wanted to deal with in any way.

Nate sent a note to Pete that if the GM really wanted to meet with him, he'd be available Sunday morning at ten. Sure, it was a diva move, but he was pissed off and he wanted to make them work for it. Yeah, he got how important it was for a brand-new team to start off clean, but he had absolutely zero control over this situation and wasn't sure what they expected him to do about it. And, honestly, he'd known the people involved for a long time—it would have been nice if they'd been a little more supportive, even if only behind the scenes.

He threw his phone on the table and tried to concentrate on the beauty of the sunrise again, but to no avail. After an hour's run that only had him doing more useless thinking, he jumped in the shower and then got himself the hell out of there.

Half an hour later he was on Main Street. Telling himself that he was just there to check up on Jules, he headed to her café. She looked up when the door opened, her smile an indication that they were on their way back to being okay.

It took almost half an hour for him to walk from the front door to Jules, thanks to all the well-wishers. Which was…good. Not unexpected. He'd always had unequivocal support from the people in town and, it appeared, that hadn't changed even with the whole NateGate thing. At the same time, it was exhausting. If he had to shake one more hand as he confirmed to yet another acquaintance that, yes, it sucked to have this going on, and, no, he wasn't worried about his knee…

Inspiration was hands down a better place for him to be than Chicago was right now, but it still wasn't quite the escape he'd been seeking. Except when he was with Dorie. Her apartment, the library… Inspiration felt pretty good then.

When Nate finally got to the counter, Jules brightened her smile. "Nate, hi. Do you remember Barb O'Reilly? Her husband coaches the boys' basketball team."

He turned to the woman standing across from his sister. "Coach is doing a great job this year. They might actually take it all the way."

Barb's face froze. Then she broke into a huge grin. "You follow the team? Oh, my *God*."

Laughing, Jules reached out and touched Barb's arm. "Didn't we tell you he did?" She rolled her eyes. "Why doesn't anyone ever believe us when we say that?"

Clutching Jules's hand, Barb turned to Nate and said, "Will you come to their game today? They're playing at 3:30 in the gym. You know—the gym that, um, you guys built for them."

Nate started to open his mouth and give the same nonanswer he'd given to Tuck a few nights before—but then he suddenly realized that thinking of Dorie had put him in a much better mood and he kind of actually *wanted* to go. With a genuine smile, he answered, "I think I could swing that. But you should probably let it be a surprise." That way he could just sneak in the back, hang out with the coaches and not have to talk to anyone except the kids playing.

After Barb left, Nate ordered a coffee for himself and then decided that it couldn't hurt to bring some over to his aunt and uncle. And, yes, Dorie. If she ran away again? He'd deal with that if he needed to. "I'll take some muffins, too."

A few minutes later he found himself in front of the library, pastry box in one hand, tray full of coffees in the other. He had no idea whether Aunt Laura and Uncle A would be working this morning—wasn't entirely sure he wanted them to be. But he was one hundred percent working under the pretense that he was here for them.

It did bother him that he wasn't sure of the reaction he'd get from Dorie—that he was actually manufacturing reasons to see her. Heading up the walkway he decided it didn't matter. Right now he just wanted to see that smile again. To feel the weight lift off his chest when she looked his way. If his motives weren't pure, so be it. It wasn't like he'd made her any promises he couldn't keep. He wasn't even sure he'd see her again after this week. Except the second he walked in the door, he knew he was fooling himself. His blood ran cold at the sight of her sitting up on Wash's shoulders, laughing as she almost lost her balance while reaching up to change a lightbulb. As she steadied herself by wrapping her arms around Wash's head, clamping her thighs down on his shoulders.

"Need a little help?" Nate asked, the door snapping closed behind him.

The amusement in Wash's eyes as he turned did nothing to settle Nate down.

"Oh, my gosh." Dorie reached her arms out to Nate, completely unaware of any tension, sexual or otherwise. Nate, on the other hand, practically dropped the coffee and muffins on the floor in his rush to grab her. Luckily, there was a step stool nearby to catch them so he didn't make a total fool of himself. Thank God he was used to moving on instinct rather than thought. Being an elite athlete had its perks.

She fell into him, gripping his shoulders as his hands went to her hips. His eyes locked on to hers and everything came to a thundering halt as the earth stopped spinning on its axis. The building could have fallen down around them and he wouldn't have cared. He had to count to ten in Japanese, for fuck's sake, in order not to dip his head down and kiss her. No, *claim* her.

Fuck.

Two days, he'd known her. Two days. He'd known Courtney for two *years* and he'd never felt like this.

He lowered Dorie to the floor and took a step back. "I, uh, brought coffee. For my, um, aunt and uncle. And you. Cream, light sugar, right?" He couldn't stop his tongue from tangling itself up with words. *Jesus.*

"Thanks," she said, not looking at him as she pulled away. She picked up the tray. "I'll bring it to them."

It wasn't until she'd disappeared from sight that Nate noticed Wash staring at him. "Shit, boy," Wash said, a smile erupting as he clapped Nate on the shoulder. "You have it bad."

Even if he wanted to deny it, Nate wasn't sure he could. His heart was racing so fast that he felt dizzy. A picket fence suddenly appeared in the corner of his mind, and it scared the hell out of him. He pushed it right back out.

"Just a momentary distraction," he mumbled, trying more to convince himself than Wash.

"So you wouldn't mind if I threw my hat into the ring?"

Nate only barely resisted throwing Wash up against the wall. Since they seemed to have overcome what-

ever tension had built up over the past two years—farm
chores went a long way in rebuilding bonds—that would
have been a seriously bad move. It also would have sent
a message he wasn't at all ready to send.

But Wash wasn't fooled, even though he gave a decep-
tively easy smile. "I mean, you're heading back to Chicago soon and you can be damn sure someone's gonna
be stepping in if there's a void." He bent down to pick
up the box Jules had packed. Opened it up and lifted the
tissue paper. "Hell, if she's there tonight?" He shook his
head. "Only reason she hasn't been snatched up is because no one's met her yet."

Trivia night. Right. Nate had planned on making an
appearance, but only briefly. Stopping in at the Bombers's game this afternoon was already more than he'd
planned. But Wash was right. From what Nate could
tell, Dorie had been either at work or in the apartment
pretty much since she'd arrived in Inspiration. It was a
small enough town that anyone new stood out. If anyone else had even a fraction of the reaction to her that
Nate was having…

Nate shook his head. "It won't work." He needed
to hear the words in order to absorb them. There were
snowballs in hell, and then another ten stops down that
road was the chance of something happening between
them.

But then Wash's snapped, "Why?" got his attention.
"Getting ready to cut and run again?"

Because, of course, all that talk had just been Wash
goading him. Not to be an ass—Wash wasn't like that
and never had been. But he was one of the few people
in the world who could get past Nate's walls, could get
him to admit something personal.

And, yes. Even though it had only been a matter of hours—at the farm that first day back, and then working at the library yesterday—Nate had his brother back. So for the first time in longer than he could remember, he spoke God's honest truth. "I have no idea what in the fuck I'm doing."

He truly didn't. Because, yes, 'cut and run' had been his MO for a long time. Pretty much from his first days in college all the way up to when he'd met Courtney. And when it came down to it, his relationship with Courtney had been the exact same thing—yes, he'd been involved with only one woman. But that's really all it had been. They'd been perfect on paper, both at the top of their fields, completely untouchable. But, Nate was beginning to realize, it had been a business relationship more than anything else. Business with benefits.

He'd played his part well, and so had she. But into each other the way two people about to be married should be? Not even close. It had been all body, no soul. And she hadn't cared enough to chase him down; if anything, she'd deliberately pushed him away.

To actually be invested in someone? To want to stick around merely because being in their presence made everything...*better*?

Nope. No fucking clue what to do with that.

The smile came back into Wash's eyes. "You should probably figure that out." Taking a muffin out of the box, he took a bite as he closed the lid.

"No shit," Nate muttered. Sinking back against the wall, he watched Wash turn and walk off in the same direction as Dorie.

So what exactly could happen? He'd had no intention of staying in Inspiration longer than a week, two at the absolute outside. Even if it turned out his playing days were coming to an end sooner rather than later, he'd… Well, there had been some vague conversation when they'd been negotiating the new contract—coaching, maybe. Player development. Whatever it was, it was highly unlikely he'd be spending much time in Iowa.

So, yes. He'd damn well better figure out what he was doing. Because it wasn't exactly a foregone conclusion that Dorie even *wanted* to stay in the picture. He'd never seen anyone run from hot to cold and back again as quickly as she did. If he wanted to be doing whatever-it-was with her? He had some major work to do.

What was *that*?

The fact that Dorie was able to carry the coffees to the back room was a miracle; she wasn't sure how she was breathing, much less walking. She handed off the drinks, grabbed her own and then practically ran to her office and locked herself inside so that there was no chance she'd bump into Nate and Wash on the way.

Leaning back in her chair, she forced herself to do a few cleansing, count-to-ten breaths. Of course, she could only ever get to four and usually made herself cough her lungs out in the process, so she put an end to that quickly and grabbed her coffee instead. Yes. God, yes. It was as perfect as he was. Eyes closed, she let its warmth seep through her. Calm her. Bring some normalcy back into a life that suddenly had her sitting a few rooms over from one of the greatest athletes in the history of baseball.

Which was all well and good until she sat up, sputtering, as she realized that the coffee was indeed exactly as she liked it. And that freaked her out more than the time her brothers had made her sit through a *Paranormal Ac-*

tivity marathon. In their grandparents' freaky middle-of-the-woods-no-one-will-hear-you-scream house. On Friday the thirteenth.

She cleaned the coffee off her sweater as well as possible and stood up. She couldn't hide in her office all day. And besides, he'd probably left ages ago. He'd found his aunt and uncle and then gone off on his merry way.

She stopped short when she came around the corner to see him sitting on the stairs leading up to the second floor. Although the grin he gave her acknowledged her presence, the phone call he was on seemed to be taking up enough of his attention that he didn't notice her shock. Or at least he didn't let on.

"Yes, I know," he was saying, patience obviously being tested. "Saturday morning. Where we met the wedding planner." The irritation broke free entirely when after a brief pause he snapped, "Are we bringing dates?"

Dorie tried to get past him before he hung up but she didn't quite manage.

"Fine," he said sharply. Then he muttered a few choice swear words and stood up, effectively blocking Dorie's way.

Since it was impossible to pretend she hadn't heard his end of the conversation, she said, "Your ex?"

"Yep," he answered. "That would be her."

When he didn't elaborate, she said, "So you're seeing her this weekend?" To cover up the flash of jealousy that she had no right to feel, she quickly followed that up with, "Here in Inspiration?"

Falling into step with Dorie as she walked toward the reading room, he shook his head. "Chicago."

She stopped short again. "You're going back?"

Of course he was. He lived there. What, did she think he was going to stay around because he'd cooked for her? And yet she added, "So soon?"

And that right there was why this was a colossally bad idea. She'd never been desperate or whiny over *any* man.

Realizing she was no longer with him, Nate turned and looked down at her, a slow smile coming over his face. Then he softly asked, "Will you miss me?" He was close enough for his breath to sear her skin.

Chest tight, heart stuttering, she forced herself not to back away from him. "Why?" she asked, trying to inject a lightness she didn't feel. "Because you're...gorgeous?"

His hand went to her chin and he tipped her head up in order to meet his gaze. The smile turned to a full-out grin. "Is that all I am to you? Just another pretty face?"

She meant nothing more to him than a challenge, she reminded herself. It was all just a game and she had yet to be conquered. But that did nothing to stop her from wanting him; from wishing she had enough time to get him, foolish as that may be.

She stepped back. Pretending that his touch hadn't affected her in the least, she said, "The face is fine, but what I really need is the brute strength." She gave his arm the most sisterly punch she could manage—pausing only briefly to appreciate the rock-hard biceps—and then started walking again, not looking back to see if he'd follow. "There's a lot more work to do. Is Wash still here?"

"Christ, woman," he muttered, catching up to her with no problem thanks to his long stride. "You sure know how to wound a guy."

As though he cared.

"Wash had to leave," Nate continued, as unwounded

as could be. "And anyway, it's just for a couple of days. I'll be back Sunday. Feel free to make a list."

Relief washed over her even as she told herself that nothing was actually changing, she would just be that much more attached when he left. Then she almost laughed out loud. Several days ago, Nate Hawkins was just a guy on TV, and, um, maybe about twenty pictures that were plastered on the back of the door in her bedroom at her parents' house. Now, here she was, shoulder to shoulder—okay, her shoulder to his chest—with him saying he'd be back and helping out again in a few days.

Despite her insisting that he didn't need to stay, he spent the rest of the day with her in the library packing and moving the rest of the books; dismantling damaged shelves; cleaning, prepping and then helping her paint. By the middle of the afternoon, it was looking so beautiful that Dorie almost cried.

Her vision. *Her* library.

"You're doing a great job here, you know," Nate said from the other side of the room, where he was wrapping paintbrushes with plastic.

She smiled and ducked her head down, embarrassed that the compliment almost made her cry. More embarrassed that she'd let on how much it meant to her to make something of this little corner of the world. She'd told him all about growing up in the noisy, crowded house spilling over with sports gear and Hot Wheels and how hard it had been to get a word in edgewise, much less have someone actually pay attention to—or be able to afford—something she wanted. So when her brothers would go down to the local Y to play basketball, Dorie would go to the library instead. Every time she walked in the librarians had put aside a stack of books they thought she might like. Even now as a fully grown adult, the armchair in the corner of the teen room felt as much home to her as the house her parents still lived in.

"I'm going to have big, comfy chairs just like that one *everywhere*," Dorie said, gathering the stray supplies from the corners of the room and bringing everything over to the pile Nate had made. "I'm going to make this a place where people can't wait to be."

"That's what the basketball court was like for me," Nate said, sitting back against one of the undamaged bookshelves and stretching his legs out.

Oh, *no*. It was one thing to work together all day; another entirely to settle in.

But as if he could sense her urge to bolt, he just reached up for her hand and tugged it so she had no choice but to sit down next to him as he went on, "Ella and Jules had me playing Fairy Tale with them as far back as I can remember. I was so psyched when I got promoted from Coachman to Prince. I think I was eight or nine before I realized that they wanted nothing to do with sports and I could make my escape."

"Escape?" she echoed faintly as she stared down at his hand still holding hers. As she held herself still when he gently caressed the skin at the base of her thumb. It was either that, or shudder herself into a pile of goo.

Sharing childhood memories wasn't doing anything to help remind her that he was not her friend—that she did not want an actual relationship. That even if she did, it couldn't be with him. But she probably shouldn't have snatched her hand away and snippily said, "Playing Prince Charming is a lot better than being thrown around, I'm guessing."

Nate laughed. He thought she was kidding. Or playing hard to get.

She carefully put her hands in her lap so that they were out of his reach. "No joke. They called it Toss the Toddler. They gave each other extra points when I was really squirmy. I got really good at the tuck and roll."

"I don't know," he said, a twinkle in his eye although he managed to refrain from laughing again. "I think I'd rather be tossed around than have to ferry my sisters and their friends around in the wheelbarrow every day. Or kiss them."

Oh, God, no, they couldn't start talking about kissing.

Yet she went ahead and answered, "You can't seriously think that having to kiss your sisters' friends comes anywhere close to being used as a ball."

"Uh, no. Not when you put it like that." He was no longer able to stifle his grin. "Although I do stipulate that kissing girls when you're eight is not the same as kissing them when you're eighteen."

Dorie should have responded with something clever and cute. Should have changed the subject already. But instead her gaze drifted down, her lips already tingling. And then she looked up to see him watching her closely. The tip of her tongue darted out—she honestly didn't know if it was intentional. She couldn't think past the part about how he might taste.

She should stand up. Stand up and get as far away as was humanly possible. But instead she brought her eyes up to meet his. And when his hand cupped the back of her head, she let him guide her to him.

"Or now," he said softly as her bones melted away. "I *really* like kissing now."

Then his mouth was on hers and she nearly cried.

Nothing had ever tasted so sweet—felt so right. His tongue found hers and her body took over, molding itself to him. Her hands went to his chest, fingers skimming over the surface of his T-shirt, her thumb seeking out his hard, flat nipple. When she flicked it, he went still—except for his head pulling back, breaking the kiss.

Rather than pull the rest of himself away, a rumble of laughter moved through him. And then his hands were on her hips and she was suddenly being lifted through the air before being brought down hard against him. Her legs fell apart all on their own. Straddling him as he ground her hips into his, she almost came right there. A sob racked her body at the feel of him anchored against her.

Oh, my freaking *God*. Her arms went around his neck.

It wasn't as though she'd never had sex. She'd had far too much of it as far as Christopher was concerned and an acceptable amount as far as she was.

But…this. Oh, God, *this*.

When Nate held her against him, tremors ran through her. When his thumbs brushed the underside of her breasts, the only thing keeping her from shooting straight up into the sky was his hands holding her down. And when he broke off the kiss and pulled away slightly, muttering, "Holy fucking shit," and looking into her eyes in a way that made her think he'd been as taken by surprise as she was, well…

If her thundering heart wasn't about to explode, she would have been muttering right along with him. She hoped to God she was just overdue for a serious vibrator upgrade. Because if that wasn't the case?

Oh, *God*.

When he gently ran his thumb across her lower lip—when he again pulled her close and traced his tongue around the curve of her lips—tears came to her eyes from sheer bliss. And before she could even recover enough to part her mouth, he dipped his head down to the curve of her neck and pushed her shirt aside so that he could put his lips directly to her skin.

Even as her eyes fluttered closed, a part of her knew she was no different than anyone in the long line of women who had come before her, and, no doubt, every single one who would come after. And yet the only thing that saved her from stripping naked right there was the vague awareness of chimes ringing, the sound of foot-steps in the hall.

She pulled away abruptly. It was bad enough that she was the cliché—the very least she could do was not be freaking making out with Nate Hawkins at work.

It seemed to amuse him. He was much less concerned about being caught with his pants down, possibly liter-ally. Especially when it was Wash who appeared in the doorway less than a minute later, seeming neither fazed nor surprised to see them disentangling themselves from each other's arms.

Or, rather, to see Dorie disentangling. Nate clearly had no concern about how things appeared.

Well, of course he didn't. This probably happened to him all the time.

With this whole damn stupid charade, however, she couldn't even be angry at him. Or, at least, she couldn't tell him why she might be.

She resisted the urge to check whether all her clothes were still in place. "Wash. Hi. I, uh, thank you for all the help this morning." She cringed at the babble coming out of her mouth. It was like a water fountain gurgling up in a rush and then spilling over. There was nothing she could do to stop it. "Sorry I didn't get a chance to say anything before you left. I can't tell you how much your help has meant. It's beyond anything I ever—"

Then Wash turned to her, his gaze finally leaving Nate's, and the look in his eyes silenced her in a way that mere common sense couldn't. Her face flushed.

As though she hadn't spoken, Wash turned back to Nate. "So are we going to this game or not?"

Nate's expression was an odd mix of anger and challenge. Without so much as glancing her way, he answered, "Going. I told Barb I would."

Flushing even more deeply, Dorie wanted to disappear. She had no idea who Barb was—maybe one of the sisters' friends who he'd spent so much time kissing? But it was clear from the unspoken part of the conversation that Wash was almost daring Nate to break whatever promise he'd made to whoever the woman-of-the-moment was. That neither one of them even tried to gloss it over with an invitation, halfhearted as it would have been, hurt more than it should have.

Wash gave a curt nod, then looked back at Dorie. Whatever camaraderie they'd built up this morning was entirely gone. "If there's anything else you need this week just let me know. I'll be happy to send someone by."

"Thanks," Dorie mumbled, an odd feeling settling into the pit of her stomach as he left the room. It was bad enough that she was just a number on Nate's list no matter how much he'd seemed to like that kiss. With Wash she'd been feeling like they might actually become friends.

Then she realized what she was thinking and almost laughed. What a fool. The idea of being friends with Wash Fairfield, a legend in his own right, was as much of a joke as a relationship of any kind with Nate Hawkins. There must be something in the water; it was making her delusional.

She even thought there might be some actual regret in Nate's eyes as he took her hand. "Sorry. I do have to go." Then he gave her that grin that almost made her want to forgive him. "I think I hate that not-breaking-promises thing as much as I like the kissing."

Hmph. She didn't believe him one bit.

He moved in closer, his hand going to the small of her back. Cupping her chin, he seemed to be deliberately ignoring her stiffness and lack of answering smile. "Can I see you tonight?"

Now it was her turn to use the not-breaking-promises excuse. As much as it pained her to give up what could possibly be the best night of her life, she had more self-respect than that. Still, it took everything she had to lightly shrug him off and step back. "Sorry. Trivia night, remember? I promised Fitz."

Except, if anything, he seemed to see that as the next step in the game. "Right," he answered, smiling. And then he was gone.

A shiver ran down her back as the iceberg drew near. It was time. She had to tell him; she had no choice. She simply couldn't take this anymore.

It wasn't until fifteen minutes later when, desperate to get rid of the phantom grazing of his lips, she was in the bathroom splashing water on her face, that she realized she hadn't exactly taken a stand. He'd be at trivia night, too.

Chapter Ten

Oh, shit.

Shit, shit, *shit*.

Nate got himself as far as the front hallway before he was able to stop and get a grip. Or, rather, run his hands over his face in hopes that he could get himself back to where getting a grip was in the realm of possibility. Back to that first night when she was just your run-of-the-mill woman who'd be happy to engage in some mutually satisfying together time and then move on. Or even your run-of-the-mill woman who'd be happy to engage in some mutually satisfying together time and then dig her heels in until she'd negotiated whatever her terms were for moving on. Because pre-Courtney, that's how it tended to go.

Except, if he was being honest, she hadn't been run-of-the-mill since the moment she raised that bat.

And now that he'd been able to touch her? Taste her? He was sure as hell getting past the robe that haunted his dreams. But even if he could just sit with her; talk with her. *Laugh* with her. He honestly couldn't remember the last time he'd laughed with a woman he wasn't related to.

Nate pushed off the wall and forced himself to head outside rather than right back into Dorie's arms.

Not that she'd welcome him—he'd seen grown men trying to steal home who weren't moving as fast as she had to get away from him when Wash had come into the room. He'd played it like he hadn't noticed, but damn that wall of ice had come down hard. He didn't know what put it there—wasn't entirely sure what he'd need to do to break it down—but hell if he wasn't going to try. He had every intention of…

Nate stopped short when it suddenly occurred to him that he was going to have to tell her who he was. He hadn't fucking told her. She knew things about him that he'd never told anyone outside of his family and closest friends. Even Courtney didn't know half of it.

Fuck.

He wanted to believe that she wouldn't care, that she'd understand the person he'd been with her these past few days was one hundred percent him in everything but name.

Except, well, she did know his name. She just didn't—

"On the floor of the library, Hawk?"

Nate looked up to see Wash leaning against his truck.

"Kind of ironic," Wash was saying. "Have you ever even been in a library before this week?"

Appreciating that Wash wasn't pushing the cut-and-run thing, Nate just got into the truck.

Unfortunately, as soon as they were on their way to the high school, Wash asked, "So what's someone as smart as she is doing with you?"

Nate laughed because that was the expected response. He even managed a wry, "You're hilarious, man. You planning on taking that on the road?"

And they kept up the lamest trash talk on the face of the earth all the way to the school, which made Nate irrationally happy, enough so to actually come out and admit, "I like her, Wash. A lot." Too much, although Wash knew Nate far better than anyone else on the planet and was therefore already well aware.

They were pulling into the parking lot when Wash spoke again. He attempted a grin but his expression was far too serious to pull it off. "I've been out of that game for a long time now, but I haven't forgotten what it's like. That whole ride…" His voice trailed off as he no doubt thought about the time he'd spent in Miami, then LA.

Yeah. It wasn't just living your life on the road; it was another dimension entirely. The parties, the women. The crazy shit that went down behind the velvet ropes and bright lights, things Wash knew better than anyone else from Nate's life here since they'd been drafted out of college together. Different sports—Wash had gone the basketball route instead of baseball, and he'd only stayed in it for a few years. But he knew.

"You think she can handle it?" Wash continued, bringing home the point that it wasn't just who Nate was that was a problem—it was what he'd be asking her to sacrifice by getting involved with him. Which, incidentally, would be everything, since her life would no longer be her own once it came out that she was with him.

Before Nate could even finish that thought, Wash added something that had never even crossed Nate's mind. "Hell, you think she can handle Courtney?"

Courtney. Nate had never even considered that.

"Fuck," he muttered, getting out of the truck and slamming the door shut. As much as he wanted to say that Courtney didn't give a rat's ass, he couldn't. It didn't matter that she'd been the one to end the relationship; she'd make Dorie's life a living hell.

"*Fuck*," Nate said again, this time with a lot more conviction behind it.

He wanted to say that Wash was exaggerating. Or that Dorie couldn't care less about any of that. But, yeah, it was even worse than he'd been thinking before.

So, I'm really into you. Crazy into you in a way I don't totally understand.

The timing sucks. I mean I'm kind of Public Enemy #1 at the moment—currently the media's punching bag for a car accident that I can't actually remember. It almost killed a single mom, and her son may never walk again. Plus it may have killed my career, but let's not get into that. It caused my ex to lose her baby, a baby I thought was mine, but wasn't because she'd been sleeping with one of my best friends. None of which actually matters since she'll still be off-the-charts pissed if she ever finds out that I can't stop thinking about you.

That I'm thinking things I have no right to think about a woman I've known for all of two days.

So, you know, drama and life-altering notions aside— wanna go out sometime?

Nate wished he had his mask on so he could slam it down on the ground. It was better than jamming his fist into the concrete bench that Wash was now leaning against.

Damn it.

He was beyond grateful that Deacon and Pike appeared right then. With only the slightest hesitation, they came forward, smiles, fist bumps and hugs all around. And, easy as that, the walls fell away. For the first time in two months—no, two *years*—Nate felt his world begin to settle back into place around him. He headed in to the game feeling on top of the world—in a way that was beginning to feel solid again. Like he was truly finding his way home.

But as they made their way to the coach's office, Nate realized that something was pushing its way out of the depths of his consciousness—something he'd locked down and away with good reason.

Not that he was pretending it didn't exist. He hadn't risen out of the rubble and raised himself to the top of his game by burying things in the sand. No. He'd done the same as with any other threat that had come his way over the past sixteen years: he'd neutralized it.

Car accident did some damage to your knee? You sucked it up and did the PT.

The haters saying it was the end of your career? You pushed your way past the doubts. Studied the hell out of your game—every team on your schedule, every player on the roster. You didn't just visualize success, you fuck-ing *ensured* it.

And when a woman came along who was as smart and sharp as Dorie—a woman who didn't say much about sports but who, thanks to her brothers, had lived and breathed it for most of her life…

Who had a perfect batting stance and, no doubt, a hell of a swing?

You did not under any circumstances allow yourself to wonder how in the *fuck* it was possible that she didn't know your name.

As Dorie sat cross-legged on the floor in the middle of the reading room, she finally accepted that she wasn't going to get anything done. Not after that kiss…

She looked down at the book in her lap. She had no idea when she'd put it there or why. It wasn't even about her being in over her head at this point. That was such a given it barely even mattered. She was just hoping to come out of this without being burned alive.

As she got to her feet, the chimes rang. She'd just turned to face the door when Fitz came charging in. "Oh, good, you're here," she said, reaching out for Dorie's hand and pulling her toward the hall.

"Um…" Dorie stumbled a little, just barely managing to put the book down rather than throw it to the floor. "What are you doing?"

"You're coming with me."

"I can't…" Dorie looked behind her. She couldn't just leave. Could she?

Well, she'd already sent Mr. and Mrs. Grimes home, and it *was* 4:30, but…

Fitz practically stamped her foot. "Come *on*."

Fine. Fitz was practically her boss, after all. And a distraction would be welcome. Dorie hurried into her office to get her things, shut off all the lights and locked up, and then ran out to where Fitz was waiting out in front of the library, her car running. The second Dorie got in, Fitz pulled out. There was absolutely no traffic, which seemed odd—until they got about a mile away from the high school to find cars parked all along the road. For Inspiration, that was the equivalent of a ten-mile backup on the Southeast Expressway back home. There was definitely something strange going on.

"What…?" Dorie asked.

She didn't have to be a Boston-born, impossible-parking expert to know there'd be exactly zero spots closer to the school. Fitz drove straight up to the main doors and pulled her car up on the grass.

"You're going to get towed," Dorie said.

But Fitz just ignored her and said, "Let's go."

The halls were as deserted as the roads were and Dorie was starting to get an uneasy zombie apocalypse-type dread. But there was a faint buzz of noise from somewhere down the hall. When Fitz pulled Dorie through a door in the hallway and up a set of stairs, the source of the noise became clear: they'd come out into the back row of seats, just below the rafters of the gymnasium.

"A basketball game?" Not really Dorie's thing. Sure, she'd been a high school basketball fan back when watching sixteen-year-old boys running up and down the court at least had some benefits. But now? Not so much.

But she followed Fitz, winding down through the seats, working her way to… Wonderful. Jules. And another ridiculously gorgeous woman, who Dorie was hoping was Nate's other sister.

"Dorie, Ella," Fitz said by way of introduction. "Ella, Dorie."

Nodding, Dorie was about to ask why they were here, when the buzzer went off and the crowd cheered. Apparently the home team had won. Puzzled, Dorie clapped along with everyone else.

As the teams returned to their benches after shaking hands, a thirtysomething man in a police uniform came out to the center of the court. Microphone in hand, he said, "Hey, everyone. Thanks for being here today. How about another hand for the kids?" Once the clapping had died down, he continued, "For those of you who don't know me, my name's Tuck, and I've had the pleasure of working with Coach O'Reilly for a while now. They're having a great season, no?"

There was another round of applause, although this

one a little less enthusiastic. At least Dorie wasn't the
only one with no clue.

Clearly aware of that, Tuck gave a big smile. "As all
of you know, we've got a history here with the whole
high school basketball thing." No puzzlement involved
in that round of cheers. It took a full minute for the noise
to die down, stopping only when Tuck finally held his
hands up. "So, uh… He's probably going to kill me for
this, but I know it would mean a lot to everyone to get a
word from a special guest we have here today. And, to
be honest, he's had a rough couple of months. Considering what he's done for us, I think that it wouldn't hurt
for us to maybe welcome him home."

Dorie glanced over at Fitz, who looked right back at
her and smiled. "Wait for it…" Fitz mouthed. Or maybe
said, because the noise had already started up again, and
words were lost entirely. The rumble began down at the
court as the kids on both teams jumped to their feet and
started cheering—screaming—at the tops of their lungs.
It built up to a roar as hundreds, no, thousands, of people
began stomping their feet. Dorie was afraid the building might actually come down. The entire gymnasium
erupted into a frenzy as Nate stepped out on the court.

He had on a baseball cap that he hadn't been wearing when he left the library, and Dorie was pretty sure
he'd used it to blend into the crowd. As though a man
like him could possibly blend. When he finally took the
cap off and gave a little bit of a wave, the frenzy became
something else. It was as if love was being rained down
upon him. As though the town had ripped its heart open
and tucked him inside.

Taking the microphone, he began to say something
but could barely get out, "Thanks, but…" before some-

one yelled, "We love you, Nate!" and the noise started up again.

Without even realizing she'd done it, Dorie found that she was on her feet and cheering along with everyone else in the place, including those still streaming in. It took Nate a while before it occurred to him that he was the one who needed to stop it. Unlike everyone else, he was speechless, his hands at his sides. He finally brought the mic up again and held his hand up, just as Tuck had before. Even with that, it took him a few starts before the crowd started to quiet down.

"Tuck's right," he said, once the noise was at a manageable level. "I'm going to kill him."

Although he smiled, Dorie didn't think he was kidding.

"But he was also right about this meaning a lot to me," Nate was saying. "More than you can know. So thank you."

Watching him closely, Dorie drew her arms tightly around herself, wishing she could hug him instead. In fact, on the outside, he seemed no different than he had in any other public appearance he'd ever done. *The Tonight Show, Late Show with David Letterman*—hell, he'd hosted *Saturday Night Live* once upon a time with that same grin. She'd come to see another side of him, though, and to her surprise, she could tell he was only just barely managing to hold himself together.

"I'm pretty sure you're not interested in a speech from me," he continued, "and as I've been standing here for, um, a while—" His quick grin drew a laugh from the crowd. "—I've been thinking that maybe you'll all indulge me for a few minutes of reminiscence. Guys? Want to join me out here?" He turned his head to the end of the court and for the first time Dorie realized that it wasn't just Wash that had come to the game with him, but Max Deacon and Jason Pike, as well. Eyes widening, she turned to Fitz.

With a huge smile, Fitz just nodded as another round of stomping and applause accompanied the men out onto the court.

"Tuck? Coach O'Reilly?" Nate said, gesturing for them to come out, as well. Then he said four other names and two of the boys from each of the benches got up and practically floated to the center of the court.

"So I know I'm just a dumb jock..." Nate grinned. "But I do know what it means when there are ten guys on a court." He looked down the line he'd just assembled, his eyes coming to a rest on the boys. "You think you could maybe pretend we're not fifteen years too old for this?"

It took a few seconds for the boys to realize they'd just been asked to play basketball with four-fifths of The Dream. The light dawned on them at the same time it dawned on just about everyone else in the gym. And this time the noise didn't stop until every one of the boys on each of the teams had their moment on the court. It took well over an hour, but it felt as though it had been no time at all. Watching The Dream play in person was unlike anything Dorie had ever experienced.

And watching *Nate* play in person was unreal. The Dream had happened so long ago that she hadn't remembered that part—and watching him play baseball was, yes, a perfectly fine way to spend a few hours. But the TV cameras couldn't catch how amazing an athlete he truly was. Nearly everything he did—from effortlessly sinking a basket from halfway down the court to coaxing and coaching through his interactions with the kids—he elevated those around him rather than outshined them. And when he, Wash, Jason Pike and Max Deacon went two-on-two after all of the kids cycled through, it was as beautiful to watch as the best choreographed dance. No one wanted to leave.

When the gym finally began to empty, Dorie chose to follow the crowd out rather than accept Fitz's invitation to meet up with "the boys" and have dinner.

Opening her arms wide as if to capture the euphoria in the room, Fitz smiled. "I don't think we can hide it anymore."

"No," Dorie answered, trying to keep from crying. They wouldn't be able to hide anything after tonight. And since that meant Nate would know she'd been lying to him, she also couldn't imagine he'd be able to forgive her. "But I think it would be better if he didn't know I was here." She bent down to grab her things.

Not being an idiot, Fitz grabbed Dorie's arm. "Hey," she said warmly, "he can't be mad after this."

Though Dorie was pretty sure Fitz was wrong about that, she wasn't going to argue. Instead she shrugged, trying to make it appear as if it was the most casual thing in the world. "Maybe not, but I'd rather he not have to find out right now."

Nodding her understanding, Fitz pulled her hand away. "You'll still be at trivia night?"

"Sure," Dorie said, maybe a little too quickly. At Fitz's glare, she rolled her eyes. "Okay. Yes. I'll be there." After an even stronger glare, she was actually able to laugh. "I *promise*."

Then, before she could change her mind, she stood up and let the crowd carry her away.

Chapter Eleven

Nate sat back in his chair, the sounds of Deacon's Bar and Grille ringing out around him. He pushed his plate away and smiled, his gaze traveling over the friends and family who surrounded him.

He really had been ready to kill Tuck. So much for *Let me just hang here in the background and not make it into a big deal.* Fitz, too. As he'd found out soon after the crowd had dissipated, Tuck had given her a heads-up, enough so that she'd be able to get their family there, too.

But he hadn't been exaggerating about how much it meant to him. Honestly? If his knee wasn't as much of a lightning rod issue as it was at the moment, he'd have sunk down right there in the center of the court. One-on-one was overwhelming, yes, even when it was words of support. That gymnasium, though, was like being in a different universe. It was the one place in the world where he was on equal ground with everyone else. Yes, the constant flow of his money into the Foundation helped sustain the people in this town. But whatever he gave they gave right back. Not with money, of course. Nor was it adulation—not the misguidedness that crashed down as soon as there was a nick in the pedestal. No. They were each other's life force, survivors through and through.

And it reminded Nate that this was where he belonged. In just two short days, everything had changed. He'd been right about them going easy on him, and it had been a little stilted at first. But as he'd begun to settle back in it seemed they had, too. As he sat here at this table, with the people he loved most in the world surrounding him and talking around him—not about or at him—it was almost as though the distance had never been there in the first place. Fitz had even given him a huge hug "just because" on their way out of the gym. And if the past six weeks had taught him anything, it was to appreciate those kinds of moments. To trust that what he had here was solid. That it would be here for him. And that maybe someday that circle would expand by one more.

His smile faded as he looked around the room. He'd spooked her; he knew that. Hell, he'd spooked himself. Which made no sense. He'd been engaged up until two months ago—to a woman who could be downright frightening when crossed. Yet the idea of being married to Courtney hadn't scared him half as much as kissing Dorie. But the only thing he found more terrifying at the moment was the thought of never kissing her again.

Well, no, there was that other not-exactly-inconsequential thing, the idea that maybe she did know who he was, that she'd been playing him all along.

And yet, despite the fact that that was actually the most logical explanation—too many people had wanted too many things from him over the years for him not to be surprised—he just didn't believe it. Couldn't. Maybe after Courtney he just *wanted* to think that Dorie was aboveboard. Or maybe it was just his dick talking.

At just that moment the door swung open and Dorie walked in. Her hat and coat were dusted with the snow that had started falling; her cheeks and the tip of her nose were bright red. After a few stomps of her feet, she took a tentative step farther into the building, stopping as the hostess greeted her. Although she was clearly on the fence about being here, she gave a bright smile.

Though her eyes lit up when Fitz waved, she hesitated, masking her discomfort by pausing to take off her gloves and unbutton her coat. If Nate hadn't been watching her so closely, he probably wouldn't have noticed that she gave a little shake of her head and then squared her shoulders. His first thought was that she was adorable. His second thought was that he needed to take a step back and at least acknowledge that this insane attraction might be coloring his judgment.

"Hey, Librarian!" Wash yelled, standing up but not bothering to make everyone else stand so he could work his way out from behind the table. He grinned and opened his arms wide. "You coming in or what?"

Dorie's face relaxed into a genuine smile. This time she didn't have to shore herself up; Wash's invitation was clearly all she'd needed. It pissed Nate off, not that Wash gave a damn. All his glare at Wash got him was a chuckle as Wash sat back down. The man redeemed himself by gesturing for the hostess to put the extra chair next to Nate.

Although Dorie had gone tense again, she nodded her thanks when Nate stood up and pulled the chair out for her. She went entirely still when he put his hands on her shoulders to help her with her coat. When his thumb happened to brush the skin at the nape of her neck, he did, as well. Everything else disappeared and time froze as he was struck by how right it felt to be here with her in this moment. Like the absolute certainty when the pitch was about to hit the sweet spot, that the ball was already on its way out of the park.

He couldn't help it. He let his hand brush her cheek. "This is a good thing," he said.

"It's not," she whispered, although he took comfort in the fact that she didn't immediately pull away. "It's really not." Then she neatly took her coat from his hands and stepped around him, smiling brightly as Fitz made introductions.

"You know most everyone. Jules, of course," Fitz said, "and our sister, Ella. And this is Jason and Deke."

Dorie muttered something under her breath, but by the time Nate turned to her, she had a smile on her face. "Deke as in Deacon?" she said, ignoring him completely. "Of Deacon's Bar and Grille?"

Turning on his considerable charm, Deke smiled. "As in grandson-of-the-Deacon-who-started-the-place. But, yeah, that would be me."

Dorie's quick grin was mirrored in her eyes. "They let you sit down and eat?" Her family apparently owned a few restaurants in Boston, and Deke was all over that.

Nate was so busy trying not to be irritated at how animated she'd become with Deke that he almost missed the land mine. The tradition was that after a game, Deke could be like any other customer. And, well… Fuck. If this was all just a charade it was a good one and Nate wanted it to last for at least a few more hours.

The waitress came to take Dorie's drink order and conversation went on from there, although Dorie was more subdued tonight than he'd seen her. For as much as the questions were now lingering in his mind, Nate sat back and spent the next half hour actively restraining himself from reaching down and taking her hand. From draping his arm over the back of her chair. As it was, he couldn't help but occasionally glance down at her, the curve of her neck drawing his eyes down to the swell of her breasts. A hint of midnight blue lace was peeking out from underneath the V-neck sweater she wore and it took everything he had not to dip his head down and run his tongue over it.

Sweet *Jesus*, he wanted her.

Thank God Fitz finally drew Dorie into the conversation, asking, "So how are you with the whole trivia night thing?"

Dorie grinned. "I'm a librarian. I do just fine."

"Excellent." Fitz reached across Deke for a buffalo wing. "Because we could use a ringer tonight. Nate is frighteningly good at filling in the holes the rest of the boys can't quite manage."

"Oh? And what holes would those be?" Dorie asked. And then immediately blushed and choked on her sip of water as she realized what she'd said.

Nate found himself grinning, as well. He took a sip of his own water as Wash good-naturedly answered, "It's their own damn fault. Raise the boy as a girl, and the boy's gonna be able to answer all the girl questions."

To Nate's surprise, it was Jules who threw the chip at Wash as everyone laughed, Nate included. "One of these times we're going to beat you guys," she said, "and you'll all be the ones buying *us* dinner."

"Girls against boys?" Dorie asked. Finally—*finally*—she turned to Nate and gave him a smile. "I think you may have met your match." Then she turned back to Fitz and Jules and raised her glass in a toast. "Six older brothers, ladies."

Even his mom joined in on the loud catcalls as the 'ladies' all leaned forward and clinked their glasses together.

And before Nate could think too much about what that meant, Deke's sister, Lola, who'd taken over quizmaster duties from Mrs. Deacon, got up on the stage. "We got off to a bit of a late start tonight, so let's have everyone get into teams and see if someone can unseat the Dream Boys tonight!"

Although he knew exactly what her response would be, Nate turned to Dorie. "A kiss for good luck?"

"Not on your life," she laughed. Then she was pulled up and out of her chair by Fitz as the tables were rearranged.

They did trivia nights a little bit differently in Inspiration. The first few rounds were exactly what Dorie was used to: write the answers down on a sheet of paper and turn them in. But here in Inspiration, those were just the elimination rounds. Now they were "down to the serious players," Jules had explained—her disapproval of Dorie apparently relegated to the background now that they were on the same team together.

Now in the final round, it was the Dream Boys, i.e., Nate, Wash and co. versus the Sisterhood, i.e. the team Dorie was on, which consisted of Nate's sisters and her. Not awkward at all. Although, she had to admit, the more time she spent with Nate's family and friends the more they became actual people, as opposed to The Dream and Co., and the more she liked them—the more she liked *him*.

She didn't like to think of herself as a shallow person. Yet she'd obviously—and without realizing it—pretty much thought of Nate exactly as he'd so self-deprecatingly called himself at the basketball game: dumb jock. Dumb jock with a beyond gorgeous shell, but still... Definitely beneath her in the brains department.

He wasn't, though. Not even a little bit. He was funny and quick and smart...

And far too perceptive for her to let her guard down for even just a little bit. So rather than laugh and joke and generally let herself be grateful that she got to spend an evening like this, she closed herself off since it was obviously going to be her only one. She didn't even want to think about how he'd react when he found out she'd known everything all along. Hell, given the way the crowd had responded to him at the game, she'd probably be lucky to escape being tarred and feathered before being run out of town. She couldn't relax at all.

And she was completely unprepared when Jules outright asked, "So what, exactly, is going on between you and my brother?"

Dorie choked on her drink. "What?"

Jules took a sip of her much more elegant glass of white wine. "He doesn't generally date. Or hang out. Yet he's spent two whole days with you."

Dorie resisted saying that she was as bewildered about that fact as just anyone else in the world would be. She also resisted saying that she wasn't interested in *dating* per se. But telling someone that you really just wanted to have some seriously good sex with their brother didn't usually go over well.

Fitz, who had been helping Dorie deflect questions all evening, was unfortunately in the midst of a heated conversation with Deke and Wash about something. And Ella, though not quite as forthright as Jules, just sat back in her chair, as interested in the answer as Jules was.

"Nothing," Dorie finally said. Because that would be true sooner rather than later anyway. "I—"

"Ready?" Fitz thankfully interrupted. Her gleefulness belying her words, she said, "So this is where things start to get ugly." The ugly part, apparently, being partly due to the fact that the categories were stacked with questions provided by the opposite team.

Ella said, "It's a miracle that either team is able to answer *any* of the questions. We usually end up with a pretty pathetic score, and the guys somehow always manage to come out ahead."

With a frown, Fitz added, "This wasn't going to be my best week to begin with—I went easy on them. And now that Nate's here? He knows all the same stuff I do; he's pretty much going to kill it."

Before Dorie could ask for more details, the quizmaster called for everyone's attention. And it truly was everyone. The bar was full. Trivia night as spectator sport.

"So you all know how this goes," Lola was saying. "Shall we see who goes first?"

Dorie expected a coin toss, maybe rock-paper-scissors. But, no.

"Arm wrestling?" she nearly shouted out when Lola announced how they'd be proceeding. From the looks of her teammates, she had no doubt that she'd be the one sent up there to represent them. Thank goodness it was fully recognized that no one stood a chance at actually winning an arm wrestling match against any one of those guys. All she had to do to win was last five seconds.

"Scared, Librarian?" Wash said, a wicked grin on his face.

"Hell, no." She smiled right back. Her only real concern was that they'd put Nate against her. That kiss had nearly pushed her over the edge of sanity, right into dreams of children clamoring at their feet. The only hope she had was to stay as far away as possible. To her relief, it was Deke who stepped up.

Then she nearly laughed out loud. The fact that she was now on nickname terms with him—with all of them—was beyond her comprehension.

When he sat down at the table in front of Lola, he gave Dorie the kind of smile that had no purpose other than to reduce a woman to a slobbering mess. His ruffled dark blond hair practically begged for hands to smooth it down, and his eyes were such a beautiful green that it was almost impossible not to drown in them. When he put his arm up to the ready, she finally did laugh, just at the sheer impossibility that this was truly happening.

"Right," she murmured, beating back another nervous giggle as she sat down and put her arm up, as well. She closed her eyes and bit her lip, readying herself for the same jolt that passed through her every time she came this close to Nate.

When Deke's hand closed over hers, however, she was surprised by the lack of shock. Her crush on Max Deacon, after all, had been a close second to her crush on Nate Hawkins. The response should have been the same. Yet she felt…nothing. Not even a little buzz that she was essentially holding his hand.

Nothing whatsoever—until she made the mistake

of glancing over to where Nate sat. And a whole field's worth of butterflies gathered in her belly and took flight. It threw her so much, in fact, that when Lola counted down from three, Dorie almost lost just because she hadn't been paying attention.

She sat up straight in order to hold her ground, then turned her attention to the task at hand. Deke was no lightweight. But Dorie wasn't either. Though it felt like the longest five seconds of her life, she managed to keep the back of her hand from hitting the table.

"Holy shit."

For some reason it surprised her that Deke had spoken. She'd been so intent on not thinking about Nate that she'd just stopped thinking altogether. Now she looked up to see Deke staring at her and murmuring, "Okay, then," as his gaze darted over to Nate and back.

Trying not to pay attention to Nate, who was now leaning forward with an unusual amount of concentration focused on the coaster for his drink, it took a minute for Dorie to realize that the room had erupted into a roar and everyone was still screaming. Fitz was jumping up and down, Jules had thrown her arms up in the air, and Ella was trash-talking the other table.

Fitz clutched Dorie's arm as she came back to the table. "Oh, my God. We've never beaten them at the coin toss."

Which wasn't a coin toss, of course, but that was neither here nor there.

Laughing, Ella shook her head. "We've never beaten them at anything, period."

Jules raised one of the shot glasses that had been delivered to the table while Dorie was up at the front. "Cheers, ladies!"

Although Dorie had already had more to drink than was wise, she took the tequila, clinked her glass and then downed it. She'd earned it, hadn't she?

Lola raised her own glass and interjected a loud, "Woo-hoo!" as she downed it. Then she pulled out a bunch of index cards from the table as Fitz sadly said, "It would have been the perfect night…"

"Except that Nate's going to answer every damn one of the questions," Jules finished for her.

Ella sighed. "At least we'll always have the coin toss."

Chapter Twelve

First Wash, now Deke. Was he that obvious?

Well, yes, probably, given that Nate was now tearing his coaster apart in order to avoid getting into it with his friends. What the fuck? It was arm wrestling, for heaven's sake. It wasn't like Deke was out there stripping her clothes off. He was barely even flirting; it was just Deke being Deke.

Yet the idea of *anyone* else's hands on her—for whatever reason—made Nate want to leap up on the table and start a whole beating-his-chest-and-marking-his-territory kind of thing.

He could feel Deke's gaze as the man came back to the table, a shit-kicking smile on his face as he said, "I get it, man." His grin widened as he took in the reaction that Nate couldn't seem to hide. "Damn."

And you haven't seen her half-naked, Nate thought. Except then Wash and Jason started smiling, too, and Nate realized he'd said it out loud. Fuck. At least Dorie hadn't heard him, thanks to the screaming going on all around them. Nate took another drink.

Jason, sitting with Tuck across the table, leaned forward. "You remember how this goes?"

Sure it had been a few years since he'd done the trivia

night thing, but Nate had never met a competition he didn't like or excel at. "Lightning round. Ten questions in a category chosen by the other team; two minutes to shoot them down. Whoever answers the most questions in the least amount of time wins."

"Hopefully Dorie doesn't kill Deke's questions, too," Wash laughed.

"Mmm," Deke mumbled grumpily. "Thanks for that."

Lola, who was getting as much enjoyment out of seeing her brother beaten as Nate's own sisters, quieted the crowd. And it was definitely a crowd. Inspiration came out to cheer no matter what the game, although Wash did mention there was a bigger turnout than usual tonight. To Nate's surprise, he hadn't minded.

"Ready, boys?" Lola said, commanding everyone's attention.

Deke, who was back to his jovial self, called Fitz out. "You're going down, Baby Hawk."

"Baby Hawk?" Nate said, eyebrows raised as he watched Fitz's cheeks turn bright pink. He turned back to Deke just in time to see the kind of smile he was *not* ready for.

Deke met Nate's gaze with a stare that got Nate's back up, especially when it was accompanied by Deke's slow grin. "It pisses her off."

Yeah, they were gonna have words.

There wasn't time to dwell on that, though, when the questions started rolling in. The first few were run-of-the-mill stuff. Given Jason's tendency to binge-watch TV before that term was ever in existence, and Tuck being a few years older and able to handle two early 80s questions, they were already starting off strong. But, as Fitz had admitted, she'd had no idea Nate would be here until too late for her to change the questions she'd already handed in. And even though Fitz was his half-sister and hadn't come to live with them until she was fourteen, her cultural education had pretty much been the same as Nate's and largely fueled by Jules. The only thing that surprised him about the next question that came up was that it hadn't come up before.

"What's the 'sport of the future' according to Lloyd Dobler? Name the movie and actor who played him."

"Kickboxing," Nate answered before the words were fully out of Lola's mouth. "*Say Anything*, John Cusack."

"Danny Zuko's best friend?" Lola asked.

Grease? Really, Fitz? "Kenickie."

"Runner-up to Kelly?" Lola said, adding, "Points off if you have to ask who Kelly is."

With a laugh, Nate shook his head. Fitz had been obsessed with *American Idol* for years. "Justin Guarini."

Her lips curving up into a smile, Lola—who was as much Nate's big sister as she was Deke's—said, "I hope for your sake you don't know this one, Nate. I don't think you'll ever live it down. Name the members of NKOTB."

Nate had no shame. Not when it meant winning. "Jordan Knight, Jonathan Knight, Joey McIntyre, Danny Wood and Donnie Wahlberg."

Even Dorie was laughing at that point. "New Kids on the Block? I'm from Boston and I don't even know all their names," she said, raising her glass to him. Her sparkling eyes threw him enough that he almost didn't hear the last question, which would have been a travesty, since it was from one of his favorite movies of all time, despite how much he'd protested every time Jules insisted on watching it.

So, yes, he had a thing for chick flicks. It was Jules's fault and it didn't bother him one bit.

"According to Westley, what 'cannot stop true love'?"

True love. Nate grinned, although he deliberately didn't look Dorie's way. "Death."

Lola smiled in response. "As long as we're there, finish the quote—'My name is Inigo—'"

"'Montoya,'" Nate said, speaking over Lola. And since he'd had a tendency to yell that very saying at the men around this table as he schooled them in basketball, it was the whole group of them standing up and high-fiving each other as they yelled, "'You killed my father. Prepare to die.'"

Trivia night wasn't exactly game seven of the World Series; it wasn't even pennant league. But Nate hadn't heard those kinds of hoots and cheers in a very long time. Even Fitz was clapping. Looking around as he sat back down, Nate realized he hadn't had such a good time in years.

Until he looked at Dorie and a sinking feeling hit his gut. He sat back down.

"Impressive, boys," Lola said, her voice carrying over the microphone as she shook her head. "Sorry, ladies. Ten questions in seventy-two seconds. That'll be tough to beat."

"So. Not. Fair," Fitz groaned. She straightened up and looked at Dorie. "No pressure, but I hope you know some esoteric facts about cars and sports. Deke's been on a roll lately."

Now it was Dorie who was smiling, although in a lop-sided, not-very-happy kind of way. "A little," she mumbled, her eyes down at the table. Then they came up and she caught him watching her and the churning got worse. The ping of a rock hitting the windshield before the crack started to spread.

It started off innocently enough in a trivia kind of way, with the questions that a decent sports fan—or, say, the sister of several—could probably get an answer or two. About hockey, for example, a sport that Nate was sure at least one of six brothers from Boston Bruins-land may have mentioned at some point.

Like, for example, the goalie with the most shutouts in his career. "Martin Brodeur," she answered without hesitation.

Basketball, another sport of which Boston fans were well aware: most points in a game. "One hundred," she said. "Wilt Chamberlain."

Even NASCAR, although that was less of a New England thing, but with all those brothers, of course it was possible.

"What color do rookie NASCAR racers have on the back of their race cars?"

"Yellow."

By seven questions in, the room was quiet. Quite a feat given how many people there were. It embarrassed Dorie; Nate could tell from the way she was sitting in the chair, as though she had to remind herself not to hunch her shoulders and curl into herself entirely. What she didn't seem to understand was that the reaction was pure awe. Nate hadn't been around in a while, but he was well aware that this town didn't take to outsiders easily—not after they'd seen themselves on national TV time and again, long past the novelty of being touched by fame had died down. And Nate's family—both blood relatives and non—were, though friendly, even less likely to open up their ranks.

Yet here Dorie was, owning it. And, embarrassed or not, too much of a competitor to let it stop her from putting herself right there on the front line and getting it done, a quality Nate admired deeply.

But if he'd stayed home—if he'd insisted she stay with him—they could have gone on pretending they weren't each living a lie. Because, yes. Question answered. Resoundingly so. As much as he was trying to convince himself otherwise, he'd been fooling himself since the moment he'd met her.

"The Spyder is a limited edition supercar," Lola read. "Name the company that manufactures it and the total of cars manufactured."

Nate looked over at Deke and glared. "Really?" He'd had to use Nate's car?

The man at least had the good graces to look apologetic. "If Fitz had no clue you'd be here tonight, do you think there was a chance I did?"

Looking down at the coaster again, Nate could hear the hitch in Dorie's voice as she answered, "Porsche. Nine hundred and eighteen."

Damn it.

Question nine didn't seal the deal. Nate couldn't imagine there was a Boston sports fan out there who couldn't answer the question, "Before their 2004 win, when was the last time the Red Sox won the World Series?"

"1918," Dorie said, the roll of her eyes evident in her voice.

Deke smiled sheepishly. "So sue me. That one was a gimme. How was I supposed to know she was Bob Freakin' Costas?"

But it was the last question that was a knife to

Nate's gut. The one that he knew was coming, but hoped against hope would prove his doubts wrong. His heart came to a slow, painful stop as the words came out of Lola's mouth. "This player led the Yankees in RBIs in every season from 1949-1955. Name the player and, as a bonus, name his claim to fame from the 1956 World Series."

He wanted her to bungle it. To give an answer just about anyone else in the world would give hearing those words. Mickey Mantle. Joe DiMaggio, hell, even Babe Ruth, although the timing was off by about twenty years. So many famous Yankees that even a Red Sox fan knew them all; so many names that someone could throw out and think they had a shot of getting it right. But what most people didn't realize was that the man whose quotes provided laughs on a regular basis was also one of—if not *the*—greatest catchers of all time.

"Yogi Berra," Dorie answered quietly. "He caught Don Larsen's perfect game."

Once again cheers erupted around her, but all Nate could do was close his eyes and breathe.

Fuck.

When he opened them it was to see her staring at him. To see her flinch at the power of the look that passed between them and then turn away as her tears began to fall. The rush of sound that overwhelmed him had nothing to do with the crowd closing in. Instead, all he could think of was that he had to get to her before she ran away. He had to…

He had to fucking *understand* why she would lie to him like that.

He stood up so quickly that his chair would have

overturned if not for Wash reaching out to grab it. No, to grab Nate. "Dude, what…?"

Nate yanked his arm away. When he pulled back, he practically tripped over Fitz, who should have been celebrating with Jules and Ella but wasn't. He put his hand to his forehead and squeezed his eyes shut. As a general principle, he didn't get angry with Fitz. He'd tried to ignore her, once upon a time; had hated the idea of her. But not once in over fifteen years had his anger been directed at her. Not the day he heard the first whispers, not the day his mother told him the rumors about his father were true and not the day his mother brought her home to live with them because they were the only family she had left, ironic as that may have been.

Yet right now, for the first time in his life, all he could see when he looked at her was red.

He pushed past her.

"Nate…"

"Goddamn it, Fitz."

"No, Nate," she snapped, getting in his face. "Goddamn you. Let her explai—"

"Let *her* explain?" That was rich. Fucking perfect. "You—"

"Yeah, well, I'll be happy to explain my part later." She grabbed his arm and pushed him back toward the kitchen, muttering, "Don't make a scene. That's the last thing you need."

"Seriously?" He let her lead him away from any curious eyes, right through the double doors and into the alley. He was highly aware that this…*rage* had as much to do with everything that had been going on over the past two months as it did with what Dorie had been hiding. But that didn't stop him from coming right at Fitz the second they were outside. "What the fuck? Has she known all along? Have *you*?"

She wrapped her arms around herself. It was the end of fucking January and they were standing outside without coats on. Yet despite the snow still coming down, all Nate felt was fire.

"I decided not to tell you," Fitz said, not even close to apologetic. "And I would do it again in a heartbeat."

He couldn't look at her. He didn't need this, not from her. If his career hadn't so recently been on the edge of being in the toilet, Nate would have rammed his fist into the wall.

As though she read his mind, she said, "I hate what's happening to you. I hate that there's nothing I can do about it."

He spun toward her. "And you thought *this* was going to help?"

"Yes," she snapped, back in his face. "And you weren't all up-and-up, either, so don't be a dick about it. You can be pissed at me later but don't take it out on her. Just go find her and don't screw it up."

Nate had no idea what to say. His mouth actually dropped open. So rather than say something he'd regret—starting but not coming close to ending with, *That's the biggest load of bullshit I've ever heard*—he turned on his heel and left.

Chapter Thirteen

He wasn't coming. Five episodes of *House Hunters* and one pint of ice cream later, and that was the conclusion Dorie had reached. She should be happy about that. She *was* happy about that.

She hugged the pillow to her chest as she tried to keep herself from crying.

This was ridiculous. It wasn't like she'd expected it to go anywhere in the first place. But her heart hurt— there was an actual ache in her chest. Her insides felt like they'd been turned inside out, and it wasn't because the ice cream hadn't sat right with her stomach. There had been plenty of guys in her life and at least that much ice cream, although rarely because of a man. And now, after only one kiss, it felt like her world had been turned upside down. What if they'd actually…?

She went still at the sound of a knock on the door, halfway hoping she'd imagined it, while desperate to hear it all the same. Unsure which would be worse, she went the denial route and turned up the TV.

There was another knock, much louder this time. No mistaking that one. But she turned the volume up louder once again.

Okay, yes, she wanted him here—but she was so

freaking scared at just the *thought* of having this conversation. And she was excellent at avoidance.

"Dorie! Let me in!"

Dorie closed her eyes. Definitely scared.

"I will fucking break down this door!" he shouted. And then, as if he realized how crazy that made him sound, he amended, "Okay. So I won't break the door down. But unless you tell me to go to hell, I'm using my key to open it and I'm coming in." His voice faded in and out a little as if he was pacing back and forth in front of the door.

Though she shook her head, she did turn the TV down a little bit. "I'm sleeping," she said.

There was a moment of silence, and then, "That wasn't a 'go to hell.'"

With a sigh, she let herself fall back into the comfort of the couch. No. No, it hadn't been.

She heard him say, "Fuck," before the sound of a key turning in the lock and then the door opening. Although she very deliberately kept her gaze on the TV, she could feel him standing there and looking at her. When she wrapped her arms around herself tightly enough to focus on that rather than crying—or, well, him—he closed the door gently, paused for a moment, and then came across the room, with a muttered, "Well, at least you don't have the bat."

"Only because I didn't think about it," she muttered back.

He made a sound that might have been a muffled laugh. Or maybe not.

Doing everything possible to ignore the way her heart was skipping beats, she unwrapped her arms from her body, as if she hadn't just been holding herself in a death grip, and attempted to look casual as she rearranged herself on the couch. Hoping desperately he wouldn't notice the ice cream or the wad of tissues on the floor, she tucked her feet underneath her and nodded her head toward the TV. "If you're going to stay, you'll have to deal with *House Hunters International*." If this was a fight with her brothers, that in itself would have been enough to send them running out of the house screaming.

But Nate sat down at the other end of the couch, far too close for comfort. "I prefer the US version, but international will do."

She resisted the sudden urge to swing her head in his direction. With great effort, she pouted, "Too bad. I changed my mind. How about a *Full House* rerun?"

"Fantastic." And in case his enthusiasm wasn't enough, he added, "Joey's my favorite. How about you?"

Dorie had no response. The only time she'd ever watched *Full House* in her life was when she'd been forced to stay overnight at the neighbor's because the babysitter fell through. "You really are a girl," she muttered.

Rather than respond to her insult, he snapped, "Want to do our hair and nails, too?" He grabbed her heel and put her foot in his lap. "I'll do your toes first and then you can do mine?"

She'd have given anything to have a comeback that would have laid him out cold. But the second his hand moved up to her ankle she lost all ability to speak.

That thought was shattered when he let go, practically pushing her away.

"Tell me why," he demanded quietly.

"What?" She dragged her gaze away from his mouth.

"Tell. Me. *Why*," he repeated, his voice raw. His hand

clenched against his thigh as he very deliberately didn't look at her. "Why did you lie to me?"

Right. Now it was her turn to look away. "Because you're Nate Hawkins."

The words escaped before she even realized she'd spoken. Words that revealed far too much than she intended, thanks to the sob rising up in her throat.

"I know who I am." He jumped to his feet and turned his back on her. "I just want to know why you pretended you didn't."

"Oh, excuse me, Mr. Pot," she said, jumping to her feet as well, her hands going to her hips. "Hi, Kettle. My name is D.B. Nice to meet you."

He went still and then made another one of those laughing-type sounds, although she couldn't imagine that's what it actually was. Not that it mattered. She was on a roll and she was going with it. "Oh. Why, hello, Mr. D.B. It's nice to meet you, too. I mean, I'm not at all thrown by a random stranger coming into my apartment while I'm taking an amazing bath—" *leaving out the Nate Hawkins component, of course* "—and eating my—"

"Dinner," he finished for her, turning around as she glared and continued, "Yes, dinner. That I was saving for—"

He cut her off midsentence by saying, "Could we do this without you wearing the glasses?"

"I... What?" Puzzlement turned to irritation. She glared up at him. "Um, *no*. If you're going to yell at me then I'm sure as hell going to see it."

"I'm two freaking inches from your face." He actually took her glasses away—that she'd been *wearing*. "Trust me, you're going to see me."

It was more like ten inches given the height difference, and his features were already a blur. She punched him in the stomach and grabbed her glasses back, then jammed them back on. "What the hell is it to you?"

When he was the one to step away she found that, for the first time in her life, she wished she hadn't won her argument. At least when he'd been yelling at her, he'd still been engaged. Now he was just standing there, staring at her blankly as if she was just another random groupie, desperate for his attention. Which she wasn't. Which she refused to ever be.

"Just go," she started to say as she bent down to pick up the remote again, willing the tears to stay contained until he was out of her way.

But when she waved him away with her arm, he grabbed it. "You really didn't know," he said, more to himself than to her it seemed. "The other night. When you were in that ro—When I thought it was Fitz's apartment I was coming into."

Technically it was still Fitz's apartment. Dorie gave him as evil an eye as she could muster. "Do you honestly think I would have set myself up for this?" They may have only known each other for a few days, but she hoped he knew her well enough to know that at least.

He went still for a second. Then, gruffly, "Take off your glasses."

There was something in his eyes that cut off her protest. Something about the way he stepped back and ducked his head down.

She had no idea what compelled her to comply this time. Maybe it was because he seemed a little lost, maybe it was because it was just easier not to see the disappointment on his face so clearly. But this time she did as he said.

After a much longer pause, he repeated, "Tell me why." Except this time it sounded more as if he was pleading.

She closed her eyes and shook her head. She hated this. "I heard your voice and thought one of my brothers had some misguided idea that they'd come out here to check on me. And then I could tell it wasn't any one of them so I grabbed the bat, and then you said your name was D.B."

Already off and running, the babble took on a life of its own. "Then I got my glasses and by the time I realized who you were, you were already talking to Fitz—oh, and by the way, your little sister's name is Angelica according to the rest of the world. How was I supposed to know that she goes by Fitz? I mean, whoever came up with *that* as a nickname?" Dorie looked away. "And you just seemed so *sad* and—"

"I seemed sad?" he said. "When I was talking to Fitz." That second part was a statement more than a question.

Good, Dorie.

Tell the nice beautiful billionaire baseball man that he sounded sad when talking to his baby sister.

"Well, maybe more…defeated." Lonely, she only barely managed to keep herself from adding. "I told myself it didn't matter who you were because you obviously still needed a place to stay so I went to change the sheets and I was *totally* going to say something when I came out, but then I turned around and the way you looked at me…" Like he'd wanted to eat her right up. And she'd almost let him.

"How did I look at you?" he asked, just as quietly as

he took a step toward her. He reached for her glasses and put them back on.

He was so close she could feel the heat radiating off him.

"Was it like this?" he asked gruffly, cupping her chin in his hand and forcing her to look into his eyes and see the stark hunger within. Because, yes. That was exactly the look. Seeing it all over again overwhelmed her. She grabbed behind her for the couch's armrest just as he bent down and kissed her.

Her lips ignored every red flag her brain was throwing and opened for him as he devoured her mouth. He grabbed her hips and lifted her until she wrapped her legs around him. He seemed frantic, as desperate as she was, and it made her even hotter. Her moan had him gripping her even tighter, and his need for her had her clutching him to her. When he ground against her, hitting her in just the right spot, she broke from the kiss and gasped for a breath. God, she was about to come right here, in his arms and fully clothed.

"Wait! *No*," she finally managed to say. It was too much. Except her hands betrayed her, threading up through the hair at the nape of his neck.

He groaned when she shifted, her hips tilting up a little, her body wanting more from him as her brain kept telling her to run away. Far, far away. She could not get involved with this man. With Nate Hawkins. There were so many reasons why that she… That… She tried to pull away a little so she could think straight, but instead she just managed to push up against him harder. Oh, God.

"Please don't mean that," he said, nuzzling the crook of her neck, his lips and tongue doing amazing things. "But if you do? You need to tell me now. And the glasses would have to come off. For good this time." His hands, too, one now in possession of her ass while the other worked its way up her back. "If you really mean the no, then you can't ever wear those glasses again."

Dorie pulled away abruptly. "You like my glasses?"

He pulled back, too, a grin on his face. "Christ, woman. I *love* your glasses."

That was it. She was gone. "Couch. Down. Now."

This was a bad idea. Terrible. And yet…

She threw her arms around him and shifted her weight in a way that would throw him off balance. It caught him by surprise and he fell down to the couch, his low laugh rumbling as he reached out to stop their fall, cradling her in his other hand and gently lowering them down the rest of the way. And then he was on the couch and she was straddling him and it felt better than she'd ever imagined it could.

It had never occurred to her, however, that he might feel the same way. That his hands might shake a little as he raised the hem of her sweater and lifted it up over her head. Or that, just like her, he wanted to see and taste and worship. Stopping her from unclasping her bra, he took hold of her wrists and pinned them to her back while he slowly traced the curve of her breasts with the tips of his fingers. When he did it all over again, this time with his tongue and with agonizing deliberation, she was so desperate for him to ease the ache that when he finally sucked her nipple into his mouth, she gasped in relief.

Surging forward and pulling out of his hold, she took his face in her hands and kissed him. He responded by putting his hand to the back of her neck and pulling her the rest of the way down. She dragged his shirt up past his waist.

Sitting back, she let her hand trail slowly down what was, possibly, the most beautiful body she had ever seen in her life. "You're perfect," she whispered. "This can't be real." It felt like a fantasy. It *was* a fantasy. And yet there was so much more to him—to this—than she'd dreamed it could be.

"I'm not," he practically growled, obviously not happy with what she'd said. His hand closed over hers. "And this is."

She raised her eyes to meet his. He made her feel beautiful. Powerful. And when she reached down to unbutton his jeans, when she ran her fingers down the length of him—when she felt him tighten and twitch against her hand—she almost came out of her skin. "This is because of me."

His hands settled loosely on her hips and he smiled, clearly amused. "It is most definitely because of you." She felt his gaze on her face as sure as a caress when she took him fully in her hand.

She loved the feel of him. Loved how intense his gaze was as he dropped back against the couch as she played. But when she pushed herself up to her knees to lean forward and kiss him, he put his hand out to stop her, commanding, "Stay." Then his hand went to her thigh and he nudged her legs wider apart. Her heart nearly exploded out of her chest, sending a surge of heat straight down to where she could do absolutely nothing about it other than beg him to move his thumb—now teasingly exploring the inside of her thigh—just a *liiitttle* bit higher.

His laugh when her hips bucked forward was a good indication that begging wouldn't help. Nor was his actual response. "Gotta be patient, baby. Don't they teach you that in Boston?"

He wasn't unaffected by any means. She could tell that much from the way he was pulsing in her hand. But then he took that away, too, taking her by the wrist and placing her hand flat against her stomach. Shifting it down so that her fingers dipped under the waistband of her jeans.

When she whimpered, he bent closer, his lips brushing the curve of her breast, then traveling up her skin.

He ran his fingers down the slope of her shoulder. Her nipples hardened painfully—visibly—which made him smile. He let his hand drift farther down, playing with one, then the other. She was about to dissolve into a throbbing, panting mess, and he appeared to be completely calm. Overwhelmingly cool.

Except for the rasp in his voice when he said, "Undo your jeans."

Thank You, God.

Her heart pounding in time with the pulse between her legs, she did as he said. Her eyes fluttered closed when he reached out and pushed her jeans farther down her hips, when his hand trailed up the inside of her thigh, right to—

This time she could only breathe her, "*OhmyGod.*" Her hips jerked forward as he pushed her underwear to the side, then slowly slid his finger in. "So wet," he murmured as a second finger joined the first.

She fell forward, over him. Clutched the back of her couch as he worked magic with his fingers. She was incoherent, delirious with need. And when his tongue rasped her nipple at the same time his thumb brushed her clit, she shattered and screamed.

His fingers eased out of her still-pulsing heat, as she panted her way back to earth. She felt his mouth on hers—felt, rather than heard, him murmur, "Beautiful," against her lips—as he twisted and gently laid her down. She only vaguely realized he was stripping off the rest of her clothes. Luckily she was still off in another dimension somewhere, one where her poor decision not to wear the one pair of lacy panties she owned didn't matter.

Sighing, she let her hand drift to his hair—such thick, beautiful hair—and smiled as his hand lightly brushed her ankle, then her knee on his way back up. But she went still when she felt the stubble of his chin against the inside of her thigh. She wasn't ready for that. It felt too intimate. Not what she usually allowed during a one-night stand—not something most of her one-night stands even had an interest in doing.

Nate laid his arm across her waist and held her down. "Just one taste," he said, so close she could feel his breath against her, and yet his eyes met hers, seeking permission.

If anything, that frightened her even more. Not that there was any question of his desire—he was practically vibrating with tension, holding back only because he'd sensed her hesitation.

This was not who she'd imagined him to be. Sexy, yes. Going after what he wanted, absolutely. But connected enough to be aware of her limits before she even said them? Caring and thoughtful and almost reverent?

How was she supposed to keep her distance from someone like that?

"Just because you like my cooking," she whispered, "doesn't mean you get to have everything in the kitchen."

He pulled his head back and she suddenly understood the power of Nate Hawkins's gaze. Goose bumps popped up all over her body as he stared at her, seemingly seeing every iota of doubt and vulnerability she kept bottled up inside. Then he smiled. "Guess I'll have to keep coming back until I've licked the cupboards bare."

He pushed her legs open a little wider, and without breaking the look between them bent to run his tongue ever-so-slowly along the crease where her thigh met her hip. Exhaling enough for her to feel the warm, hot air between her legs, he moved to the other leg and did the same, before laying kisses on her navel, her ankle, her knee.

He pulled away and she sat up on her elbows just in time to see him rip open a foil packet and put on a condom. He moved over her, his hand traveling up her leg on his way. And time stopped when he looked down and caressed her cheek, murmuring her name.

No.

No, no, no. She could not do tenderness. Not with him. "I think I need to get a dog."

He froze. His eyebrow arched up at, yes, her completely out-there thought.

"You know," she explained, trying to keep her traitorous body from weeping with need. "To take care of cleaning all those cupboards so that the guests won't have to do it."

"Mmm." His eyes sparkled with amusement. "Kinky."

Before she could say that that wasn't what she'd meant—*obviously*—he was sinking into her and any chance of speech was gone. Her head fell back at the sheer bliss of having him inside her. With her neck exposed, he took full advantage, kissing her and smiling against her skin every time she moaned. He pulled her knee up alongside his hip, a rumble of pleasure running through him when she gasped, then again when he went so deep the tremor traveled up her spine. She thrust her hips up, crying out when he pulled almost all the way out and then right back in. With every ounce of her being she wanted it to last longer, but she'd been on edge for centuries and couldn't take any more. She put her hands on his shoulders and squeezed.

He got the message. With the slightest shift he rubbed up exactly where she needed him to. She clutched him to her as she exploded. As he drove into her one, two— oh, God; *so freaking good*—three times before he followed her over.

It was a full five minutes before either one of them could speak—and she loved every second because they were spent with him collapsed on top of her, every single inch of him deliciously warm. She refused to let him pull away.

He shifted so he could look her in the eyes. "I don't want to hurt you," he whispered, brushing her lips with his thumb.

"No chance," she said. It was a flat-out lie. He had the potential to hurt her more deeply than any man she'd ever known. That would have been true if all he'd been was Nate Hawkins, the fantasy. But when fantasy combined with the reality of the man she was coming to know, it could be devastating.

She pushed the thought out of her head, concentrating instead on the way his skin felt beneath her hands as she ran them down the sleek, strong muscles of his back. "You think maybe we could try that again?" she asked. "I'm not sure it worked."

Clearly aware that it had worked impossibly well— three times—he threw his head back and laughed. Then he bent down to kiss her. "Well, then, I guess we'll have to make you scream."

Chapter Fourteen

The sound of his phone ringing woke Nate up. He rolled over, reached for it...and knocked a whole stack of books onto the floor.

He sat up suddenly, blinked at the completely unfamiliar room and then realized... Right. He'd spent the night at Dorie's. His phone, which had stopped ringing for all of two seconds, started ringing again. And now he was realizing it was in his pants pocket in the living room since, by the time they'd made it to the bedroom, clothes had long been shed.

The phone stopped ringing once again. Then, also once again, started ringing after two seconds.

Recognizing the pattern, Nate swore as he wrapped the sheet around his waist, swore again as he stumbled over the books now strewed across the floor—nearly twisting his knee in the process which would have been a freaking nightmare to explain—and made his way to the living room in order to stop the phone stopping and starting yet a fourth time. Failing thanks to his pants being tangled up on the floor, he snatched it on the second ring of the new cycle and glanced at it only to confirm it was Pete, as expected.

"I'll call you from the car," he snapped.

They'd been down this road before—Pete nagging at Nate until he'd received verbal confirmation that Nate was on his way to somewhere Nate didn't want to be going—so Pete's only response to that was a chuckle before hanging up. Nate threw the phone down to the coffee table.

Now that he was fully awake, he took a look around. The apartment wasn't big enough for Dorie to be in it without him knowing, so he came to the obvious conclusion that she'd gone to work.

"I do have a job, you know," she'd said to him when, probably around 5:00 a.m., he'd tried to convince her that spending the entire day in bed was a perfectly reasonable thing.

Well, yeah, but it had surprised him that that's what her answer was. It also surprised him that he wasn't entirely happy about it.

He'd always actually preferred waking up alone, even with women he'd been with more than once. Until this morning he'd convinced himself that it was just the way he was; that his job was so physically and mentally demanding—even during the off-season—that he couldn't quite perform it if he didn't wake up in the zone.

Turned out that was all a crock of shit. Even today, of all days, when he had to pull himself together and get himself to Chicago to finally face the music, he didn't give a crap about the zone. Maybe that was a lie he'd been telling himself so he wouldn't have to confront the fact that he really was an ass for wanting to fuck a woman and then spend the rest of the night alone.

With Dorie, though, having sex pretty much until the sun came up, he already wanted her again. And again after that. And then again and again and again until he was a hundred years old and all the Viagra in the world wasn't going to help but he wouldn't give a damn because as long as he could be touching some part of her he'd be fine.

Christ. He'd just liked holding her. Touching her. *Laughing.*

Yeah, the laughing part was definitely new. When she'd gone into the whole pot and kettle thing—when he found himself trying desperately to hold back his laugh despite how angry he'd been… Hell, when she'd thrown out the comment about getting a dog—he'd known he was in trouble. Like, this-is-a-woman-I-could-possibly-fall-in-love-with trouble. Having barely cracked a smile in two months and then laughing during both fighting *and* sex?

This was definitely not part of the plan.

Okay. He was getting ahead of himself. Maybe a cold shower would help. She was amazing, yes. Sex with her had been playful and breathtaking and hot as hell. But that was all it was, no matter how many times he'd begun to think about things he couldn't possibly mean.

And he was pretty close to convincing himself of that, right up until he read the note she'd left by the coffee machine.

Hey, there. Sorry I have to run, but, well, I kind of literally have to run. Marathon thing and all that. And I know you have a long drive, so I'll just head straight to the library after that. Wouldn't want to interrupt your beauty sleep, after all, especially since you have that whole gorgeous thing going on. And, um, I can't believe I just wrote that. I can't believe I ever said that. I hope Chicago treats you better than it did last time you were there. But just

in case it doesn't, don't forget that I have a bat—
and I know how to use it. So I guess I'll see you
when I see you.

XOXO DD

Oh, and P.S. That was the most amazing night of
my life. For your sake, I won't breathe a word about
it to my brothers.

Nate was driving and talking to Pete on the phone, just
about to turn onto his aunt and uncle's road, when he
suddenly realized Dorie had given no indication she intended to see him again. It was an art he'd perfected.
Send 'em off with such a big smile that they had no idea
you'd just given them the blow-off.

"See you when I see you?"

"Shit." He came to a complete stop in the middle of
the road, only barely registering the squeal of brakes
and honking horns around him.

"Nathan Hawkins, your mother will hear about this!"

He looked up to see his fourth-grade teacher waving
her fist as she drove around him.

Jesus.

"Sorry, Mrs. Bellevue!" he called out.

He pulled over to the side of the road, shaking. He'd
done some stupid things in his life, but never anything
that idiotic. What the *hell*? "I gotta go, Pete," he said,
realizing that Pete had stopped talking at the sound of
chaos, but that Nate had no memory at all of what their
conversation had been about.

Oh, right. "Yes, I'm coming back tonight," he promised. "Tell Courtney not to worry about her fucking car."
For heaven's sake. Did she think he was going to run
off to Canada with it? He hung up before Pete could say

anything else. The man knew him too well; the questions would be relentless.

As well they should, considering Nate was pulling a U-turn with only a little bit more awareness of the cars around him than when he'd stopped in the middle of the street.

Having driven like a bat out of hell, it wasn't surprising that he made it back to the library in less than fifteen minutes. It was probably better for everyone that there was a spot right in front. God knew what he would have done if he'd had to look for parking. He got out of the truck and slammed the door.

Had Dorie seriously been saying he should have a nice life? *Thanks for the fuck, or four, but now that I've crossed that off my bucket list, you can go on your merry way?*

Nate's hand was on the door handle when he finally came to his senses. Realizing that his heart was pounding in his ears, he rested his head against the window. Yes, maybe that's the way it had been for him in the past. The women who wanted his name notched on their belts, who wanted a story to tell their grandkids one day.

Well, probably not about the fucking part.

But that wasn't Dorie. He still refused to believe that.

Yes, she'd pretended not to know who he was. He hated that she'd let him stay with her that first night because she felt *sad* for him. *Christ.* But if anything, he'd done the pursuing. Not once had she done anything that came even close to the predatory shit he was used to. Hell, even her underwear spoke volumes. He'd been with a lot of women and every single one of them had been wearing matching lingerie, usually red, black or a combination thereof. And, more often than not, see-through. All of which he found incredibly appealing, just to be clear. But Dorie had known exactly who he was—

exactly what he wanted from her and how many women he'd already had it with—and she'd still been wearing plain cotton panties and a dark blue bra. That was as far from belt-notching, predatory as it got.

He opened the door and walked inside, steeling himself for seeing Wash or Deke or any other guy who may have decided to make a move. But it was just Dorie, stretched out on her back in the middle of the floor of the reading room, eyes closed and hands holding a notebook nestled against her chest.

"What marathon thing?" he asked, not meaning to scare the bejesus out of her—she had those damn chimes, didn't she?—yet doing that all the same.

"Oh, my *God.*" She threw her notebook straight up in the air as she sat up. When it dropped back down, she threw it at him. "What the *hell*?"

Catching the notebook against his chest, it occurred to him that she had a surprisingly good arm. "Sorry," he said. And he truly was. But they'd spent nearly the past three days together and he wanted to know why she'd never mentioned anything about a marathon. "Was that just an excuse to get far the hell away from me, or are you really running a marathon?"

She avoided the first part of the question, something he tried not to read too much into, and skipped right over to the second. "I'm in training. With Colin and Christopher."

"That's…" Amazing. She was amazing. But he only managed the one word before his mind went blank as he remembered how adeptly she'd used those muscles last night, clamping her legs around him and drawing him in. Yeah. He should have realized there'd been some kind of training involved. "You didn't think to mention it?"

"Of course I thought to *mention* it." She got to her

feet and glared at him. "And then I realized that would be the most asinine thing ever, because then I'd have to also mention that the marathon we're training for isn't Boston, since it's a Donelli family tradition to go to the Red Sox game on marathon day. And then I might have needed to admit that I actually know a thing or two about baseball. That if you hadn't signed with the Watchmen, you would have been playing against us that day."

He felt his mouth settle into a grim line. Okay, yes. She had a point. And he definitely would have made the connection. He'd played that game in Boston a few times over the years—the 11:00 a.m. game that Boston always played at home so their fans could head straight to the marathon finish line a few blocks away. He loved that game, loved that tradition.

But he didn't care about any of that right now. "Anything else you haven't mentioned?"

"I…" Her brow furrowed. "What?"

For all that they'd talked, he was realizing there was a lot he didn't know. "Well, you clearly know a lot about sports."

She sat down again, then shrugged. "I didn't have much of a choice. My parents had already bought every type of equipment known to man—it wasn't like they were going to run out and buy me a tutu just because I didn't want to play hockey."

The thought of her in a Bruins jersey and nothing else… "You played hockey?"

The corner of her mouth twitched and a sparkle came to her eyes. "Is that better or worse than the glasses?"

The thought of her in a Bruins jersey and *glasses* and nothing else? Holy *shit*. "Better," he groaned. Oh, Christ, was it better. He took a step toward her. "What else?"

"Karate. Boxing. Soccer. You're looking at the best pitcher in the Allston-Brighton Little League circa 2002." She gave a sly smile. "Why? Were you thinking of approaching the mound?"

He was on her almost before she could finish. His hands were in her hair, under her shirt, then on her hips as he pulled her to him. He was so hard that it hurt and he didn't give a fuck that they were in the middle of the main room of the damn library.

She didn't either, apparently. She nipped at his neck and he brought her to the floor, pulling her down on top of him. He pushed her jeans down past her hips far enough for her to wiggle out of them. Today she was wearing those boy short panties and he was pretty sure it was the sexiest thing he'd ever seen.

No. The sexiest thing he'd ever seen was her peeling them off and then reaching down to undress him before bending down and closing her mouth around his dick.

She swirled her tongue, then her hands closed around his ass. It took everything he had not to come. He didn't want to want her this much. He should be on his way to Chicago right now, not hauling her up by the shoulders until his lips were finally back on hers. He arched up into her, reeling as her wet heat closed around him; pushing away the words dancing around in his head. She rose up until she was nearly free of him. Then, smiling wickedly, eased back down so slowly that he was afraid he might actually come out of his skin. She did it again, and then again, faster and faster until his whole body was humming with need.

She pulled away from him and he felt like she'd taken his air away. "Dorie…"

But then she was straddling him again, right at his

knees, bending down and taking him in her mouth, and his eyes nearly rolled back in his head.

"Condom?" Her voice sounded as ragged as he felt.

Right.

Christ. His head fell back against the floor. "Wallet."

He should have gotten it himself but he was so fucking tight that he couldn't move right now. The next thing he did had to be burying himself in her or he was going to die. No fucking lie.

He heard her tear the packet, felt her place it on him, slowly roll it down his cock.

She was playing with him. Fucking playing. A low laugh ran through her and it nearly undid him.

He wrapped his arms around her and flipped them over. He'd make her pay for that. Later. Right now, though, it took every ounce of control he had to wait until she was the one writhing and pleading. Until she came, screaming. But then she pulled his head down to her neck and moaned his name, and, his hands fisting on either side of her head, he was gone. When he finally collapsed against her, he kept his weight off her as best as he could, but he didn't want to move away.

Christ. He didn't want to move away.

After a minute or two, he brushed the hair away from her face and kissed her. "Come to Chicago with me."

Eyes widening, she went still beneath him. Then she bit her lip and looked away. "Why?"

Rolling to the side, he ran his hand slowly down her back from her shoulder to her hip, caressing skin so soft and smooth that he wasn't sure he'd ever get enough of it. Then he reached around for her clothes and handed them to her so she could get dressed as he did the same. "Because I don't want to be there if you're not there with me."

"Don't say things like that," she snapped, scrambling away from him.

He hadn't meant to. *Fuck*, how he hadn't meant to. He grabbed her hand. "Just come. Please."

The pause was nearly unbearable. If she said no...

But then she smiled, and she took a handful of his shirt as she pulled him to her. "I'm pretty sure I just did."

She made him wait until 3:00, a time she declared was an okay time to leave, especially since she'd decided yesterday afternoon that so much had been accomplished that she'd given his aunt and uncle the day off.

Thank God, since he'd taken her in the middle of the damn room without a thought as to who else might be around.

Although the apartment was well within walking range for someone who, apparently, ran upward of seven miles a day, he waited around so he could drive her back and then they could get on the road straight from there. He didn't push her again about the blow-off note; he thought he was beginning to understand where she was coming from. And they'd figure it out later. Because, yes, he did wonder if this need he had for her was more about the freedom she'd offered by being one of the few people in his life who didn't treat him like Nate-freaking-Hawkins, especially considering she'd actually known who he was the whole time. She was smart enough and kind enough to give him the benefit of the doubt, but she needed to be able to trust that his heart was in the right place.

And so did he.

Chapter Fifteen

The Porsche was beautiful.

Not that Dorie went around waxing poetic about cars on a regular basis, but she didn't think she'd ever been in the presence of something so spectacular and so incredibly out of her league. Other than the man standing next to her, of course. If she started thinking about that, however, she'd start hyperventilating. It was better to focus on the car.

Clearly amused, Nate asked, "So which of the brothers is into cars?"

"Seamus," she said absentmindedly, her hand running over the top. "Cars and baseball."

She couldn't believe she'd agreed to go to Chicago with him. That did not a one-night stand make. Plus, the library reopening was in three weeks. Sure, they'd made huge strides this week thanks to all the help, but there was still so much to do. And she had the five thousand dollars in seed money from the Foundation that she still needed to decide how she wanted to use. But how could she not say yes to him? He was her fantasy—by actual definition.

Except the Nate Hawkins in her dreams didn't laugh at her jokes. To be honest, Fantasy Nate wasn't even that smart. He certainly didn't cook dinner for her or get turned on by the way she looked in her glasses.

Her dream man, did, though. And that was terrifying.

"Right," Nate murmured. "The Yaz fan."

Dorie's head jerked up. "You remembered."

He wrapped his hands around her waist, pulling her to him, back to front, and making very clear that despite pretty much having had sex straight for the past twelve hours, he was still hard. For her. She was pretty sure her mouth was wide open but she was too stunned to move. When he leaned close and whispered, "I remember everything you say," it did not help matters one bit.

Then his lips brushed down her jaw and it no longer mattered.

She closed her eyes.

"Every…" He kissed her neck. "Single…" His hand slid down her belly. "Thing." He reached down between her legs, stroking her through the jeans that were supposed to protect her from this very thing, and a moan rumbled up through her.

"Nathan, is that you?"

Dorie froze at the sound of Mr. Grimes's voice from the driveway.

"I saw the truck and—"

His voice cut off as he came through the garage door and saw Dorie standing there with Nate, although, thankfully, no longer with his hand nearly down her pants.

Oh, God. So she'd gone from being the baby girl of the Donelli family to being the slutty new librarian who had taken all of three days to hook up with her employees' nephew. Awesome. She moved a few steps away from Nate and hoped that this did not look like, say,

she was spending the weekend with a man she'd just
had mind-blowing sex with on the floor of the library.

"Hey, Uncle A," Nate said, not a care in the world.
"Sorry. I called first, but I just got the machine."

"Oh," Al said, looking over at Dorie and then glancing away. "Just dropped your aunt Laura off at your
mom's place."

With a nod, Nate handed a set of car keys to his uncle.
"Thanks for the use of the truck this week."

An oddly grim look settled over Mr. Grimes's face
as he grunted and pointed vaguely at the Porsche. "So
you'll be taking care of this mess, then?"

"Yes, sir, I will." In an unexpectedly sweet gesture,
Nate leaned down and hugged the older man. "Love
you, Uncle A."

After a long hard look at his nephew, Mr. Grimes
turned back to Dorie, nodded his head, and said, "See
you Monday, I guess."

Shoving her hands into her coat pocket, she smiled
and nodded back.

When he left, Dorie whirled around to face Nate. "I
can't—"

He palmed her cheek and silenced her with a kiss.
Not the carnal, I-can't-stand-another-second-without-
you kisses he was phenomenally good at. Instead, this
was more along the lines of *I won't force you but I know
you're thinking twice right now and I'd rather you didn't
think at all.*

*Except maybe about all of the things I can do to you
with this ridiculously hot body I have, and these amazing hands, not to mention a mouth that, as promised,
made you scream.*

She whimpered in protest when he pulled away.

"You were saying?" he asked, his hand going down to her ass as he pulled her up against him.

She rested her head against his chest and sighed. "Never mind."

Nate grinned and went to get their bags from the truck. He put them in the trunk and then opened the door for her, closing it behind her after she got in.

As they drove away from the farm, a quiet came over him that didn't appear to be a happy one. She didn't say anything at first, deciding that he had enough to deal with.

Her restraint lasted all of ten minutes. "If I had a car like this," she muttered, "I'd be a lot happier when I drove it."

"I don't have a car like this," he answered. "That's the whole point." Then he looked over at her, as though he'd just remembered who he was talking to. As if he wasn't sure how much he wanted her to know.

"I know pretty much everything about you," she admitted. Exactly why she'd run away from him this morning. Another conversation she didn't want to have, but it was too late for that now. "If you have an issue with that, then you'd better turn around right now."

His knuckles turned white as he gripped the steering wheel; the muscle in his jaw twitched. After a few minutes, he gave a bitter laugh. "So, you don't mind driving around with the drunk-driving asshole who killed his fiancée's baby."

If her heart hadn't already been broken for him, that would have shattered it.

Reaching for his hand, she didn't pull away when he flinched, waiting instead for him to finally lace his fingers through hers. "I think it's very easy for people to assume the worst and I think that you paid the price for that. I never thought you were that guy. I'm not that good at pretending." She looked away, giving him a little space. "And just for the record, I wouldn't sleep with 'a drunk-driving asshole who killed his fiancée's baby,' or did any of the other things they're saying you did."

He swallowed hard and she felt the pressure as his fingers gripped hers, but he didn't say anything so she added, "That said, I would consider a guy with a bum knee."

She smiled when he gave an incredulous laugh before saying, "As long as we're on record, my knee is fine."

Um, yes. She'd seen it in action under somewhat strenuous conditions. She squeezed his hand. "I know." From there she didn't push. That was maybe enough for now.

When 'for now' stretched into another hour, she decided it was time to do something about it. "So have you ever had sex in this car?"

She had to grab the edge of her seat when the car jerked to the side. He looked at her, eyebrows raised. "What?"

"I *said*, did you ever—"

He cut her off with a laugh. "You are such a guy."

Okay. She supposed she deserved that, considering she'd called him a girl last night. But she wasn't going to let him redirect her. "Well?"

He pulled his hand out of hers in order to place it squarely at two o'clock on the wheel. "It's a little too small inside for that to work, don't you think?"

Well, yes. Probably. With a shrug, she answered, "The hood's pretty big." She looked at him, then out at the road passing by. "Big enough."

This time his laugh was tinged with disbelief. "No. That isn't something I've ever done."

"That's a shame," she said, thinking that the tips of his ears turning red shouldn't be so appealing. "Seeing that it's going back tomorrow morning and all."

Gripping the steering wheel even harder, he tightly said, "It's thirty degrees outside."

She smiled. He was getting the point. "Hood should be warm."

"Engine's in the back," he answered. A big smile came over his face. "Too bad that wasn't one of the trivia questions."

Right. She knew that. It was just that he was distracting her. But two could play at that. "Shouldn't be that hard to warm it up."

The silence lasted a little too long for comfort, broken finally when he said, "Why would you want to do something like that?"

He sounded so suspicious, like she was going to pull something over on him.

With a sigh, she realized he had good reason. "Because this is far too nice of a car for you to hate it as much as you do."

Obviously surprised, he swung his head to her. "I don't—"

"Yes, you do."

Two minutes later they were off the highway. He took a turn off the exit ramp, then another soon after that, and then they were in the middle of nowhere, surrounded by cornfields and with no one else around. When he pulled to a stop on the narrow dirt road, he didn't look at her. "You're sure about this?"

With a roll of her eyes, she answered, "Well, not if

you're gonna make it sound like such a chore. The whole point is that it's supposed to actually be fun."

"Fun," he muttered, as though it wasn't a concept with which he was familiar.

Again with the glowering silence. Turning so that her back was against the door, she asked, "So tell me, Nate. What exactly is it that you do to have a good time?"

His entire body stiffened. "I play ball for a living." His voice was ten times colder than it was outside. "How can that not be a good time?"

She wondered if the bitterness was something that he'd been dealing with for a while or if it was a relatively new development; either way, his public persona hid it well. Here, in the confines of the car, it was hard to miss. "You tell me."

Since he didn't seem inclined to do anything of the sort, she unbuckled her seat belt and got out of the car. Her eyes stung at the blast of icy wind and it did occur to her that this wasn't one of the smartest things she'd ever suggested, especially as he was right about the damn engine and all its warmth being at the back of the car. But she wasn't about to back out now.

She'd left her parka in the car and she shivered as another gust of wind hit her. Deliberately not looking at Nate, she hitched herself backward and looked up at the darkening sky. It took Nate all of five seconds to come out after her. He put his jacket over her shoulders—denim, with an incredibly soft Sherpa lining—and said, "You're going to freeze to death."

Closing her eyes, she pulled the coat tighter and breathed in the amazing scent of him. "How is it possible this smells so good?"

"You're crazy," he muttered under his breath. Then

he gave a laugh that was equal parts wonder and appreciation, although she didn't realize it was for her until she opened her eyes to see the intensity in his.

His hand trailed from her jaw, down her neck, down over her breast, its peak hardened by cold and anticipation. His fingertips alone sent heat coursing through her. She was already at the point of not breathing when the smile died on his lips and his eyes darkened. "You're a fantasy come true. You know that, right?"

"Me?" The only time the word *fantasy* appeared in the same sentence as she did was when she was having one.

But then he was holding her, cradling her as though she was the most precious thing on earth. "You even taste too good to be true," he murmured into her neck as he proceeded to nuzzle his way down the center of her body, covering her skin as quickly as he exposed it—wrapping her in his jacket, the sinfully soft lining tickling her bare skin. He rolled her jeans and panties down her hips to her thighs while keeping her warm with his sinful hands and tongue. He nipped and teased, tantalizingly close enough to let her know he was following the letter of the law if not quite the spirit, goddamn him, and within moments she was begging. And then, with just one brush of his thumb, he broke her. Shattered her entirely. It took her a few moments of breathless recovery before she realized he was just sitting there, practically in his catcher's stance, looking up the length of her as he grinned.

"This was supposed to be for you," she said, the words coming haltingly as the air slowly came back to her lungs.

He ran his hands from her ankles up her legs, stretching out over her as his grin grew wider. Reaching in under the jacket, his hand covered her breast. "That *was* for me."

She shifted a little to give him access; no need to make him work too hard.

"And anyway," he was saying, "the angle of the hood isn't really that conducive to—"

"Stop talking," Dorie said, grabbing him by the collar and yanking him into a kiss. She wasn't strong enough to flip him onto his back the way he'd done to her twice the night before, but she sure could nudge and nuzzle him there, especially if she distracted him enough by fumbling with the buttons of his jeans. And he was sure as hell strong enough to keep her steady as she got to her knees and flung her leg over him. She sank down just enough to tempt him before saying, "I mean if you don't want to…"

He reared up and grabbed her. Half-glaring, half-hungry, he reached into the pockets of his coat and pulled out a condom. He sheathed himself with it and then she quickly sheathed him with her body. It worked out perfectly as far as she was concerned. Except that, when he collapsed back against the car, pulling her down with him, he touched his forehead to hers and looked deep into her eyes. "I am so totally fallin—"

"No," she snapped, hearing the words before he actually said them. Her heart leaped to her throat. She clutched at him, resting her head on his shoulder before he could finish the thought. She couldn't even for a *second* allow herself to believe she'd heard what he was clearly about to say. "Shut up." She squeezed her eyes shut. "Please just shut up."

Okay, so obviously, not a one-night stand. But still just a…fling. With someone who'd spent his life in the extremes and whose life was so out of control at the

moment that he was just looking for something—someone—to ground him.

Honestly. They'd known each other for a matter of
days. Less than a week! She didn't believe in love at first
sight, or even love at multiple-and-increasingly-naked-
sightings over the course of several days. She certainly
wasn't about to derail her life plans based on it.

Unlike most men she knew, he didn't try to shy away
from what he'd obviously—*inconceivably*—been about
to say. At the same time, he didn't try to say it again. He
laughed softly, then stroked her hair for a minute before
lifting his head and kissing her. There was still a smile
in his voice when he said, "Okay, fine. Shutting up." He
shifted a little, slanting his mouth so that he could go
deeper into hers.

She was well on her way to telling him to ignore
what she'd said about shutting up when he asked, "Do
you want to drive?"

Her eyes went wide as she sat up straight, nearly sliding right off the hood in the process. Was he *kidding*?
"You realize I learned to drive in Boston. Who knows
what damage I could do?"

He laughed. "A Red Sox fan *and* a Boston driver. You
pack a mean punch, Donelli." But he sat up, too. Looked
over at her and smiled. "I think I'll take my chances."
He held out the keys. "What do you say?"

Seriously? "I say that you'd better be ready to pay
some speeding tickets, because I sure as hell can't afford
them." She snatched them out of his hand and jumped
off the hood before he could change his mind.

Dorie turned the car back over to him right before they
got on the main highway. She fell asleep soon after,

which, as far as Nate was concerned, was a good thing. He needed to get ahold of himself, and luckily he had the next four hours to do it. Half the time he found himself desperate to get her out of his head and the other half he wanted to grab her and hold on as if his life depended on it. Which it might, considering he'd felt his whole body come alive the moment she raised the bat over her shoulder and stared him down without an ounce of fear—defending her dinner, no less.

He'd turn his attention back to the road in front of him and his eyes would drift down to the hood and the vision of her laid out in front of him. Even the fact that he'd had a split second of wondering if maybe she was setting him up, if maybe there was some photographer on standby, didn't seem to matter. Because that's all it was: one split second of doubt, followed by twenty minutes of driving need. And to his dismay, he was now contemplating the idea of true love and happily-ever-after-type endings, which was ridiculous, of course—because no matter where his career was headed, his life was in Chicago and hers wasn't. Reality would soon intrude.

Although he didn't want to wake Dorie, he should check in with Pete. He had no interest in the cavalry—be it his ex herself or one of her minions—showing up on his doorstep, even though the plan was to meet in the morning. Courtney was unpredictable that way. He hit the button for the phone and pulled up Pete's number. Thankfully, he got voice mail.

"Trip took a little bit longer than I expec—"

His voice cracked and he nearly swerved—again—when he felt Dorie's hand close over his thigh. He finished his message, the words practically running together as one. "…Than I expected. Keys'll be with the doorman by eleven."

Making sure he'd ended the connection, he grabbed Dorie's hand as she worked her way up farther. *Sweet Jesus.*

Through clenched teeth, he said, "Do you *want* me to be in another accident?"

She yanked her hand away. "That was crazy dumb. You shouldn't let me out in public."

Why her reaction turned him on even more, he had no idea, but his voice cracked again as he practically growled, "I have no intention of letting you out in public."

If he could spend the entire weekend with her naked in his bed, he'd be entirely content. Knowing she was there would make the meetings he had to endure go that much more quickly. Hell, knowing she was *here* made the prospect of heading back to Chicago a palatable one. He grabbed her hand and put it right back on his leg, just a little farther away from where it could do damage.

"You weren't, you know…" There was a question in her voice as she squeezed his hand briefly. "Right before the accident."

The harsh laugh escaped. "No."

He'd been distracted by Courtney, yes, and was one hundred percent sure that if he hadn't been so thrown by her words, he would have been able to avoid the other car. But, *hell* no. "Not even close."

Though he could feel Dorie's eyes on him, he wasn't planning on sharing more than that. That said, just because he was clearly sending that message didn't mean that she'd be accepting it. So he was completely prepared for her to say something. He just wasn't expecting it to be her commenting, "So that was Pete."

Hearing something off in her tone, he glanced over, surprised that her mouth had settled into a grim line. Which, come to think of it, was often Nate's response when it came to Pete. It was almost as though she knew him.

A sinking feeling came over him. Oh, *fuck*.

"Please tell me you don't know him."

She pulled her hand away. Crossed her arms across her chest, closing herself off. "I was kind of hoping you didn't know about any of that."

That. The waiver. Right. Just because he hadn't thought about it in two years didn't mean it wasn't still out there. How Pete had known about Dorie, though…

Of course. Fitz had known Nate was with Dorie that first night. She must have mentioned it.

"It was a joke." He cringed the second he said it, wishing he could take it back.

Unsurprisingly, Dorie mumbled, "That's so not the right answer."

No, it wasn't. And with anyone else he wouldn't give a damn. With Dorie, though… He took a deep breath. "I was twenty-three. Came out to Chicago and had that ridiculous year." He'd broken records that had stood for decades, had heard his name put up there with those of his heroes, and had been the shoo-in for Rookie of the Year. "They put Ox and me in a room—" Ox, as in Jack Oxford, one of the best pitchers in the league and also Nate's ex-best friend, "—and gave us a list of, well…"

He couldn't say it. Couldn't even put into words what had taken two bewildered, out-of-nowhere "rookie sensations" a bottle of tequila and an entire afternoon to acknowledge, much less actually write down.

"What would be acceptable," he finally managed. "And what wouldn't."

There was a very long and heavy silence. He didn't even realize he was holding his breath until Dorie said, "I guess I get that."

Hell, at least she wasn't already ditching him.

"But if you have him put that thing in front of me again," she added, "I will shove it exactly where, according to section 4B, you don't want it to go."

His coughing fit provided a reprieve for a few minutes, which was good, because he honestly had no idea what to say. He'd been too drunk to remember what he'd written down, too embarrassed to have looked at it since. He did have some ideas, however, of what she might be referring to.

"You didn't sign it?" She was the only one in the entire history of that stupid thing who hadn't, with the exception of Courtney.

"Seriously?" Dorie said, whipping her head around and glaring at him, clearly misunderstanding his reaction. "I will literally jump out of this car if you're about to tell me you want me to."

No. What he wanted to do was close his eyes. Capture the essence of the fire blazing in her eyes, the you-may-be-Nate-fucking-Hawkins-but-there's-no-way-in-hell-you'll-pull-that-shit-on-me attitude. It had been years since he'd seen that, since someone hadn't put him up on a pedestal. Even his sisters, who he'd used to be able to count on for putting him in his place whenever required, had been treating him with kid gloves of late, Fitz's alley-lashing notwithstanding. He goddamn hated it. And it was probably why he'd come back to Dorie's that second night—because even after being accepted back into the heart of his family, he'd felt the distance. Felt that, for as much as they were happy to have him home, they didn't quite know how to talk to him anymore.

So he'd gone back to Dorie's and she'd treated him like any other guy. More like one of her brothers than he'd preferred, to be honest, but there wasn't a kid glove or a pedestal anywhere to be found.

"That's not what I'm telling you at all."

Obviously confused, she asked, "Then what are you saying?"

He took her hand. Tried not to get lost in the way his breath caught as soon as he touched her. "I'm saying—" gruffly, as it turned out, "—that this is one those times you should be telling me to shut up."

Dorie's mouth dropped open as she stared at him. "You're not mad."

Working not to smile, Nate said, "No."

Although she frowned, she came to a decision, it appeared. If he was willing not to say the actual words, she was willing to let it go.

Or, rather, willing to let some things go.

She smiled. "Well I suppose that's good, then. You know why?"

Ah. Right. He figured this was a subject that would come up again. "Because you'll knee me in the balls?"

With a happy little sigh, she squeezed his hand, then let go. "Damn right I will."

The smile he'd been holding back turned into a laugh. "And here I thought you were getting attached."

She laughed, then reached out and let her hand slowly drift down his jaw. "How about if I promise to kiss and make it better afterward?"

Okay. This was no longer a laughing matter. He stepped on the gas, never before so eager to get home.

Chapter Sixteen

If there was one thing in the world that Dorie was an expert on, it was men—their thoughts, what they wanted and how they behaved. Hell, she knew so much about men that she could barely relate to women, the main exceptions being only two that she could think of: Sean's wife, Claudia, who had also been Dorie's babysitter until Dorie was able to be a babysitter herself. And Sophie, Tommy's on-again, off-again girlfriend since middle school, the closest Dorie had ever come to having a sister. But Soph was in law school and crazy busy so it had been weeks since they'd talked, and whatever Dorie told Claudia ended up with Sean, too, so Dorie had to be careful about what she said.

Maybe if she had more girlfriends she'd have more of a clue how *they* thought men thought, and then maybe she'd be closer to understanding Nate. Because she didn't get him. He *confounded* her. She had no idea what she was supposed to do.

He was obviously misguided about falling in love with her—holy *hell*. But she was starting to get what Fitz had meant the other day—that he seemed happier. Lighter. And if that was something Dorie could do for him, she was more than okay giving up her weekend to the cause. So, knowing that despite his knowledge of all things girlie he was, in fact, a man, there were two ways to dissuade him from his clearly delusional idea: his stomach and his dick. She had no interest in cooking anything now that they were nearing his place, so she was left with just the one. And making promises like the one she'd just made seemed to be the only way to get his mind back to where she was comfortable.

But she didn't want to get into a car accident any more than he did. So she kept her hands to herself for the rest of their trip, and sat back and looked out the window, enjoying the sight of the city as they drove into the heart of it.

They got to his building about ten minutes later. And it was beautiful, of course. Right on the Magnificent Mile. He drove down into the garage, to a spot that was right in the middle of all the other ones.

"Don't you get something special?" Dorie asked as they got out. "I mean… That's, like, a million-dollar car."

He just looked at her. "This is the spot they gave me. I'm not about to cause a scene so I can get something better."

"Not a *better* one, just one that…" She looked around at the cars surrounding them, which, admittedly, were of the luxury variety. Still… "It's a *million* dollars."

"Yep," he said, slamming the trunk.

Now it was her turn to stare. "You really don't like that car."

"Nope." Then he turned and started walking away.

"Wait…" After one last look at the *gorgeous* car, she hurried after him and pulled at her tote. She didn't need a valet. "So you don't even want to say goodbye to it? After tomorrow it's gone, right?"

Calling It

He stopped short, exasperated. "It's a car. I'm not going to tell it *bye*. I..." He reached down for her hand as he stepped closer. "I have exactly one thing I like about that car." He ducked his head and nuzzled her neck. "The memory of *you*. On the hood. With me."

And then he was kissing her. His mouth on her jaw, on her neck...

It felt... Oh, *God*. How could it be better?

How could it keep getting better?

In a kiss-induced haze, she let him lead her through the parking garage. "Huh?" she asked after realizing he'd just spoken.

Chuckling, he pushed the button for the elevator. "I asked if there was anything special you wanted to see while we're here in Chicago."

Without hesitation, she answered, "The library."

"The library?"

She nodded. "Harold Washington. It's the main branch of the Chicago Public Library."

The elevator came right then and she started to walk forward, only to be jerked back thanks to her hand still being attached to his and him not moving. The elevator doors closed again. "What?" she asked.

"Not the Willis Tower, not Shedd Aquarium or the Art Institute or Grant Park," he stated. "You want to go to the library."

She jabbed the button for the elevator and was happy to see the doors open right away. "Well, sure. Those things, too, if there's time." Tugging him forward, she watched as he pushed the button to the thirty-eighth floor. "But I looked it up on my phone and the library does tours. It might just be for groups, so we can just grab a brochure or…" Her voice trailed off as she realized he was staring at her, completely amused.

"I'm pretty sure I can get someone to give us a tour of the library." He smiled.

"Oh." She frowned. "I hadn't thought of that." It felt, well, wrong. Then again, Nate Hawkins walking into the main library on a Saturday was probably a bad idea all around. So maybe it would be better if—

"I can't decide if I should be happy that it never occurred to you to use my name…" They reached his floor and stepped out into the hallway, the doors closing behind them. "Or the exact opposite because of the look that came over your face a minute ago."

Right. Of course he'd noticed. "It's just so complicated."

"It doesn't have to be," he replied, placing his hand on her cheek. She leaned into it without a shred of resistance.

Still, she tried to break the stare—she didn't want to see the emotion in his eyes, or the evidence that he might truly care for her as deeply as he was telling her. It would poke holes in her whole this-can't-be-real defense. So for safety's sake, she responded, "Says the man who's in town to return the limited edition Porsche to his billionaire heiress ex-fiancée and taking in a meeting with the Chicago Watchmen management while he's here."

His lips quirked into a smile. "You just don't give up, do you?"

"Well, you're all, 'Let me just tell the woman I met all of three days ago that—'" She squealed as she was suddenly being lifted into the air and thrown over his shoulder. "You did not just do that!"

Except he had, obviously, because she was now hanging upside down and being carried in a fireman's hold. And being *tickled*. "I'm not ticklish!" Unfortunately, her giggling and trying to squirm away from his hand gave her away. He just laughed.

She pummeled him on that nice and firm backside of his as he stopped to open the door to his condo and then, because it was right there, took a big bite through his jeans.

He didn't even react. Instead, he came to a stop after only a few steps through the doorway. Every muscle in his body—at least the ones she could feel—tensed. Nate slowly lowered her to her feet as a man whispered something in rapid-fire Spanish from somewhere to her left. Something that roughly translated into, *Who the fuck is she?*

About to ask the same, she whirled around.

The man who had spoken was, among other things, a three-time Cy Young Award winner. And the man he'd been talking to was a two-time World Series MVP. Her mouth dropped open as she looked around her and realized she was standing in the presence of a Who's Who roster of professional sports.

"What…?" Nate asked, clearly as stunned as she was, although his attention was focused in the other direction, at the six additional men who stood there. As far as she could tell, he hadn't even noticed the guys who'd just spoken.

Instead, his eyes were sweeping the dining area of his crazy nice apartment, which, incidentally, Dorie would be exploring in detail as soon as possible. They came to rest on a man she didn't recognize, despite his presence being solid enough to center a room's worth of majorly alpha men. His salt-but-mostly-pepper hair was cut short and he wore expensive slacks—she wouldn't dare call them pants—and a button-down shirt that practically had dollar signs hanging off it. He had amazingly beautiful deep brown eyes that she would find attractive if they weren't, at the moment, ice-cold.

"Pete," Nate said. Because of course that's who it was. "What's, uh…" He ran his hand through his hair. "What's going on?"

Pete's gaze flickered to Dorie and then back to Nate. He kept his voice even, but his jaw most definitely tightened before he flashed a smile. "Thought you might need a bit of help with the reentry. Some whiskey, a little poker…" Then his voice went so even that it practically flatlined. "But I didn't realize you'd have company."

Still a little dazed, it took a few seconds for Nate to focus back on Pete. And then on Dorie. "*Oh.* I…I mean, we…"

Under other circumstances, Dorie would have been entirely pissed off. Or embarrassed. And, most likely, unwelcome, given the group that had gathered here tonight. But these weren't other circumstances and this wasn't just any group. And, to be honest, although Pete was not at all her favorite person in the world, there was genuine concern in his eyes when he looked at Nate. It was clear he wasn't just Nate's lawyer; he was actually, it appeared, a friend.

Since everyone seemed to be deliberately *not* staring at her as they tried to figure out what exactly she was doing here, it appeared it would be up to her to move things along. So she stepped up to Pete, ignored the irritation in his eyes and thrust her hand out. "I'm Dorie." She mentally crossed her fingers behind her back. "It's nice to meet you."

As wariness, then awareness, came into Pete's eyes, she smiled. "Yep. That's the one. And just so that we're on the same page, we didn't do anal and he brought the condoms, although I am on the Pill, just in case you were wondering."

Nate looked up at her sharply as she spoke, her words bringing him out of this trance, although she wasn't sure it was her statement about the Pill that got his eyes flashing or if it was that she'd actually just said all that to Pete. At least she'd been quiet enough for only the two of them to hear it.

"Dorie," Nate exhaled. "*Jesus.*"

"Just needed to get that out of the way," she muttered while turning to the other men. And then she started introducing herself around, refusing to care about the fact that she'd spent half her lifetime watching some of these men play their various sports. This was about Nate, not her. There was no way in hell she was going to stand in the way.

To say that Nate was blown away was like saying Shaq was on the taller side.

Holy Christ.

Sure he'd met most of them before, he'd even shared a meal or two. But these guys were in his home. They'd taken the time to be here—Pete must have called in more than one favor to make this happen.

Honestly? Nate was beyond grateful that Dorie had just gone in guns blazing, because it gave him the minute he needed to compose himself before the other men started coming up to him with the fist bumps and back slaps that made it feel like all was right with the world. And, yes, this was his world.

Even more so when there was a knock on the door and more guys walked in. Three guys from his old team—Devon Haney, Tim Kozlowski and Eduardo Andrade. Then there were two players from the new one—Rico Castillo and Troy Simons. Good, solid guys he was looking forward to playing with. All five men had sent texts and left messages since the accident. Nate hadn't responded, at first because he couldn't handle yet another conversation in which no one knew what to say. But then because...

Because he'd just shut down. And climbing back out of that deep, dark hole had seemed so unattainable and impossible that he couldn't even think of where to start.

Now, though... Now he was just humbled. Grateful. Happy.

"Amigo!" Rico stepped forward and wasted no time in gathering Nate into a bear hug. A shortstop who had made the switch from AL to NL last year, he said, "I told you the sun would rise again, my friend. Now we just need to get these hombres off our backs." He hooked his thumb at Nate's former teammates. "Then we ride like the wind."

Then Kozlowski stepped forward, his eyes conveying the same laser-like focus as they did from third base even as they rolled at Rico's hyperbole. He threw his arm around Nate's shoulders. "Back off, Castillo. I'm getting my boy back."

That set off a round of trash talk—Sox and Cubs v Watchmen; baseball v basketball v football; younger guys v Pete's veterans. Several rounds of Scotch were poured, and then there was a move back to the table where packs of cards had already been broken out. Nate took a sip of his drink and let his gaze come to a rest on

Dorie, who was caught up in conversation with Eddie and Troy. And, *hell*, they seemed to be talking about the wives and girlfriends—going so far as giving her numbers to call. Shit. She was not going to like that—not one bit. He was about to go over and save her when Pete came up to him.

"You okay with this?" he asked. "I can cut it short if you want. I'm guessing this wasn't what you had planned for the evening."

Nate looked at the man. What Pete had done for him tonight was incredible. Nate wasn't about to bring up the subject of the waiver, nor was he going to even attempt to explain whatever it was that was going on with Dorie. Hell, he didn't even understand it himself.

He was taken aback by how right it felt to have her here. If she was starstruck—and he had no doubt she could name every single man in this room—she didn't show it. Nor was she in any way irritated that what had been 'planned,' as Pete had put it, was completely off the table. She just seemed to be looking for a way to unobtrusively remove herself and let Nate hang with some friends. He took a sip of his drink, watching her trying to inch away, even as she smiled at something Rico said.

"Hey, Donelli," he said, startling her. "You play poker?"

A grin came over her face, then she cocked her head to the side. "Is that the one with the chips?"

He laughed. He didn't believe for a second she wouldn't be running the table by the end of the night. That wasn't the case for the others—they all looked up at her with renewed interest as they saw an easy mark.

"Don't fall for it," Nate said, unable to hide his smile as he tried to warn them. These were some of the best athletes on the planet and she was going to take them down. "She's a wily one."

She gave a little snort of a laugh that shouldn't have been cute but was ridiculously so. "He exaggerates." But she was already working it; if she was even the least bit intimidated by the sheer power in the room, she didn't give a hint of it.

It was clear Pete didn't know what to make of it. What to make of her. But after an assessing look at Dorie, Pete just rolled up his sleeves and cracked his knuckles. "Deal the woman in."

And Nate wasn't wrong. By about three hands in, it was clear to everyone that Dorie was either very good at cards or "the luckiest chick on the planet," according to a disgruntled Haney.

"Rather be lucky than good," she murmured before laying down an ace-high flush, which irritated Haney even more.

She also, not surprisingly, had an amazing poker face, something Nate would have liked to know about several days ago. Watching her closely through the night—surreptitiously, of course—it was clear that the only tell she had was when she had a particularly hopeless hand. She'd bite her lip and roll her shoulders in a way that highlighted that beautiful rack of hers.

It was distracting enough that it took him a full two hours before realizing it was deliberate. And that it got more pronounced as Haney, who tended to be a bit of an ass when he was drunk, got more and more vocal with comments of the "little lady doesn't belong" variety. Comments that had Nate ready to throw down with him then and there, although every time he even started to respond, he felt a swift kick to his shin, which was accompanied by a death glare from Dorie.

It turned him on more than a little bit. And as much as these guys were his friends, he had to admit that he wasn't all that sympathetic to the ones who were falling for it. Not when they seemed to be fully okay with letting Haney's comments slide. If they could take the heat on the field, then there was no excuse for not being able to take it here, no matter who was dealing it.

It wasn't until the end of the night that it fully paid off. By this point—a little after 4:00 a.m.—it was down to Pete, Dorie, Nate and his friends. The pot was three thousand and change, the highest of the night, and she was biting her lip the whole way through. Since she'd taken enough of everyone's money so far, no one had a problem raising on her despite the fact that every single one of them was good enough to know exactly what that lip-biting meant. They were going to crush her and they were fine with that.

So when she laid down a full house—"Aces full of tens, baby!"—you could literally hear the jaws drop.

"You are fucking *kidding* me," Kozlowski said, throwing down his cards.

"Like my brothers always say, boys…" She leaned forward to pull in all her chips. "Never trust a pair of tits."

Nate choked on his drink. Despite the lightness in her voice, she was clearly pissed. And not a little bit triumphant.

Rico, who up until that moment had been about to go home several thousand dollars richer, let out a tear of Spanish that Nate could barely follow—and that was after being schooled in the language by some of the best pitchers in the game. You didn't have to speak Spanish to get an impression of what he was saying. But Dorie just gave a smile. A *whatever* kind of shrug. He should probably be frightened out of his mind. Should be, but wasn't, which was something he had no intention of analyzing right now.

"That's not a pair of tits," Haney muttered. "That's a wolf in chick's clothing."

"She played us," Troy said, sitting back, with a glint of admiration. Use your opponent's weakness and all that. Of course, he could afford to be generous, since he'd folded early on. He turned to Nate. "Your new girlfriend played us."

As Haney finally loosened up and joined in on the conversation, Nate came to the realization that, fuck it all to hell, he really was in trouble. Especially because he realized he wasn't nearly as interested in protecting her as he was in watching her take them all down. That he'd begun to consider her an equal in a way that only his teammates had ever been—an equal who had no interest or need for him to defend her.

"I'm not his girlfriend," she'd muttered.

As the cards were put away and the conversation turned back to Dorie's win, Nate took the cigar Pete handed him and smiled. "Can't say I didn't warn you." Unlike Dorie, he had no problem rubbing her win in their faces.

Dorie just shrugged as she stacked her chips. The sly smile she gave was only for him.

Pete, who had remained silent through all of this, held out a cigar. "Smoke?"

She looked at it and then at Pete, her eyes narrowing. Nate had no more idea of what exactly Pete was thinking than she did, although it probably ran along the lines of: this woman is going to take you to the cleaners and you're not even going to care.

She shook her head. "Thank you, but no."

Thank God. If she put one of those in her mouth and blew?

Then she stood and stretched, and he was pretty sure his head was going to explode. Both of them.

"I assume there's a bed somewhere around here that I can crash on?" she asked.

"End of the hall, corner room," Nate ground out. Christ.

She smiled and gave a mumbled, "Good night. It was really nice to meet all of you."

They all just kind of smiled back at her, though some reluctantly. When she finally picked up her bag and disappeared out of sight—not acknowledging Nate in any particular way, incidentally, which he was trying not to let bother him—there was a collective exhale and then a moment of silence.

"*Dios mío,*" Rico finally muttered.

"Christ, Hawk, that woman scares me," Kozlowski said, taking a drag on his cigar as he looked at the hallway Dorie had disappeared into. "Where did she come from?"

"And does she have any sisters?" Troy asked, setting off a round of comments that was increasingly vulgar, though that had never bothered Nate until tonight. And although the other guys were careful enough not to say anything about Dorie herself—you did not talk trash about a man's woman and expect to get away with it— it reminded Nate that what he wanted with Dorie was unlike anything he'd ever wanted before.

He almost laughed. That thing about "the life" chewing her up and spitting her out? He and Wash couldn't have been more wrong.

Unfortunately, his silence didn't go entirely unnoticed. Troy was the one who called him on it, looking down the hallway after where Dorie had gone and then swinging his gaze toward Nate. "Holy Christ," he said, his drink nearly spilling out of his hand. "You're going to marry her, aren't you?"

Nate knew he should laugh that off. And he didn't need to look over at Pete to know why the man had been so quiet. But, hell if he didn't get a rush just at the thought of her as his wife.

Not that he'd be giving that answer here tonight, of course. Hell, no.

"Dude," Haney said. "Makes sense to keep her."

God help him, if Dorie heard that.

"Shut up," Rico muttered.

"What? Like he doesn't already know what the guys are saying?" Haney went on as if Nate wasn't in the room. And since Nate didn't, actually—he didn't generally listen to crap like that—he sat back and gestured for Haney to go on.

Which Haney did. "That you were on your way out. Even before the wreck. That your head hasn't been in the game for a while now and that the Watchmen were crazy to sign you, because it was only a matter of time before you tanked."

Knowing he didn't want to end this night in a full-out brawl, Nate ground his teeth and decided not to kill the guy.

Ignoring the others' glares, Haney tossed back the rest of his whiskey and then pointed right at Nate. "But, fuck, man. You're back. You got me? You. Are. Fucking. *Back*. And if she's why then you'd better fucking hold on."

There was about ten seconds of silence before the entire table burst into laughter.

"Jesus Christ, Haney," Troy said. "What the fuck are you on? He barely even won a hand tonight."

Standing up and stretching, Haney just shook his head. "Because he spent the entire night with a hard-on."

"Like you didn't," Kozlowski said, laughing as he pushed Haney toward the door.

Good thing everyone left after that, because Nate would have hit at least one of them soon.

He cleaned up whatever couldn't wait until morning and walked through the condo back to the bedroom, turning lights off along the way. And he had to admit, Haney—crazy as he was—spoke some truth. Although his game hadn't suffered—yet—signing with the Watchmen, a team he'd get to help build from the ground up, had been partly in hope of recapturing the joy and excitement again. Because it sure as hell had been fading.

But, yeah, something had changed in the short time since he had left Chicago on Tuesday night. Even his condo felt like a new place. He hadn't even come back here after that dinner because he pretty much hated it. Thanked God it was just a sublet through June. But now, after a night that would probably rank up there in his Top Five for a very long time—with the knowledge that Dorie was in his bed—it felt like home.

Dorie hadn't even bothered to change. She'd just stepped out of her jeans and then crawled under the covers. After stripping out of his own clothes, he climbed in next to her, nudging her over. "You're on my side," he whispered into her neck.

Rather than move over, she pushed back into him—
not helpful. "*My* side," she mumbled back.

They were clearly going to have some conversations
if he managed to talk her into letting this be more than a
temporary thing. He did just have one much more imme-
diate thing he needed to clear up, however. "That, uh…
That thing you were saying about the Pill…?"

Her body went tense for the most fleeting of moments
and then relaxed. "Right," she said. "I was meaning to
talk to you about that." She turned in his arms so that
she was facing him. Did *not* look him in the eyes as she
trailed her finger down his chest. "I mean, I know it's
crazy to think you'd take my word for it. And it's not
like it makes sense since this is such a short-term thi—"

"It's not a short-term thing," he interrupted, his hand
running up the back of her leg. Goddamn he loved the
way her breath hitched.

Undaunted, she continued, "And it's really just about
sex—"

"It's not just about sex," he snapped, unable to keep
the irritation out of his voice on that one.

She ignored that, too, saying, "But I've never been
with a guy without a condom," as her arm snaked down
between them and she took him firmly in hand. "And
I'd really like for that to be different with you." Then
she started to play.

Oh, fuck. Sweet Jesus, fucking *fuck*. He grabbed on
to her shoulder. How did she do that? Although, no, he
didn't want the answer to that question, because she'd
clearly had some practice.

"And you?" she whispered as she feathered kisses
down his throat. "All clean, right? I mean…" Her mouth
was traveling across his collarbone. She threw her leg

over his and pushed up so she was straddling his thighs, stroking him the whole time. "I'm assuming that would have been headline news by now if you weren't."

A laugh escaped even as his eyes rolled toward the back of his head. How was it possible she could make him laugh right now? About something that usually made his blood run cold, no less. "Yes," he gasped. "For some reason—" Oh, *shit*, she was throwing in some tongue. "—they didn't want—" *Fuck*. Taking him into her mouth. "—that in the press—" Taking him all the way to the back of her throat. Sweet *Jesus*, fuck. "—*release*."

She did something then that nearly blew him out of his mind. He managed to keep control, but only because there was no way in hell he was coming until they were doing this bareback.

And then her mouth was abruptly gone.

Her head came up, sexy as sin—hair wild, lips full and puffy and red, eyes anime-worthy wide. "Did you just make a joke?" On hands and knees, she stalked up the length of his body looking so fucking hot that the beast inside him wanted to roar. He almost started panting like a goddamn dog.

Poised above him—so close he could feel her heat—she held still as he yanked her T-shirt over her head, as he nearly tore her panties in two. "Pretty risky move, making me laugh when I have you in my mouth."

That's what that was? He would have laughed again if the entire future of mankind didn't depend on him grabbing her by the hips and yanking her down over him and, oh, fuck, *yesssss*, driving into her tight, wet heat. He wasn't sure who took who after that, just that it was hard, fast and so damn perfect that it almost brought him to tears.

Or maybe that was because of the look in her eyes—hell, yes, she was falling just as hard as he was—right after she came. She shut it down quickly, reaching up for a quick kiss before turning around and resting back against him.

Short-term?

Only about the sex?

Hell the *fuck* no.

He wrapped his arms around her and fell asleep.

Chapter Seventeen

The sun wasn't nearly high enough in the sky when Nate woke up. He should have felt worse than he did; his head should have been pounding. But he didn't and it wasn't. There was only one thing throbbing and for only one reason.

Waking up with her was everything he'd dreamed it would be.

Literally. It felt like the second his eyes closed, he was caressing her. Shifting her hair off her shoulders, kissing the back of her neck as he ran his hand down her arm, over her hip, the smooth skin of her thigh…

She'd just called his name when his eyes flew open and he realized that the sun was out. That she was actually wearing a T-shirt that she must have pulled on at some point during the night and that her back was still to him. But that he was buried deep inside her.

"*Nate*," she whispered as she angled her hips, pulsing around him from within.

He tried to wait. He didn't want to take her like this, without fully knowing if she was as wet and ready as she seemed or if that was still just part of the dream. But then, trembling, her hand found the back of his thigh, clenching him as she gasped. Her body clamped down around him as he kissed the base of her neck.

That was all it took. He exploded into her, rocked as she shattered around him. He grabbed the headboard, desperate for something to ground him, to keep from taking flight. When she reached up and closed her hand around his, though—fell back against him with a low moan—he was lost. It wasn't just that he'd *begun* to fall, it was signed and sealed: he'd fallen full in love with her. In a matter of days.

He pulled her closer and dropped his head, wanting to breathe her in; overcome by a hunger from so deep inside that it took his breath away. "You're killing me," he finally managed to say.

"I know," she said, stretching out languorously like a purring, satisfied cat. "I'm sorry. I even contemplated the can-you-help-me-in-the-kitchen quickie last night but it didn't seem the time. And, uh, I probably would have gotten lost trying to find the kitchen."

Right. Because she was insisting it was sex only, short-term. This was seriously beginning to bug him.

But before he could say anything about it, she slapped him on the leg. "Now leave me alone and let me get some sleep." She pulled the covers up over her shoulder. "Gotta rest up for the next time," she said dreamily.

He closed his eyes and tried to sleep himself, but it was pretty much useless and he decided to take a shower instead. He was dressed and contemplating what to make Dorie for breakfast when he realized that he hadn't left the keys to the Porsche at the desk.

"*Damn* it." The thing he'd specifically come back to Chicago for and he'd forgotten entirely.

He slammed the refrigerator door and turned. And

almost had a coronary as he took an involuntary step back. Holy *shit*.

"Courtney."

"Hi, baby," she said, walking toward him. She didn't seem angry. He didn't think that was a good thing.

"Uh, hi," he answered instinctively. And then asked, "What are you doing here?" when his brain caught up. The last time he'd seen her was a few days after the crash. She'd come into his hospital room, told him her assistant had found him a place to live and was having his stuff moved out of their town house that day. That was it. If she thought she was having a come-to-Jesus talk with him now she was seriously mistaken.

His eyes slid over to the pass-through. He was so busy looking for escape routes that he didn't see the glint in her eye until she was right in front of him. "I was thinking…" she said, slowly unbuttoning her coat. Shrugging it off slowly and revealing lingerie underneath.

Jesus. "Are you *kidding*?" he asked, amazed at how evenly he managed, given she was now standing there in nothing but black lace—complete with stockings, garters and stiletto heels.

A flash of irritation flitted through her eyes, but it was gone by the time she wrapped her arms around his neck. "I should think it's obvious that I'm not." She started to brush her lips over his jaw.

He quickly disentangled her arms and set her away from himself. Looking down, he felt oddly unaffected. She was beautiful, yes. With her deep blue eyes and ash-blond hair up in a twist, she had a Grace Kelly vibe about her—with the body of a Victoria's Secret model and the mouth of a porn star. Yet he felt nothing, not even as she trailed her hand down his chest. He figured that might have something to do with the fact that he'd been having sex for the better part of the past twenty-four hours, and that Dorie had pretty much...

Well, shit. And now he was hard again. Just at the thought of her name. "Fuck," he muttered.

"Well that's what I'm trying to do," Courtney said, exasperated, "but it's taking you a while to cooperate."

Before he could stop her she reached down the front of his pants. "So," she continued as if they hadn't broken up badly two months before. "I think we made a mistake."

He was trying to figure out how to tell her that she wasn't actually the woman he was hard for when her words hit him. He grabbed her hand and removed it, then took her by the waist and set her away—again. "*We?*"

She looked up at him for a minute, considering her response. Which, apparently, was to go for the buttons instead. She jutted her chest forward, making sure that the skin spilling out over the cups of her bra brushed his arms. "Yes, Nate. We. We're two incredibly intelligent—and ridiculously attractive—people. We make more sense together than we do apart."

"Then maybe you shouldn't have *fucked* my best friend," he replied, vehemently, as he latched on to her wrist and attempted to—

"Um, hi. Hello."

Courtney's head whipped around at the same speed as Nate's did. Shit. Well at least Courtney's hand was no longer down his pants. But when he started to step away, she just grabbed the waistband and held on.

Without acknowledging him at all, Dorie came into the kitchen, her hand out to introduce herself to Courtney—just as she'd done with Pete last night. Except then she happened to notice where Courtney's hand was and she stopped short. Her face went a little pale and she jerked her hand back. "Right. Never mind."

Eyes traveling from Nate to Dorie and then back again, Courtney seemed amused. "Who's this?"

Afraid to make any sudden moves, Nate very carefully made the introductions. "Dorie, Courtney. And, uh, vice versa." Christ.

Completely unconcerned that she was standing in nothing but very skimpy underwear, Courtney gave Dorie the kind of up and down once-over that, Nate had seen firsthand, had grown men quaking. Dorie, however, seemed entirely unperturbed.

Not only unperturbed, she actually smiled and said, "Wow. You are beautiful. Seriously *beautiful*."

Honestly? That was her response? Not even a little hint of jealousy?

And not because of the beautiful thing, which Courtney was. But Dorie was, too. And he was coming to realize that what he'd had with Courtney was an alliance, whereas what he had with Dorie was…

Goddamn it. It was nothing right now because she refused to believe otherwise.

He got it. He really did. If he hadn't had something to compare it to, he probably would have felt the same way she did. But, *shit*, at the very least, he would have given it a chance.

Aw, *fuck*.

No, if the places were reversed, he probably wouldn't have. But now that he recognized it, he wasn't about to let it go.

"So," Dorie said, coughing a little to clear her throat. "Does anyone want breakfast?"

"Courtney isn't staying," he said to Dorie, glaring. Then he turned his glare to Courtney. "She's leaving as soon as I get her the keys."

"*What?*" Courtney snapped. "You can't seriously…" She looked back at Dorie with a combination of disbelief and disdain. "She's just the rebound girl."

Nate didn't even look over to see Dorie's reaction. He didn't doubt that was one of the things she was telling herself.

"I'm entirely serious," he answered, looking directly into Courtney's eyes.

She stepped back, her gaze never leaving his even as her eyes widened. This thing with Dorie was different; something he'd never felt with Courtney. Having them both here in the same room only drove home that point. And Courtney wasn't an idiot. She was, in fact, one of the smartest women Nate knew. The flicker of emotion in her eyes as the understanding came over her was the first sign he'd ever seen that what she felt for him might actually be something close to love.

Dorie, on the other hand, just narrowed her eyes, then rolled them. She came all the way into the kitchen and brushed by both of them on her way to the fridge, where she opened the door and took out the orange juice. "Listen to her, Nate. You make a lot of sense together."

A lot more than we do, she didn't add, though it was clearly in her voice. Even Courtney gave a little snort at that.

He reached into the cabinet and handed Dorie a glass. "Really?"

Not at all happy to have been shut out of, well, everything, Courtney straightened out her coat with a loud snap and put it back on. While buttoning it up, she said,

"We have some things to discuss. I'm free for dinner tomorrow night."

Whatever was going through Dorie's head right now—and Nate was aware he wasn't coming off in a favorable light—she wasn't about to let Courtney call the shots, which was…interesting.

"Uh-uh," she snapped, probably something Courtney had never in her life heard. "You can catch up when pitchers and catchers report. That's when he goes back to his old life."

Pitchers and catchers. Less than three weeks. "Good to know," he murmured.

Dorie frowned, realizing she'd just given him her end date. He didn't like it, but now he knew. Realizing Courtney had no idea what they were talking about, he added, "February thirteenth." And he was going to make every minute count.

"Fine." Courtney pulled her gloves on with a snap. "And just leave the keys at the desk. I'll have someone pick them up." Then she whirled around and walked out. The door slammed shut a few seconds later.

"Well," Dorie said at that point. She raised her eyebrows, drained her glass, and then put it in the sink. "Beautiful. Seriously."

Nate opened his mouth to respond, but she held up her hand and said, "Don't." She grabbed the edge of the counter. Not meeting his eyes, she said, "I don't play games, not like that. And I'm not about to be a pawn in yours."

No. He stepped toward her, stopping only because she went rigidly still as he got close. "You're not a pawn," he answered, wanting so badly to take her into his arms, yet knowing that was the exact wrong move. "I want to make you my damn *queen*."

When her head came up, there were tears glistening in her eyes and for once she didn't deny what he said. It just turned out that had been the wrong move, too.

"But that's the problem, Nate. I don't want to be the queen of your world. I want to be the king of mine."

Well, shit. She'd rendered him speechless for, possibly, the first time in his entire life. Or, actually, not the first time, since she'd tied up his tongue that first night, too. Goddamn he was fucked.

She mistook his silence for capitulation. "See?" she said, smiling despite the sadness in her eyes. "It's so much easier if it's just about sex."

"It's not—" he started to say, but she cut him off by peeling off her shirt—no bra—and dropping it.

"The really…" she said, lowering the PJ pants—cotton panties again, neon pink—and stepping out of them.

"…good…"

She kicked them to the side.

"…sex."

Nate let out the breath he hadn't realized he'd been holding. "I know what you're doing," he said, trying to take the high road as she hitched herself onto the counter. "We're not done talking."

With an evil smile, she merely grabbed hold of his shirt and pulled him to her.

His brain went fuzzy as his dick surged forward to take the lead. "Fuck," he muttered yet again. Then her hand dropped down and all bets were off.

Was there anything the man wasn't good at? Dorie honestly didn't know how she could walk, much less run nine miles, yet here they were on mile two and she was on such a high from all that amazing sex she'd been having that she felt like she could go ten times that without breaking a sweat.

"Are we going to talk about this?"

She glanced up as he ran next to her, which was something she'd been trying very hard not to do. She still wasn't entirely sure what she was doing here.

He misunderstood her silence. Rolling his eyes, he said, "Are you going to tell me I think like a girl again?"

She wasn't, but that would be as good an excuse as any. She shrugged. "There's nothing to talk about."

And there wasn't. That was doubly clear after last night as the men in his world had closed ranks around him—supporting him, reclaiming him. And then Courtney, of course, pulling him back to the land of *Nate Hawkins*, and reminding Dorie that the Nate of this fantasy didn't truly exist. That even if it did, guys like him did not get all hot and bothered for women who meant what they said when they threw out words like king.

But that didn't mean she wasn't determined to enjoy the rest of the weekend.

"How about we start with Courtney?" he asked, as if putting small-town librarian Dorie in the same category as a trust fund heiress slash morning news anchorwoman made sense—which it didn't. She knew that, Courtney knew that, everyone in the hemisphere knew that; it was only Nate who didn't seem to.

Though she felt his glance she didn't look up to meet it.

"So it didn't bother you that she basically had her hand down my pants when you walked in."

Dorie's cheeks flushed and she found herself running faster. Of course it had bothered her. It had been a slap in the face. But Dorie wasn't going to tell him that. "If I were her and I'd done what she did to you and was trying to get you back, then I'd probably be putting my hands down your pants, too."

"Jesus," he said, obviously irritated. "Do you even want to *try* to make this work?"

She stopped running. Hadn't they already had this conversation? "Make what work?" For heaven's sake. "We've known each other for four days. There isn't a real *this* to talk about."

"Five," he corrected, coming to a stop and glaring down at her.

"Okay. Fine. Five." Whatever. She'd give him the half hour from Tuesday night even though it was technically Wednesday morning by the time they'd actually begun talking. "Do you have this conversation with all the women you sleep with before you've known them for a week?"

His eyes flashed with anger. "I've never had this conversation with *any* woman before. I've never *wanted* to have this conversation. Why do you refuse to believe that?"

He truly needed her to spell this out for him?

She jabbed at his chest. "Because you get paid millions of dollars in a year and I can barely scrape together my car payment. Because you go to benefits for a thousand dollars a plate, but the best dress I own is from the Anthropologie clearance rack. Because..." Oh, *hell*, no tears. Please, no tears. "Because your ex-*fiancée* is the most beautiful woman I've ever seen and she wants you back."

And when he was bored with this little interlude into

normal life—which he would no doubt be the second he was on his way to spring training—it would just be Dorie all by her lonesome, watching *House Hunters* marathons and bingeing on ice cream again. After blowing her chance to finally do something with her life because she'd spent all her free time following him from place to place rather than stay and do the job that she'd left her whole family behind for.

But she wasn't going there with him. She wasn't going there, *period*, because this was only a short-term thing. Only se…

Goddamn. The tears won. She angrily brushed them away.

As he started to protest, she cut him off. "And even if you don't want her back, too, there's another hundred women just like her waiting to beat down your door." Wrapping her arms around herself, Dorie took a step back. "And I don't want to always be in a competition for the man I lo—"

When he looked up sharply, she realized what she'd almost just said.

Oh, double goddamn. "You know," she mumbled, wanting to kick at the ground but settling for rubbing her toe in the dirt instead. "If it ever became more than sex."

"At the risk of getting my balls chopped off…"

"*Kneed*," she corrected, glaring up at him only to see his eyes practically dancing with laughter.

Undeterred, he carried on, "Kings are always fighting off someone." He raised his hands in surrender as her jaw dropped. "Just saying."

But then he got serious, wrapping his arms around himself as well—they were like the poster children for the Body Language of a Tense Conversation. The gaze he directed toward her was an appraising one. Assessing. He swallowed hard, then looked down at the ground.

"Okay," he finally said, raising his eyes and giving her a look so piercing that she took another step back. Then he turned away from her and started running again.

Um, well, good.

Glad he was on board.

They were practically back to his building when he finally spoke again. "You need to know something. I've lived half my life like this, and sometimes *I* can't even believe it. And you're right—the women…" His voice trailed off as he shook his head. "That part has been beyond surreal."

He slowly came to a stop, waiting for her to draw up next to him. "But it's been fifteen years, and in that whole time…" He shook his head as he looked down at her. "You say I'm going to get tired of this. I say maybe I've waited my whole life for whatever this is. And if you think that you scared me off by saying you want to go all alpha on my ass?" He grabbed her by the elbows and hauled her close. "Then you'd better start coming up with a better excuse. Because you are so off base you aren't even on the field."

Then he leaned down and *owned* her with a kiss so searing it left her breathless. When he pulled away, he smiled. "I also think that the reason you're resisting is because you're afraid I'm right and you're wrong. So maybe you'd better man up and get over it so that we can get on with our lives."

Still thrown by the kiss, it took Dorie a few seconds to realize what he'd just said. She sputtered, "Did you just… Did you just call me *chicken*? Is that your idea of *romance*?"

That made him laugh. He gave a shrug and then reached down for her hand, looking both ways as he stepped forward to cross the street. "Maybe I've been taking the wrong approach. Maybe the only way for me to convince you that—"

He stopped suddenly, his eyes on a cluster of people in front of his building. "*Shit*." He let go of her hand and dropped down to one knee to tie his shoe. "Please don't take this the wrong way, but I have to pretend that I don't know you. If I thought it would do anything other than make your life a living hell, I'd take you with me. But right now, I have to go."

Then he was off and running down the street, leaving her standing there. Bewildered. Breathless. She opened her mouth to call his name, but realized someone else had just done that for her. And suddenly the small group of people turned into a frenzied mob, swallowing him up into a sea of flashing cameras and shouted questions. Their intensity was frightening, even from here. With a deep breath, she sank back against the wall behind her and closed her eyes.

He'd just torn the rug out from underneath her, shaken it out and then laid it back down in front of her, daring her to take that step.

She squeezed her eyes shut and brought the heels of her hands up to them. It was a one-night stand. A weekend, at most. This was too much, too soon. She didn't want something with complications and concessions and compromise.

So rather than attempt to make sense of any of it, she pushed off the building and started running again.

* * *

It was a little after four in the afternoon and Nate was going out of his mind. It had been two hours. Had she run all the way back to Iowa?

"You planning on joining us?" Pete said from the table. He and Mark had laid out what looked like a hundred different contracts and proposals to go over and Nate couldn't have cared less.

"I'm sure she's fine." Mark cast a concerned glance over at Pete. They obviously had no idea what to do with Nate pacing a hole in the floor and Nate obviously didn't care. "She's a big girl. If she can hold her own against Haney and Pete, I'm sure she can manage not to get lost."

"I'm not worried about her getting *lost*." Nate ran his hands through his hair. He'd had her; he'd seen it in her eyes. And then the fucking vultures had showed up, killing his whole point and proving hers entirely.

"So then call her. Text her. Whatever," Pete snapped. "We've got work to…" A smile came over his face as he looked at Nate. "You don't have her number, do you?"

Feeling like the biggest fool in the world, Nate just folded his arms. He'd spent every minute he possibly could with her; it hadn't occurred to him to get her number. Of course this meant she didn't have his number either, so there was no way she could get him if she needed to.

"We could call Fitz," Pete offered, laughter in his eyes.

Right. Because that's exactly what Nate needed right now. "Hell no."

Pete raised his eyebrows, then looked at Mark. Turning back to Nate, he said, "Okay. Let's deal. You work with us for half an hour, and if she's not back by then,

I'll get it from Fitz. No one needs to know." That was bullshit, though. Nate was never going to live this down.

Nate looked at his watch. "Fine. Half an hour."

It was twenty-eight minutes exactly when the call came from the front desk. "Miss Donelli is here."

Great. They let thirteen raunchy guys and one mostly naked ex up without blinking, but Dorie they needed to announce. He refused to acknowledge that was exactly the kind of thing she was talking about.

"Please send her up," he said through gritted teeth. "And you don't have to announce her again."

Only half caring that he'd cut Mark off midsentence, he went out to the hallway, pacing in front of the elevator until the doors opened. Dorie appeared amused, which wasn't the reaction he was going for.

First things first. "Phone," he said, holding out his hand.

Or, actually, that wasn't the first thing. Reconsidering, he pulled her into a hug, clutching her against his chest and muffling her surprised, "Wha—?"

He honestly wasn't sure she'd come back to him. Knowing he still wasn't out of the woods even though she'd all but admitted that she was thinking in terms of love, too, he breathed her in, ignoring her laughter as she tried to push him away, saying, "I stink. Please don't—"

"Come sit in the Tampa Bay dugout in August." She smelled like heaven as far as he was concerned. He let go and held his hand out again.

Outright laughing this time—thank God—she eased it out of her arm band and handed it to him. But her tone seemed a little off when she gave him the code. "One-five-three-three."

He plugged it in, smiling. 15, 33. Two very good numbers. Then he looked up. "Thurman Munson and Jason Varitek?"

Her cheeks went from zero to hot pink in less than a second. "What can I say? I've always had a bit of a thing for catchers."

Tek he got; the guy was career Red Sox after all. But… "You know who Thurman Munson is?" As in, 1970s-era Yankees catcher and captain. Yankees, for one thing. Before she was born, for another.

With an uncomfortable shrug, Dorie looked at him, clearly unsure of how he'd respond. "He was my baby-sitter's first love." She smiled. "Well, she loved the entire 1978 Yankees infield, and drove my brother crazy about them until he finally married her and made her a Red Sox fan."

And that made *Nate* smile. It didn't hurt to know that mixed marriages could work—not that he was about to verbalize that thought right now. So instead he said, "Even Lou Piniella?" He could've gone with Reggie Jackson, but that would have been a little too obvious for a woman who clearly knew baseball.

Dorie's eyes narrowed. "You're *testing* me?" Then she grinned and playfully jabbed him in the chest. "I said infield, Hawkins. Piniella was the right field guy."

His heart thudded in his chest. He put his hands down to her waist, drew her in closer. "How can you doubt that we're made for each other? How can you doubt that I lo—"

"Uh-*uh*." Though she shoved him away, she was back to laughing. "However…" She walked a few steps away before turning back to face him, suddenly serious. And for the first time he realized she was holding shopping bags. "I decided that maybe I wanted a few more dresses. You know, in case I have to go to a benefit or any—"

He was kissing her before she could finish the thought. And he would have kept kissing her, except there was a cough from the doorway to his condo. He closed his eyes—one last kiss—and then pulled back, letting his forehead come to a rest against hers.

She glanced over at the door and then back at him, her hand running down his chest, which in itself shouldn't set off fireworks but did. "Oh, honey," she said. "You didn't tell me we had company." Then she ducked under his arm and smiled sweetly. "Checking up on me, Pete?"

Pete smiled back. "Never trust a pair of tits is what I say."

With that throaty laugh that went straight to Nate's dick every time, Dorie patted Pete on the chest as she walked by him into the apartment. "Good one, lawyer man. Glad you're learning." Turning so she was walking backward down the hall, she held up the bags she was carrying. "Oh, and thank you for giving me all your money last night. I had myself quite the shopping spree."

Pete gave a sharp laugh. "Careful there, Dorie. You're actually starting to grow on me."

Her laughter carried as she turned the corner to the master suite. "Don't get too attached."

On the one hand, that wasn't at all what Nate wanted to hear her say. On the other hand, Nate had known Pete half his life. And there'd never been a woman in Nate's life that Pete had actually liked. Nate couldn't help but smile.

"Shut up," Pete snapped although he was smiling, too. "Let's get back to work."

She came out of the shower half an hour later, just

as Pete and Mark were trying to convince Nate that he needed to hire a manager.

"Pronto," Mark was saying. "Or personal assistant, or even just a new publicist. With this week's news we should have been capitalizing on you being fully exonerated. We managed to hold on to all the endorsements, but just barely. And we tried to keep up with the mail, but we were so busy fielding calls that I have no idea what we missed."

Out of the corner of his eye, Nate saw Dorie wander through the living room and over to the windows, looking amazingly hot in black yoga pants and a formfitting T-shirt. Boston Red Sox—Pedroia, unfortunately—but he'd let that slide. He didn't intend for her to be wearing it for very long. He tried to turn his attention back to Pete and Mark. "I have a publicist. Alexis. She called me the other day."

"Right," Pete said, a glance passing between him and Mark. "She actually called you Wednesday and Thursday, but the firm fired her because she wasn't able to manage the client."

"What? Because of *me*?"

He'd taken off for less than a week. For just a few days he hadn't wanted to think about anyone else. And because he hadn't returned her calls he'd gotten her fired. "Well, then, hire her." Screw her firm. She'd been at dinner the night he left Chicago and she'd actually held her own against him.

Mark nodded. "I can set something up. Then maybe Pete and I can go back to our real jobs."

Chastened, Nate looked down. "I, uh…" *Damn.*

Hell. He owed them so much. Because they *had* stuck by him, even though he hadn't exactly made it easy to do so of late. They were on the payroll, yes, but they'd never wavered in their support. Nate finally had enough distance from it all, that he could see that loud and clear. "This has been a really shitty couple of months. And I…" *Damn* it. "Thank you." It came out more gruffly than intended, but there you go.

A ghost of a smile appeared on Pete's face. "You are a spectacular pain in the ass," he said, "but somehow we love you anyway."

"*He* loves you," Mark grumbled, "because he's had a crush on your sister since their law school days. I just want to take your money."

Nate ignored the first part of that comment; he did everything possible *not* to think about Pete and Ella. But in terms of Mark, well, Nate didn't believe that for a second. Mark had been with him from the beginning, just like Pete. Of course, Dorie didn't know that. And when she stopped suddenly on the threshold upon hearing those words, Nate could feel the daggers coming out of her eyes.

Mark could feel them, too. He held up his hands in a gesture of surrender. "I come in peace, I swear." His gaze slid over to Nate's. "She knows I was only kidding, right?"

She did now—the daggers had disappeared, replaced by a look of apology. But Nate wouldn't forget that unbridled fierce protectiveness for *him* for a very long time. He couldn't take his eyes off her as he introduced her to Mark.

"I see what Rico was talking about," Mark muttered with a grin. "You're quite the spitfire, aren't you?"

"Rico Castillo talked about *me*?" she said, clearly taken aback.

"Does she seriously not know?" Mark asked, this time looking at Nate.

"Not know what?" Nate said, clueless himself.

Mark laughed. "Check today's trending topics."

"What?" Dorie snapped. She edged closer as Nate looked at his phone.

#natesnewgirl

Fuck.

"How do they get this stuff already?"

Though Pete was an expert on a lot of things, Twitter wasn't one of them. Unfortunately, however, he was studying Dorie in a way that made it clear she was at the top of his list in terms of leaking the news.

Before Nate could defend her, Mark answered, "Rico and Troy had a bit of an exchange this morning." He smiled at Dorie. "It appears that if things don't work out with Nate, you have other options."

Nate was happy to see that, though Dorie's face had gone deathly pale, she had enough wits about her to snap at Pete, "So only the girls have to promise not to talk?"

Pete, at least, had the decency not to snap back.

"I'm sorry," Nate said, shutting off his phone and taking her hand. He didn't want this; he'd wished for anything *but* this.

"It's fine," she said with a laugh that had an edge of hysteria laced through it. "Totally fine."

It wasn't fine. And this wasn't even the worst of it—there would be a whole legion of fans more than happy to weigh in. They tended not to be kind. And there wasn't a goddamn thing Nate could do to stop it.

Pete sat back, still watching Dorie as she shot to her

feet and ran a hand through her hair. "I, um... Dinner," she said. "I'll cook us all dinner."

Nate did not want dinner. He most definitely did not want dinner with Pete and Mark. What he wanted more than anything right now was to grab her and wrap her in a cocoon until something much more newsworthy came up.

"Unfortunately, that's not going to work," Pete said, actually sounding sorry; Nate had to give him that. Leaning forward again, Pete looked at Nate. "Bobby and Lou—" i.e., Nate's former bosses who he'd spent his entire career with up until now, "—heard about your meeting tomorrow morning and they saw an opening. They want you to join them for dinner."

Now it was Nate's turn to sit back. "Tonight?" They wanted to talk to him *now?*

"Seven thirty," Pete was saying. "Morton's. You, Mark and me."

Nate could feel his face tighten with irritation. "Dorie, too." He wanted to spend the weekend with her. He had until the thirteenth to get it right. Three weeks, and he didn't want to waste a second.

But she wasn't exactly excited about the prospect. "Or maybe I could just stay here and get some work done."

Right. That would make the most sense. They could each focus on their jobs and he'd come home after dinner like they were any other couple in the world. Except they weren't a couple, as Dorie had made clear. And he had a feeling that part of her resistance was because she was trying to talk herself out of the fact that she felt something, too—something a lot stronger than the "short-term" fling she was insisting this was.

He didn't want to force her. This was a woman who

refused to let him tell her he actually saw a future with her. The last thing he wanted was to let on that she was exactly right about the role people would expect her to play: trot her out for decoration at dinner, and then let her sit there quietly while the serious talk took place.

At the same time, he wanted her there, more than just a little bit. He hated dinners like this. She may be the decoration, but he was the commodity. A thing to be sculpted and trained—sometimes supported, sometimes not—and used until his body gave out. It was all part of the job and he made sure not to complain about it, especially when he had it better than most—when he was paid a whole hell of a lot to put up with it. But having Dorie there would make it bearable. Given the way she surprised him with how her mind worked, how she made him laugh when it seemed impossible to smile, it might even be enjoyable. Plus, to be completely honest, he didn't want to waste a minute he had with her.

Hell. "What if I just meet them for a quick drink? Or maybe coff—"

To his surprise, though, Dorie cut him off. "Can you make sure no one gets any pictures of me?"

He looked up as she came to stand in front of him.

No one? Meaning the mob that was always lying in wait?

"Yes," Nate answered before Pete or Mark could intervene.

Her eyes narrowed, which was a good call since Nate had no idea how to make good on that promise. But he would stop the freaking Earth from turning if that's what it took. Still…

He took her hand and tugged her closer. "It's okay if you don't want to. We can just stay here."

The fact that neither Pete or Mark contradicted him wasn't necessarily a good thing. It was an important meeting and neither would be happy if it had to be canceled. The silence meant that he was in for a big talking-to when all was said and done. But it also meant they were aware this wasn't negotiable. Dorie came first no matter what anyone else said.

There was a moment of silence as she considered it. Then a big smile came over her face as she leaned down and kissed him. "Okay," she murmured.

As she pulled away, though, Pete said, "Hey, Donelli. Just one thing." He rested his elbows on the table and made a steeple with his hands. "Don't pull a stunt like you did last night. It won't go over well."

Irritation flashed through Dorie's eyes. Demonstrating exactly the kind of thing Nate wasn't allowed to say he loved about her, she let go of his hand and glared at Pete. "Fine. Two things right back at you. First of all, I'm a grown-up. I know what's appropriate and when, which is something some of your baseball player friends could learn a thing or two about. Second of all…" She pulled back her shoulders and drew her entire being into what Nate now knew was a five-foot-five-inch don't-fuck-with-me tower of strength. "I have to tell my family about, um, us—" She was clearly uncomfortable with the term as she glanced over at Nate then back at Pete. "Whether you like it or not. I need to prepare them." Then she spun and left the room as Nate watched Pete's and Mark's mouths practically drop open.

"She hasn't told anyone about you?" Mark asked, looking at Nate in clear disbelief.

"She thinks it's just a fling."

"It is just a fling," Pete said.

"No," Nate said. "It's not."

Pete, knowing when not to push it even though he wasn't happy about it, just sat back in his seat, his arms crossed.

Mark asked, "No pictures? Not even just of you?"

"I'm trying not to take it personally." Nate smiled. "Can we be done for now? I'm beat."

With a sharp laugh, Mark started gathering up papers. "I'll bet."

Pete was just staring at him, though. "Please tell me that you at least considered the fact that she could be taking you for a ride."

He hadn't, not seriously. Not even after finding out she'd known who he was all along. So he did as Pete asked and considered it.

Went with the gut instinct that had gotten him to where he was and dismissed it entirely. "You guys will see yourselves out, right?"

Shaking his head, Pete turned his attention to the rest of the papers and waved his hand distractedly. "Seven thirty. Morton's on State. Don't be late."

Chapter Eighteen

Thank God she'd gone shopping. Thank *God* she'd done well at the poker game the night before or she wouldn't have been able to go shopping. She hadn't been exaggerating about the car payments.

Dorie looked at the array of bags she'd spread out on the bed in front of her. What she *should* have done this afternoon was hop on a bus and head straight back to reality. Yet here she was, completely violating her only-about-the-sex point by going to his dinner with management.

With a sigh, Dorie reached into one of the bags. The dress was fine—maybe not Morton's fine, but nice nonetheless. The shoes, though? Not nice. Not nice at all.

Do-me shoes? Claudia had texted when Dorie'd sent her pictures of the pairs she was considering.

Just don't show them to your brothers and everyone will go home alive.

To be honest, Dorie hadn't intended to ever show them to anyone other than Nate. She'd planned to cook him dinner, maybe in nothing but an apron and some completely-unlike-her shoes, and then they'd—

"I'm sorry."

Dorie nearly shrieked with surprise when she saw Nate standing in the doorway. For goodness' sake. "You need to stop doing that."

He smiled. Damn, he had the most gorgeous smile. He came toward her and put his hands on her waist, bent down to touch his lips to her hair.

She closed her eyes. She was trying not to get used to this. She was trying so very hard. "Sorry about what?"

"Dinner, to start with." His hands went through her hair and he eased her head back so she was looking into his eyes. Eyes that were even more gorgeous than his smile, if that was possible. "I get that that's outside the lines."

She appreciated that. She really did—which was partly why she said she'd go. She wasn't used to anyone putting her first, and the fact that he was willing to completely throw a wrench in everyone's plans—for her—meant more to her than she was ready to admit. The other part, though, was that she wanted to be there for him. To be the one person who had no agenda whatsoever except to be there for Nate.

"But I can also stay here. I mean, maybe it's not such a great idea for you to be seen with me so soon after Courtney." She wasn't an idiot. No matter how hard Nate tried, someone would get a picture of them together. She was a freaking trending topic, for heaven's sake.

Her response did not make him happy. That was clear enough from the glare he was throwing her way. But just in case she didn't get the hint, he added, "Courtney left *me*. I don't give one iota of a fuck if people think it's too soon. You're the only one whose opinion on that matters." He took a step away, his back to her as he paused for a minute before turning to face her again. "I know you don't believe for a second that what I feel is—"

When she started to hold up her hands to stop him he grabbed her wrists and continued, "...is *real*. Whatever it is," he conceded, not saying the *L*-word. "It's real. I *want* you to tell your family. I *want* people to know." He let go of her, then ran his hands through his hair. "If you'd rather not come to dinner tonight I totally understand. And, trust me, I get all the reasons why you'd want to stay home. But it would make me really happy to have you there."

Well, um, okay.

It wasn't that she thought he was lying about how he felt; she didn't. He so obviously and wholeheartedly believed it. But he was coming off the rockiest six weeks of his life—and they hadn't even known each other for a full week. And when he came to his senses, it would be awful. Which was why she was trying so desperately to keep boundaries around it all. If she could keep it physical and with an end date, she could cherish it for what it was and then just move on in the end.

Right. As if that was even close to possible.

But dinner? Yes. If he said he wanted her there, then she was going to take him up on that. She smiled. "I hope a dress from the Gap is acceptable."

The corner of his mouth twitched. "As far as I'm concerned, anything that doesn't say Red Sox on it is acceptable." As if to make his point, he fisted his hand in her T-shirt and pulled her closer. "In fact," he murmured against her neck, "I may need to take care of this one right now."

"Uh-uh." Laughing, she pushed him away. "I have

some major work to do here. You'll need to make yourself scarce for a little while."

She wasn't lying. She cleaned up pretty well, but it did
take some time, especially since it wasn't something she
did on a regular basis. Hair, nails, makeup, dress, heels.
It was a good hour before she was ready. Enough time
that she was on the verge of making them late. But even
with that being the case, she still had to call her family
just to be safe. There was no way she was letting them
hear about this from someone other than her.

She'd just fastened the buckle on her right shoe and
was tapping the call button on her phone as she straightened up when Nate hissed, "*Jesus,*" from the doorway.

She ended the call before anyone picked up. "What?"
she asked, her hand dropping to her side. "Is everything…?"

Her words died in her throat as he came toward her.
She took a step backward and would have fallen against
the bed if he hadn't caught her by the elbows and steadied her. Because she *saw* it. She saw in his eyes how
deeply he felt for her.

It was infatuation, she'd been trying to tell herself.
Lust. Even a little bit of I-can't-believe-you-just-said-
that. But just now she'd seen love. Honest-to-God,
he-might-be-telling-the-truth-about-how-quickly-he'd-
fallen love.

"You're stunning," he said. "Beyond beautiful. If you
believe nothing else I tell you, at least believe that."

To be honest, having been adored by six older brothers and the best parents in the world, she did believe
that—she'd felt it all her life. She'd even had men tell
her that, had them show their appreciation in intimate
terms. And yet she was entirely unprepared for the emo-

tion that nearly choked her. She could *not* fall in love with this man.

"I do," she said. "Believe you, that is. When you look at me like that I do."

His hands went to her jaw; he angled her head up so gently—touched his lips to hers so tenderly—that the tears fell. Again.

Thank God she'd gone for the waterproof mascara.

As his kiss deepened, her arms went around his neck and she pulled him close. Maybe for just this one night she could pretend that he was right. That this would never end.

But before she could get too far into the pretending, he broke off the kiss. Not to create a distance between them—if anything, the way he held her to him, his hand at the small of her back, was even more intimate. Then his other hand came up between them and—

"What's that?" Her entire body went still as her eye caught the flash of Tiffany blue in his jacket pocket.

"Had to do something with myself while you were making me wait." There was a twinkle in his eyes.

She'd never in her life been given jewelry by a man. Not even from her father, whose special gift of choice was a pair of tickets to a Red Sox/Yankees game.

What was he thinking? "I can't accept this."

With a laugh, he muttered, "I'll pay you to say that again in front of Pete."

She glared at him.

"Would it help if I told you it cost me less than what I lost to you last night?"

Her mouth twitched before she could stop it. "Marginally." Except she was lying. It helped a lot. And it scared her out of her wits that he understood that. With a deep breath she pulled at the end of the ribbon and opened the box.

It was the most beautiful necklace she'd ever seen. A rope of tiny pearls that joined together in a tassel of even tinier beads. It took her a minute to speak. "This is for me?"

His voice was gruff—almost irritated—as he answered, "Of course it is." His touch was gentle, though, as he turned her to face the mirror on the wall, her back to him as she lifted the hair off her neck. She watched as he undid the clasp and then brought it over her head, letting it fall gently to her chest. Never in a thousand years would she have picked this out for herself—and yet, somehow, nothing had ever suited her more perfectly. *He* suited her perfectly.

Oh, God, no he *didn't*.

When he looked up and caught her eye in the reflection, he smiled. His arm draped down the front of her as he pulled her against him, his fingertips brushing the hollow at her hip. Though he didn't speak, she could see every word she wouldn't let him say aloud written on his face.

Afraid that she might say something that would betray everything she'd managed to hold back so far, she murmured, "This is so not the Julia Roberts movie I thought I was living."

"Careful there, Donelli," he said softly, laughter dancing in his eyes. "I know how every one of those movies ends. The odds are in my favor."

Her phone rang. She reached for it blindly, her voice barely a whisper as she said, "Hello?"

"Luce... *Fuck*. Are you okay?"

"Sean." It came out a croak. Eyes still on Nate, Dorie cleared her throat and tried again. "Sean. Hi."

"You're okay?" he snapped, the background noise of the restaurant a dull roar. "You're not in the hospital or anything?"

Dorie tore her gaze away from Nate's so she could focus on, say, speaking. "Um… I'm fine. Is—"

"You're *fine?* Goddamn it, Luce." He must have put his hand over the phone because his voice was muffled as he said, "Did you hear that? She's fine. No. Hell. *Yolanda.* Don't get my dad. I've got it." His voice louder, he came back on the line. "Luce. Please tell Yolanda you're fine."

Yolanda. She'd been the hostess at the mother ship since the restaurant had opened. "Hi, Yolanda. I'm fine."

"But why would she call us on a Saturday night and then just hang up?" Yolanda said, clearly unaware that she could ask Dorie directly rather than go through Sean. Phones weren't her thing.

"Well, that's an excellent question, Yolanda," Sean answered in his well-honed, annoying I-am-the-oldest voice. "Especially since she knows that even just calling the restaurant on a Saturday night is grounds for calling out the National Guard."

Pulling out of Nate's arms, Dorie turned away from the mirror as her brother went on, going so far as to re-cite Golden Rule #1 from growing up. "Do not call the restaurant during dinner rush unless you're bleeding. If it's during *Saturday* dinner rush, then it better be because you've lost a limb."

Dorie sighed and sat down on the edge of the bed. She was glad when Nate leaned against the dresser rather than joining her. Sitting next to Nate on his bed while talking to *anyone* in her family was a singularly bad idea.

Sean finally closed with, "…so you'd better have a hell of a good reason for calling on a Satur—"

"I got the point, Sean," she snapped. "Can I—"

"Oh, shit," Sean muttered. "It's the shoes. Crap, Luce. It's a guy, isn't it? Are you pregnant?" With every question, Sean's voice grew more belligerent. "Is he at least man enough to—?"

"Geez, Sean! I'm not pregnant." Nate's head jerked up at that last part. Great. Trying to get the upper hand in the conversation, she added, "And how do you know about the shoes?"

Nate stifled a laugh. He was enjoying this.

"My wife is the most beautiful, smartest, sweetest woman in the world," Sean replied, "but the woman says three Hail Marys if she forgets to tighten the top of the milk. She practically gave herself a nervous breakdown trying to hide those pictures from me."

Dorie looked down at her feet. She stuck one leg out and twisted her foot a bit so she could get a decent look. "For heaven's sake," she muttered. "They're just shoes."

The words nearly died in her throat when she realized that Nate was looking at the shoes, too. And then at her ankle. And then her calf. Her thigh…

A whimper escaped as heat pooled between her legs.

"What the hell, Luce?" Sean sounded even more irritated than before. He was growling, too, except not in a good way. "His hands better not be on you right now. I will—"

"I need to talk to Daddy," Dorie snapped, cutting him off. "*Now*, Sean."

There was a moment of silence before Sean said,

"Fine. I'll call you from my cell. We've already tied up this line long enough."

Yes, that was true. The problem was that she *had* known it was an awful time, and that no one in her family would pick up their phone right now, so she'd needed to call the restaurant's main number. Dorie very specifically did *not* look at Nate as she waited. She was already close enough to losing her nerve.

When her phone rang again she was ready for it, about to launch into an explanation immediately when her father's voice boomed in her ear, "Lucinda? Is that you? How's my baby's new job? How is Kansas?"

"Iowa, Daddy," Dorie said, rolling her eyes. He knew, of course. He just refused to get it right. "And I'm actually in Chicago this weekend." It was as good a non sequitur as any. "Which is kind of what I needed to talk to you about."

"But Sean says you're okay?" This time it was Dorie's mother speaking.

"Hi, Mom. Yes, I'm okay." For the love of Pete. "*Please* tell everyone I'm okay."

"You can tell them yourself. It's report card night. Everyone's here. I'm putting you on speaker."

What? "No, Mom. Please don't—"

"Oh, wait. Look at that! I can see you! Don't I have the smartest grandson?"

Groaning, Dorie said, "Mom, *no*. I don't want to Face-Time you."

"Dorie!"

At least her mother had remembered not to call her Lucinda. That was something.

"Is that your *bedroom*? Are you in a hotel? Why are you in Chicago?"

Without thinking, Dorie glanced over at Nate. Except that made everything worse. "I'm, uh—"

"Are you there with a friend? Is it someone you met at your new job?" Forgetting she was on FaceTime, she put her hand over the phone as she turned to Dorie's father. "She's there with a friend. Do you think it's a man?"

"Mom! Dad! *Sean!*" At least her brother would have some sense.

Which he did. Too much of it, in fact. He took the phone out of their mother's hand, positioned it so that Dorie could see that, as her mother had said, practically her entire family—right down to the niece and nephews—was sitting at the huge table in the private room in the back, all staring expectantly at Dorie as Sean laughingly backed away.

"Oh, Mommy," Dorie could hear her niece saying in a hushed yet overly loud whisper in the background. "Auntie Luce looks like a princess."

"Not with those shoes," Sean muttered, his arms folded across his chest.

"So what's your big news?" her father was saying. "I gotta go back to the kitchen, so you'd better spit it out."

Right. Dorie took a deep breath and once again deliberately did not look at Nate. "So there's this guy…"

The questions erupted before she could get even those few words out. Most of them had already been asked, the are-you-pregnant one being the clear favorite. And when Dorie once again gave a resounding, "No!" there was clear puzzlement as to why she'd be calling otherwise, since there wasn't anything else that could be quite as momentous enough to call right now.

"Is he…" Her mother looked over at her father with concern. "Is he a Yankees fan?" With an apologetic look at Claudia, she added, "Sweetie, you know your father has a hard time with that."

Sean falling for a Yankees fan had broken their father's heart. Literally, at least according to Dad. After Sean's announcement that he was marrying Claudia, their father had gone into cardiac arrest. Though the doctor insisted it had everything to do with the blockages in his arteries after eating pizza almost every night for fourteen years, the family was suspicious. And Claudia, after spending almost a whole year in church for penance, was now converted.

"No, Mom." Dorie checked on Nate. To her relief, he appeared to be amused. "But he is, actually, really into baseball. Which is why I'm calling."

Her family was looking at the phone expectantly.

"He's kind of, well, I think you'll recognize his name." Understatement of the year, given that she'd spoken of him nonstop from the ages of thirteen to seventeen. "He's pretty…famous." Her heart started pounding. "And there's a little bit of a chance that you might hear about it, so I wanted to make sure that I was the one who told you first."

"Then maybe you should actually tell us," Christopher yelled from the back of the room, his grin far too wide and evil.

"Yes." Dorie nodded her head. That's exactly what she was planning to do. "I'm, um…" *What?*

Seeing?

Sleeping with?

The woman-of-the-moment for?

"I'm…I guess you could say that I'm going out on a date with him, um, Nate. Nate Hawkins."

There was a moment of stunned silence. And then

nearly every single person in the room burst into laughter. Sustained laughter. So much so that she couldn't get a word in edgewise.

"Great one, sis!"

"Best. Punk. Ever."

"I just snarfed my spaghetti. Spaghetti just came out of my nose. Did you see that? Did anyone see that?"

Dorie glared at Nate. This was all his fault.

No longer nervous and now supremely irritated, Dorie stood up. "Don't say I didn't warn you!" she shouted into the phone. Oh, how she wished she had one of those ancient phones where you could slam the receiver down in its cradle. People were actually crying they were laughing so hard. She'd been thinking she might have him wave to everyone but there was no way in hell they were getting that now. "I have to go!" She couldn't help but add, "And I love you all, damn it!"

"Oh, sunshine," her mother said, having recovered enough to only hiccup once as she spoke. "You're my favorite daughter in the whole world. Have a wonderful time in Chicago. Call me when you're back at home."

Okay. So maybe she didn't blame them. Even she found this situation entirely laughable in a ludicrous sort of way.

"They're adorable," Nate said, coming over and wrapping her in his arms. The fact that he was shaking with his own muffled laughter did nothing to help matters. At least he was trying to hide it, Dorie supposed.

He took the phone from her and she expected that he'd put it on the dresser or throw it on the bed. But instead he sat down on the bed, pulled her into his lap and held it up over them. It was second nature for her to try to snatch it back—that's just what you did when someone decided to play keep-away. But the moment she looked up for it, he snapped a picture.

When she leaned her head back to look at him, he bent down, kissed that one spot on her neck, then snapped another one.

"Mmm," he said gruffly. "That's the one I'm keeping." He pushed a few buttons, sending it to himself, and then smiled as he handed the phone back to her.

It wasn't until ten minutes later, when they were in the basement of his building waiting for the car the doorman had arranged, that Dorie had a chance to look at the pictures he'd taken. The one he'd kept for himself wasn't anything she'd be sending home, that was for damn sure. With her eyes closed and her head thrown back and Nate practically devouring her skin, it looked carnal. Primal. Freaking amazing.

Dorie sighed. Leave it to Sean to ruin her I-am-woman moment with an incoming text.

I don't give a flying fuck who he is. If he even thinks about touching you, I will take that heel and ram it through his balls.

Chapter Nineteen

Dorie's family was a kick. That was a damn good thing, because they clearly weren't the type to hold back their opinions. The texts had started coming in about the time Nate and Dorie got into the elevator. One after another, through forty floors—basement parking levels included—a five-minute wait for the car he'd called and, now, three cycles of the light at Chicago and State thanks to a bus that had stalled in the intersection.

Hell, if traffic didn't ease up, they'd be late, which would piss Pete off. If it wasn't for Nate's promise to avoid the media, he would have just gotten out and walked the half a mile.

Well, the media, plus there was no way she'd be able to cover the distance in those shoes.

Holy shit, those shoes.

"Christ," he muttered, shifting as his already uncomfortable meet-with-the-boss pants grew that much more so.

"Sorry," she murmured, misinterpreting. She shrugged apologetically as she held up her phone. "The shock's wearing off."

"Mmm," he said, happy to turn his attention back to something a little less hard-on inducing. "I can see that."

And he could. His eyesight was excellent and she wasn't making much of an attempt to hide the messages. He'd caught more than a few:

JCD: U weren't serious were u?

Mom: HI m3y Buechler baby!!!

Mom: *beautiful

JCD: Holy shit. Christo just told us ur 4 real WTF????

Tommy: !!!!!!!!!!!!!

Shay: Be careful with his knees. I've got $150 riding on him.

JCD: *Were* u?

#1 Niece: Does he know Koji? Can he get me an autograph?

Sophie: Holy crap. Tommy just called me. No freakin' WAY!!!!! Does he know about…

Now *that* was intriguing, especially when Dorie's cheeks turned a bright enough shade of red that he could see it in the darkened backseat of the car. And of course that one got cut off.

Christo: cat—> bag—> BAM.

Shay: On second thought, you shouldn't have anything to do with his knees.

#1 Niece: P.S. Liam wants to know if he's going to be our uncle. We'd rather have Ellsbury. Can you date him instead?

Col: Dad's not looking so good. If he has another heart attack, you're out of the Super Bowl pool and Claudia's in.

Tommy: !!!!!!!!!!!!

Shay: And no riding of any kind. I'd hate to kill my best player, but I'll do it if I have to.

And then there was Nate's favorite:

Sean: I don't give a flying fuck who he is. If he even thinks about touching you, I will take that heel and ram it through his balls.

Just thinking of that one made Nate laugh. "Your family really has a thing about balls."

Her thumbs flying across the touch screen, Dorie replied, "'No head, no nuts.' That was what the doctor said after every one of their checkups. So, of course, that's what they aim for. Literally, figuratively, the whole shebang. It's a bit of an obsession."

Of course. Nate laughed again, although this time he managed to turn to look out the window and keep it to himself. Yes, this was crazy. No, it made no sense. But all he could think was that she was the whole damn package. She was beautiful, smart *and* she made him laugh. Plus there was her overall excellence in just about any pastime he could think up, her competitive streak...

Without thinking, he reached over and rested his hand on her leg. He wanted more of her—wished he could wrap his arms around her and just pull her close—but he'd settle for this for now. He couldn't just keep sitting here and not be touching her.

She went still beneath his hand. He turned back to see her staring at him, her eyes wide and lips slightly parted.

"A little scary," she said quietly. "Aren't they?"

Well, Hawk. Do-or-die time. She'd given him the opening; an excuse to tell her what she expected to hear, that this was, in fact, more than what he wanted to sign up for.

And yet he found himself leaning toward her, his hand going to the back of her neck as he drew her closer. "It takes more than that to scare me." Just as he was about to bend down to her, though, the phone rang again. "They are, however, starting to piss me off." They'd had a whole lifetime with her; he'd had less than a week—and was on a hard deadline. He wasn't ready to share.

He took her phone and slid his thumb across the bottom of the screen to answer it. But before he could get a word in edgewise, he was met with a torrent of words. He wasn't paying attention to the words themselves so much as the fact that they were in Spanish—which, since the woman on the other end of the line had expected Dorie to be answering the phone...

Nate's eyes met Dorie's. "You speak Spanish." That meant she'd understood Rico's rant the night before.

She shrugged. "A little."

There was also a pause in the Spanish. And then, "Who is this?"

"This is Nate." He ignored the sharp intake of breath. "And you?"

"Nate," the woman repeated. "Nate Hawkins." Not *her* name. Obviously. According to the readout on the phone that was Claudia, who, from the little he had paid attention to as she'd been speaking, was big brother Sean's wife.

"That would be the one," he replied.

Another pause, before a whispered, "*Dios mío.*"

He supposed he shouldn't have been surprised when, after a muffled side conversation, a man came on the line, a whole hell of a lot of challenge in his voice. "So you're really Nate Hawkins. As in I-just-signed-a-contract-for-hundreds-of-millions-of-dollars Nate Hawkins."

"That would be me." Settling back against the seat, Nate forced himself not to be defensive. Or, for that matter, to go on the offensive. "I'm guessing you're Sean."

Dorie somehow managed to snort and give a little laugh of disbelief at the same time.

"You know who I am?" Sean asked.

"I know you're obsessed with my…" Nate stopped talking when Dorie's hand clamped around the very body part that he'd been about to mention. The look in her eyes was pure death glare: the hand giveth and the hand taketh away. Gripping her wrist, he managed to say, "…interest in your sister."

To be honest, Nate couldn't entirely blame him. If he was talking to a man who wanted to do the things to one of his sisters that he wanted to do to Dorie, well…

"She's special," Sean said quietly. "She deserves so

much more than a love-em-and-leave-em kind of guy. Even if that guy is one of the richest men in the world."

That was an exaggeration. Nate wasn't even in the top hundred in the US. Granted he was ranked as one of the top-earning athletes, but that wasn't the point. And, unfortunately, he understood exactly what Sean was saying. "I agree. One hundred percent."

He reminded himself that Sean was just looking out for his sister when he answered, "I'm hoping you're a nicer guy than they make you out to be. But if you're not, do not for one second think that we won't come at you with everything we've got."

Damn it. Nate definitely needed to get someone back on board to handle his PR because he was, actually, a nice guy. He had no intention of hurting Dorie.

Then again, he wasn't exactly thinking the warmest thoughts about her family at the moment.

"*They* don't know a thing about me," Nate answered.

"Yeah, well," Sean replied, "I hope that's true. Can you put my sister on?"

Not letting go of Dorie's wrist, he held the phone out, closing his eyes against the unwanted emotion that had suddenly come over him. It wasn't until she threaded her fingers through his—after releasing her deathly hold, incidentally—that he felt the calm come back.

"Yes, Sean," she was murmuring. "I know… For heaven's sake, I'm not *twelve*… Let me talk to Claudia, damn it!"

From there followed a diatribe in Spanish about how Claudia was a saint among saints for putting up with the Donelli men. And maybe, just maybe, if Sean and company hadn't been so ridiculously overprotective, she would have settled down by now with a nice, safe guy who *hadn't* slept with half of the *SI* swimsuit models and—

"Stop." Not sure whether to laugh or be offended, Nate took the phone from her once again. This time—in Spanish—he said, "Claudia? We're hanging up now." And then he did that very thing.

Mouth open, Dorie seemed about to protest but then she said, "*You* speak Spanish."

He hadn't mentioned that? He supposed they were even. "And Japanese." Plus he'd been picking up some Portuguese. Tools of the trade.

She folded her arms in front of her chest. "You didn't say anything last night when Rico went off."

"Because you kicked me every time I started to speak up for you." He nearly laughed at the look on her face. She clearly couldn't decide whether to apologize or tell him that she was entirely capable of defending herself.

He supposed he shouldn't have been surprised that she took it in an entirely different direction. "Well, I wasn't about to let Rico know that I understood what he'd said. It would have embarrassed him."

"But you had no problem cleaning everyone's clocks instead."

There was that low laugh of hers. "Nope. That felt *good.*"

Which, of course, had Nate thinking of all the ways *he* could make her feel good. "Any other special skills hidden up those sleeves of yours?"

Although it was a rhetorical question, she paused to give it thought. "I once did 532 chin-ups in a row, although I'm not sure I could even do half that now. But I can still Hula-Hoop for three hours straight."

That stopped Nate cold. "That's, um, a lot."

With a smile, she leaned into him, pulling his arm around her shoulders. "When I was too old for Toss the Toddler, my brothers needed something else to get me out of their hair, so they convinced me to go for the world record." When Nate didn't answer—for sheer lack of ability to speak as he considered the stamina required—she added, "You know, as in Guinness?"

"I know," he answered, half wanting to laugh, half still caught up in thinking about three hours of her hips moving like that.

"Kept me busy for hours," she said. When his laughter won out, she whirled around to glare at him. "What?"

Bending down to kiss the top of her head, he had to admit, "Your brothers are geniuses."

The glare held for all of two seconds before she laughed, as well. "Tell them that and I'll—"

"Knee me in the balls." More content than he'd ever known he could be, he pulled her close against him. "I know."

Chapter Twenty

True to his word, Nate had the car pull around to the back of the building the restaurant was in, avoiding the photographers at the front. They were then escorted through underground hallways and up through a back entrance to the private dining room. She felt like James Bond.

Or, rather, the Bond girl. Who didn't even have a name.

Dinner wasn't exactly a reality check. It was like she'd won one of those radio contests where you got to go to a meet and greet with, like, Bono. She felt all goofy and tongue-tied; terrified she'd say something foolish. After a while she found that if she managed to think of the owner as her uncle Sal and the GM as her cousin, Stephen, she was able to be coherent. Luckily, Uncle Sal and Stephen—or, rather, Bobby and Lou, as they'd insisted she call them by their actual names—seemed intrigued that Nate had brought a rabid Red Sox fan to dinner, not to mention that they were both highly amused by the outcome of the previous night's poker game.

Everything was going great, in fact, right up until the moment Bobby said, "We'll be hosting the Watchmen in July. How about you come up and watch the game in the box?"

The box. As in the one the owners sat in. She actually laughed. "Thanks. But I, um…" She ducked her head, not quite able to look Nate's way as she mumbled, "I don't think I'll be at the games."

Though Bobby seemed a little surprised—probably didn't get many noes—he just smiled as he looked between her and Nate. "Well, anytime. You just call my office and let them know you're Nate's, uh, friend."

With Nate tense beside her, Dorie made every effort to smile. "Thanks. That's very nice of you."

Things were a lot less enjoyable after that, especially as Nate shifted into professional ballplayer mode—surly, and kind of, well, cold—when talk turned to his contract. Dorie forced herself to just sit back and observe rather than let on how knowledgeable she was about the subject of Nate Hawkins. The pitchers he worked best with, the way he could read an opposing lineup like nobody's business…

She found it fascinating, in fact…until she fully processed what they were saying.

"We couldn't gamble that kind of money, son," Bobby said, not even trying to beat around the bush about why they hadn't fought harder to keep him. "Not at your age. And you know the reason they did is because they want you to bring up the new kids and then move you over to management."

Dorie didn't realize she'd let out a little squeak of outrage until everyone turned to look at her. Nate was hands down one of the best players in the league. Completely in his prime. Hell, the Watchmen were building a whole *franchise* around him.

They'd clearly passed the Dorie-speaking part of the evening, however.

"You manage a game like nobody's business," Lou was saying. "There's a place for a player like you. And we'd like that to be with our organization."

When Nate didn't respond—when he looked down at the spoon that he was twisting around in the fingers of his right hand—Mark stepped in. "Well, right now his place is on the field. But we'll be sure to remind you of this conversation when the time comes."

Though Nate smiled vaguely, he'd gone distant in a way that Dorie hadn't seen before. She let her hand drift toward him, brush his side just to let him know she was there for him if he needed her. She was surprised that he actually reached down for it, entwined her fingers in his and then brought their hands up to rest on the table for anyone in the world to see.

Dinner ended shortly after that, to Dorie's great relief. It was emotionally exhausting—and she was only a bystander. A fact, incidentally, that she did not point out, given Nate's mood. The back entrances and underground tunnels felt ridiculous this time around and she couldn't believe she'd made him arrange it. She was so ready to take off these damn shoes, change into pajamas and climb into bed. But she hated how quiet he'd been on the way back, even though they were alone. *Especially* since they were alone.

"What can I do?" she finally asked when they were safely inside his condo.

His head jerked up as though he'd forgotten she was there, even though he'd been holding her hand. Up until she spoke, that was, at which point he let go. His eyes went dark and brutally hot. "Don't ask if you don't want to hear the answer." Then he yanked his tie loose and headed toward his bedroom.

Oh, my. Dorie took a deep breath.

Well, no one had ever accused her of playing things safe. She hung up her coat and then walked down the hall.

His jacket was thrown over a chair and he was unbuttoning his shirt by the time she got to the doorway. "Do you want to talk?" she asked.

Glaring at her, he finished with the shirt, tossed it over the jacket and walked past her into the walk-in closet that was bigger than the bedroom she'd grown up in. She followed him in there, too.

"About what?" he snapped, untucking the T-shirt he'd worn underneath. "How I've probably only got a few more years in me, and that's only if my knees hold out? Or maybe about the idea of what my life looks like when this is all gone. With…" He sank down to the bench that ran against the wall, legs spread apart, and leaned forward, resting his elbows on his knees. "With nothing to come home to." He ran his hands over his face and then just let his head rest there. Voice muffled, he said, "So, no, I don't want to talk right now."

Closing her eyes, she reminded herself that this was exactly the problem. It wasn't so much that he wanted *her*, it was what she represented. A warm body in a bed. A smile to welcome him home.

Then he added, "I especially can't talk about this with you." His voice cracked a little at the end there and something inside her broke right along with it.

Okay. So maybe she really was a little bit more to him than a passing thing. It still did nothing to change the fact that he was at a crossroads and she was just a way station. She supposed she could call him out on that.

Or not.

"Well, fine," she snapped right back. "I don't want to talk, either." She walked over to him. Nudged his leg over a little so that she could stand right there in front of him; right up against him, forcing him to lean back against the wall and look up at her.

"What are you doing?" he asked warily.

"Luckily," she answered, "*my* knees aren't the problem." Then she dropped down to them, her hands going to his belt.

He stopped her, grabbing her hand forcefully enough to leave a mark. "This is *not* a good idea," he said. "I'm not in the mood to be nice."

Looking up at him through her lashes, she gave it right back. "Did I ask you to be?"

He glared down at her. There was a beat of silence, then two, before he said, "I want my mouth on you tonight. I want all of you."

She went still. It wasn't like she *didn't* want that. It was just that it was a very big step for her—it was a level of intimacy and trust that she guarded closely. And she was afraid that if she said yes, he'd see it as a commitment she wasn't ready to make, because he knew exactly what he was demanding. He was well aware it went beyond the physical.

And yet she couldn't deny that she wanted this with him. As foolish as it made her, she wanted everything.

The second she nodded he grabbed her face in his hands and hauled her up against him. The kiss, as he'd warned, was not nice. It wasn't tender. It was violent and brutal and on the edge of painful. She'd never wanted anything more.

Her hands went back to the waistband of his pants and she fumbled with the button and zipper, suddenly very tight against him. Just as she managed to get it open, he roughly took her by the shoulders and set her back. "Stand up."

Though she wasn't usually one to follow orders, she was finding that he was the exception. She did as he said. His eyes took her in as his hand went to the end of the wraparound belt. With one pull, the dress fell open. Surging forward, he gripped her hips as his mouth closed over her breast. His tongue glided over the rough lace of her bra, an appreciative growl rumbling through him. Or maybe that was her, humming with anticipation— then crying out when his teeth closed down over her nipple and tugged.

Knees buckling, she dropped back to the floor, pulling his pants down over his hips. Breathing heavily as he continued to run his hands up and over and around her breasts, she finally freed him, moaning as his erection twitched against her tongue. Then his hands were in her hair as he thrust inside her mouth.

He was on the edge; she could feel it. Taste it. But he pushed her away before she could take him over. He held her at arm's length until he got his breathing back under control and then stood up, taking her with him. Dress hanging open, she watched as he drank her in, for the first time seeing that she wore thigh-high stockings with lavender lace trim that matched her panties—a thong, as he would soon find out—and bra.

"Sweet Jesus," he murmured, trailing his hand past her knee.

She was already soaking wet when his fingers skimmed over the silk of her panties. Her breath came in shallow little gasps as he pulled the dress down over her shoulder, her arm, as he guided her by the small of her back until she was up against the wall. He leaned in, kissing her; pinning her in place as the dress, still hanging off her right arm, didn't seem to want to come free. He was pulling at it and twisting it and it just kept getting caught. With an irritated little grunt, she tried to shake it—

Her eyes flew open when she realized that was by design rather than mistake. "What are you doing?" she asked as he took her now thoroughly bound wrist and raised it over her head.

He gave her a devilish, unapologetic grin. "Not being nice." He took her other hand and raised it over her head.

Looking up above her, she gave a nervous laugh. "The chin-up bar? Really?"

"Careful, Donelli," he said, utter concentration on his face as he secured her wrists to the bar. "I have some records of my own for you to break."

"Like, um, what?" It was hard to worry too much about what kind of plans he might have when he was skimming her neck with his lips and tongue, when he hooked his thumbs in the sides of her panties and let them fall down to the floor. He bent down to help her step out of them, his hand closing around one ankle as he gently lifted her foot up, then the other.

"Guess you'll have to see," he said, humming against the inside of her thigh as he spoke.

And then he was pulling her up to him, his hands molding over her hips as though her body was a chalice and he was dying of thirst. The stubble of his chin was rough against her as his tongue lashed over her clit. She lost her footing entirely, trembling and twisting with need. His tongue and teeth and, oh God, *fingers*, were teasing and tempting her, bringing tears to her eyes as she ached for—began to *plead* for—release.

His mouth vibrated against her as he laughed, lifting her legs up over his shoulders and tilting her back, controlling her entirely. Holding on to the bar so tightly that she was afraid it might break, she was begging and bucking and trying so desperately to make him allow her to just *come*, damn it, that when he pulled away abruptly—just faded back, letting her legs fall away from him as he let her go—she screamed in frustration.

Breaths coming in ragged gasps, body limp yet trembling, the only thing that kept her from just hanging there was the death grip she had on the bar. That, and the dress that bound her to it.

Head so heavy she could barely lift it, she looked up to see Nate staring down at her, his hands braced against the wall on either side of her head. He was still wearing the T-shirt and his pants were back up around his hips, though unbuttoned and resting loosely. He was, to put it simply, gorgeous. That she stood there bound in front of him, his plaything in four-inch heels, thigh-high stockings, a bra and a pearl necklace—should have made her feel cheap and used.

But it didn't. She felt powerful. Beautiful.

Stunning.

Smiling slowly, she leaned forward and let the tip of her tongue slowly circle his nipple through the cotton of his T-shirt. Voice hoarse and ragged from all that begging she'd just done, she said, "So, Hawkins, you just going to stand there? Or are you planning to fuck me?"

He surged forward, hitching her legs up around his waist and twisting her. Slamming her back against the doorjamb, her spine aligning with its frame. Though she wanted to wrap her arms around him, she had to make do with clamping her forearms against his neck as he pushed his pants the rest of the way down. And then he was inside her. Her legs a vise around his hips, she gave as good as she got, tilting her hips and brushing against the base of his cock with every thrust he gave. She came in a frenzy of cries. He followed quickly, his head falling against her forehead as he gave a shuddering groan.

"Holy Christ," he finally said.

After another few minutes he reached up to untie her. Then he cradled her in his arms and carried her to the bed.

Chapter Twenty-One

For the third morning in a row, Nate's first waking thoughts centered around Dorie. He was alone, like he'd been after their first night together—was that seriously only three nights before?—but unlike Friday morning, he could feel her presence.

He rolled over onto his back, his hands going behind his head as his eyes caught sight of the chin-up bar, just past the closet door.

He had no idea what had come over him. He'd been possessed. Hell, he'd *wanted* to possess, which was ironic since Dorie was the last woman on earth who'd allow it. And yet last night that's exactly what she'd done. She'd let him take everything he wanted; she'd opened herself up and let him in.

Of course, she'd also made it abso-fucking-lutely clear to Bobby and Lou that she wasn't planning on sticking around. Maybe if they hadn't gone immediately into the whole contract thing he would have handled it better.

Okay, fine. New day, new game.

Nate pulled on a pair of sweats and went to find Dorie. She was in the kitchen—not a big surprise. What did surprise him enough so that he stopped short was that the T-shirt she was wearing didn't say anything about Boston. It was a Chicago jersey; with his name and number on the back.

Not that he hadn't seen a thousand other people wear that shirt. Though it had taken some getting used to way back when, it no longer shocked him. But to see it on her, to see her wearing his name…

He'd covered the distance to her, wrapped her in his arms and buried his head in her hair before he even realized he was moving.

She laughed and leaned back into him. "I hope you like eggs and bacon, because whoever grocery shops around here hasn't done it in a while."

That was one hundred percent true. "I tend to order in a lot." Leaving one arm in place to hold her against him, he let his other hand travel down the front of her, brushing between her legs on his way back up and underneath the jersey.

Turning in his arms, she laid her head against his chest. Now it was her arms going around him, her hands cupping his ass—none too gently—and pulling him up against her. "So what's on the agenda for today? More ordering in?" Then she reached down the front of his sweats and lightly slid her hand down the length of him.

And somehow, despite having sex more times with her in the past several days than, possibly, he'd had in years, he was ready to go again. Up until a few days ago, he would have said that wasn't physically possible. Yet here they were.

He closed his eyes and gave in to the sensations rippling through him. For just a minute. Okay, maybe two, he thought, as he bent down to kiss her, her lips so sweet and soft that he could happily spend his life tasting them.

"I wish," he said. Maybe groaned, although for a second he did wonder if perhaps she was just determined to get in as much as she could before the deadline she'd set for them to be over. "But there's another meeting."

The sigh she gave was just dramatic enough for him to realize that she was neither surprised nor overly disappointed. "Wait, let me guess... The mayor? The president? Or maybe just Brad Pitt, saying he wants to do a movie about you."

The mayor, maybe. The other two, however, he was pretty sure that Mark would have been beating down the...

He belatedly realized that she was laughing.

"The scariest thing about that?" she said, a huge smile on her face as she elbowed him away from her and turned back to tend to the eggs and bacon. "You actually had to think about it."

"I didn't—" He started to protest, but then he started laughing, too. Giving her a little space, he went about the business of setting the table, pouring the coffee and OJ... All the little domestic-type things that he was used to doing alone. That he didn't want to be doing alone any longer. That he didn't want to think about because his throat turned scratchy and raw. With an effort, he lightly said, "Just for the record, I've only met the president twice. And Brad Pitt doesn't know me from Adam. Now Ben Affleck is another story entirely..."

The sharp laugh she gave was full of both delight and resignation. "I don't even want to know if you're joking." She shut off the burners and brought the skillet and plate of bacon over to the table. Sitting down, she placed the napkin in her lap as she let him serve her. "So, give. Who's the meeting with today?"

"The Watchmen. The GM and coach."

Bacon halfway to her mouth, she sighed. With a faint smile on her face, she shook her head. "Of course it is."

This time they walked. Or, rather, snuck out the back, jumped in a cab that they took for two blocks, and then Nate gave the driver a tip that was about five times the actual fare and they got out and walked the ten or so blocks to Mark's office. Although they did get a few double takes along the way and there were at least five 'Is that…?' head turns as they walked by, no one stopped them and, Dorie tried to tell herself, it was just like any other walk she'd ever taken. Except not.

She gave a deliberate shake of her head. She was beginning to understand why run-of-the-mill fun was so hard to come by. "This isn't what it's like in Inspiration, is it?" she said.

Nate laughed softly. He didn't question what she meant by "this." "No. Not quite."

When he didn't say anything else, she asked, "Is it hard?"

Though his hand tightened briefly around hers, he didn't answer right away. He waited until they were halfway across the street before he said, "I can't say it's my favorite part of the job, but let's be honest. I get paid a *lot* of money to do something I love. How many people can say that?"

She had a feeling he had no idea that his hand had betrayed him or that the smile he gave her didn't carry to his eyes.

They window-shopped their way down the street and it didn't take nearly long enough. Coming with him had been a much bigger issue than she'd realized. She wanted more of this; more of *him*. She hadn't expected to feel so…happy. In a euphoric, walking-on-air kind of way. It even made her start to think that maybe this could actually work. She'd been able to put the finishing touches on a grant proposal this morning while he'd watched a video of the pitchers on his new team, and later today they'd be visiting the library. So, hello, having her cake and eating it, too. Look at her being all professional and the supportive girlfriend at the same time.

Fling. Not girlfriend. It was still just a fling. But yes, she was pretty sure she could do this for at least a few weeks.

Until the moment the elevator doors opened up onto the reception area of Mark's agency. And there, right opposite the doors, was a larger-than-life—honestly, it was at least fifteen feet tall—copy of the *Vanity Fair* picture. It took her breath away. Literally. She felt her chest tighten. And she suddenly felt faint. Very, very faint. She may have actually squeaked.

Nate's arms went around her. "Shit. I…I totally forgot about that. That's… Just… Nothing. It's nothing."

She was shaking her head. Shaking *everything*, her body trembling uncontrollably. "I don't…I'm sorry. I just…I forgot. I forgot who you were." Though she couldn't believe she was capable of it, especially given the men she'd played poker with the other night and the fact that she was now aware of what it meant to have to evade the press.

"Don't say that." His words came out in a whispered rush. Hands gripping her shoulders, he was suddenly bending down so he could look her in the eye. "You *know* me, Dorie. You know who I am. That's just a picture. That's all it is."

A bark of hysteria-tinged laughter escaped her mouth.

"Right," she murmured, trying to get her breathing under control. "That's all."

Before he could do anything to try to convince her further, there was the soft sound of a door swishing open. "Mr. Hawkins?" a woman said, her footsteps drawing near. She stopped abruptly when she realized that there was, well, a moment happening. Not wanting to draw any more attention to herself than she'd already done, Dorie turned her back on the woman and tried to step away. But Nate wouldn't let her. He'd moved his hand from her shoulder down to her hand, his firm grip making it clear he had no intention of letting her escape.

"Jacqueline," Nate said. "Hi. They, uh… They made you come in today?"

With a deep breath or four, Dorie regained enough control to turn back—just in time to see the surprise cross over his face.

Jacqueline gave him one of those *'You're kidding me, right?'* looks. Except that he was, in fact, Nate Hawkins—not "just Nate"—and Jacqueline, with her cute little skirt and perky blouse, was clearly a woman used to attracting a man's attention. So what in ordinary human standards would have been a look to kill, came off more as an if-you-weren't-so-beautiful-I-might-have-to-hurt-you-but-since-you-are-who-you-are-we're-going-to-let-it-go type thing.

She smiled as she said, "We're here whenever you need us to be."

"Christ," Nate muttered, bewildered enough that Dorie truly believed he had no idea that when he said jump, people didn't just ask how high, they killed to be the ones who had the chance. "I'm sorry. I didn't realize—"

"Hawk!"

They all turned to see Mark striding down the hall, a huge smile on his face. He clasped Nate on the shoulder, then bent down to give Dorie a kiss on the cheek. "Good to see you again, Dorie. Quite the dinner last night, huh?"

"Um, yes," Dorie answered, glad that his appearance meant that Nate had let go of her hand. Her now clammy, lifeless hand. "That it was."

But now Mark's hand was at the small of her back, propelling her down a hallway full of other larger-than-life-size, equally iconic photographs as he chattered on. There were other athletes, actors and actresses...a former president.

"Seriously?" Her eyes found Nate's and he quickly looked away, his face unreadable.

His only response was a muttered, "Christ, Mark, shut up," after several minutes' worth of the agent going on about Nate's talents, including a lot of emphasis on him being their number one client. Or, to be specific, "numero uno *cliente*." Nate just rolled his eyes.

They came to a large glassed-in conference room in which stood a young woman. More conservatively dressed than Jacqueline, she was talking emphatically to Pete, whose benign and slightly amused expression didn't quite match up with the tension in his arms, clasped tightly around his chest. Both Pete and the woman turned when the door quietly opened, Pete with relief and the woman with, well...apprehension, maybe. A little bit of anger, possibly. The thought passed through Dorie's head that this might be another ex-girlfriend, but Nate's reaction was entirely unexpected.

"Alexis," he said, more relieved than anything else, although there appeared to be a little apprehension on his side, as well. He moved forward, though, giving her a hug that was almost brotherly. "I'm sorry. I had no idea that..." He took a few steps back and shook his head. "That you were fired. Because of me."

Dorie looked behind her, trying to judge how far the door was and whether or not she could get back through it without anyone noticing. She shouldn't have come this morning. Flings didn't do this kind of thing; girlfriends did.

Before Dorie could make an escape, however, Alexis drew herself up and, though her eyes filled, managed to hold herself together. "I appreciate the apology. But you were clear about wanting some time away. It's not your fault no one wanted to accept that. And I..." Her lips trembled a bit. After a few seconds, though, she regained her control and said, "I appreciate your giving me this opportunity."

Although it was clear Nate was uncomfortable, he just nodded and briskly said, "You earned it. The other night." Then he grinned. "You made an impression."

Her cheeks turning bright red, Alexis said, "Um, then as one of my first duties, let me say that you should never, *ever* tell a woman that she earned anything 'the other night'." That last bit she put air quotes around. "Not in front of anyone else, at least."

Dorie couldn't help but laugh at that. When everyone turned to her, she smiled. "I'd just leave it at 'ever'."

"I didn't..." Nate stammered. "That's not what I..."

Cutting him off, Dorie leaned forward to shake Alexis's hand. "I'm Dorie. It's nice to meet you." One of these days, Nate was actually going to introduce her to someone before she had to do it herself.

"I… Yes," Alexis said, turning her attention to Dorie. She gave a flash of a smile. "You're the new girlfriend."

Oh, how she wished everyone would stop saying that. "I'm not his girlfriend."

Undaunted, Alexis gave Dorie an assessing gaze as she shrugged. *Whatever.* "You're not Courtney. That's a good thing."

"Um…okay," Dorie answered, not sure what else she was supposed to say. And if she thought too hard about it, she might start laughing. Hysterically. So she didn't.

Impatiently, Pete gestured for everyone to sit. He glanced up at the clock. "You made them come to you, Hawk; they're going to make you wait. I figure we have about twenty minutes."

And Pete clearly wanted to use that twenty minutes. With only a brief glance Dorie's way, he pulled out what appeared to be Nate's contract. "There are a few things we should go over before they get here."

Dorie started to get up. She couldn't imagine Nate wanted her to hear any of this; it was too private. Yet the look he gave her—after a blank yet somehow challenging gaze at Pete—and the firm grip he took of her hand, it was clear he wanted her to stay. And she had to admit; it wasn't boring. The figures they were talking about were truly mind-boggling. She was pretty sure this was the only time in her life she'd be part of a conversation that involved the words *million* and *paycheck* in it and wasn't a joke.

She drew the line, however, when Jacqueline came in to say that "the guests" were waiting in one of the other conference rooms and everyone stood up. This time when Nate wouldn't let go of her hand, she pulled him back. She shook her head. "I can't."

He nodded for Pete and Mark to go ahead, then sat back against the table and pulled her close. "These things are a lot more fun when you're sitting next to me. Come with us."

Nope. She closed her eyes and melted a little when he nuzzled her neck. Still… "Not this time."

She felt him go tense. Felt him pull away. When she opened her eyes, it was to find him staring at her. "Why?"

Right. Of course he wouldn't let it go at that. He was tenacious if nothing else. But the thing was, he saw too much. And she had no doubt he'd see right through her because no matter how hard she was trying to fight it, she was already invested. And the second she stepped foot in that room, she wouldn't be able to deny it anymore.

Bottom line was that they hadn't been there for him. They should have been out there fighting for him from the moment the questions started coming in. Their doctors should have been out there reassuring everyone that his injuries hadn't been career-threatening, and the GM and coach should have been adamantly in his corner about the Breathalyzer test. The two lame statements they'd made hadn't been nearly enough.

And it hurt him. Even back when he'd been her pretend boyfriend, she could tell as much. Anyone looking at his eyes could see glimpses of it. But being with him over these past few days… She'd seen how badly he'd needed to know that he wasn't alone. Because that, probably more than what had actually happened with Courtney, had nearly destroyed him.

Lowering her gaze, Dorie tried to shrug him off.

"*Why?*" he said again, gripping her shoulders tightly enough that she couldn't help but look into his eyes.

She was already beginning to believe that he might actually be falling in love. It was hard enough to keep her heart protected from an onslaught like that. He was giving it his all right now because he had no other focus, she had to remind herself. The moment he stepped on that field again he'd be back in his world and everything would change.

But even knowing that, she was physically incapable of holding herself back. He was already too important to her. And as soon as she opened her mouth, he'd know how close he was to getting through and he'd take full advantage; full-court press and all that. She wouldn't stand a chance even though she had absolutely no doubt it would all go bad in the end. Going into that room would open her up in a way she simply couldn't allow.

Unable to turn away from the intensity of his gaze, she answered, "Can we leave it at 'because'?" She tried to put enough attitude in it that he wouldn't question her further. And that was all she said.

He didn't protest, didn't pry any further and didn't try to convince her otherwise. Instead, after another few seconds of staring into her eyes, he slipped one hand down to her waist as he cupped her jaw with the other.

And he smiled. He knew she was weakening. Knew her armor was falling away.

Her eyes filled as he leaned in and touched his lips to hers. When he pulled away, she pursed her lips, kind of like she was blotting lipstick, except she was really just trying to keep him there. Permanently. So that she could always remember the way he tasted.

Because this was going to end soon. It had to. Before she could fall for him all the way.

"Be here when I come back," he whispered. "Please?"

How did he know that the only way she could think of to protect herself was to turn tail and flee? That she was fighting against his pull with every ounce of her being.

How was that possible?

Unable to trust her voice, she just nodded, her forehead bobbing against his chest. His voice rumbling against her ear as he only reluctantly let her go, he said, "A word, Alexis?"

She sank down into the chair when they left the room, her head going to the table. What on *earth* did she think was going to come of all this? And if she felt like this now, how was she ever going to manage after he left?

Chapter Twenty-Two

She cared. A hell of a lot more than she wanted to let on. Nate should have been elated about that; instead it just depressed him. She had no faith in him—in them—at all. None whatsoever.

Yes, this was an incredibly and, okay yes, surreal situation—it hadn't even been a whole *week*. She thought he was infatuated—which he was. Saw her as a challenge—which he did. But didn't she get that no one had ever interested him as much as she did? Excited him?

The answer to that was, clearly, a big fat no.

And although she was obviously falling as hard as he was, that just seemed to make her more determined to run farther and faster away.

"Fuck," he muttered, tipping his chair back and tapping his pencil against the table furiously.

Glaring, Pete spoke loudly enough to talk over him. "Of course Nate's willing to meet with the trainer before he starts. That's not a problem at all."

Oh, for Christ's sake. They'd been talking about his health for the past twenty minutes, time he would so much rather have spent with Dorie. Damn it, he wished she was in here, going at them. That would have been a sight to see. Hell, she could have backed him up and told them his knees were fine. Except for a little rug burn.

"Great," Coach was saying. "We'd like for you come down to Mesa a few days early, maybe have you meet up with Casti—"

"No," Nate snapped. No way in hell he was leaving Dorie before the thirteenth. He hadn't agreed to that.

Except he had. Goddamn it, he had. He'd had no reason not to. Chicago, Arizona, they'd pretty much been the same to him since the day he'd signed his first contract. And up until about a week ago, he couldn't have cared less. But now...

He buried his head in his hands. "Shit."

He could feel the silence settle in around him. No one knew quite what to do with it. Hell, *Nate* didn't know what to do with it. Though he'd stayed away from playing the asshole for most of his career, he wasn't above it now, even though the last thing he wanted to do was start off on the wrong foot. He liked these guys; he genuinely liked them. Other than the part where they'd hung him out to dry for two months.

But just as he was about to open his mouth, Mark leaned forward. For the most part, Mark played the affable, back-slapping, man-about-town good guy. He played it well enough that, unless you'd witnessed him in a negotiation, you wouldn't have a clue how he'd gotten a reputation of being one of the best in the business. And the fact that Pete played a much larger role in every conversation revolving around Nate had some people wondering what exactly it was that Mark did.

Nate didn't care about those people. Mark didn't care about them, either. The only thing Mark did care about was his clients, most of whom he considered friends as well as business partners. And right now he was Nate's favorite person in the world.

"Let's cut to the chase, shall we?" He leaned forward, got that ice-cold look in his eyes. "You screwed him. None of us want to talk about this, but you know it. We know it. And as of a few days ago, everybody in the fucking world knows it. The *only* thing Nate did wrong was pay more attention to the kid in the other car than to the damage that he might have done to his knee. You want to hold that over him, you have every right. Your lawyers and Pete can go at it until it's far too late for Nate to help you do what every single one of us in this room wants—start off this franchise's history with a World Series win." He shrugged matter-of-factly. "My team will make you look like coldhearted assholes for pursuing that course of action, but have at it. I honestly don't care."

Then he gripped Nate's shoulder, clasping it like a good old boy. "But here's the thing. Nate is one of the best there is, on the field and off. You know it doesn't get better than this. Hell, you built your fucking team around him. So why don't you cut him a little slack—which you know you goddamn owe him—and let us tell you when and where he can be available between now and February thirteenth."

Nate didn't want to be anywhere other than Inspiration between now and February thirteenth, but he knew when to keep his mouth shut. He also knew that it was flat-out unbelievable that the GM, even if he'd been a drinking buddy of Nate's on occasion, sat back thoughtfully.

"You're right," the man finally said, turning to look at Nate head-on. "We played this wrong. I can't tell you how sorry I am that you've had to go through this." He shook his head as his gaze dropped down to the table. "Alone. That you had to go through this alone." Looking back up into Nate's eyes, he added, "And I am *personally* sorry that I haven't been standing right beside you the whole time." After holding Nate's gaze for long enough to show Nate he meant it, he turned back to Mark and Pete. "We need Nate to meet with the trainer twice a week and we want a full physical—with our guys— by Thursday. You tell us when and where; we'll make it happen. And we'd like to see some public appearances, too." He stood. "Other than that, we're good."

He reached across the table to shake Nate's hand. "I can't wait to get you started. I've been looking forward to this for a long time." With a smile, he added, "And I seriously can't wait to meet this woman."

If Mark hadn't already laid into them, Nate might have chanced an introduction right away. He wasn't sure what kind of mood Dorie would be in, though; hell, after the way she'd reacted to that picture when they first arrived, he wouldn't have been entirely surprised to find she'd bolted.

It wasn't until he came around the corner that he felt the tension ease away. She was talking with Alexis, each of them sitting with various stacks of paper in front of them at the conference table. Although... Was she really saying...?

"'...every long, hard inch of you into my mouth and suck you until you beg me to stop. And then I'll climb on top of you and ride you so hard that you'll be begging me to stop. And then I'll get up on my hands and knees, and you can fuck me until—'"

"No, wait," Alexis said, giggling. "'Until you're begging me to stop.'"

"Uh-uh—'until *I'm* begging *you* to stop,'" Dorie answered, laughter in her voice. "People seriously write this stuff? Do they think he's going to be, like, 'Oh, hey, I need some action so why don't I dig into this fan mail and see if I can find some hot little number to fuck my brains ou—'" She stopped talking abruptly as she looked up from the letter to see the three men standing there.

"Holy fuck," Mark muttered, eyebrows raised in amusement as he looked over at Nate.

"Oh, please," Dorie said, rolling her eyes. "I mean, what is a 'long, hard inch' in the first place? It's either an inch or it's not. And—"

"Dorie." Nate sucked in a deep breath.

She swiveled her chair toward him with the evilest of grins. "What? Are you begging me to stop?" She turned back to the table. "So. Look what we found." She held out a letter.

Nate practically had to shake his head to shift gears and was still in a bit of a daze as he took the letter. It was in Spanish and, to his overwhelming relief, had nothing to do with body parts of any kind.

Except… "Holy shit." Everything else faded away as he sank into a chair and began to read. He looked up at Dorie. "Where did this come from?"

She gestured to the piles of paper on the table. "It was just in one of the bags, in with everything else."

As he began to read, he heard Alexis softly tell Mark and Pete, "It's the woman from the accident."

She was coming to him, asking for his help; asking him to help heal her son.

I know I have no right.

I understand what my actions have cost you and wouldn't blame you for wishing on me any punishment you think I deserve.

But Roberto hasn't spoken since that night.

He may not ever walk again.

I beg of you—he believes in your dream.

Please help him see that miracles can happen, even to boys like him.

Paz,

Marcela Perez

Ducking his head down, Nate folded the letter carefully. He'd stayed as far away from all of this as he could, deliberately not seeking out anything beyond the barest of details. The boy was stabilized; the mother was out of her coma. And once he'd gotten out of the hospital himself, mentally and physically beaten and bruised, he'd held the world at bay. It had been easy enough back when he'd been painted as the bad guy. Pete was the only one he'd let through his door in those first few weeks. Mark and Ella the only others for weeks after that. And then he'd gone home.

Although he still couldn't remember much about the accident itself, the police report that had come out the other day put Marcela completely at fault. Her letter made it clear she accepted that blame. But he felt no anger toward her even now.

Instead he just felt reborn.

Maybe Dorie was right. Maybe the only reason they worked was because he'd been so broken that he'd needed something—anything—to hold on to, to bring him back to life. Or maybe she was trying to talk herself out of something she knew as well as he did was extraordinary. Because the reality was that he wanted more out of life than what he'd seen flash through his eyes that day. He wanted the excitement and possibility that soared within him when he looked at her. No regrets, nothing halfway.

He looked up to find her staring at him, her expression unreadable. "I have to do this," he said.

She didn't answer right away and he hated that he was putting her in this position. She'd had one thing she wanted to do in Chicago and this meant that she wouldn't get to do that today.

But even though she had every right to protest—or even tell him that it was fine, she'd just go to the library on her own—as he'd somehow instinctively known deep down inside that she would, Dorie smiled, her eyes going dark and warm. "I know."

The rest of the day was a blur from there as the team went to work. Pete was on the phone to the hospital, Mark had Jacqueline calling for a car and Alexis was—

"No press," Nate snapped, not realizing what she was doing until it was almost too late.

Making the one argument Nate was even willing to consider, Alexis said, "She needs it as badly as you do. *More* than you do, especially now. People hate her. They think she blew your chance at another World Series trophy."

Right. Even though he had specifically *not* been paying attention to the news these past few days, Nate knew exactly what it was like to be on the receiving end of that crap. "I know. I just… That's not what she needs today."

With a glance in Pete's direction, Alexis reluctantly nodded. "Then what can I do?"

"I…" Nate scrubbed his face with his hand. He'd planned to buy a car later this afternoon, yet another thing that probably would have freaked Dorie out. But they needed a way home. So… "Can you arrange for a plane to take us back to Iowa tonight?"

Then he went through his contacts. He'd just text his buddy, Mike, who ran the dealership back home so that there'd be a car waiting for them at the airstrip in Inspiration.

"Not tonight," Mark said, shaking his head. "You've got the trainer tomorrow at eleven, and we've got the show in New York tomorrow night."

Late-night TV. Right. The redemption tour, Mark had told him earlier.

Shaking his head, Nate said, "I promised I'd get Dorie back for work tomorrow morning."

Out of the corner of his eye he could see her straighten up. "Us?" she asked. "As in, you and me?"

"Of course." He really hoped that at some point she'd stop being so surprised. "I mean, I like these guys a lot, but I really don't want to go home with them."

And now she was gripping the armrests of her chair. "I don't do planes. Just drop me off at the bus station. I can—"

"No one's dropping you off at a *bus* station." Exasperation warring with amusement, Nate shook his head. He hooked his foot on her chair and pulled it toward him until their knees were touching. "Let me get this straight. You moved halfway across the country from your family and you don't fly?"

She shrugged completely unconvincingly. "There are trains."

That made him laugh outright. Oh, fuck, he loved

this woman. And he hoped to God she'd start to see that as a good thing. Soon. He took her hand. "Fly with me tonight. Come to the hospital and then we'll go home."

She obviously wanted to tell him no; it was written all over her face. But something convinced her to change her mind.

Thank God. Because it was the only thing that got him through the day. The moment he stepped into Marcela's hospital room he almost lost it. She had the bed on the far side of the room and didn't turn to them until he cleared his throat. But the second her eyes met his, things he'd buried so deep they'd only been the faintest shadow of a dream came suddenly roaring back.

The car taking flight with thundering power and grace...until it wasn't.

The heart-stopping realization that they were tumbling through air and space, and there was nothing he could do to control what was about to be a very hard, very abrupt stop against the unforgiving cement wall.

Reaching for Courtney—for the baby he'd just learned wasn't his—and almost laughing at the thought that...

That that was it. That was what his life had come to, how it would end.

Except it didn't end. The car rolled itself upright and, for who knows whatever reason, every car coming at them at seventy-five miles an hour managed to stop before slamming into them or each other. Lungs on fire, he'd jumped out of the car, gasping for air and standing there in the middle of the Ike. What felt like an eternity had probably only been a second or two before he'd realized the horrific sound cutting through the confusion, traffic and the swelling of pain in his goddamn knee was a mother screaming for her son. And, yes, wrenching his knee further as he'd twisted himself to get close enough to the kid to at least try to stop some of the bleeding, as he held that same woman's hand while the metal was pried away from her nearly lifeless boy.

As she herself began to slip away.

He found himself gripping Dorie's hand as Mrs. Perez closed her eyes and made the sign of the cross before looking up again.

There simply weren't words. She reached for his hand and then cried in his arms. They'd survived. And somehow, though all of this, Dorie—a woman who, yes, he'd only known for a handful of days but who had already seen deeper into his soul than anyone he'd ever known—was his rock. She grounded him through what ended up being the single most emotional day of his entire life.

And by the end of the afternoon, with her in his lap, his hands over hers on the controls through a rousing game of Madden NFL against Marcela and her son, he realized that it was also the best. His only complaint, in fact, came at the very end of the day when she refused to have sex on the plane.

"If we're having sex, then who's going to keep the plane in the air?"

Nate had to laugh. "The pilots? The laws of physics?" At the same time, he nudged his foot forward a little. Let his knee brush hers.

Clutching the armrests of her seat, she glared at him. "Don't distract me." But she parted her legs just enough to let him in. God, he just needed to touch her.

The nice thing about a Gulfstream was that the seats were huge, roomy enough even for him. Once they'd been in the air for a good ten minutes, he convinced her she could still hold on to the plane if she was sitting in his lap.

"No sex," she murmured, relaxing into him as he ran his hand lightly up and down her spine.

Reclining the seat a little bit, he grinned. He closed his eyes and let his head fall back. Just sitting here like this was heaven. Pure and simple.

She was so quiet for a little while that he thought she'd fallen asleep. Just as he was drifting off himself, she whispered, "I think you saved that boy's life today. Maybe the mom's, too."

Emotion swelled up within him from nowhere, setting fire to his lungs. He'd come to a similar conclusion, but in reverse. Not that he'd ever want to go through that particular wake-up call again, of course. Christ, no. But he hadn't even realized he'd gone off track—not until the shock of the past few months hit it home. And not until this past week when he'd been happy again. Truly happy.

Realizing what—who—he wanted in his life. Not wanting to waste any more time.

When he could speak without betraying himself, he gruffly said, "Yeah. This was a pretty good day."

Dorie hugged him tightly. "Not just a good day. The best day ever."

Chapter Twenty-Three

The first morning after having sex for three days straight started out with Dorie's new favorite thing: more sex. After three more orgasms—bringing her total for the past four days to more than she'd had in her entire life, thank you very much—he'd brought her coffee in bed, kissed her goodbye and headed off on his private plane.

Right.

The freak-out began while she was brushing her teeth and her eyes fell on the bathtub where, less than one week ago she'd been getting all hot and bothered by her imaginary boyfriend, and... Holy shit.

Holy *shit*.

Had that really happened?

After a few minutes of nearly hyperventilating, she pulled herself together and went about the rest of her morning routine. She was about to shut off the TV on her way out the door when she heard the news anchor say, "Nate's new girl." Mouth falling open, she turned up the volume.

"If you were one of the lucky few who captured a glimpse on film—"

She laughed in both horror and relief as a picture with

Nate, at the hospital, holding open a door for Alexis, was displayed in a little box about the anchorman's head.

"We hear you might be set for life. Now back to New York."

It was maybe five minutes before Dorie was able to snap her mouth shut and get on with her day.

The freak-out picked up steam during her ten-minute walk to the library. It had only been the local morning news segment—highly unlikely that it would have made its way east to Boston—but if she had to it wasn't going to be any fun to explain to her family that, no, she hadn't been lying, and, yes, she had actually been there, too. She was even in the photo, albeit a blur on the other side of the door as she'd cleaned the spilled coffee off her shirt. Honestly. Thank God no one had gotten a picture of Nate's actual New Girl in that particular moment.

The third and final stage of the freak-out came after she got to the library and ran into Mr. Grimes in the front hall. After the slightest of pauses, he'd just smiled and made small talk about the weather while she tried to pretend that he had not seen her between bouts of sex with his nephew. With the exception of that pause, he hadn't treated her any differently than any other day since she'd met him. But all she could see was her father's disappointment reflected in his eyes.

Her dad knew how much this job meant to her—he knew how hard she'd worked to put herself through graduate school and how much he'd hated that he couldn't do it for her. Yes, he liked to tease her about the Iowa thing and, no, he wasn't at all thrilled that she'd moved so far away. But when the rest of her family was giving her hell about picking up and moving he'd been the one who, in a rare moment of temper, slammed his fist on the table to silence them all. Then he'd turned to her and said, "If this is what you want to do, you do it. No one else gets a say."

To throw that back in his face because of a fling?

She whirled on her heel, marched straight into her office and picked up her phone. Knocked her head on the desk when she saw it had gone dead since she'd forgotten to charge it on the plane. Plugged it in, waited the eternity it took to finally have enough charge to power on again…and groaned when she saw how many texts and calls were waiting for her, half of which were just strings of exclamation points and questions marks from Tommy, who seriously needed to find a new thing.

She'd closed her eyes, taken a deep breath, and proceeded to send Nate a text because, thank God, he was still on the plane and therefore couldn't talk on the phone.

Thx for the amazing weekend. I know I said the 13th, but we both know it would be simpler to just leave it at that. See you next time you're in IA. XOXO DD

There. Then she'd cut off all contact by shutting off her phone.

Within the hour she was dying to turn it back on, although she wasn't sure if she *wanted* to see that he'd called—because that meant that she'd need to actively tell him she couldn't see him again—or that she didn't want to, which would confirm that it was all just a heat-of-the-moment kind of thing for him and would make her feel miserable.

Although she'd managed to keep it off the rest of the

day, and had stayed at work as long as she could stand it, she couldn't help but turn the TV on to watch his interview once she was in bed. And if it was just the heat of the moment, it appeared that the flame was still on.

He'd been adamant about no press in the hospital, but he'd let the kids from Robbie's floor take pictures and they'd gone viral. When he was put on the spot about it on live TV, he'd smiled, a glow lighting him up from within. He'd talked a little about Robbie and Marcela, a lot about how wonderful the EMTs and other first responders had been. About everything but him.

Then there'd been a little quiz of Chicago sports trivia that he'd aced, of course. The final question, though, was the one that had Dorie's heart racing: *So, is 'Nate's new girl' a Sox, Cubs or Watchmen fan?*

Nate had given that laugh that rumbled up from inside him, the one that made Dorie want to lay herself out in front of him and purr. "She's a Sox fan. No question."

With a huff, she fell back against her pillow. Then she picked up her phone and powered it up to see that the number of texts was now in the triple digits, seven of which were from him. There were a few pictures from New York of the 'wish you were here' variety, and one that, well, kind of made her think she maybe needed to get back into her bathtub with all those frisky jets.

Um, *no*. She drew on her superlibrarian powers and wrote, Did you get my text this morning?

Wow, he replied right away. I figured it would take you at least 10 mins before you yelled at me.

That was his response? That is not me yelling.

THIS IS ME YELLING.

And...? he texted back. Nothing else?

I don't think there's anything else to say, she responded.

Ah, so we're going nonverbal? Works for me. I like it when you moan.

And now she understood a little bit more of Tommy's brain, because all she wanted to do was type "!!!!!!!!!!!!!!!!!!!!" for days.

Before she could come up with something better, he wrote, FYI-I HAVE TIL 2/13 (just saying) Night, D.

Damn him. She threw the phone down and tried to get some sleep.

She failed miserably, so by the next day she was practically dead on her feet. Or, rather, on her knees, since she was down on the floor looking at pictures.

"Lucinda, dear, is this what you mean?"

Dorie looked down to see the photograph Mrs. Grimes was holding and shook her head. "Not the same ones that everyone's already seen." She shuffled through the pile—past all the ones of the Iowa Dream, although that was as much self-preservation as making her point—to one of the high school boys' basketball team from a few years back, just as the winning basket had been sunk. "Let's use this one instead."

The idea had come to her in the middle of the night. She'd already decided to use some of the seed money for a huge leather chair—that plus a nice throw rug and a lamp would help her transform the corner of the reading room into a cozy nook reminiscent of the one in the library back at home. But she kept coming back to those life-size photographs that had lined the halls of Mark's office. Trying not to dwell only on the *Vanity Fair* picture of Nate, she'd begun to see herself as a little girl, sitting in that chair in the library with all of those hopes and dreams.

She wanted to recreate that feeling here, with the life-size photos to serve as inspiration. Except rather than blow up the iconic Dream pictures, she wanted to find photos that captured the amazing moments of everyday life.

"How about this?" Mrs. Grimes asked, pointing to one of a teenage girl in jeans and a flannel lumberjack shirt, her arms crossed in front of her chest and her head thrown back in sheer exhilaration as she spun on the ice.

"Exactly," Dorie replied.

By the end of the afternoon, they'd settled on a few more: a picture of three big, burly firefighters, proud smiles on their faces as they held out their prize-winning pies. Really—firemen plus pies? That was a no-brainer.

There was one of an older couple sitting on their porch at sunset, his arm around her shoulders as she leaned against him, and Dorie's personal favorite: a young girl, seven or eight, stepping up to home plate with a bat that had to be bigger than she was. But she was wearing a Hawkins jersey—also way too big for her but so damn cute that Dorie decided it superseded any cliché—and the determined look on her face made it clear that nothing would get in her way.

After Mr. and Mrs. Grimes left for home, Dorie stayed to arrange a second tier for Mrs. Grimes to choose from when she heard, "*There* you are!"

Dorie turned to see Fitz standing in the doorway to the reading room. "I… Yes." She smiled uncertainly as she got to her feet, not sure how to react to the obvious concern on Fitz's face. "Is everything okay?"

"That's what I was going to ask you." Coming into the room, Fitz glanced at the photographs on the floor, then back up at Dorie. "I've been texting you. For days."

"Oh." Dorie reached into her pocket and closed her hand around her phone, even though it was still off. "I've been on a bit of a phone fast."

Fitz stared at her for a few moments. "Any particular reason?"

"Um, home stuff."

Did Fitz know Dorie had spent the weekend with Nate and was now in major avoidance mode? From what Dorie could tell, there weren't any pictures of her and Nate out there—just a few more of him and Alexis. Maybe Fitz was just trying to figure it out.

Fitz edged her way around the room. "Did you happen to watch TV last night?"

"I did, actually." Honestly? It was all still a little surreal.

"Nate seems like he's getting back to his old self," Fitz said.

If by that Fitz meant that Nate seemed happy, well then, yes. Because he was still a bit delusional about them seeing each other again. But he was a big boy; he'd get over it.

She forced her reply to Fitz. "That's good."

"But you're okay," Fitz said flatly.

Dorie bit her lip and nodded. "I am."

Before she could say anything else, the door chimes did their chiming thing and, ten seconds later, Wash strode into the room. He stopped short when he saw Fitz. "Oh. Hi."

"Hi, yourself," Fitz said, frowning. "What are you doing here?"

Also frowning, Wash answered, "Same thing you are, I'd guess." He turned to Dorie. "Just checking in to see how things are going."

For heaven's sake. What was this, a pity party?

Oh. Oh, God. Dorie closed her eyes and forced herself not to feel flustered. Not to *be* flustered. Because that's exactly what this was. They didn't realize "Nate's new girl" had been *her*. They thought she'd locked herself away after fleeing trivia night because he'd realized she knew who he was. And that made things all the more infuriating.

They were his friends—who he obviously hadn't spoken a word to about the fact that he'd been with her. Except it was a temporary thing, so to explain it now would make no sense.

"I am so totally fine," she said with maybe a little too much enthusiasm. They both looked at her strangely. Now what was she supposed to do? She liked them— and she was touched that they'd cared enough to seek her out. She didn't want it to be awkward for them, though, especially when Nate was their actual friend.

"Well, good then," Fitz stated.

With a look at Dorie and then at Fitz, Wash nodded. "Sure. Good."

They all just stood there looking at each other. Not awkward at all… "So, um…" Dorie looked down at the floor—she really should be working. There was so much to do. But then her eyes fell on the pictures they'd chosen earlier, all those people smiling and living out their dreams. And she realized, this was part of why she'd come here. She'd opened the door, but Fitz and Wash were the ones inviting her in.

And then they all spoke at once.

"I guess I'll—"

"We should—"

"Would you like to come to dinner?"

That last one was Dorie, of course, and she'd gotten it all out before realizing they were both gearing up to leave. Not necessarily inviting her along. "I mean—"

"Jason and Deke, too?" Fitz asked, kind of as if she didn't think she'd heard Dorie's question right.

"We're not exactly light eaters," Wash added. "Just to be clear."

Dorie couldn't contain her smile. "I have six brothers, remember?" It would be nice to cook for a crowd again. Plus it had the benefit of keeping her mind off Nate. It was a win-win.

Right?

Once Nate decided to charter the plane, his life got a lot easier. He'd been able to spend Sunday night with Dorie and then head back to Chicago for another meeting before more time at the hospital with Marcela and Robbie. From there to New York for the show and then his own personal red-eye to Arizona where he'd met with the trainer as requested. He'd come straight to the house he had here and was now happily soaking in the hot tub and…

And…hell. Thinking of Dorie. Trying to be amused rather than irritated that she was trying to blow him off again.

By text, no less. Really?

When his phone buzzed a few minutes later, he

hoped it was her coming to her senses. But, no, it was from Deke.

Dude. Poker night. U in?

Nate smiled. He hadn't been invited to poker night in years. Even when he'd been back for one reason or another, the invites hadn't exactly been flowing; case in point, the week before. Because at some point he'd decided he had better things to do and had stopped saying yes. What an ass.

Unfortunately, that was going to be case yet again.

In Scottsdale tonite. On to LA in the morning. Next week?

You're on. Holding you to it. Call if ur back b4 then.

He'd be back on Thursday morning, but he wasn't making plans with anyone other than Dorie for now. She'd been the one to give February thirteenth as their end date. He was at least getting that. So he'd be spending every moment humanly poss—

Hold the fucking phone. What the *hell*? He had a plane at his disposal, nowhere else to be until tomorrow at noon, LA time. That was actually doable. And the thought of watching Dorie run the card table again gave him a rush.

On second thought, count me in. Ok to bring a +1?

Is she pretty? was Deke's return text.
Beautiful. Gorgeous. Funny. Sexy as hell.

There was a bit of a pause. Then, Sounds good as long as she can run the Fitz/Wash gauntlet. C u tonite.

Dorie had already managed the Fitz/Wash gauntlet; Nate had no concerns about her fitting in. Hell, she probably fit in better than he did. He grabbed a towel as he got out, then tried to call her. Her phone went straight to voice mail, of course, which was full. Goddamn it.

Fine. He had no problem just appearing at her door. It had been working for him so far.

Fifteen minutes later he was showered and dressed, his keys in his hand as he walked out to the truck he kept here. He would stop to pick up some food for the crew he'd just roused out of their hotel rooms and then he'd be on his way.

He tried to sleep on the plane, thinking it would help him stop obsessing about Dorie. But closing his eyes just made it worse. He could feel her. Smell her. Hear the sounds she made as she broke apart beneath him. He was afraid he might actually fall asleep and end up jacking off in front of the crew without even realizing it.

Shit. If she really didn't want to see him again?

No.

Visualize success.

Just don't get off on it.

When they finally landed he didn't even bother trying to call or check in with anyone. He got in the car he'd left at the airstrip the day before and headed into town. It was just past seven when he got to her place, and he was eager enough to see her to take the steps three at a time. Just as he was about to knock, however, he heard a man's voice followed immediately by Dorie's laugh. Nate froze.

Could she be seeing someone else?

She laughed again.

Well, tough shit. This was not one-sided, no matter what she said. Texted, for Christ's sake. Nate wasn't going down without a fight. Pitchers and catchers was what she'd told Courtney. He still had fifteen days.

With renewed determination, he took a deep breath and knocked. Straightening his shoulders, Nate put on his game face—one of the best in the bigs—gearing himself up for whatever was on the other side of that door.

What he was not one bit ready for was it to be… "Fitz?"

"Nate," she said, stepping out into the hallway, eyes narrowed and angry. She stuck her head out as though she was looking for someone. The fact that no one else was there seemed to anger her even more.

"What th—?"

"What's that?" she snapped, cutting off his question. She pointed to the bag he held in his hand.

"Chimichangas," he answered. "From Arizona." He lifted the bag up over her head when she reached for it, even though he knew it pissed her off immensely. "For *Dorie*."

Frowning, Fitz said, "There's, like, four containers in there."

"The woman likes her food." And he was not above using that fact. As he stepped forward, Fitz put herself in front of him. "What the *fuck*, Fitz?"

"That doesn't make up for anything," she hissed.

He reached around her in order to push the door open. "Am I supposed to know what you're talking about?" he asked as he went in.

Stopping short, he felt his blood go cold again. Wash

and Deke? It was bad enough to think of another man moving in on her—to have it be one of his best friends? Been there, done that. Got the six weeks' worth of media coverage.

It didn't help that when Dorie turned around and her eyes met his, she glared and whirled away. He glanced at Fitz again, then up at Wash. He hadn't exactly pictured having an audience.

Deke was either oblivious to the tension or experienced enough at diffusing bar fights that he could pretend that was the case. "Nate!" He came over and clapped Nate on the shoulder, a big smile on his face. "Glad you got my text."

Uh… "What text?" Nate asked, his hand automatically in his pocket for his phone. Pulling it out, he saw that, yes, Deke had texted. We'll be at Dorie's. C u when we c u.

Great.

As Deke turned to head back toward the counter that separated the kitchen from the living area, he whispered, "Women are on the warpath. No clue why."

Fitz was on her own for the moment. Dorie, however…

Ignoring Wash's glare, Nate walked toward her. Though every cell in his body ached to touch her, they clearly had a few things to get straight. Going over to the kitchen, he put the bag on the counter. His eyes on her and her alone, he turned his back to the others and quietly said, "What. The. Hell?"

Her eyes flashed. She was the one avoiding his calls, yet she was angry with *him*. Not flustered, like after the first time he'd refused to let her blow him off. Just pissed.

With a glare thrown in his direction, she neatly

walked around him. She reached past Wash—far too close for Nate's comfort—then, holding a plate heaped high with breaded chicken, turned back to Nate. "I'm making dinner." With a smile far too bright to be genuine, she added, "Do you like chicken? Maybe you can stay, too."

Seriously? "I like anything you cook." He nodded to the bag. "I brought you a present."

She looked at the bag, then back at him. "Thanks. That was very nice of you." Then she walked back around him and over to the stove.

Okay. This was *The Twilight Zone*. Nate ran his hand through his hair. He had no freaking idea what was happening, but it had better stop soon. He didn't have time for this shit.

There was another knock on the door—which for some reason made Dorie flinch—and, with a huff, Fitz turned on her heel to answer it. Jason, who got a much nicer reception than Nate had.

"Oh, hey, Nate," Jason said, a smile on his face as he brought over a six-pack and placed it on the counter. He took a quick look around. "So where's your date?"

"My *what*?" Nate asked as Fitz hit Jason on the shoulder and Wash took a step toward Dorie. A protective step.

With a frown at Fitz, Jason rubbed his arm. He'd never been great at reading hints, even entirely unsubtle ones. He turned back to Nate. "Your plus-one. You know, the one you said was—"

"Jesus, Jason!" Wash finally said. "Shut it, ok?"

Nate closed his eyes. He almost laughed. He might have if the relief weren't so staggering. Because if she was this pissed at the thought of him bringing a date? And she was—he could practically feel the daggers.

Still in business, baby.

"No, wait," Dorie said, her eyes narrowed. "I'd love to hear about his date."

With a smile too wide to hide, Nate took the plate out of her hand and placed it on the counter behind him. "Gorgeous. Funny."

"Nate!" Fitz shouted as Wash, glaring, said, "Really, Hawk?"

Ignoring them, Nate reached out for Dorie and pulled her to him. Inhaling her scent—*finally*—he ignored her protest as he lifted her up to the counter and nuzzled her neck. "Sexy as hell."

He wasn't surprised at the way she stiffened for a second—she wasn't one to easily let things go. What did surprise him, though, was the hurt in her eyes. It humbled him.

He wasn't used to vulnerability. Usually, it was just a game. Literally—the one with the list of impossible hookups. He was on that list for a lot of women and he'd even happily played along on occasion. But even if he *had* given any credence to Pete's suspicious thoughts about her motives, it was obvious that Dorie's games were in her own head. She couldn't allow herself to believe.

Well, he'd just have to believe enough for both of them.

Confirming his assessment, her eyes welled as she whispered, "They said you were bringing a date." Becoming very occupied with something on his shirt, she wouldn't meet his gaze. "And since you didn't tell them about me, I figured…" Her words died off as she shrugged.

He took her hand. "You figured I was bringing someone else." If it wasn't for the tears, that would have pissed him off.

Her lower lip quivered. "Because we're short-term," she whispered.

"No," he said into her ear. "We're not."

Even more faintly she persisted, "It's only sex," still unable to look him in the eye.

He honestly didn't know what to do to get through to her. Gritting his teeth, he said, "Agree to disagree." They were going to talk about this. They had to. But now was not the time. And because he couldn't wait a second longer, he bent down and kissed her.

From the way her hand flattened against his chest, he could tell she was debating whether to push him away. He could even taste the salt from her tears on her lips. But then she grabbed a handful of shirt and pulled him closer.

She was the one to break away, her eyes still closed as she bit her bottom lip. When she opened her eyes again, there was still uncertainty.

So, after running his thumb over her cheek he took a step back. In a voice loud enough for everyone to hear, he said, "So, Dorie. My friends are playing poker tonight. And although I want to spend every minute I possibly can with you, I kind of love them too, so I was hoping you might want to join us."

Though she huffed a little at the "too" part, she didn't contradict him. He took that as a good sign.

Dinner was amazing, of course. The ease with which she handled four big men and one not-so-big woman who had fairly decent appetites shouldn't have surprised him but did. And, after about half an hour of settling in, she even started looking happy.

He liked that her gaze kept sliding toward him when she thought he wasn't looking. And the way she entwined her fingers with his when he let his hand fall down to her leg.

"I can't believe you didn't tell us," Fitz said, glaring at Nate as she gave his shin a hard kick under the table. "And *you*," she said, jabbing a fork in Dorie's direction. "If you replied to even one of our messages…"

Dorie's face flushed again as she looked away.

Which didn't stop Fitz, who turned back to Nate and said, "At least she was replying to *you*."

"Not quite." Nate let out a bark of a laugh. "You think I would have let her for a *second* think I'd be bringing someone other than her? She was too busy breaking up with me."

"We're not together," Dorie insisted, shaking her head.

He grabbed her hand and deliberately placed it on the table—with his. "We are."

Their eyes met and he held her gaze until she relented, murmuring, "February thirteenth."

Hell, yes. "Now that's what I'm talking about," he said, leaning in to kiss her. A quick touch to her lips—nothing more than that. And yet it felt so completely natural that it wasn't until he pulled back that he felt it ripple through him and take root somewhere deep inside. He smiled as she gave an exasperated sigh.

Pulling her hand away, she changed the subject. "Does anyone want more chicken?"

As everyone else went for the food, Wash murmured,

"Holy *shit*." Sitting back in his chair, he looked from Dorie to Nate. Despite the distance that had been there over the past few years, he knew.

"It's only been a week, man," Wash said.

"It only took two days," Nate answered.

He felt like he'd shouted the words. Roared them. But it was something only Wash heard; everyone else had moved on.

Even Fitz, who was usually more in tune to things like that, was saying, "Well, how the hell were we supposed to know? All we knew was that he was off gallivanting in Chicago with some new girl. And you'd disappeared for days so we thought you went and locked yourself up so you could avoid us."

"Hey—I haven't gallivanted in a while now." Nate reached out for Dorie's hand again, taking it in his.

Wash, back to being happy-go-lucky Wash again, smiled and lifted his beer to Dorie. "Just say the word and we'll bust his ass if he gets out of line."

Before that could go any further, Nate steered the conversation away from anything relationship-related. They were already too far down that road. "So are we playing poker tonight or are you all just stalling so I won't take you to town?"

As everyone stood up and started gathering dishes, Deke turned to Dorie. "I guess we should have asked before. Do you know how to play poker?"

With a smile that hit Nate like a bolt of lightning, Dorie looked up and into his eyes. "Poker? Is that the one with the chips?"

Chapter Twenty-Four

Every day of the next week and a half was like Christmas. Dorie got to know the local UPS and FedEx deliverymen so well that she was trading marathon training tips with one and helping choose between engagement ring choices for the other. Mrs. Grimes had been processing the books as fast as they could come in, and Mr. Grimes—with help from Wash, Deke and Jason—had assembled the new shelves. Even Mayor Gin had gotten involved, heading down to Des Moines with Dorie and Fitz to buy new furniture for the children's area.

Plus, even though the library wasn't open yet, it felt like half the town had dropped by to welcome her. She'd apparently made quite a name for herself at trivia night—that tended to be what they opened with—but they also wanted to meet "Nate's New Girl." Awesome. Because that was going to be so freaking fun the first time he showed up in the press with another woman on his arm.

Though she felt a little like the main attraction of a road show, it gave her a chance to show off the library. And she kind of loved making up batches of biscotti every night for the hordes. She was getting into this whole small-town-life thing.

And then there were the photographs. They'd been delivered yesterday, huge panels with frames that fit the trim on the library's windows. It took a whole day to hang them throughout the building. They were beyond beautiful. With the exception of some trivial prettying-up, they were actually ready for next week's reopening. So, workwise, things were just fine.

It was Nate that had her in free fall.

Dorie frowned as the butterflies took one of their increasingly frequent rolls through her stomach. Although she'd tried to convince herself it was about the ceremony, she knew full well her nerves had nothing to do with that. No, they were all because Nate had not let up his attention one bit. And because she was falling for it.

After showing up at her door the night she'd had everyone over, he'd been back five times. And despite swearing to herself after every single one of those times that she was not letting him in again no matter what she'd said about February thirteenth—that she was fully capable of keeping her heart tightly encased in a protective titanium box—she hadn't once been able to turn him away.

And now she was stealing glances at her watch because she'd agreed to go away with him for *another* weekend. It was yet another in a long line of mistakes—she clearly hadn't gotten the *How To Manage a Proper Fling* handbook. But she simply hadn't been able to bear the thought of a last time with him.

She was just finishing up an email when she heard him beep. Snapping her laptop shut, she put it in her tote and slung it over her shoulder. She was going with him on the condition that he'd let her do work on the plane. His condition was that she do it naked. They were still working out the details. She grabbed her suitcase on the way out of her office and detoured into the reading room to see if Mr. or Mrs. Grimes needed anything before she left. "I can tell Nate he has to—"

Mrs. Grimes held up her hand before Dorie finished her sentence. Then she held up her phone and, without a word, showed Dorie the text from Nate.

Don't even try it, D. I will carry you out if I have to.

"Okay," she laughed. She said her goodbyes and headed outside.

He was leaning against the car, waiting for her, when she came out the door. "You're terrible," she said.

That amazing grin flashed over his face as he came toward her. "Just covering all the bases." He took her bag and then bent down to kiss her. "I love the way you taste." Pulling her closer, he said, "So if I handcuff you to the armrests, does that still count as holding up the plane?"

Her head jerked back as her cheeks flushed. *"What?"*

Guiding her to the car, he laughed. "Just say the word."

The frightening thing was that she was tempted, even as they got to the plane and the pilots, two almost-as-pretty-as-Nate flyboys, greeted them.

"You weren't serious about the naked thing," she whispered to Nate as they sat down across from each other. Was he?

Fastening his seat belt, the corner of Nate's mouth twitched up.

Well, alrighty then.

She waited until they were in the air to ask him—

again—where they were going. All he'd told her was
that it would be totally casual.

"This is okay?" she asked now, gesturing down at
her jeans and sweater.

He frowned a little at the V-neck, although that wasn't
generally his reaction when there was cleavage involved,
but just shrugged and looked down at his phone. "It's
fine."

"*Fine?*" She kicked him. "That's the best you can
do?"

Putting the phone on the table next to him—because
Gulfstream jets had actual side tables rather than tables
of the tray kind—he finally looked up at her. The look
in his eyes made her throat go dry as he answered, "I'm
trying really hard not to be thinking about what you look
like in that sweater so, yes, unless you're reconsidering
the sex-on-the-plane thing, then that's the best I can do."

"Oh," she said. Okay, more like gasped. "Is it…is it,
uh, warm in here?"

He smiled. Not nicely. "Very."

"Um…" She fanned her face with her hand. "I'm not
really holding up the plane, am I?"

The smile grew wider. "Not at all."

Her eyes drifted to his mouth. His amazingly kiss-
able mouth. Email could wait. "And those guys are probably pretty busy…" Her gaze slipped down to his chest.

He waited a beat before he rasped, "They are."

She was out of her seat and in his lap two seconds
later. They were well on their way to being naked when
he pulled away from her, a string of curses on his breath.
"Dorie. Damn it. I didn't think…"

She kissed him at the base of his throat. It was a thing
for him. "Don't you dare tell me you don't want this."

His hands went to her wrists. "I do want this. *Hell*, I can't tell you how much I want this."

She pulled back. "But?"

He closed his eyes and let his head fall back. After a few steadying breaths, he opened his eyes again and looked straight into hers. "But in about an hour and a half, we'll be in Boston and although I'm not afraid of your brothers, it's probably not the best idea for me to meet them quite that soon after being inside of you."

The flush at his words came as fast as the tears to her eyes. "What?" she whispered.

Letting go of her wrists, his hands fell to her hips. "I know how much you miss your family. And I know you don't like to fly, but here you are. So I thought that maybe…" His voice trailed away. Leaning forward, his lips brushed her cheek. "But I also know that we're not exactly at the meet-the-brothers stage."

Which she'd had no intention of being at, as he well knew.

"So," he was saying, "we have reservations in Quebec and Miami, too. I even have tickets to the Super Bowl if that's where you want to go. We have another forty minutes before you had to choose."

Her hands flew up to her mouth in a steeple. She was, literally, speechless. Her lungs had nearly deflated and her heart was Energizer Bunnying its way out of her chest. "Why?" she finally managed to ask.

His eyes met hers head-on and she could see his intentions plain and clear. Not that he'd ever tried to hide them. No, unlike her, he'd taken his heart and handed her his sleeve. "You know why."

And, God help her, she wanted desperately to believe that this could work. That he could go off and live his baseball life during the day, and then come home to her castle at night. But that truly was a fairy tale. And no matter how pure his intentions were, the reality was still that she'd be the one off to the side while he was living out his dream. His work would always be more important—he'd given Robbie back his life, for heaven's sake—and she'd always be the one trailing behind him, scrambling to get her work done on the plane.

Waiting until she could speak without breaking down, she said with as much conviction as she could, "We are a short-term thing."

He turned to look out the window and swallowed hard. It took him a minute, but when his eyes came back to hers, they were clear and unwavering. "We're whatever we want us to be."

Of course she *wanted* this to be. But arguing with him was a lost cause. She bit her lip as her eyes filled. "You're not playing fair."

"I'm not *playing*," he snapped, his hand clenching the armrest. Then he leaned forward, his arm wrapping around her waist as he looked up at her. "But if I were, then I would definitely be operating under the Everything's Fair principle."

As in love and war, she was assuming. Of course he would manage to get that in there. With a great deal of effort, she looked out the window. "I don't want to fight about this."

He gave a little laugh—not a happy one—as he let go of her and sat back. "Neither do I. It would be nice if we could actually have a conversation about it, however."

Ugh! The man was infuriating! "I don't want to *talk* about it, either!"

"No," he snapped angrily. "Because to you it's only about sex!"

Before she could respond to that, he let his head thunk back against his seat. Scrubbed his hand over his face as he muttered, "Christ. I can't believe I just said that."

When she shifted forward—reached out for him, honestly not knowing what she could do to get him to just *stop* insisting that this could be something, her heart actually hurt because of how much she wanted it to be true—he just looked her in the eye for a moment. She could see the second he relented.

"So," he finally said, his fingers inching up her thigh, demonstrating exactly why she had, as of yet, been entirely unable to tell him no, "if this happened to be one of those times you decided to try to distract me with that mouth of yours, I probably wouldn't complain."

Oh, thank goodness. She gave a grateful grin. And then that mouth of hers got down to business.

Boston was a gamble. Dangling a trip home to her family in front of her could go either way. But the stakes were high and his time was short. And when you were in the bottom of the ninth, with two outs and the bases loaded, hell, yes, you did what you had to do. Especially when she was smart enough to see right through it. Straight-out manipulation wasn't his thing. But the closer they got to Boston, the happier she became, and he was glad he could at least give her that. Even if this did go bad.

"Do they know we're coming?" she asked as they started their descent.

Nate shook his head. "Not from me."

"Awesome!" When they landed, she borrowed one of the pilot's phones and proceeded to place an incredibly complicated food order, ending the call before she gave her name.

The mother ship, as she called it, was in an area that managed to be highly upscale and neighborhoody at the same time. There was a knot of people at the entrance despite the winter chill. Goddamn media.

It didn't seem to bother Dorie, though. When he sat back in the seat and turned to look at her, she was just staring at him. "What?" he asked. Was it too much to hope that she'd finally come to her freaking senses and was about to tell him that, yes, she loved him, too?

Yes, apparently. She shook her head as she put her hand to the back of his neck and drew him down into a kiss.

And he didn't want it to end; he never wanted it to end.

When she pulled away, he reached for her, cupping her face with his hands. *Don't leave.* He heard the words in his head; wasn't sure he'd managed to keep them there until he saw the question in her eyes.

Now it was his turn to shake his head. Though he didn't think of himself as a man who begged, if he'd truly believed it would make her stay, he'd do it in a second. He wasn't kidding himself. Dorie wasn't wrong. The odds of this working were low to begin with. Subterranean. If she wasn't one hundred percent there with him, then, well, just call him Frosty and send him to hell. But his entire life had been a one-in-a-million shot. And no matter how much she was trying to talk herself out of it, there was a future for them. He believed that with everything he had.

He pulled back. Only then did he realize that the

crowd of people wasn't the press, it was her family. "That order you called in…?"

Confusion flashed through her eyes as she lagged a little bit behind him in switching gears. Then she glanced outside the car and smiled. "It's been my order for years." That glint came into her eye and she shrugged. "This is so much better than calling them and saying I was coming."

Though the car pulled up to the curb, no one came close—although they were doing a horrible job at pretending they weren't trying to figure out who was behind the tinted windows. Knowing that he probably wouldn't have another chance to hold her the way he wanted to for a while, Nate pulled her up to his lap, smiled as she, clearly thinking the same thing, leaned in for the kiss and let her hands wander.

They were interrupted by a sharp rapping at the window. He looked, and the hand was attached to a very big, very surly-looking, impatient guy. "Lucinda Dorinda! If you don't open up this door we're coming in to get you—and if his hands are anywhere near your ass it's not gonna be pretty!"

"Sean?" Nate asked, tempted to yell back that it wasn't *his* hands that were the issue but deciding that probably wouldn't get them off to the greatest of starts. Especially since he had, in fact, come inside her and although they'd cleaned up on the plane, he had no doubt every single one of her brothers would be able to tell.

With a grin, she shook her head. "That one's Seamus."

Refusing to remove his hands from her hips right away, Nate said, "Probably shouldn't make them wait any longer."

Cocking her head, she looked at him, curiosity still

lingering in her eyes. But then she gave him a quick final kiss, shifted across him to the other side of the car and pushed open the door and let out a whoop of joy.

Getting out and closing the car door behind him, Nate watched as the mob absorbed her, more people pouring out of the restaurant as it became clear that, yes, it really was Dorie coming home. Other than a few curious glances, not a single one of them could have cared who he was. And that was perfectly fine with him.

Chapter Twenty-Five

One softball team, two former professors and four neighbors later, Dorie sat at the bar of her father's restaurant, looking at her drink. She had to admit that a part of her wondered if the turnout had something to do with Nate even though no one seemed to be paying him much attention.

Her brothers, of course, were the exception. They'd run him through several rounds of darts and were now well into an intense game of pool. She was thinking about whether she should go rescue him when someone's arms went around her. There was a flash of red hair and then a squealed, "Lucinnnnnnnnnnndaaaaaaaaaaaaa!"

"Soph?" She whipped around on the barstool. "Oh, my God! Sophie! You're supposed to be in New Haven."

"And you're supposed to be in *Iowa*!" Pulling out of the hug, she punched Dorie in the arm. "Are you kidding me? My best friend in the world swoops down out of the blue with the love of her life and she doesn't think I'd drop pretty much *everything* to come see her?" She dropped her bag to the floor, took off her coat and plunked down on a barstool. "Holy shit, Donelli. What the hell?"

"He is *not* the love of my life," Dorie hissed. And

when Sophie raised an eyebrow in protest, Dorie added, "Don't you dare say anything like that when I actually introduce you."

"Like what?" Sophie asked innocently as she signaled for her own drink. "You mean you haven't told him that you made me and Kelsey O'Reilly add him to our prayer list every night when we were thirteen? No worries. My lips are sealed. I promise."

"Good," Dorie muttered as Claudia came and sat down on the other side of her.

Sophie laughed and turned so that she was leaning back against the bar. "Oh, *my*. That is a mighty fine specimen right there."

As Claudia murmured her agreement, Dorie decided to turn, as well. After all, the man had brought her halfway across the country; she supposed she didn't have to be shy about her appreciation.

The thermal shirt he was wearing stretched tightly across his shoulders as he bent over the pool table and made what must have been a beautiful shot given the look on his and Seamus's faces while Sean and Tommy winced. "How is he more beautiful in real life than he is in all those pictures?"

With a snort, Sophie said, "That Hawkins guy is all right, I suppose, but I was actually talking about Tommy. Oh, *God*, do I need to get laid."

The shiver that ran through Dorie's body wasn't a good one. "How many times do I need to tell you that you are not allowed to bring up my brother and sex in the same sentence?"

Again Sophie grinned.

Dorie elbowed her. "Claudia—will you please tell

Sophie that this isn't okay? I mean, Tommy's basically your brother, too."

Unfortunately, this wasn't an argument Dorie was going to win. Not when Claudia shook her head. "Sorry, Luce. We'll be living in your parents' house until our new kitchen is done. I'm as desperate as Sophie is."

This was the problem with your only female friends being people you were either related to or who were in love with one of your brothers. Both, in the case of Claudia. Dorie shuddered again. "You guys are doing this on purpose."

After taking a long drag of her beer, Sophie answered, "Hell, yes, we are. Why are you here with us when you could have your arms wrapped around that man?"

Yes, well, that was an excellent question. One Dorie had begun to ask herself as the crowd thinned. The answer obviously had something to do with the love-of-her-life thing. That she had once upon a time planned out his proposal—on the pitcher's mound at Fenway, of course, where he would by that point be a perennial Red Sox all-star player—was not going to convince him that they would soon be parting ways. If it came out, that was, which would be beyond horrifying.

"Actually," Sophie said almost to herself, "why am *I* standing here?" And Sophie being Sophie, she finished off her beer, placed the bottle on the bar and walked across the restaurant to do just that. Just after Tommy sank a decent shot of his own, Sophie reached around him from behind—her hands settling just this side of decent over the button on his jeans—and murmured something into his ear that made him smile.

"Baby," Dorie could see Tommy say in return, leaning back into her with an intimacy and ease Dorie had always envied. He turned just enough to throw his arm around her shoulders and pull her into a kiss. Then, after a questioning glance over at Dorie, he shifted a little in order to introduce her to Nate.

Oh, God. If that wasn't enough to get Dorie across the room, nothing else was.

She got there just in time to hear Sophie say, "...BFFs for years."

"Years, huh?" Resting his pool stick on the floor, Nate smiled. "Even during her *Full House* days?"

Sophie knew full well what Dorie's TV-watching history was and that John Stamos had never been a part of it. Unfortunately, considering the twinkle in his eyes, it was clear to anyone watching that Nate knew that, as well. Not missing a thing, Sophie laughed. "No. But I sure got my fill of high school basketball."

Nate, who like any other warm-blooded male in a ten-mile radius had turned to Sophie when she laughed, now turned back to Dorie. The corner of his mouth twitched up. Reaching for the chalk, he ran it slowly over the tip of his cue stick. "Really."

Dorie looked down at the floor. Thank God Claudia chose that moment to come join them with her children in tow.

"Time to go?" Sean asked, taking their youngest out of Claudia's arms. The three-year-old looked up drowsily, then resettled his head on Sean's shoulder. Claire and Liam, looking all of their respective thirteen and ten years, followed closely behind. Although they'd played cards for a little while with Dorie earlier in the evening, they'd spent the past few hours in the office with their iPads.

At Claudia's nod, Sean turned to Dorie. "So what's your plan—are you staying at the house?"

No, they were *not* staying at the house. That was the thing you did with your boyfriend—not your three-week, sex-only fling. But rather than say that—well, not the sex-only part, obviously—she turned to Nate. "So my brothers haven't scared you off yet?"

The second the words were out she snapped her mouth shut. Nate was the only man she'd ever even had a conversation with about that. And Nate was probably the only man in the entire universe who, standing here in her father's restaurant with three of her brothers within arm's reach, would respond with, "From what I can tell, they're not even bringing their A-game," accompanied by a kiss-my-ass grin.

After a second's hesitation, Seamus and Tommy both laughed. Sean, on the other hand, just looked at Nate.

Turning to Claudia, Claire said, "Wait, so are they staying with us tonight or not?"

"I don't think they've decided yet, *mija*," she answered gently, giving Dorie an out.

"Nate can stay in my room," Liam offered, shrugging as if it was no big deal.

To his credit, Nate didn't miss a beat. "Thanks, buddy. That's really nice of you. I might take you up on that."

Um, *no*. "*Or*," Dorie started to say, "maybe we could—"

"How about my room?" Claire asked. With a smug look at her younger brother, she added, "It's bigger."

Not only did Liam not jump at the bait—he was actually shaking his head adamantly.

"What?" Claire asked.

"You *know*..." he answered, even though she clearly

didn't. And now everyone was looking at him, which to Liam was one of the worst things that could happen. So Dorie wasn't entirely surprised when he blurted out the thing that he so clearly hadn't wanted to say in the first place. "The *pictures*."

Dorie closed her eyes, as the other shoe dropped heavily—right down onto her head—when Claire said, "What pic—" She cut herself off. Her eyes went as big as Liam's as she looked at Nate. "Oh. Right."

Because it wasn't just one picture on the back of the door of Dorie's childhood room—it was a whole collage of them. "The Shrine," as Soph referred to it. Dorie opened her eyes to everyone staring at her, Nate included. Yet for reasons unbeknownst to her, he didn't seem horrified. *Bemused* was more the word she'd use.

Sean was another story. "What pictures?" he snapped, glaring at Dorie as he folded his arms in front of his chest. "Please tell me you don't have naked pictures of Nate Hawkins in the bedroom where my thirteen-year-old daughter has been sleeping for the last two months."

"Oh, right," Dorie snapped right back. "So it's my fault you didn't do a proper inspection of *my* bedroom before you allowed Claire in?" She put her hand on Claire's arm and whispered, "Which I don't mind at all, sweetie. You know that, right?"

Used to not-so-occasional sibling flare-ups, Claire just smiled and nodded.

"And no one's naked," Sophie added, holding up her right hand. "I swear. At least not when I saw them last." She cocked her head a little as she looked Nate up and down. "I suppose there could have been some recent additions."

Good lord. Dorie wished she was close enough to

Soph to smack her on the shoulder. "There are no naked pictures," she hissed.

"Well, there is that one where he doesn't have his shirt on," Liam noted ever-so-helpfully, his expression thoughtful.

"Oh, Christ," Seamus murmured, laughing. "This just keeps getting better and better."

Trying to help out but failing miserably, Claire ignored Seamus's comment and added, "But it's from when he was, like, my age, so it's not that big of a deal."

"Not that big of a deal," Sean repeated. "He was at least sixteen, which is most definitely *not* your age."

Sophie—eyes twinkling devilishly—put in her own two cents. "I think the real question is does Nate have any naked pictures of Luce?"

This. Was. Not. Happening.

"Sadly, no," Nate answered as easily as could be, as if half of Dorie's family had not just spent the past several minutes discussing her pictures of him from seventeen years ago. As if they weren't talking about naked pictures right now.

Dorie stifled the squeal that threatened to escape.

"Do you have *any* pictures of Auntie Luce?" Liam asked. "I mean, she is your girlfriend, right?"

With a grin, Nate answered, "You need to ask her, because she gets really mad when I talk about it. But, yeah. I have pictures." He took out his phone and held it up. "Want to see them?"

"Yes!" Liam and Claire shouted as they surged forward.

"Hell," Sophie muttered. "Me, too."

The three of them gathered around Nate as he thumbed through. "That's her in her apartment. She makes the best cupcakes in the world, but you probably already know that."

Nate had pictures of her? As in, plural? From *when*?

"She has flour on her nose," Liam said.

"Yep," Nate said. "That's one of my favorites."

That would have embarrassed Dorie if she hadn't been stunned speechless by the turn this had taken.

Nate kept going. "And this is her painting with our friends…"

"Is that…?" Tommy, who was now watching over Sophie's shoulder, looked up at Dorie. "You're fucking kidding me."

Without looking up, Nate nodded. "Wash and Deke."

"I recognize them," Claire said. Which of course she would, given the shrine. "You all played basketball together when you were kids."

"Yeah, we did," Nate said softly as he thumbed through a few more pictures and then stopped, surprised. With a quiet, "Huh," he looked down at his phone. "Fitz must have taken this."

"Wow," Claire murmured, her eyes going round. "Auntie Luce looks so *pretty* in that picture."

"Yeah," Nate answered gruffly. "She does." He looked up at Dorie right then and suddenly all of the easy lightness was gone. Instead he seemed intense and determined. *Fierce.*

His focus was off enough that he didn't seem to realize that Claire had bent in to look more closely. "And happy." With far too much awareness for a thirteen-year-old, she looked up at Dorie. "You both look really happy."

For as much as Dorie wanted to see exactly what picture Claire was talking about, she couldn't move. She was rooted in place, her eyes stinging.

"Um…Claire, Liam," Claudia said, stepping in front of Dorie. "Mr. Hawkins—"

"Nate," he corrected.

"Nate. Right." Claudia took Claire by the shoulders and turned her to the door. "Time for us to go, *mija*. You'll have plenty of time tomorrow to visit more."

"But is he—"

"He'll be sleeping on the couch," Sean snapped, still clearly out of sorts. "And Auntie Luce will not be."

Her eyes going to the ground, Dorie grumbled, "That's Daddy's line."

When Seamus and Tommy started laughing again, Sean glared at them. Then he gave Nate and Sophie a curt nod goodbye and followed Claudia out.

Fuck, he had screwed up big. Nate had brought her to Boston to show her what he could give her. What he'd gotten instead was a glimpse of a future he was doing everything he could to secure, completely unsuccessfully.

He'd watched Dorie with her niece and nephews throughout the evening—teasing them, hugging them, her love for them entirely uncontained—and been nearly overcome by how much he wanted that. How much he wanted that with *her*. Any doubts he may have had were pretty much shot to hell at the sight of utter contentment on her face when the three-year-old reached his arms out to her and refused to let go until she'd agreed to carry him to the car.

He turned his back to the door and chalked his cue stick. Seamus also turned back to the table right then, bending over to take his turn after Tommy failed miserably at what should have been an easy shot. "Thanks, Soph," he said, turning to the redhead. "Always can count on Tommy to scratch when you're around."

Sophie was not at all what Nate had expected in terms of Dorie's best friend. The woman was raunchier than hell—Nate had been close enough to hear what she'd whispered in Tommy's ear and it went about four steps past the typical locker-room conversation. At Seamus's comment, she stuck her hand in Tommy's back pocket, pulled him up against her and looked into Tommy's eyes. "You can scratch my itch anytime you want, baby."

"They've been that way since they were fifteen," Seamus muttered as he took his shot. "It freaks Sean the hell out, as you can imagine."

"Claire's how old?" Nate asked, watching the seven ball slip into the pocket. "Thirteen?"

Straightening up, Seamus nodded. "It was bad enough watching Luce grow up…"

Luce.

Right.

"Watching Claire?" Seamus was saying as he shook his head. "Kind of makes you think." He tried to sink the two ball in the side pocket. Missed.

Nate laughed as he studied the table. He was pretty sure he could get the eleven ball in the corner if he banked it right. "I have three sisters," he replied. "I've spent my whole life thinking."

"Thinking about what?" Dorie asked, having reappeared right then. She picked up the cue stick that had been Sean's, clearly ready to take her brother's place.

"Sisters," he said, watching her studying the balls rather than meet his eye. He'd just leaned down to take his shot when she moved directly into his vision, bending over enough that the sweater slipped aside to reveal a beautiful expanse of creamy skin. He almost laughed.

Was she trying to get him killed? Sure he'd used his time wisely while she'd spent the night avoiding him from the other side of the bar. Although he might not have won over her brothers entirely, they'd at least stopped full-out threatening him. He considered that a big step. But playing the cleavage card while Tommy and Seamus were right here…?

Careful to keep his eyes on the table, Nate lined up the cue ball and the eleven. "You do realize that half the games I play involve thirty thousand people threatening to kill me." He pulled the cue stick back carefully, then, with a smile thrown in her direction, knocked the eleven in. Straightening up, he grabbed the chalk again. "If you're trying to distract me, it's not going to work."

She came around to where he was standing—came to stand directly in front of him and looked up at him from under those lashes of hers. Her hand went to his chest. Began to trail downward. "That's not what you said on the plane."

Nate had barely managed to grab Dorie's wrist when Tommy snapped, "No," as he practically spun Sophie into a topspin in order to get right up in Dorie's face. "None of…" He waved his hand from Dorie to Nate and back again. "*This*. Not in my place."

"'This'?" Dorie mimicked. "Are we back in medieval times, my lord?" She yanked her hand away from Nate, elbowed Tommy out of the way and then, without even taking two seconds to line up the shot, knocked in the ten and fourteen balls. "Should I clear off the table for you and Sophie and then just go back to my corner, *sir*?" There went the thirteen, then the twelve.

Nate raised his eyebrows. Seamus, laughing, shook his head. At which point Dorie turned on him. "And *you*..." The nine went in, then the five. "A different woman every time I turn around. You're worse than *him*."

"Me?" Nate said belatedly. Uh, hold on... "I haven't..."

The rest of the balls went in. She didn't hesitate, didn't miss one. The one, four, two, and then the eight. Then she shoved the cue stick at Tommy. "So if I want *this*?" Just like Tommy had, she waved her hand toward Nate and then to herself again. "Even if it makes no sense in the world that he seems to want it, too?" She took hold of Nate's waistband and yanked him toward her so hard that he almost lost his balance. But the pool table was there, and although his hip slamming against it was the only way for them to remain upright, he honestly didn't give a damn. She was beyond hot when she was pissed.

She clamped her hands around the back of his neck and drew his head down, obviously still making her point to Tommy. "Then I'm going to do whatever the hell I want to." She raked her hands through Nate's hair, pulling him down the rest of the way as her lips touched his. It took everything he had not to throw her down on the pool table she'd just so handily cleared. Especially when, breathing raggedly, she pressed herself up against him, making no effort to hide her sigh as she felt him hard against her.

She hitched herself up on the edge of the pool table and curled into him. "I'm sorry," she said, dragging her hand down to his waistband. "But my brothers are going to kill you in the morning."

So, yes, that apparently was her intention after all. Which was fine with Nate. If she didn't want to play nice, there was no reason he had to.

Resting his hands on her hips, Nate shifted just enough to show that he'd registered every move Tommy had made since the moment Dorie had put her hands on him. Looking into Dorie's eyes, he had to admit, he was also maybe searching for signs that she was drunk. Still, he smiled. "I can handle your brothers."

He felt the step forward that Tommy made. Fixed his gaze on Tommy while slightly turning his head. If Tommy was seriously going to make a thing of this, then Nate was ready to respond in kind. He had no idea what Dorie was up to and no interest whatsoever in a bar fight with Dorie's brothers but he'd do whatever was necessary.

Sophie was having none of it. She grabbed Tommy by the shoulder. "For Christ's sake, Tom. Quit being a Neanderthal. A juvenile *idiot* Neanderthal."

Seemed kind of redundant to Nate, but no need to fan the flames.

Stepping between Tommy and Nate, Sophie reached around to touch Dorie's knee. "Good for you, hon. It's about freaking time." Then, like Claudia had done with Claire—except for the force involved—she spun Tommy around and pointed him toward the door. "You want to get all riled up, you work it out with me."

With one last glare at Nate, Tommy put his arm around Sophie's shoulders. "Hurt her and I'll kill you. Don't think I won't."

Well, at least it wasn't anything about Nate's balls. He hid his smile and nodded. "Understood."

The second they left, Seamus shook his head as he hung up his cue stick. "What the hell, Luce?"

"Just tired of the double standard, Shay." Dorie jumped off the table and out of Nate's arms, pouting.

"Tired of watching him and Soph go off together while I'm stuck here cleaning up the place." Although the weariness in her voice made clear how true that statement was, the kick she gave the pool table was hard enough for Seamus to wince and glance down to check for damage. "Tired of watching all of you pair off, leaving me to fly solo."

That last part sounded sad enough that Seamus's head came up sharply. When he looked over and realized Nate was well aware of the undercurrents, he stuck his hands in his pockets and looked down. "Yeah. We've never made it easy for you, have we?"

Folding her arms across her chest, Dorie ducked her head down, trying—and failing—to not let on that she was crying.

"Well, *fuck*," Seamus said, looking up again after a minute. "I guess you really did need to move all the way out to Kansas, didn't you?"

Dorie's head snapped up. "*Iowa.*"

"Iowa," Seamus repeated with a grin that made clear he knew exactly where she'd moved. "Right." Now it was his turn to fold his arms in front of him. "Fine. Go have some fun with pretty boy, here." With a nod in Nate's direction, he reached out for Dorie and pulled her into a hug that seemed to affect him as much as it did Dorie, although he gave Nate a don't-you-dare-ever-tell-her-as-much glare. "And don't pick fights with Tommy, okay? He's still bigger than you."

"I can kick better," she mumbled.

Seamus's response to that was a noogie.

With an elbow to his gut, Dorie said, "You did not just do that to me in front of Nate."

Not bothering to respond, Seamus turned to Nate. He

reached out to shake hands and then pulled Nate toward him. Just close enough to be heard when he quietly said, "I don't care how blue your balls are. If you think that stunt she just pulled gives you license to…"

Nate pulled back. "Are you seriously giving me the 'no means no' talk?"

With a pat on the back and friendly-as-can-be grin, Seamus turned to Dorie, who obviously had been straining to hear whatever it was Seamus was saying to Nate, and gave her a big hug. "Love you, Luce." Then he walked away.

Now it was Dorie's turn to put her hands in her pockets. She looked down at the floor. "Sorry, I'm not… I don't…." She wiped her eye with her sleeve. "I didn't mean to throw you under the bus."

Leaning back against the pool table, Nate just looked at her. "You sure about that?"

If it wasn't for her tearstained face, he might have made a bigger deal about it. He didn't get off on being used—well, not in the overall scheme of things—even if it was just to make a point, and their nonconversation on the plane had left him unsettled. But he could see how badly she'd needed that. How she was flailing about and grabbing at the only thing steady enough to hold, even if a part of that meant deliberately trying to push him away.

But if she finally came around to where he was? "You can try to throw me all you want, Dorie. I'm not going anywhere."

"Don't go making any promises you can't keep." She sniffled. "You haven't actually seen the shrine yet. It'll have you running in no time."

Yep, she was going all in. And he wasn't about to let her.

"Hmm," he said, taking her into his arms. "When I think shrine, I think worship. Like on your knees and all that. Last thing I want to do is run."

He felt her huff against his chest, part laugh, part cry. But then she gave a halfhearted shrug as she pulled away. He kissed the top of her head, and then walked her out the door and took her home.

Chapter Twenty-Six

Dorie woke with a start, sitting up straight in the moon-lit room. It took her a few seconds to remember where she was: back in Iowa. In her bed, with Nate.

He lifted up his head and gave a sleepy, "Hey." Threading his hand through the strand of hair that brushed her shoulder, he asked, "You okay?"

Okay?

No. Not even close. She felt like she was headed down a mountain in a car with no brakes and no steering.

"You weren't supposed to make them love you," she said, quietly enough that she wasn't sure if he heard it. Wasn't sure she wanted him to.

From the way he went still against her, it was clear that he had. "I'm pretty sure Tommy would argue that I was in any way effective," he tried to joke.

But she could hear the strain in his voice; could hear that he knew it wasn't a joke for her.

"Is that your plan?" she asked, emotions all tangled up inside and yet still unable to keep from running her hand down his chest. "Whisk me away on a private plane so I'll forget that this is only short-ter—"

"Don't you get it by now?" he said, gripping her wrist. "This isn't short-term, not for me."

"But it is for me," she answered, even though her heart was tearing in two. Slowly, painfully, no matter how much she'd tried to keep it whole. "It has to be. Except now you've won them over—the one man in the history of the world to do that, by the way—and they won't understand why I let you go."

"They're not exactly my concern at the moment." It was obvious that he was angry. His pulse was beating wildly against her even as he quietly added, "So maybe you could explain it to me instead."

She wished she could. She wished it more than anything. Because as she let herself inhale his warm, masculine scent—let herself appreciate the hard and lean muscles as she edged her leg over his—the thought of never seeing him again almost killed her.

But giving in to this? Giving in to him and then having him walk away in the end?

It wasn't happening. It was her car, damn it, and she was getting those brakes fixed ASAP.

"Tell me what you need," he said gruffly, as close to pleading as a man like him got. And the tear went deeper.

She rested her head against his chest; burrowed into the hollow of his neck.

She wanted him like this. The two of them alone in the dark without anything else to stand in the way.

But what did she need to be able to believe?

"I don't know," she answered, even though with everything in her heart she wished she did.

The next day dawned crisp and clear. Dorie was up with the sun, completely unable to sleep. She rolled out of bed quietly, careful not to wake Nate.

She threw on her running gear, laced up her shoes and then was out the door. Even at this early hour in the middle of February, there were signs of life everywhere. The doors were already open at Jules's café and the gas station on the edge of the town center was doing a booming business of trucks from surrounding farms. Everyone she saw waved and smiled, some even calling out her name.

For the first time since arriving in Inspiration, Dorie felt, well, not that she actually belonged, but that she might someday, and not just as a roadside attraction. Plus Fitz and Wash were going out of their way to make her feel at home. Sometimes, she thought, in spite of her relationship—*fling*—with Nate. Not that they didn't approve; it was more like they were looking out for her. Making sure that no matter what happened she had a place to land. Which was good because she was going to need it. Tonight was the reopening ceremony, which meant that the thirteenth was the day after tomorrow.

She stopped running when the air abruptly left her lungs. Bent over as the pain shot through her and she tried to catch her breath.

Two days.

This would all be over in two days.

No. She could *not* be upset about this. How could she look at something this incredible as anything other than a gift? She'd always cherish the memories of this time with him: the night he'd shown up at her door to cook her dinner. The trip to Chicago...

The way he looked at her every single moment they were together. That alone might sustain her for the rest of her life.

So, no. *No.* She wasn't going to be sad about this.

Not. Sad. And she was going to turn her butt around and get back to him.

She could hear the shower running when she opened the front door. With a smile, she slipped off her jacket and toed off her shoes, then headed down the hall. The bathroom door was open a few inches; she eased it the rest of the way. The shower curtain wasn't all the way closed, either, and she had to admit, his reflection gave her pause. His hands were flat against the wall in front of him, his head hung down directly beneath the showerhead, the water flowing down over his shoulders and back. If he hadn't looked so tired—no, *weary*—she might have feasted a little bit more on the eye candy.

Well, okay, she did feast a little bit. Who could blame her? The absolute perfection of the man's body still got to her every time.

She stripped off the rest of her clothes and quietly stepped into the shower behind him, her hands wrapping around his hips just as he looked over his shoulder and smiled. "Hey. I thought you went to work."

Touching her lips to his shoulder blade, she murmured, "Couldn't sleep. Went out for a run."

His muscles tensed under her tongue as she licked the water away. "You didn't want company," he said, a statement rather than a question. And the second his eyes met hers she looked away. If she gave him an explanation, he'd take it wrong.

He gripped her chin and turned her head so she was looking up at him. Staring down into her eyes it looked like he was going to say something, but instead he... God, she couldn't even call it a kiss. His tongue swept through her mouth and the intensity of it sent her reeling. She fell back against the wall, flattening her hands against the cold tile behind her. Her eyes went wide as he pulled away. "Nate…"

But he bent down to kiss her again, cutting her off. Then he was lifting her, holding her high enough for her to be looking down at him, her arms resting on his shoulders. His mouth went to her breast, his tongue lapping at her nipple before he gently bit down. When he wrapped her legs around his waist, she pushed up against him and moaned. She was already wet when he eased inside her, slowly at first, then roughly enough for her to cry out.

"Too much?" he said into her neck, his teeth scraping at her skin as he pulled out.

"God, no," she gasped, holding his head against her as he pushed back inside of her. Tilting her hips just enough for him to… "Oh, *God*." Her head fell back as he thrust again, spreading her, spearing her. A tremble ran through her as every nerve ending stood on edge.

How could she tell him that she wasn't ready to let him go? That she wasn't sure she'd ever be?

"Dorie…"

She gave herself over to him entirely, his hands guiding her, playing her, sliding up and over her hips, up her sides, over her breasts until they came to a rest where they'd started, cupping her face. She opened her eyes to find him watching her. Everything stopped as he held her gaze… Until his eyes closed, and his head dropped down, and he sent her flying. Everything burst around her, her body coming to a shuddering stop just as his arm shot out to the wall to brace himself and he groaned his own release.

He rested his forehead against hers for a minute, not saying anything. And she was incapable of speaking after he eased her down to stand on her own and then wordlessly stepped out of the shower. Closing her eyes, she turned her face to the water, knowing that if she gave in and said the word, he would—

"Dorie?" he said, his voice hoarse, and she realized how badly she wanted to hear the words. How much she needed to hear him tell her he loved her so much that it was somehow all going to all work out, even though that made no sense whatsoever.

The shower curtain swept open and, heart in her throat, she looked into his eyes.

Except what he said was, "Mark just called. He got me on a radio show in fifteen minutes, and then I'm having coffee with Fitz. I'll meet you at the library at ten." Then he leaned in and gave her a quick kiss on the forehead.

Um...

"Okay," she said to the shower curtain as he closed it. "I guess I'll see you then."

Chapter Twenty-Seven

Nate had woken up that morning knowing he needed a plan—especially given what she'd said in the middle of the night. It had gotten to him, he had to admit: she was possibly the one woman in the world who not only didn't want any of the things he could give her but actually held them against him.

Yeah, the Boston trip had backfired all right, although not just in the ways Nate had considered. He'd wanted to show Dorie that he could handle her family, that he could give her things no one else could. What he hadn't anticipated was how much deeper *he'd* fall. Because the truth was, he'd loved that they couldn't have cared less who he was. Loved that it hadn't given him an automatic pass, but instead was as much of a strike against him for them as it was for Dorie. Loved that Dorie gave it right back to them, teasing and goading them instead until they'd completely forgotten about whatever plans they had to test Nate, and were back to teasing her. It was quite the cycle.

He loved it so much, in fact, that he'd even spent an afternoon helping Sean hang cabinets in his kitchen. Which in itself had been fine—in the big-brother-interrogating-the-man-sleeping-with-his-sister way, of course—right up until the moment when Sean had said, "She's been in love with you since she was thirteen. Every asshole from here to Cape Cod fell in love with her but the only one she ever had eyes for was you. Which worked at the time."

Nate had been thinking that, yes, he was trying to make it work for him now, too, when Sean had gone on to say, "My *point* is that she's never been in love before. Not for real."

And it had struck Nate that maybe the real issue was that, beyond her slipup that day in Chicago, Dorie had never even come close to indicating that she was, actually, in love with him. The real him, as Sean had so helpfully pointed out.

But as Yogi had said, it ain't over 'til it's over. Dorie wanted him just as much as he wanted her—he believed that a hundred percent. She just couldn't get her thoughts around the logistics of it all. And as he'd gotten into the shower that morning, he'd decided that he wasn't going to make it easy for her to walk away. Not that he was going to pressure her into something she didn't want; he was just going to show her that he wasn't going anywhere. Not for good, at least. Pitchers and catchers, yes. Obviously. But he had every intention of coming back.

Then she'd been there with him, a vision he hadn't been entirely sure he hadn't conjured up just from pure desire. Of course then she'd told him she'd gone out for a run alone and it was clear it wasn't a vision at all. If it had been, then she wouldn't still be running away from him—literally—whenever he got too close. So he was pretending that it hadn't bugged the shit out of him. That it was just like any other day in the world rather than two days before what she'd decided was The End.

And here they were at the library where she was buzz-
ing around making last-minute adjustments—straightening a picture here, plucking a book off the shelf and
displaying it on the table there—as the clock counted
down to four thirty. At the moment, she was biting into
one of Jules's chocolate-covered strawberries, laughing
as the chocolate broke apart into pieces that she lightly
brushed off her sweater where it hugged the curve of
her breast.

"Oh, my God," she said to Jules, closing her eyes
as she licked the strawberry's juice from her lips. And
then she had to go and add, "That's orgasmically good."

"Mmm," Jules murmured, the sparkle in her eye well
known to Nate as an indication of nothing good. "Speaking of orgasms, when are you going to—"

Oh, shit, no.

"Where do you want these tables?" Nate asked loudly
as he came all the way into the room. The last thing
he needed right now was for Jules to decide that if she
couldn't fix her own happily-ever-after she'd work on
Nate's instead.

Blushing furiously, Dorie gratefully answered, "Right
over there. Let me help you." Before he could stop her,
Dorie lifted up one of the six-foot tables folded up
against the wall and hoisted it over her head.

With a glare thrown back over his shoulder at Jules,
Nate went after Dorie. "*Help*," he stressed, reaching over
her and taking it out of her hands. "The intention being
that two people are involved."

"And yet here you are, going all he-man on me." She
folded her arms in front of her chest, a hint of a smile
in her eyes. "So what's my part in this?"

"You tell me where to put it."

"I'm sorry, but that's just too easy." The smile broke out into a full-out grin. "You know exactly where I want you to put it."

Hell, yes, that was too easy. He put the table down on its edge, using it as a screen as he backed her up into the wall. Pressing up against her, he bent down and nuzzled her ear in the way that made her curl up into him. "Don't tempt me, woman." It made her giggle, too.

He loved it when she giggled.

She nudged him away with her knee even as she pulled his head over to kiss him square on the lips. A playful nip that turned into something a whole lot deeper when she tilted her head just so. Still holding the table upright with one hand, he used the other to draw her knee up and wrap her leg around him.

"Mr. Hawkins, this is not proper behavior for the library." She ran the tip of her finger down his chest, coming to a stop at his waistband, a mere inch away from his dick.

"You're right," he said, unable to keep the huskiness out of his voice as he ran his hand up underneath her skirt, right up to where he was cupping the curve of her sweet ass. "But just the other week the librarian was a whole lot friendlier."

Her chest heaved as she took in a deep breath of air, and then she closed her eyes and grasped his shirt in both hands. With one hard yank, her mouth was on him, her tongue claiming his. Her kiss was as hard and hungry as his was, and when she finally tore her head away, they were both breathless.

After a minute she put her finger to his lips. "Hold that thought." Then she slipped out from under his arms and, smoothing down her skirt, walked away.

Shit. Nate let his head clunk against the wall. When he finally managed to get his bearings again, he pulled away the table to see that, not only was Jules still standing there, she'd been joined by Fitz and Wash. And now all three of them were just staring at him.

"Not a word," he snapped. He wasn't out of the woods yet. He'd done everything he could possibly think of and yet he wasn't out of the goddamn woods. He *had* to get her to talk to him tonight. If he had to tie her down to make her listen to him, he would.

Although, to be honest, that sounded good regardless of the circumstances.

The night was spectacular. *She* was spectacular. She welcomed everyone as if they were an old friend, even those she hadn't yet met. Every child who walked in got a hug or a high five, and every family got handed a big shiny Mylar balloon. "The other kind isn't safe for the littlest ones," she'd said, shrugging. "And I got a good deal on the framing; I had money left over."

"Bet you've never had a girlfriend who bargain-shopped," Jason had teased after that.

He still didn't, unfortunately. Not by a long shot. But Nate just smiled as if he was entirely okay with the state of their relationship.

Though Nate couldn't honestly say he'd spent much time in this building up until these past few weeks, even he could tell that what she'd done was transformative. Everything looked like the balloons: big and shiny and new. But at the same time, the rooms were as solid as they'd always been. As though the building itself knew that it was one of the few that had been there from the founding of the town itself. One of the beacons of hope that had remained standing while over half of the rest of the town lay in shambles around it.

And seeing everyone come out reminded Nate of how much he loved Inspiration. Not just because it was one of the few places on earth where no one really cared who he was—as long as he kept bringing in bags of ice and unloading trays of food for Jules, at least. It was more that everyone showed up. That everyone wanted to be there—wanted this to be a success, whether it was the basketball team or the reopening of the library.

There was the sound of someone clinking on a glass and Nate, along with everyone else in the room, turned to see Fitz standing on the newly polished and gleaming circulation desk. Once she had everyone's attention, she jumped down to the floor.

"Thanks, everyone, for coming tonight. In a few minutes you're going to hear from our newest addition to Inspiration. But before we introduce her, Mama Gin would like to say a few words."

Nate leaned back against the wall, unable to take his eyes away from Dorie.

From the other side of Wash, Deke laughed softly. "So is this just a temporary thing, or do we make sure everyone else is hands-off even after you're down in Mesa with all your groupies?"

"*Boys*," Mrs. Bellevue hissed.

"Sorry, Mrs. Bellevue," they all chorused.

Nate was actually more than happy to be scolded into silence. He knew what his answer to that question was, but he still wasn't sure that Dorie agreed. And anyway, his mom was talking.

"…tonight. Before she begins, however, I wanted to…"

There was a rustle in the crowd behind Nate as people parted to make way for a new group of arrivals. For some reason, this group had attracted more attention than usual and even his mother looked up. From where Nate was standing he couldn't see who it was, but a look of surprise came into Dorie's eyes, and then a radiant smile over her face as she blinked as though she couldn't believe what she was seeing. Then she whispered something to Fitz who, in turn, said something into his mom's ear.

Curious, Nate leaned forward in order to see who the new arrivals were: Claudia, Christopher, Seamus and Mrs. Donelli.

Well...*shit*.

The irony of it was almost enough to bring a smile to his face. *Almost.* They were here because of him. Because he'd told them about tonight when they'd been in Boston—Dorie hadn't, as crazy as that had seemed to him. But he'd known how important it was to Dorie and he'd done everything possible to make sure her family knew it, too.

But their being here meant that he wouldn't have this one last night with Dorie. This one last night to make his point—thoroughly—that this didn't have to end.

Jamming his hands in his pockets, Nate was glad as hell he'd spent years perfecting his game face.

"I understand that some of Dorie's family members have just arrived from Boston," his mother was saying with a smile. "Welcome. I'm so pleased that you've joined us." Taking in the rest of the crowd, she continued, "As you all know, the library has unfortunately fallen into a bit of disrepair over the past few years. For a place that means as much as it does to us, we just haven't been able to give it the love it deserves. And when Aunt

Laura came to me and said that we'd need to shake things up a little, my original idea was that we might have to look as far as Ames, maybe even Des Moines." There was a ripple of laughter. "Imagine our surprise when this came in the mail." She held up a piece of paper and then turned to Dorie and smiled. "Yes, dear, I'm afraid I'm about to embarrass you a little bit."

Leaning back against the wall, Nate could see the deep breath Dorie took in before throwing an apologetic glance his way. That was interesting. Brave, actually, especially as she probably had no idea that his mother would never do anything of the embarrassing sort. Still, Dorie straightened her shoulders and glared at him when he smiled and turned his full attention to what his mother was saying.

"'Your community has meant so much to so many people,'" his mother began reading. "'I can't even begin to explain what it meant to us halfway across the country watching five boys our own age take hold of a nation. Through teamwork and dedication and plain old hard work, they ignited a fire inside of us—inside of a thirteen-year-old *me*—and showed us that even if everything you'd known lay in ruins around you, or if you'd never quite built up anything beyond that foundation to begin with, that it didn't matter.'"

Nate could feel Wash shifting uncomfortably next to him. It was always odd to hear about those years from someone else's perspective, even when they had something nice to say. But hearing Dorie's words from months ago—from before they'd met—just made it sink in even further. She got that it was about the five of them, about what they'd done *together*. About taking that fire and making it work for you. For something good. Which may have been why the only thing that had bothered him about that shrine of hers was how many pictures of Deke had been included in it. There was something about her that ran deeper; he might not have been able to put words to it so quickly, but he'd known it from practically the moment he saw her. Once she'd put some clothes on, at least.

"'Because a dream doesn't need walls or a pretty coat of paint. It needs the barest of foundations, a friend (or four), and a spark just strong enough to ignite the flame.'" His mother looked up, gave Nate a hard stare for whatever reason, then smiled as she started reading again. "'I know that most people wouldn't compare the story of The Iowa Dream to a now thirty-year-old girl's love of libraries. But I'm not most people. If it was The Dream that ignited the fire inside of me, it was my library that fanned the flames. The stories there showed me how to lay that foundation and how to build those walls. The stories there inspired me, and it's where I learned to dream.'"

Another look as his mother flipped over the page before continuing, "'I realize that you may not have expected any applications from Boston, and I'm sorry to say that, despite my affinity for all members of The Dream, I am—and always will be—a Red Sox fan through and through.'"

That statement got some loud laughs, and there was more than one person who turned back to look at Nate. "Sorry, buddy," one guy called out. "You can't get all the girls," said another.

Right. Hell. It took everything Nate had to give the easy smile that was expected when all he really wanted to do was pick Dorie up and carry her out of there. He wrapped his arms around his chest and jammed his hands into his armpits so hard it actually hurt. Wash looked at him curiously; Nate didn't look back.

He did look directly at his mother who could, unfortunately, read every emotion playing over his face. Having been the mayor for thirteen years, she took it in and moved on. "'But I've been carrying a piece of your town inside me for so long that it already feels like home.'"

His mother folded up the paper, her eyes surveying the crowd as she gave a knowing smile. "It's hard for us to let someone in from the outside. I know that's not something we generally say out loud. I certainly don't." She laughed along with everyone else. "But we've all been through a lot together. Some horrendously awful times followed by some truly wonderful ones." With tears in her eyes, she looked over at Nate, her gaze taking in Wash, Deke and Jason next to him, before turning her attention back to the crowd.

"You know, when Nate decided to move forward with baseball, I asked him why he chose that over basketball as so many of us had expected."

And now it was Nate's turn to be surprised. Though he knew exactly what conversation she was talking about, he wasn't entirely sure what it had to do with tonight.

"What he told me has stayed with me since then." Her smile grew warmer. "He said that playing basketball could never be as good as it was when he was playing it with Wash, Deke, Jason and Cal. That it could never be as good as it was when he played it *here*, with us. Because they were his brothers; because we are his family. And because he couldn't imagine anyone ever understanding that what happened here had nothing to do with a game. That it truly *was* a dream."

This time Wash didn't just shift beside him, the man actually straightened up and whipped his head around as he muttered, "You never told me that." Deke and Jason seemed equally stunned, which Nate supposed shouldn't come as a surprise. His mother was the only person he'd ever given a straight answer to for that question because she, unlike the rest of the world, had actually wanted to understand rather than talk him out of it as if he was about to make the biggest mistake of his life.

As if.

By the ripe old age of twenty-one, he'd already watched his house blow down around him as he huddled in the basement with Ella and Wash. As he'd spent that harrowing hour praying everyone else he loved was okay.

He'd learned the truth about his father, whom he'd thought was long gone, only to find that the man had been living three towns over with his replacement wife and daughter.

He'd struggled with the idea of Fitz and with his own reaction to her; had somehow made it to the other side of that, finally becoming the brother she deserved.

And when the scouts came calling and the offers had been made, he knew that the only thing that had kept him going through that horrific time had been his family and friends. The idea of playing basketball without his brothers—with Wash on an opposing team—hadn't appealed even a little bit. So he'd gone the baseball route. He'd been handed more money than he'd ever seen—and that was after the Iowa Dream book and movie deals—to hit a ball with a stick and make a career out of it.

Choosing baseball over basketball was the biggest mistake he'd ever made?

It was laughable. With a shrug, Nate turned to Wash. The truth of the matter was, "You never asked."

After a few seconds Wash just smiled. "It was magic, my brother. You don't talk about that kind of shit or else it goes away."

That made Nate laugh and shake his head. Magic. This was starting to sound like a Jules conversation. "Yeah."

Placing the folded-up piece of paper in her pocket, his mother took off her reading glasses. This time she directed her smile at Dorie. "The first time I read what Dorie wrote I was reminded of that conversation with Nate all those years ago. To be honest, it's the first time anyone from the outside has ever come close to capturing what those of us who have been through it all together know to be true. But not only did she capture it with what she wrote, tonight she's truly captured it in spirit."

She turned back to the crowd and gestured to the oversize photographs hanging on the walls around them. "When I walked in and saw these pictures I was also reminded that, for too long, now, we've defined ourselves by what happened seventeen years ago, both the bad and the good. Although anyone who was at the high school watching the boys play a couple of weeks ago doesn't need to reach for a distant memory to bring back the good, if you happened to have been at Deacon's later that night to watch our newest citizen run them to the *ground*—" She gave a wicked grin as everyone laughed, the "boys" standing next to Nate included, "Then I'm sure you'll agree that we have more good things ahead of us. It's time to start dreaming again."

There was a moment of silence as her words were absorbed. And then the entire room burst into applause as Fitz nudged Dorie forward, right up to where his mother was standing and saying, "And since she's proven so well that she's not an outsider so much as one of our own who just happened to have been born and raised halfway across the country, we have a small token of our affection." At her nod, Tuck came forward and held up an Inspiration High basketball jersey for everyone to see. Although the applause grew even louder, it was clear that Dorie had no idea why until he turned and showed her the name on the back: Donelli.

"Wear it proudly, Dorie," his mother said. "No matter where you go from here, you're one of us."

It wasn't until that moment that Nate turned back to look at Dorie and realized she had tears running down her face; hell if his own cheeks weren't a little wet. As the applause became deafening as the crowd signaled its approval, Fitz nudged her the rest of the way forward, right up to the front.

Dorie's hands shook a little as she took the jersey from Tuck and stared down at it. She looked up at where her family was standing, no doubt beaming with pride. Her gaze turned to Ella and Jules, both of whom were shouting her name and yelling over the rest of the crowd, then to Wash and Deke and Jason, all roaring their approval. She was getting the Inspiration home crowd welcome. Nothing like it on earth.

Then her eyes connected with Nate's and it was like everything else faded away. She seemed so small and vulnerable while, somehow at the same time, fierce and strong and larger-than-life. As though she'd found her rightful place without even realizing it and was there to claim it, not about to let anything stand in her way. She was the most beautiful woman Nate had ever seen. She was the one. There would never be anyone else for him.

Except then her eyes clouded over and she looked down, and, right there in that moment, he knew that she was done, that he'd gone down swinging. No matter how hard he'd tried to convince her otherwise, tonight she'd be telling him goodbye.

She wiped the tears away from her face and looked up again, this time careful not to look his way. As she appeared to be realizing at the same time Nate was, the noise had died down and everyone was waiting expectantly for her to give some kind of response.

"I, um…" She shook her head as though she was shaking out cobwebs. With a self-conscious smile, she said, "Mama Gin, I'm sorry to break this to you, but that wasn't just a few words."

That got the biggest laugh of the night so far, although her cheeks flushed enough for Nate to be pretty sure she hadn't intended it as a joke at all. And other than her, there were only two other people not laughing—Nate, because hearing the words *Mama Gin* come out of her mouth had just cut him to the quick, and his mother, who hadn't been offended by any means, but who had looked up at Nate. He saw on her face the moment the final pieces fell into place as she figured it out.

He'd avoided this conversation for weeks, having already invested too much into what he'd hoped was happening but not wanting to speak the words out loud. And now, here it was crashing and burning, and he was going to have to have it anyway. Absolutely fucking perfect.

Unaware of what was happening between Nate and

his mother, Dorie shook her head again. "Sorry. I'm… I'm honored. Thank you. I don't know what to say."

"That's a first, Luce," Seamus yelled out, which got another laugh from the crowd.

With a glare at him, Dorie looked down at the jersey, her eyes sadder than anything he'd ever seen.

And it pissed Nate off. There was no reason she should be sad. No reason at all. She was the one who'd set a deadline, right? She was the one who had gotten everything she'd wanted. And the worst part was? She'd been entirely up-front that what she wanted wasn't him.

Clearly working hard at fighting off a new rush of tears, Dorie squeezed her eyes shut for a moment. Then she opened them up and pasted a huge smile on her face. "In that case, then, come dream with me. We have a lot more stories to write togeth—" She cut herself off as emotion took over her voice. Biting her lip again, she took a deep breath in through her nose and then exhaled. "Together."

Chapter Twenty-Eight

Dorie smiled and hugged her way through the next few hours, so close to a breakdown that she didn't allow herself to stop moving for even just a second. But the feeling of emptiness grew inside her, seeping through her veins and clawing at her gut.

She watched as Seamus and Christopher greeted Nate as an old friend. By the end of the night, in fact, when just about everyone else had gone home, it was as though his family—Wash, Deke, Jason and Tuck included, of course—and her family had been friends forever.

She had put up her boundaries order to protect herself from this very thing, yet her family had slipped into his world as easily as she had. She was overwhelmed with emotion, not sure if she was angry—at him? At herself?—or just sad. Bone-deep sad. It was killing her.

This day—no, these entire three weeks—had been magic. But it had worked because they didn't need to fit their lives together, diamond-encrusted square pegs into your run-of-the-mill holes. Here, in their little honeymoon period of infatuation, they were great. The second it moved into long-term, though... They just didn't mix.

Why was it that he refused to see that?

"Dorie," Mayor Gin said when Dorie returned from

escorting the last of the guests out the door, "you've done an amazing job tonight. Why don't you leave the rest of the cleanup to us so you can spend some time with your visitors?"

She shook her head. "I should be saying the same to you. And Mr. and Mrs. Grimes, you've put in way too much time today—you should be the ones going home. I can finish this up on my own."

Meaning with Nate, of course. She needed to see this through. Needed to get it over with before she gave in to the fantasy and gave up everything else.

"That's crazy," Fitz said. "With all of us here, this will be done in no time."

Which it was. All too soon, everything was cleaned up, packed away, all ready to greet the crowds Dorie hoped to see the next day.

"So, honey," her mom said as she was getting on her coat. "Point us to the closest motel and we'll see you as soon as you open up in the morning."

"You don't have rooms reserved?" Jules asked sharply, though not unkindly. "There's a big basketball game in Ames tonight. I'm sorry to say, there probably isn't a room around for miles."

As everyone was bending over backward to offer her family a place to stay, Dorie brushed aside her sinking feeling and said, "Don't be ridiculous. Mom and Claudia can stay in my bed. Shay, Christopher and I can camp out in the living room just like old times." Though she deliberately didn't look at Nate, she could feel tension running through him.

Or maybe she was imagining it. When he spoke from beside her, his voice was as easy and friendly as always.

"My car's right outside. Between Wash and me, we can get you all over there with no problem."

Good-nights were said, hugs and smiles were given, and before she knew it, Dorie was sitting next to Claudia in the backseat of the car while Nate gave her mother the history of just about every building they passed. It was all too much. Dorie avoided Claudia's questioning look and stared out the window instead.

Thank God Wash was there, too, because focusing on him was the only way she could get through getting her family into her apartment and settled. And when he looked from her to Nate, saying that it was time for him to head back home, Dorie gratefully followed him out the door and closed it quickly behind her so that she didn't have to hear Nate say goodbye.

"Nice job, librarian," he said with a smile. "Best thing we've done in years was to steal you away from Boston."

Considering that was one of the nicest things anyone had ever said to her, the proper thing was most definitely *not* to burst into tears. But that's exactly what she did, which prompted him to pull her into a hug. "It's okay, D. Whatever it is, it'll be okay. You just call us and—"

She felt him stiffen before she heard the click of the door as, presumably, Nate came out into the hallway and closed it behind him.

Wash pulled her in tighter. "Just call us. We're here for you."

Although she kept her back to Nate as Wash went to him, she heard him clap Nate on the back and tell him, "Same with you, my friend. Don't be a stranger."

"I don't intend to be," Nate said, his voice echoing in Dorie's ears. Because of course he wouldn't. She'd seen him rebuild the bond with his friends and family over the past few weeks. She couldn't imagine anything would keep him away. Seeing him when he could make it back in town was just something she was going to have to live with.

Live without.

She waited until Wash was down the stairs and the door to outside had been opened and closed before turning to Nate. And it was time.

Arms tightly around herself, she said, "Please don't make this harder than it needs to be."

"Than it *needs* to be?" He shook his head and leaned back against the railing to the stairs, carefully keeping his distance even as he said, "I want to be with you. You want to be with me. How could that possibly be a bad thing?"

"Because it's not *real*." Her voice went shrill—she felt a bit light-headed—as though something had possessed her in order to make sure she said the words out loud.

Why was he pushing this? Why couldn't he just do what every other man in the world would do, especially the billionaire, superstar ones: take the gift she was handing him and walk away? She was trying to be reasonable here. One of them had to be.

She had to sniffle back what was threatening to come out as huge, messy sob. "This was a dream. That's what this is. That's all it can ever be."

There was a heavy silence before he responded.

And when he did, he was *pissed.* She took a step back as he pushed away from the railing. "That's bullshit," he said, his voice laced with rage. "How can you stand here and tell me this isn't real?"

Her heart tearing open, she tried desperately to keep

the tears at bay. "It was supposed to be short-term!" she shouted. "Only about the sex!"

"It doesn't work that way!" he yelled right back. Then he took a few steps away from her, clearly attempting to calm down. "I'm in love with you, Dorie. *In.*

Love. I've never felt anything like this before and I'm a hundred percent certain you feel the same way."

Hearing him say the words—actually come out and tell her—was exactly as powerful as she'd known it would be. And it slayed her. Her chest went tight and she couldn't breathe, especially because he was right. She did feel that. She was head over heels.

"I *have* felt this way before. That's the problem," she cried, the anger and frustration spilling over. "I've been in love with Nate Hawkins for nearly my entire life. And then… And then you come along and you're *perfect*. Like I dreamed it up and there you were. And it's sucking me in, the thought that *you* could actually be in love with *me*. But then the season will start and…"

She could picture it clear as day. He'd want her to come and be with him, but she had her life here so she'd eventually start telling him no. And sooner or later— most likely sooner—he'd realize it wasn't worth it. *She* wasn't worth it.

And that would destroy her.

"We've known each other for three weeks," she said, the tears raining down. She had no way of stopping them. "You can't change your entire life for someone you've only known for three weeks."

"Yes. I can," he said, strident in his clearly delusional belief. "I *do* know you, Dorie. And I know I can make you happy."

"The way you made Courtney happy?" she spat out.

His head jerked back as though he'd been slapped.

Oh, God. She had *not* just said that.

"See?" she mumbled, hating herself for the words that had come out of her mouth. "That's a Week Four Fun Fact. I say awful things."

To no one's surprise, he didn't smile. She looked down at the floor.

But she couldn't deny that the words had some truth, that it was her greatest fear. If one of the most perfect women in the world—okay, kind of bitchy, but still—hadn't been able to survive a relationship with him, then Dorie didn't stand a chance in hell.

Not that it mattered. She'd severed the cord. Not the way she'd intended, but what she'd done nevertheless.

"So that's it, then," he said, his eyes full of ice, body rigid. "Pitchers and catchers report the day after tomorrow. Everything's all wrapped up in that pretty little bow, just like you wanted."

Dorie wrapped her arms around herself. "Nate…"

"What, Dorie?" he snapped. "Are you going to tell me again that I don't know what I feel? That, whoops, thank *fuck* you told me this isn't real because now I can go jump back into bed with Courtney? Play poker and smoke cigars with my friends?"

Well, yes. Ultimately. But she wasn't going to say that. She dropped her gaze as he pulled his jacket around him, stalked past her to the stairs. When she finally raised her head, he was just standing there, his hand on the bannister, his eyes on the floor.

He swallowed. Hard. Then, without looking at her, he softly said, "The guy you've been in love with half your life doesn't exist, Dorie. But the one that's standing in front of you was willing to give you everything he had. If that's not enough, though, then you're right. It really was just a dream. Too bad the wrong one came true." Then he drank her in, from her head down to her toes, with one last—agonizing—look. "I won't ever forget you. Think what you want, but since the moment we met, it's been you."

Then he ducked his head, shoved his hands in his pockets and headed down the stairs. Out of her life forever.

She dropped to the floor and cried like a baby.

Chapter Twenty-Nine

He did everything in his power to forget her.

The first week of spring training came and went with Nate working harder than he ever had before. Although he'd always been one hundred percent ready out of the gate, he jacked it up so much that even players who hadn't had to report yet—both from his own and from other teams—were coming out to watch, just to see what was going on.

After four days of it, management brought him in and put him through every test they had because they didn't believe he wasn't on anything.

"Not even painkillers for the knees?" they'd asked amid rampant debate. His old friends Jim and Marco were having a field day. NateGate on Steroids, they were calling it.

Fucking assholes.

But his knees were freakin' fine; it was his head that was the problem. Dorie was still his first waking thought every day; the last thing he thought about when he went to sleep.

Had he been that wrong about her? Was what he had to give her really not enough?

When working hard didn't do the trick, he decided he

may as well play even harder. He started going out with
Rico and Troy after practice, just for dinner at first, but
then, after a few days, to the bars afterward. He even
spent a few nights partying with the new kids, guys in
their rookie season, suddenly making more money than
God and blowing it the only way they knew how.

Didn't matter one goddamn bit. Every morning, every
night, she was still there, haunting him.

By the middle of week three, he was bone tired just
from the energy of trying to keep her out of his head. It
wasn't the easiest thing to do since, thanks to the drugs
being a nonissue, Jim and Marco had moved on to the
topic of Where Is Nate's New Girl, and What Has She
Done to His Career?

He wasn't about to tell them that he no longer had a
"new girl," so instead he'd destroyed every radio in his
house. The fact that it was a useless gesture—the only
radio he listened to was in his car and he wasn't about
to smash in his dashboard no matter how tempting it
was—hadn't escaped him.

He'd been doing better, though—right up until he'd
played his first few games in his new uniform and had
gotten a text from Wash: Nice to see you back in form.
Homestead says hi.

The Homestead. Did that mean his mom? Fitz?

Did it mean *Dorie*?

Christ.

For the next four days in a row he played worse than
at any other point in his professional career, which, incidentally, was pretty hard to do during spring training.
And now here he was in his big empty house, sitting at
the island in a kitchen that was practically big enough

to fit his entire childhood home—before it had blown down, of course—alone. Well, except for good ole JD.

Yep. Just him and Jack, although a lot less of Jack than when he'd started out.

When the doorbell rang, it took a few minutes to register. A few more for Nate to make it to the door and fumble it open.

"Oh, man," Rico said, standing there and shaking his head. He turned to Troy. "This is even worse than I thought."

No. Nate did not need this. Did. Not. Need. This. *Shit.*

He started to close the door, but Rico easily brushed past him. Easily herded him down the hallway no less, directly into an ice-cold shower, with all his clothes on.

"What the fuck, Castillo?"

Shoving open the shower door, he probably would have thrown a punch if it wasn't for the towel that flew at his face.

"Did that sober him up?" Troy asked as if Nate wasn't even there.

Toweling dry his hair, Nate snapped, "Yes, unfortunately." He stayed away from booze for the most part, but tonight he'd been planning on sinking into that haze. Tomorrow, well… That was another day.

"Good," Rico said from where he sat against the vanity. "Because I'm jonesing for that hot tub of yours and I don't need you passing out on me."

The man had a hot tub of his own. Hell, everyone did. But Nate supposed it was better than getting piss-ass drunk all by himself.

Of course it only took ten minutes before Rico was on the phone, pulling up various pictures from throughout the week. Hinting that maybe it was time for Nate to get his cojones back. Going beyond hinting as he dialed the phone, started to invite someone whose voice was way too high-pitched and giggly to—

"No," Nate snapped, snatching the phone out of Rico's hand, fully ready to drop it in the water. "Not happening."

Although Rico shrugged it off good-naturedly, there was no missing the glance he and Troy exchanged.

"Hey, man," Troy said, taking over. "We just figured you could use some cheering up." He took a pull from his beer as he nodded at the phone. "Swimsuit models, Nate. This year's cover. They were at that party the other night, remember?"

Spreading his arms out along the cool tile rim at his back, Nate just closed his eyes and let his head fall back. He didn't want to hang out with any models. He didn't want to hang out with any women, period. Hell, at the moment, he was seriously reconsidering allowing Rico and Troy to stay. "Doing just fine, guys. Don't worry about me."

Which was bullshit, obviously. But he had no intention of acknowledging otherwise.

Goddamn it. When was this going to end? It really had to fucking end.

After a few more attempts to get him talking, Troy and Rico had gone on to dissect this afternoon's game, and Nate was gratefully on his way to passing out when he realized that he wasn't hearing a jackhammer in his head, but instead the click of heels along the stones.

"Nate! What the *hell*?"

His head came up and he opened his eyes to see the last person he'd ever expected standing over him. "Courtney?"

She was wearing something off the runway, no doubt. But even as he took in the bright red dress that showed off every curve, both natural and man-made, he thought of Dorie. Of how her curves—all natural—would fill it out. Of how it would feel to take it off her.

He let his head fall back to the tile again and closed his eyes. "Go away."

Her steps—and voice—came closer. "6:30. You obviously forgot."

Fuck.

Dinner. Right. She was broadcasting from Arizona this week, in honor of the opening games of the season, and she'd talked him into dinner with the reminder that it was after February thirteenth. As if he hadn't realized that particular fact. "That's tonight?"

"Yes," she snapped, nodding curtly to Rico and Troy. "I'll be in the car. Don't make me miss the sunset." She turned on her heel and walked away.

Under other circumstances, he probably wouldn't have let her get away with that. She was long past the point where she could order him around. But, well... fuck. It was better than hanging here. Who knew what other brilliant ideas Rico and Troy would come up with?

He scrambled out of the hot tub and threw a towel around his waist. To Rico, he said, "Lock up when you leave."

The restaurant was high-end, of course. Five-star rating, award-winning, gorgeous setting. The table they were shown to was right up against the railing with an unobstructed view of the desert on two sides.

They placed their orders and, since Courtney had clearly wanted to watch the sunset, he decided he'd be nice about it and wait until the show was over before bluntly asking, "Why are we here?"

Completely unruffled, she smiled. "I wanted to resume our discussion."

Discussion? "What discussion? Last time we talked, you were attempting to seduce me into..." Shit. He'd walked right into that one.

"Exactly." She smiled smugly. "Into getting back together." She moved her salad around on the plate, then put her fork to the side. "If we pick things up where we left off, we can still have the October wedding we planned."

Thankfully, the waitstaff swooped in to clear their first round of plates right then. It kept him from killing her.

"The World Series is in October, Courtney," he said as calmly as possible. Pitchers and catchers, yes; it was completely believable that she hadn't known that date. Unless you were a true baseball fan—which, incidentally, the fiancée of an MLB catcher should be, although that was neither here nor there—it probably didn't cross your mind. But the woman wasn't stupid. And she was being deliberately obtuse about this. "I can't plan a wedding for then."

She rolled her eyes. "There are so many teams in baseball," she said. "The odds of you getting into the World Series are probably very small."

He could tell her the exact odds of it if he took two minutes to check his phone, but that wasn't the point. "We're not getting married."

Courtney leaned back as their main dishes came, throwing a shrewd look his way. "If I thought that I actually hurt you by sleeping with Ox, I'd apologize." She lifted her wineglass and stared at the deep red liquid as she swirled it.

Stretching his legs out in front of him, Nate did pretty much the same thing with his water, albeit without the swirl. Leave it to Courtney to make it so that he was the one who felt like a jerk even though he was the only one of the three who was completely innocent.

Because she was right. Losing the baby he'd just begun to see a future for hurt. Finding out that one of his best friends had been with his fiancée hurt. And he'd been irritated as hell that it all came out so publicly that he had no choice but to deal with it. But if he was being honest, he'd have to admit that not once did he wish that it had turned out differently. It was almost a relief, in fact.

When he finally looked up into her eyes and saw the tears she was desperately trying to hold at bay, however, his chest tightened. It wasn't that he'd never cared for her, he just…

Hell.

"Why did you do it?" he asked before he could stop himself.

Although it had taken him awhile to remember details about the car accident itself, the one thing that he'd been able to recall with absolute clarity was the moment Courtney had turned to him and told him the baby wasn't his. It was only the next moment—when Marcela's car swerved in front of him—where everything had gone blank.

Her lips quivered slightly as a single, perfect tear slid down her cheek. She turned to look at the darkness rapidly falling beyond their table. Though she brought the wineglass to her lips, she didn't drink from it. After a minute, she put it back on the table, still not looking his way. Hand on the stem, she softly said, "I just wanted to feel *something*."

"And you chose *Ox*?" Nate snapped. The man was ice personified. He was even colder than Courtney was.

But, Christ, no, Nate didn't want to actually know the answer behind that question, so as Courtney started to say something, he held his hand up. Because he got it. Now that he'd had a taste of it he could see what he and Courtney had lacked. And Dorie had been right; what he'd given Courtney wasn't enough. His voice even broke a little as he said, "Courtney…"

She shook her head to warn him off. Even now, in this moment that was probably more honest and open than any moment they'd shared while they'd been together, she refused to let him in. Unlike Dorie, who'd given so much of herself despite fighting him every step of the way.

Had he loved Courtney? Given how much the opposite had been true over the past few months, it was hard to think about what came before. She wasn't a warm person. Wasn't particularly nice, even. She had a wickedly sharp sense of humor, an IQ off the charts and was, as Dorie had said, "beautiful, seriously so." And, as she herself had so recently said, they did make a good match. On the surface, at least. He'd just forgotten that what everyone else saw wasn't actually who he was.

Or maybe it was that he'd lost himself.

"I'm sorry I couldn't do that for you," he finally said. She'd mattered to him. He'd enjoyed their life together. Maybe if Dorie hadn't happened, he wouldn't even have known he was capable of anything more.

Obviously hearing even what he wasn't saying, she

turned to look at him, her eyes questioning. "You know," she finally said, pulling her shawl around her as she leaned back, "this is probably the most romantic date we've ever had." She gave him an oddly serene smile. "Are you sure you don't want to marry me? We really are perfect together in almost every way."

Settling into his seat, he actually laughed. "Almost."

But no, it hadn't been enough. It wasn't even close to what he'd felt with Dorie. And he had no doubt that if they *had* had that she never would have strayed—despite what Dorie obviously thought.

He caught the waiter's eye, handed over his credit card and was glad when the waiter had it back right away.

Just as he was signing his name, Courtney asked, "Why aren't you fighting for her?"

The pen slipped out of his hand. "What?"

"That woman. The one in Chicago. Dorie." Her eyebrow quirked up. "The Sox fan."

Nate picked the pen up off the floor and laid it down on the table, suddenly unable to breathe. "I'm not sure what you mean." That was a lie, of course. After Jim and Marco couldn't get anything on Dorie—the town had closed ranks around her, apparently—they'd moved on to a daily comparison of his stats while with Courtney v those since. Dorie wasn't faring well.

Even though he could feel Courtney's gaze on him, he didn't look up. Not until the silence dragged into a full minute and it would have been ridiculous not to.

A look came into her eyes, one that was both wistful and wicked at the same time. "I don't take kindly to being second best. You know that."

"According to the radio, you're winning," he couldn't help but say.

Although she gave him a thin smile—yeah, he didn't think it was that funny, either—she added, "If I didn't know I'd still lose in the end, I'd fight harder for you. I'm just wondering why you're not doing the same. I mean, that was the real thing, right? What we never had?"

His mouth opened and then closed, all on its own accord as a series of excuses ran through his head, the strongest of which was that Dorie didn't love him. That she didn't want him as much as he wanted her. Or, rather, "She fell in love with a picture on the wall," he said. "Not me."

Courtney leaned forward and reached for him. "Oh, baby." Her hand cupped his jaw. "You couldn't be more wrong. It just scares the hell out of her. It scared the hell out of me and I'm as perfect as you are."

Right. There was the Courtney he remembered. "Humble, too."

With a smile, she gathered up her things. "Take me home, Nate. We've both got early calls in the morning."

Standing up and pulling her chair out, the thought occurred to him, "Dorie has six brothers, you know."

"Oh, God, no," Courtney muttered. Then she plastered that blinding smile on her face, turned away from him and dazzled her way out of the restaurant.

But she'd gotten him thinking. And for the first time since that last night with Dorie, he tried to see beyond the words she'd said to him and instead to what they actually meant. He'd been so focused on convincing her that his feelings were real, that he'd never tried to understand why she was so adamantly working at not admitting hers were, too. That, as had been made so painfully clear, she'd never been in love before, except with the idea of someone she'd never met.

And then he'd come in guns blazing, telling her that he was falling in love with her all of three days after they'd met. Right after he'd taken her on the hood of his million-dollar car in the middle of a cornfield, no less.

Christ. He'd been freaked and he'd known exactly what was happening. But rather than allow for her to let it all sink in, he'd let pride and anger carry him away.

Unbelievable. For over fifteen years he'd spent day in and day out building relationships, working at trust and reading the playing field. He knew full well that it took a good long time for a team to come together; a hell of a lot of effort on everyone's part to make it into something sustainable—something great. Three weeks wasn't a winning season, it was just a streak, especially for someone who couldn't quite bring herself to believe.

And then he'd gone and done exactly what she'd expected: no matter how many times he'd told her he wasn't going anywhere, he'd still been the one to walk away.

Chapter Thirty

Two days after Rico and Troy had done their interfering bit, Nate was sitting in the locker room and staring at his phone. He wanted to call her; he truly did. He just couldn't quite get to that next step. It still burned that she'd refused to even try.

For as distracted as he'd been, he wasn't paying attention to the guys' chatter and it wasn't until Rico slapped him on the back that he even had a clue something was wrong.

"What?" he asked, warily taking note of Rico's grin.

"You should've told me you got yourself back in the game," Rico said, nodding at Troy as the other man joined them.

Belatedly, Nate noticed that two of the younger guys were hanging on every word. When one of them actually smiled and bowed down to him, Nate's blood ran cold.

What the fuck?

Telling himself that he was clearly just misreading something, Nate took off the shirt he'd worn this morning and replaced it with his jersey. "What are you talking about?"

Rico's face froze. "You, uh…you don't know?"

Not missing the glance Rico shot over at Troy, Nate

shook his head. "Not a clue." The sinking feeling sank even further when a voice carried across the room. "Wait, *Sports Illustrated*? Two of them? Not the chicks from *Playboy*?" When Nate turned to see who had said it, he was almost blown over by the swoosh of wind as everyone quickly turned their heads away, trying to pretend they weren't talking about him.

He got up close and personal with Rico, practically hissing, "What's going on?"

Holding up his hand, Rico said, "Don't kill the messenger, okay, bro?" Then he took out his phone, thumbed through a couple of screens and handed it over. And…

Shit.

Nate sank down to the bench as he stared down at the images. At the images of *him* with two women he barely even remembered meeting at a club he'd been at for all of thirty minutes. If it weren't for Rico and Troy's visit two nights before, he wouldn't even have known who they were. But yes, there he was, his head bent down in a way that made it seem he was a hell of a lot more involved than the reality of the conversation that night, which had essentially been: nice to meet you both. Yeah, congrats on getting the cover. Time for me to head home.

Alone.

Shit. "Please tell me this is the worst of it."

Wordlessly, Rico took the phone, maneuvered through a few more screens and then handed it back.

Goddamn it. Some fucking gossip site had gotten hold not just of those pictures but also one of him and Courtney at dinner. And, of course, the copy they were running was: *Anyone still wondering where Nate's golden glove has gone?*

#NatesGotHisOldGirlBack

#MakeThatThree

He wasn't actually too concerned with the picture of the models. He was pretty sure Dorie wouldn't believe that one. He could even picture the laughter in her eyes as she rolled them. *Really, Hawkins?*

Swimsuit models?

Try to be a bit more original next time.

But the one with Courtney… The one that made it look like he and Courtney were together again…

"*Fuck*." He stood up and slammed the locker door. Opened it and slammed it shut again for good measure.

Nate got ejected in the second inning. The coach was furious. "I don't care how much you're making, Hawk. I'll send you down to Iowa so fast you won't know what hit you. Get your head out of your ass and start *playing*, for fuck's sake."

The problem, of course, was that Iowa was exactly where he wanted to be. But with Dorie in Inspiration; not playing Triple-A ball half an hour from home.

Even though he'd probably be fined for it, he left the park after that. Went home, changed into shorts and a T-shirt and went off for a run that was more like a ten-mile sprint. He got home, stood in the shower until the water ran cold and then spent the next three hours watching *House Hunters International* and thinking about how he'd managed to get it all wrong with the one woman he wanted it to be right with. A woman that he still wanted. *Needed.*

But God, how he did. He was driving his career directly into the ground and he couldn't have cared less. At this point, it almost didn't matter whether she believed him or not. He'd take whatever punishment she dealt out. He didn't even care how pathetic that sounded; he just wanted her back.

Well at least he hadn't hit rock bottom; he wasn't watching *Full House*. Yet.

When the doorbell rang he almost didn't answer it, especially considering what had happened last time around. But, hell. He needed something to distract him.

FedEx, it turned out to be. A package from his mom. Nate took out the note first and unfolded it.

My sweet Nate.
I never knew you to give up on what you wanted.
    This doesn't seem the time to start. Love you,
honey.
Mom.

Then he reached in and took out…

His heart thudded to a stop in his chest. The box looked older than sin, its velvet worn and faded. When he opened it, though, the ring inside sparkled. Thankfully, his dining room chairs were solid. It didn't even budge when he dropped down to one.

How could she know? He'd done just about everything possible not to let on to his mother what was going on. The night at the library had been the first time he was even sure that she knew there was something between him and Dorie in the first place.

But, clearly, she did. And, equally clearly, despite what had passed since then, she seemed to think that it was something salvageable.

He tried not to read too much into that. His mother wouldn't interfere; not in a tracking-down-Dorie-and-making-her-have-a-talk kind of way. She was observant, though, the original Hawk. He had to believe that if she'd gone so far as to send him his grandmother's ring, then there was a chance—even if it was just the slightest one—she knew something he didn't. That maybe Dorie might be willing to hear him out.

Chapter Thirty-One

Dorie was fine. One hundred ten percent. Two hundred percent. As many percentages as there were, that's how fine she was.

The reopening of the library had been more successful than Dorie had dreamed and she threw herself into building upon that. Storytimes, visits from school groups, meetings with the local civic organizations. You name it, Dorie did it. She had to. There was all this rocket fuel burning up inside her and if she didn't burn it off, she'd combust. Especially since when she stopped moving, she...

She remembered what it felt like to be in Nate's arms and she was afraid she might actually die.

Which was ridiculous. She'd known him for three weeks—barely—and it had been more than that since he'd gone. Plus she'd been completely rational about all of it, thank you very much. He'd been the one to blow things out of proportion. And he should be grateful she hadn't turned into a psychopath on him and demanded he follow through on all the things he'd said.

So she tried not to think of it. Not to think of him.

Pretty damn hard to do when there were reminders of him everywhere she turned, including the communiqués from Boston, to her dismay. Her brothers had informed her she was a topic on sports radio, although they'd kept it from her as long as they could. They'd finally had to tell her because although she didn't listen to those shows their father did—he tended to have it on all day. They'd enlisted the kitchen staff in keeping him away from *The Jim and Marco Show*, but it was only a matter of time.

Wonderful. But that wasn't the worst of it.

Even limiting her entire life to the library and home wasn't enough. The library was, of course, an issue because of Mr. and Mrs. Grimes, the rooms he'd helped paint, the reading room floor... The list went on. The only saving grace was that his sisters and friends had mostly stayed clear.

To be safe, however, Dorie kept to her office whenever possible, and then headed directly home. But that hadn't helped tonight when, after flipping the TV on to watch as she'd cooked dinner, she'd been too far away from the remote to fast forward through the commercial for the MLB channel. *30 Clubs in 30 Days*. One glimpse of him was enough. She'd sat straight down on the floor and started crying. Sobbing. It was worse than the night she'd watched *Toy Story 3*. So she'd picked herself up and gone right back to work.

Which was why it was so strange that her alarm clock was ringing. And it was even stranger because it was still dark out. It was the middle of March and, as of the week before, she was no longer supposed to be waking up before the sun.

She fumbled for her phone, finally managing to shut the damn thing off. Except as she was doing so, she realized that she'd fallen asleep at her desk in the library. It was 12:52 a.m.

As she was brushing off the two paper clips that were stuck to her face, she was also realizing that it wasn't her cell that she was holding but, rather, her office phone. She put it to her ear. "Um… Hello?"

Just as she was about to hang up, she heard, "Dorie?"

Her heart suddenly pounding in her throat, she was glad she was already sitting down. Oh, God. Oh, *God*. "Nate?"

He didn't speak right away and she had a moment of wondering if she was still asleep. No matter how much she'd tried to keep him out of her head during the day, she hadn't been able to keep from dreaming about him every night. She was already on the track to Crazy Town; it probably wasn't that much further to actually hearing his voice in her head.

But, no. There he was, saying, "Dorie. You're still at work. It's one in the morning."

Yes, well, being in a place where she could actually find activities other than cry herself to sleep was a better option than seeing him on TV. Or obsessively trolling the internet. Or actually seeking out anything she could find, no matter how much it upset her.

"Mmm," she answered, working very hard at not sounding like the world had just tilted on its axis. "The perfect time to call someone's office phone if you don't want to actually talk to them."

"Or if you're trying to leave a message for someone who wouldn't pick up the call if they saw who it was on the other end," he replied, without missing a beat.

Well, yes. "There is that," she admitted, jumping up to her feet and beginning to pace. She felt dizzy. Light-headed. Probably better to stay seated, but she was already up. "So what message would that be? 'You were right, Dorie? Turns out I do like the models after all?'"

She could feel the rant coming on, what she'd tried so hard to contain for all these weeks. She knew he hadn't done anything with them—knew it in the marrow of her bones. Yet here she was, getting herself all worked up. It didn't seem to matter that he was here on the phone—that he'd actually been the one to reach out. The meltdown was coming and there was no way to stop it. She was about three seconds away from losing her shit; it wasn't going to be pretty.

"Or maybe it was more along the lines of, 'So, thanks, Dorie, for the three weeks of reminding me what I really wanted," she continued. "Like, for example, my fiancée, who's actually even more beautiful than this year's swimsuit issue cover girls. And, most likely, smarter. Definitely richer. Not that I need the money—'"

"*Dorie*," he said, cutting her off. He sounded like he was…

"Are you *smiling*?" Yes. That's exactly what it was. He actually sounded like he was smiling. "I swear to God, Nate, if you see even a bit of humor in this situation, I'm not just going to knee you in the balls, I'm going to cut them o—"

"I love you."

Her mouth already having formed the O, she just stood there, gaping. Sucking in the air to replace what had just rushed out of her lungs. "What?" she asked, her voice barely even a whisper. She would have thought that by now she'd be immune to the actual words.

She wasn't. Her whole world shattered into a million glimmering pieces around her.

"I love you," he said again, proving that she hadn't

dreamed it. "I've loved you since the moment I saw you standing there, holding my bat."

A nervous laugh escaped. He had not just said that.

"Um, okay," he muttered. "That wasn't how I meant for that to come out."

Now it was her lips curving up into a smile.

Oh, hell, no. She forced her lips straight again.

"I *love* you," he said yet another time, the words not having lost their power one bit as they were repeated. Her knees felt wobbly; she was afraid that if she didn't sit down, she might actually fall. Having paced all the way across her office, she no longer had a chair available. She plopped directly down onto the floor.

"I've spent the last month trying to tell myself you were right that we'd never work out, but you weren't," he said.

Finally finding her voice, Dorie managed to eke out, "You have a funny way of showing it."

"So then let me," he answered. "Let me show it. Let me explain."

Oh, God, how she wanted him to. She wanted that more than anything she'd ever wanted in the entire world. But if she let him in—if she let him in even a little bit, it would hurt too much. She didn't ever want to go through this again. "No."

"*Dorie*," he pleaded. "They—"

"*No.*" She got to her feet. Needed to find her strength from somewhere and sitting on the floor wasn't going to do it. She had to hang up. If she didn't hang up, he was going to—

"Have I ever lied to you?" he asked, frustration in his voice. "Since day one I've been up-front with you." Implying she hadn't been, which, unfortunately, was true. "Can you at least give me that?"

She took in a ragged breath. Although there was the whole D.B. issue, she begrudgingly said, "Well, I guess…"

He didn't give her time to add in a *but*. Instead, he shoved his foot in the door she'd just allowed a tiny bit open. "Nothing happened with—"

"Vendela the second and Tyra Banks junior?" She couldn't help it. "I mean, they're the ones who would have been on your wall growing up, right? I get it; the fantasy thing." Obviously, considering the circumstances of this conversation, which kind of made her head spin.

"First of all," he said, back to sounding amused, "it's frightening that you know that. I'll have to make sure Deke doesn't add in any *SI* cover girl questions to future trivia nights. And I was actually going to say with Courtney. But more importantly…" The amusement faded and the only thing in his voice was heat. Pure unadulterated fire, although not of the good and passionate kind. He actually sounded majorly pissed off. "I told you exactly what my fantasy is—you. Nothing about that has changed. As much as I tried to convince myself that you were right—that we were wrong… It just isn't true."

Now Dorie was sitting down and back to desperately trying not to cry. She hated this. She couldn't conceive that that was actually possible; it wasn't any easier now than it had been a month ago. She wanted so badly to believe him, though, that it actually hurt. And all she could think to say was, "What do you want from me?"

She sounded like a wounded animal; he probably heard it and had no idea how to reply. The fact that he didn't answer right away made it that much worse. Terrifying for reasons she couldn't even name. And she was afraid he'd tell her again that he loved her. If he'd even asked again for her to believe him she, well… She didn't know. It was a leap of faith that she wasn't able to make. Not right now. Not yet.

"I want to call you again tomorrow," he gruffly answered. "And I want you to promise to pick up the phone and talk to me."

The tears that had begun to well up in her eyes stopped.

Thank God. Oh, thank God, that was something she could do. "Okay."

She'd said okay.

Nate clutched the phone to his chest and squeezed his eyes shut. He honestly hadn't known which direction she'd go—and he had no idea what he would have done if she'd chosen the alternative. But she'd given him an inch…and it felt like a mile. Winning the World Series hadn't been this good.

For the first time in a month, he drifted off to sleep with a smile on his face. It felt like he'd only had his eyes closed for a few minutes, but when he opened them again, the sun was shining and the birds were chirping. He'd slept so soundly that he was still holding the phone in his hand. Which was good; he had another call to make.

For once he was glad that his name got him put immediately through. "Pete. I need your help; Mark and Alexis, too. This one's complicated."

Chapter Thirty-Two

In honor of the town's favorite son—and, yes, in an attempt to bring kids into the library no matter what it took—Dorie had designated one of the back rooms as the new media center. She'd gotten two huge flat screen TVs and subscriptions to every sports channel there was. The rule with the teens was that they could use it as a study room as long as the sound stayed off.

This afternoon, Dorie made an exception. Although she had a billion things to do, she stood in the doorway watching the game, along with just about everyone else who'd ventured into the library that day. After a string of abominably bad games, Nate hadn't just turned it around, he was on fire.

"Turn it up!" one of the kids wearing a Bombers basketball sweatshirt yelled from the front of the room.

"I will if you act civilized," Dorie answered, pointing the remote toward him like a, well, pointer.

"Yes, ma'am," he answered meekly. "Please."

She complied more happily than she let on. Having been desperately trying to ignore Nate's existence for these past few weeks, she hadn't watched a single game. But she was well aware of the downward spiral he'd been in with the exception of the very beginning of spring training. And today it was beyond thrilling to hear the commentators go on about how he'd turned it around. Not just that, how he looked like he was enjoying the game again for the first time since spring training had begun.

"A lot of people have been wondering if those first few games were just a fluke," one of them was saying. "And given the uncertainty caused by the events during the off-season, frankly, I'm not sure anyone believed we'd see the old Nate Hawkins again. But this is something that a whole lot of people have been waiting for. If he keeps it up, this could be a year to remember."

"Dare I say future Hall-of-Famer, Matt?" his partner asked.

With a smile, Dorie ducked her head down. She had to admit, she did get a bit of a rush knowing that the day after they'd spoken on the phone he was back to playing "future Hall-of-Famer" level baseball.

For the first time in weeks, the adrenaline coursing through her was a blessing rather than a curse, and she came back to her apartment in an amazingly good mood. Which was a good thing because Fitz was waiting for her when she returned. And all that buzz helped Dorie gear up for making the apology she owed the woman after avoiding Fitz for these past few weeks. She wasn't even mad that Fitz was probably here because Nate had wanted someone to check up on her.

But Fitz, it seemed, wasn't here because of that. Instead, she came right out and said, "I don't care what's going on—or not—between you and Nate. You're the only friend I have in this whole damn town who doesn't know my entire life story and I came to see if you might like to go for a run. Or hang out. Or…" She shrugged her shoulders. "Or whatever."

With a smile that was bigger than it probably should be, Dorie leaned back against her door and crossed her arms over her chest. "You realize that the whole idea of friends is that they kind of *should* know each other's whole life story. Right?"

Fitz's smile matched Dorie's own. "Let's make a deal. I won't ask about Nate and you don't ask about Deke. Other than that, everything's fair game."

Dorie only barely managed to keep her eyebrows from shooting up. She'd been so caught up in what was going on between her and Nate that she'd never really tuned in to anyone else's drama. Fitz and Deke? Really? But she resisted the temptation of asking—for now at least, no way in hell that one was staying under wraps—and stuck her hand out to shake on it. "Deal."

Although it all went out the window—well, on Dorie's end at least; she still couldn't get a single thing out of Fitz—when Nate called her not just that night, but then the night after that, and the one after that one, as well. In fact, every time they'd come close to saying goodbye, he'd make that same request of her: pick up the phone just one more time.

By the fifth day of phone calls, he didn't need to ask—and Dorie found herself spilling her guts to Fitz. Messily.

"Do you love him?" Fitz asked.

And, yes, after a week of being worn down by Nate's relentlessness, she could finally admit that this was more than a childhood crush—that what they had was strong enough to make sacrifices for, to maybe even build upon. She'd tried to deny it for so long that just allowing the words to be spoken felt like allowing herself to breathe. "More than anything I've ever known," she whispered.

"And he told you he loves you?" Fitz asked, handing over a wad of tissues.

Dorie sniffled her way through, "Pretty…much… every…day."

She looked up just in time to see the corner of Fitz's mouth twitch. "But you still don't believe him."

After blowing her nose in a distinctly unladylike fashion, Dorie could only be grateful she wasn't having this conversation with Nate. Because what she still couldn't quite get past and she told his sister, "He's Nate Hawkins. How can this possibly work?"

This time Fitz didn't bother to hide her smile. Unknowingly echoing her brother's words, she said, "Because if it's what you want, then you'll make it work."

And by two weeks in, Dorie realized that they were right. That if she was all about creating her own destiny, then, damn it, why couldn't she figure out a way to make sure her dream man was in it?

Because by that point she had no doubt that that's who he was. And not because of the picture on the wall part, although she had allowed herself to start sneaking peeks at the *Vanity Fair* photo again. No. The man who'd held her in his arms, who'd taken her to heights she hadn't ever imagined she could reach. He was right. It was real. He'd proven it to her every single one of the past seventeen nights as they'd talked on the phone.

About her childhood and his. The training camp he wanted to start when he retired from baseball—that he was actually beginning to think about his retirement. The places she'd always wanted to go; the much-more-manageable-than-seven number of kids she'd want to be dragging along with her. And so much more.

She could no longer make the excuse that it was only about the sex. Especially since he wasn't even getting any. She'd attempted the phone version—once. It had been entirely unsuccessful.

"Uh, Dorie," he had said, "I think you need to actually talk about touching yourself; not just do it."

"But I can't *talk* about it," she had whispered, looking around her darkened bedroom as though Sister Mary Pat was going to suddenly materialize.

Which was when she had realized he was laughing at her. She started laughing as well, stopping only when he quietly said, "Christ, Dorie…"

He knew she wasn't quite able to respond to anything like that yet and had quickly moved on to say, "I love you. I'll talk to you tomorrow."

But she hadn't been ready to say goodbye. Not that time. And so she'd taken a big, long leap. "Wait. I had this idea the other day…"

Chapter Thirty-Three

Boston, five weeks later

Nate hesitated before stepping into the visitors' locker room at Fenway. By now it was probably over a hundred people who knew what was going on, thanks to the arrangements he'd had to make to pull this off. If it didn't work, it would be the biggest crash and burn in the history of the modern world.

If nothing else, it would be a hell of a story to tell his grandchildren. Everyone from the owners of three ball clubs right down to the grounds crew and security teams were involved. And he had no doubt whatsoever that this would be talked about for some time, no matter how it turned out.

Having Robbie here with him helped, and that was all thanks to Dorie. He loved her all the more for suggesting that Marcela and Robbie spend a few weeks in Arizona. They'd become as close to him as his family—sharing a death-defying experience did that, apparently. But, to be honest, Nate was pretty sure he was getting more out of it than they were, and he'd been thrilled when they agreed to come to Boston and be a part of this as well. It was actually kind of fitting. The light in

Robbie's eyes when he came into a ballpark—the look on Marcela's face when she saw her son's happiness… It made everything beyond clear.

True love existed. Between a mother and her child, yes, but also between a man who had never expected to feel something so pure and a woman who resisted it almost with her entire being. And Nate had no idea what he'd do if the past month of proving it to her hadn't been enough.

So, yeah. Wheeling Robbie into the locker room was the only thing that kept him going.

With a deep breath he pushed open the door and stopped suddenly. The whole team had come out. They had a game that night and one at eleven the next morning. Coach had said a few guys would be there this morning, guys who were well aware of the ups and downs he'd had in Arizona and who wanted to wish Nate luck.

A *few* guys. Not the entire team.

There was utter silence in the room until Tim Kozlowski came over, smiling. "You're really about to do this, aren't you?"

A laugh escaped. "I guess I am."

After a hearty clap on the shoulder and a big bear hug, Tim stepped aside as the others crowded in, joking about another one biting the dust but pretty much happy all-around.

A hush came over the room as Ox walked in and, seeing Nate, stopped short.

Looking over at the man who was nearly as much a part of his history as Wash was, Nate gave the slightest of nods. There was still that flash of betrayal, but, as he'd recently come to realize, it was followed almost immediately by the biggest sense of relief ever. Just one minute in Dorie's presence had shown him he'd been living half a life. That what he'd thought was the worst thing to ever happen to him would end up being the best.

When Ox raised his eyes and met his gaze, the man nodded, as well. Then he gave the cocky grin that he was known for. "Calling all your favors in on this one, huh?"

The grin came more easily than Nate knew it could. "Hell, yes, I am."

Ox threw Nate a White Sox jersey, and then turned his killer smile toward Robbie. "Well, as long as you guys are here, suit up. Let's play some ball."

Nate wasn't sure how the union would feel about this, but stepping on the field with his old team felt as natural as it ever had been, like he'd never been away. When Rico and a couple of the Boston players came down from the stands to join them, well… It was probably the best time he'd had playing ball since he left home.

When they got back to the hotel a few hours later, Rico clapped him on the shoulder. "Don't go getting any ideas, friend. We're taking it all the way this year. You and me." Then he and Robbie went to meet Marcela at the hotel's restaurant.

Not wanting it to get out that he was in Boston, Nate stayed in the room and had just turned on ESPN when his phone rang. Expecting it to be Rico checking in on him, he almost didn't even bother to look at the phone before he answered.

"Dorie," he said, unable to keep the surprise out of his voice. She hadn't called him since, well, *ever*, really. They'd been talking every day for over a month; twice a day for the last week. But he'd always been the one to call her. "Is everything okay?"

There was silence and then, sounding a little nervous,

she said, "Um, yes. Of course. Everything's fine. Is this a bad time? I hate to bother you."

"*Bother* me?" He actually laughed, just from the sheer incredulity of it. "Sorry. You're not bothering me. It's not a bad time." He stood up and went over to the window. He knew the city well enough to know that he was looking in the direction of her parents' house. Though he'd give just about anything to be there with her right now, he had a plan and he was sticking to it. "But everything's okay?"

"Yes," she hurriedly said. "Totally okay. I mean, as long as you're not hanging out in Cincinnati with any swimsuit models, at least."

Cincinnati. Where, if he was playing tonight, he'd be taking batting practice right now. He smiled, glad she could joke about the models. "I can assure you I am not hanging out in Cincinnati with any swimsuit models." He looked toward the lights of Fenway. At least that was the God's honest truth.

"So..." she said hesitantly. "That's good."

"I think so."

He waited for another minute or two, figuring that whatever she was working herself up to say was going to be big. The longer she took to say it, though, the more on edge he became.

"For God's sake," he finally said. "Just spit it out."

That prompted the low, warm laugh that drove him out of his mind. "You really can read me, can't you?"

"I guess that depends," he said. "Because I'm gearing myself up for something big here, but I can't tell if it's a good thing or a bad one."

He heard the catch of her breath and clenched his fist

against the thought that the last time a conversation had felt as monumental as this, she'd said goodbye. "*Dorie...*"

"It was good to see you last week," she said.

"Likewise," he managed, although that wasn't even close to how it had felt to see her walk off that plane, even if the visit was officially so she could see how Marcela and Robbie were doing. She'd insisted on flying coach and staying at the airport hotel and had very deliberately, it seemed, avoided being alone with him, even on their trip to the Mesa Public Library, to which she'd dragged Rico and Troy along. The only exception was when she'd let him drive her back to the hotel and...

"And that was a really nice kiss," she added softly.

He closed his eyes and rested his head against the window. All he needed to do was think of her standing there with her back to the door of her room and he was gone. "It was."

"You're a really good kisser."

Holy Christ, she was killing him. "Dorie," he said, his voice sounding strangled even to him. "I would love to go on reminiscing about every single moment I've spent with you. But you are seriously freaking me out right now." He put his hand up against the glass just to steady himself, he was that worried about what she was trying to say.

She sniffled. "I never cry," she muttered, sounding as angry as she was upset. "Only over you."

Killing him. "*Dorie.*"

"Okay," she finally said, so firmly that he had a feeling it was more for her than for him. And then she was quiet for long enough that he was ready to break the space-time continuum and jump into the phone in order to pull a response out of her. But then she said, "So here's the thing. If it weren't for the fact that you're one of Seamus's star players on his fantasy baseball team, my brothers would have flown out and killed you by now because they were so pissed. I can't honestly guarantee they still won't hunt you down and try."

The air that Nate had had so much trouble finding was suddenly there. For fear he might actually fall, he made himself sit down. "Please tell me there's a 'but' in there somewhere…"

"But I'm about to go find them all and tell them they'll need to figure out a way to deal with it. And if it weren't for the plans I have with Robbie and Marcela tomorrow, I'd already be on a plane to tell you in person that…" Her voice broke again, but he barely even noticed. He was right there with her when she said, "That I'm sorry it took me so long to tell you this, but I love you, too."

Chapter Thirty-Four

Marathon Monday had been one of Dorie's favorite days for almost as long as she could remember. She loved everything about it from the family breakfast that started it all off to the party at the restaurant that ended the day.

And, of course, the baseball game.

This particular year the day seemed even brighter—the sky was bluer, the sun shone warmer and the flowers that had just yesterday pushed their way out of the soil seemed in full bloom.

"Has she stopped smiling yet?" Dorie heard Christopher ask Shay.

Chomping down on a piece of bacon, Shay just rolled his eyes and shook his head as he looked at his phone.

"Seamus Donelli!" their mother shouted as she smacked him on the side of the head. "I will *not* have phones at my table."

"Ouch!" Straightening up, Shay put his phone in his pocket. "Okay, okay."

Although her brothers were still occasionally throwing glares her way, everyone was in good spirits as, decked out in their Red Sox gear, they loaded onto the 57 bus, the one that would take them to Fenway.

Though they got to the ballpark a little later than

usual, they were still in time to catch batting practice. Sitting between Seamus and Colin, Dorie settled back into her seat, trying to get comfortable. She sat up straight and glared at Seamus when, for the first time ever, he missed the box of Cracker Jacks that had just been tossed at him and instead hit her squarely in the head.

"Seriously, Sha…?" she started to ask, but stopped at the look on his face as he stared down at the field. The box fell out of her hands. "*What…?*"

It seemed as though her whole family noticed at the same time, but it was the completely unrelated college kid two rows behind them who said loud enough for everyone to hear, "Is that Nate Hawkins? Didn't he sign with the Watchmen?"

She stood up. Yes, that was Nate. God, yes, she'd know that body anywhere. Even from this far away she could feel the heat rush through her both from, well, lust. Sheer lust. But anger, too, and not just a little bit.

She trusted him. He wouldn't do anything to hurt her. So there had to be an explanation as to why he would have spoken to her for half an hour last night and not mentioned that he'd be here at Fenway today. That he'd be *on the field* at Fenway. With a team he wasn't part of anymore.

She pushed her way down the steps, causing several people to bump into each other and swear. But she could barely even nod her acknowledgement, much less her apology. Luckily, Seamus and Colin weren't too far behind her so they apologized for her. She kept moving.

They were close enough to game start time that security was already blocking off the sections closest to the field to everyone except the ticket holders for those seats. "You don't understand," Dorie said, wanting to push forward but trying not to make a scene. "I need to talk to Nate Hawkins."

The guard laughed. "Yeah, lady. You and every other woman in here."

"But… But I'm…" she sputtered. Well, what was she? She wasn't sure she could call herself his girlfriend if he hadn't, oh, thought to *mention* that he wasn't in Cincinnati today.

Colin came up behind her and, being a police officer, did manage to get the guard to at least be willing to hear her out. But she still had no idea what to say.

"Look," Seamus said for her, putting on his most charming bartender-honed smile. "Nate is actually a friend. He and Dorie—"

The second her name was uttered, a huge smile came over the guard's face. "Dorie? Why didn't you just say that in the first place? Hold on." He took a phone out of his pocket and dialed a number. Nodding, he turned back to her, saying into the phone, "Okay. Yeah. Verbatim. Go." Holding up his hand—as if he didn't already have her full attention—he looked into Dorie's eyes and said, "'I'm sure that at some point today, someone's going to knee me in the balls…'" The guard winced and, it appeared, his hand dropped involuntarily to protect himself, but he gamely continued, "'…But this was the only way I could think of to make you believe.'"

Dorie's mouth dropped open. Her eyes flew to the field and… And there Nate was, standing with Tim Kozlowski on third base, watching her with a gaze so powerful that she actually took a step back. When he smiled her whole body melted. Thank God Seamus was standing right behind her, laughing as she stumbled back into him.

"Oh, and, 'P.S.,'" the guard said, his face crinkling up as he concentrated on what was being told to him at the other end of the line. "'I figure nothing's going to drag you away from your family, but if Claire and Liam want to join Robbie in the bullpen, all they have to do is say yes.'"

It was Colin who said to the guard, "Yes. They totally say yes."

In a daze, Dorie went back to her seat, leaving it to Seamus and Colin to explain what had happened. And although she didn't typically listen to the radio broadcast when she was at the game, she was grateful to Seamus when he let her use one of his earbuds.

"*...no information coming out of Chicago,*" the broadcaster was saying. "*There've been some whispers over the past few days—someone even swore he took batting practice here at Fenway yesterday morning and, as you know, he wasn't on the roster for today's game in Cincinnati—but no explanation as to why he would be here today.*"

"*I'm reading the wires now,*" the second man said, "*but it's 'no comments' across the board. Even Hawk's own people aren't saying anything. This is one of the strangest things I've ever seen.*"

Dorie couldn't agree more. She honestly had no idea what to think. Although, after a while, she decided that she really didn't want to think anyway. She just wanted to watch baseball. To know that, in a few hours' time, she'd be back in Nate's arms again. She supposed she should be wondering why he would have hidden all this. Since he'd done it for her, however—of that she had no doubt—she was going to trust that there was a good reason behind it. And she would—

Jumping to her feet, she, along with several thousand other people, yelled, "Come on, Kozlowski! Take your pitch like a man!"

But she was probably the only one who Tim Kozlowski winked at when he showed them all up and hit a grand slam.

Nate paced the locker room. He couldn't believe his presence had attracted enough attention for the media to still be hanging around; that was a complication he hadn't prepared for. He especially hadn't prepared for all the higher-ups to conspire together to make him promise to talk to the press when all was said and done. He'd finally conceded, as long as he could talk to Dorie first. But it just made the stakes that much higher.

There was a knock on the door and then Alexis walked in. "Showtime," she said.

Right.

Okay.

He followed her out. Alexis had managed everything from prepping the security teams to holding off the grounds crew so that he could have the field after the game.

She came to a stop in front of a closed door. "Ready?"

No. He absolutely wasn't. No matter how many times he'd told Dorie her brothers didn't bother him, he couldn't deny this was the one part of the whole day that had him truly worried.

Not that he was afraid they'd take him down or anything like that. But even if they didn't see things his way, there was no way he was walking out of this stadium today without Dorie wearing his grandmother's ring. If they didn't like that, well, it wasn't going to be pretty.

The second he stepped in the room, they all turned. And, yes, they were an imposing bunch, Mrs. Donelli and Claudia no less so than the men in the family. To probably no one's surprise, Sean was the first one who came over. Before Nate even had a chance to react, Sean threw the punch, hitting Nate square in the jaw. Also unsurprisingly, no one rushed to Nate's defense, not even the two women in the crowd.

"*The Jim and Marco Show*, for Christ's sake?" Sean seethed. "If you hurt her again I will *end* you."

That Sean gave not one fuck about who Nate was said just about everything. Everything except, "I won't." Rubbing his jaw, he met Sean's gaze. "I'd try to convince you that leaving her was probably the worst mistake I've ever made, but all you need to do is watch one of those games from spring training to know it's true."

Though Sean's mouth twitched, that was all he allowed. Satisfied enough with that answer, Sean took a step back, opening the floor up to Seamus. "Let me get this straight. You created a media storm just so you could see her today."

Nate hadn't really expected anyone to notice, but, yeah. It appeared the airwaves were going a little crazy at the moment. "Pretty much."

"So," Tommy continued, picking up Seamus's thread, "you had to pull in the people here at Fenway, plus your old and new teams."

Nate nodded. "From what I understand, there are some majorly big VIPs up in the owner's box today."

Now it was Christopher's turn. "And I'm guessing

this wasn't all just because you wanted to grab an ice cream with Dorie after the game."

As Alexis had said, showtime. Nate took a deep breath as he turned to Dorie's father. The man had barely spoken two words to Nate in the entire weekend he and Dorie had been visiting Boston. Nate honestly had no idea where he stood. But that wasn't about to stop him now. "I love your daughter. I'd like to spend the rest of my life with her. And I'm hoping that I can ask for her hand with your blessing."

Her dad folded his arms in front of his chest. "And if I say no?"

Right.

"Then I'll do everything I can in my power to make you change your mind someday. But I love her too much to let another day go by without asking her to be my wife."

The silence was heavy and tense, but nothing Nate couldn't wait out. He was prepared to do whatever it took. He was beyond surprised, though, when her father's response was, "My little girl is going places. You think you have what it takes to stay out of her way?" Nate gave an incredulous laugh. He'd been fending off dads since his Iowa Dream days. Yet Dorie's dad just wanted him "out of her way."

Yeah. He could do that. Hell, he replied, "I'll buy her her own plane." She could go anywhere she wanted as far as Nate was concerned—as long as she took him along.

Mrs. Donelli stepped forward right then. "Oh, for heaven's sake, Thomas. All you're doing right now is keeping your daughter waiting." She turned to Nate with a smile. "And, Nathan, that's very generous about the plane, but I think you should be saving your money for retirement or maybe a down payment on a house. You can never be too careful."

Uh… Was she serious? Nate glanced over at Seamus, who just rolled his eyes as he groaned, "*Mom.*"

With a small smile—it was still a bit unclear whether she was kidding or not—Dorie's mother took his face in her hands. "You have it," she said. "Our blessing. What a sweet boy to ask."

Just when Nate had absorbed the fact that he was the sweet boy she was talking about, she pinched his cheeks. "Now go find my daughter. And don't you dare tell her that her brothers knew first."

This had been a seriously strange day. After getting over the shock of it all, Dorie had enjoyed the game. But she understood why the players' wives sat together. She'd almost gotten into three fights with some particularly obnoxious fans over things they were saying about Nate—and he hadn't even been playing. Seamus and Colin had had to hold her back. Tommy had been assigned to escort her to the concession stand.

At the bottom of the ninth, Dorie had looked up to see Alexis standing at the end of the row. And, maddeningly, Alexis refused to tell Dorie anything.

"I'm sorry," she said, holding her hands out to the side. "But he did ask that I come get you right about now."

Since the game had not exactly gone in favor of the home team—Tim's grand slam had made the score 8–5 and Boston wasn't able to recover after that—some of the seats right up behind the dugout had cleared, and that was where Alexis took her for the last inning of the game. The same guard from before just smiled as they walked past him.

It wasn't Nate who appeared as the stadium emptied out, though, but… "Rico? What are you doing here?" The fact that she was on a first-name basis with the shortstop of the Chicago Watchmen was no more mind-boggling at this point than anything else.

Evading her question, he just wrapped her into the biggest hug ever and quickly changed the subject as the final out was made. They chatted for a few minutes, mostly about Marcela and Robbie, who, Dorie now realized… "They're part of it, too?"

Rico smiled. "Nate was concerned that you might decide not to come to Boston this weekend. He wanted you to be here for this game."

"Yes," Dorie answered wryly. "He certainly went through a lot of trouble."

He stood up right then and held out his hand to her. "Would you like to go out on the field?"

"Are you kidding?" she asked, shooting to her feet. But there were still players out there, and the grounds crew hadn't even begun their cleanup. Plus, there were security guards and stadium personnel. Everywhere. Gathered at various points, their attention on her and Rico even though they didn't seem to be looking her way. She leaned in closer to him, whispering, "They won't kick us out?"

Rico laughed as he took her hand and led her down the row of seats. "No, *querida*. No one's going to throw us out."

Not only did they not throw her out, in fact, but one of them even opened the gate for her that let her onto the field. Rico followed after her, then stuck his head in the visitor dugout. "Anyone have a glove Dorie can borrow?"

If she'd been able to speak at that point, Dorie would have. She could not stand here in the middle of Fenway Park and play catch. But that seemed to be Rico's intention as he guided her to home plate.

"Hey, Eduardo—you want to throw a few?"

Eduardo Andrade? "No way," Dorie murmured.

Though she'd met him the night of the poker game, he hadn't really said much. And considering the man had just pitched eight solid innings, she started to shake her head. But then he threw her the ball. She would have turned to see where her family was—she couldn't believe that they'd just cleared out along with everyone else, but that was their loss—except she was afraid to take her eyes off the ball for even just a few seconds.

They'd been throwing the ball back and forth for a few minutes, when Eduardo threw one so far over her head that there was no way she could reach. She turned to get the ball, and—

Nate.

She snapped her mouth shut and her hands dropped to her sides as he snatched the ball out of the air. She was so happy to see him that she couldn't help the smile that came over her face. It was like the sun had just risen in front of her after the longest, coldest, darkest winter ever. At the same time, she was also irritated enough that she kept herself from running forward and launching herself into his arms. Just barely, but still...

"You're here," she stated.

"Yes," he answered. His eyes sparkled with amusement as he came up to her, no doubt because he knew exactly how pissed off she was and was enjoying every minute of it.

Oh, no. She was not letting him get away with anything just because he made every cell in her body want to jump up and beg for attention. "You were in Boston last night and you didn't tell me."

A smile. "True."

Eyes narrowing, she started to say, "But why—"

"So here's the thing," Nate said, echoing her words from last night and drawing Dorie's attention back to him. And for a moment, she just looked at him. Stopped her mind from running and her irritation from showing and even her happiness from overwhelming her. She'd been a little afraid of this moment, truth be told. Afraid that once she put it out there into the world that she was in love with him that something about it all would fade; that maybe she wasn't, really, and it truly was just a childhood fantasy that she hadn't quite been able to let go.

But here, as he stood in front of her and looked into her eyes, she knew. Without a doubt in her heart, she knew that he was the man she had always loved and that there would never be anyone else after him.

"I, uh…" Nate stepped closer, right up to her. He was so close that she could practically feel his heart racing; or maybe that was just her own. "I know this is kind of soon, but I, well…" He took her hand. "I'm not sure how the rest of this season will go and I don't know if I'll ever have the clout for something like this again."

Though he was smiling, he was clearly nervous about something. Which was, yes, a little strange. He wasn't the nervous type. He was definitely more the take-a-majorly-obvious-day-off-to-hang-out-with-his-old-team/

rope-in-Rico-Marcela-Robbie-and-practically-the-entire-staff-of-Fenway-Park/make-the-grand-gesture type.

"The clout for wh…?" The air went out of Dorie's lungs. "Oh, my God."

She took a step back at the roar of sound in her ears so loud that she actually glanced up into the sky for the fighter jets that sometimes flew over the park. When she looked back at Nate, he was nearly eye level with her, down on one knee.

Her hands flew to her face, baseball glove included. "OhmyGod."

Laughing softly, Nate gently pried the glove off her hand. "Probably better to get rid of this before someone gets hurt."

Eyes glued to his face, Dorie felt the tears come. If she hadn't been afraid that she might miss something big, she would have tried to blink them away. But she didn't want for even a second of this to pass without her being fully aware of it.

"I know this was supposed to be the pitcher's mound," he said, "but…"

This time she couldn't even say, "Oh, my God," but she thought it. Oh, how she thought it.

Looking up at her, it appeared that his eyes were filled, as well. He nodded down at the plate. "This is my home. This is the only place where I've always known who I am, exactly who I want to be. Until I met you." He reached into his pocket and pulled out a box. A velvet, seen-better-days box that was the most beautiful thing she'd ever seen. Until he opened it, and the most beautiful ring was right there, its diamond catching the rays of the sun.

He continued, "I love that you'd go to your death to defend your dinner, although you'd stop and visit every library along the way." To her complete mortification she snorted at that. It only made him smile. "I love that you're either giving me attitude or making me laugh, sometimes—often—both, even when the idea of smiling seems insane."

Now she was crying full-out. Oh, God.

"You reminded me what it's like to have a dream— to go after it and keep fighting for it every single day." He reached up to wipe her tears away. "There is no one on this earth I'd rather call my king."

Full freaking out.

"Marry me, Dorie. Be my wife. Make me the happiest man this world has ever seen."

Still speechless, she let him take the ring out of the box and then take her hand. Her words came back in a rush of air. "What would you have done if I hadn't called you last night and told you that I love you?"

He kissed the tips of her fingers and her knees went weak. Then he smiled as his nod took in the whole park, from the Green Monster—although he seemed as surprised as she was that the words *Nate and Dorie 4Ever* were plastered across the scoreboard—to all the players filling the dugouts, all the people who worked here now openly staring and smiling, and, if she wasn't mistaken, the mob of people in the owner's box that included a very familiar-looking bunch of men, plus her mother and Claudia.

"I probably would have made the biggest fool of myself in the history of mankind," he answered. The laughter disappeared out of his eyes almost as soon as it came in, though. "But I wouldn't have regretted it, not for one second."

Dorie's tears began in earnest. "Then I guess you'd better put that ring on my finger so that I can tell you yes and kiss you."

So he did. And she was true to her word, although, to be honest, she would have thrown herself at him in another two seconds if he hadn't gotten on with it. "I love you," she whispered. "I love you so much."

His hands went to her face and he was drawing her in, kissing her like she was the air he breathed. The roar in her ears wasn't imagined this time; it was the sound of a few hundred people cheering as fireworks went off—or, rather, the simulation of them on the Jumbotron over center field.

"That, uh…" Nate pulled away from her only briefly enough to say, "That wasn't m—"

Wasn't him, she supposed he'd been about to say, considering that he'd seemed as startled as she was by the noise. Startled enough to shift his hold on her, to loosen his grip just enough for her to—

"Oh, my God," she said, hopefully for the last time in a very long while. "Did I just…?"

"Knee me in the balls?" he asked through clenched teeth. "Yes. Yes, you did."

* * * * *

Acknowledgments

Thanks to Mom, Jessica, Johanna and Jenny, without whose early comments and encouragement this book never would have existed, and Stephanie, for sharing the 807th perspective; to all of the contest judges who put in an incredible amount of work for so little reward but whose feedback is the equivalent to a master class in writing. To Adriana Anders, for giving me the exact right push at the exact right moment; and to Anna Harrington and all the rest of the Team Sarah ladies, not to mention Angela James, Kerri Buckley, Stephanie Doig, Heather Goldberg and Andrew Low of Carina Press, and everyone at the Nancy Yost Literary Agency for being there pretty much all the time. And to the raunchiest group of ladies in the world. (You know who you are.)

To Mom and Dad, Aunt MaryEllen and Uncle Vinny, Aunt Irene and Uncle Ken, and my grandparents for proving not just that Happily Ever Afters exist, but that it's something to strive for, and to Kelley, for giving me my own reason to believe. To Lucy, Will and James, for being so proud, even when you don't want to acknowledge that your mom wrote one of those books.

And a special thanks to the 1978 New York Yankees, the 2004 Boston Red Sox, the Pearson kitchen and the most wonderful family in the world, all the way down to the flakiest of the bunch.

But most importantly to the two amazing women to whom I am forever in debt: my agent, Sarah E. Younger, whose belief in Nate and Dorie made "The Dream" a reality, and my editor, Alissa Davis, who managed to make both this book and this experience more than I could ever have hoped. You are the best gift a newbie author could ask for.

About the Author

Award-winning author Jen Doyle is a big believer in happily-ever-afters—so she decided it was high time she started creating some. Jen holds an MS in library and information science from Simmons College GSLIS and, in addition to her work as a librarian, has worked as a conference and events planner as well as a communications and enrollment administrator in both preschool and higher-education environments. (Some might say that there is very little difference between the two; Jen has no comment regarding whether she is one of the "some.") She currently lives in the Boston area with her husband, three children and three sometimes-problematic cats. Visit her at www.jendoyleink.com, www.Facebook.com/jendoyleink.

Get 2 Free Books,
Plus 2 Free Gifts—
just for trying the Reader Service!

Get 2 Free Books,
Plus 2 Free Gifts—
just for trying the Reader Service!

Get 2 Free Books,
Plus 2 Free Gifts—
just for trying the Reader Service!